Coral Hare:
Atomic Agent

Inspired by actual historical events

Clive Lee

DEDICATION

This book is dedicated to the members of the 442nd Regimental Combat Team and the Tuskegee airmen, some of whom I've had the honor of meeting during my academic years, as well as all members of the Greatest Generation for their trials, tribulations, and the sacrifices they have made to preserve our way of life. Thank you!

TABLE OF CONTENTS

DEDICATION iii

CONTENTS iv

ACKNOWLEDGMENTS ix

Foreword 11

Prologue 12

1   Kappa 32

2   One Unmissed Call 34

3   Operation Z 41

4   The American Nightmare 57

5   G-men 61

6   Chasing the Man With the Blue Sapphire Ring 65

7   Wild Bill 69

8   Oh So Secret 72

9   Weaving Silk 76

10   The Big Kahuna 82

11   Ride Out the Wave 87

12   Suicide Pill 92

13   Jim 95

14   Becoming Too Old, Too Young.............................98

15   Apples to Apples 110

16   "Ooh, Shiny!"..115

17   Cigar...119

18   Infiltrator...125

19   First Encounter...131

20   They're Going to the Wrong Place....................138

21   B-san...144

22   The Unplanned Raid...150

23   Boom...155

24   Inferno 160

25   Incoming...172

26   Trapped...176

27   Gingko...183

28   The Gift 190

29   Run Mina Run...197

30   Hot on the Trail..205

31   Rain...211

32   Darkest Nights..218

33   K40 178 905 221

34   Bitter Almonds 227

35   Broken 233

36   Rude Awakening 237

37   Doomed 239

38   Out of Time 250

39   Adrenaline 255

40   Loaded for Bear 268

41   Trikie 278

42   Sapphire 285

43   Banzai 294

44   Shrapnel 300

45   Silent Vigil 304

46   Over 305

47   A Spot of Tea 310

48   Cargo To Die For 315

49   Sinking 321

50   Seeing the Wizard 328

51   Into The Briar Patch 332

52   Baptism 335

53   Takedown 339

54   Panther in the Mist...345

55   Killzone..348

56   Lucky Charm..353

57   Silent Giant vs. Sleeping Giant...........................356

58   Dragonfly...360

59   False Colors...367

60   Ascension...371

61   Kappa, Part II 380

62   New Black Ships..389

63   Father's Hat...393

64   Homecoming..396

65   Afterword and Author's Historical Notes.....................399

     Japanese-Americans OSS agents and the shadow war .399

     Japanese Americans during World War II 403

     Other Allied spies of Asian descent..............................404

     Notable real-life female spies in World War II 405

     The Japanese atomic weapons program(s)...................407

The Great Tokyo Air Raid a.k.a. Operation Meetinghouse 411

The Konan Cave Facility (in Modern day Hungnam) 412

U-Boat Uranium 413

The I-400 series submarines and Ulithi Atoll................414

Ooh, shiny! 417

Final Words 417

Epilogue 419

ABOUT THE AUTHOR...421

ACKNOWLEDGMENTS

Thanks to everyone who provided their feedback in the course of writing this book. Leanna Gong, E.T. Chen, John Shum, and Hue Banh – thank you!

And last but not least, I'd like to thank my father for providing continual feedback, suggestions, and encouraging me all the way through.

"...I will never quit. I persevere and thrive on adversity. My Nation expects me to be physically harder and mentally stronger than my enemies. If knocked down, I will get back up, every time. I will draw on every remaining ounce of strength to protect my teammates and to accomplish our mission. I am never out of the fight."

- Excerpt from the Navy SEAL Code, successors of the World War II frogmen.

"I have always assumed that the Japanese would have done whatever they could to develop the atomic bomb during the war, and if they had had it, would have used it. I have always assumed that any country that could have had the bomb during the war would have used it, the Nazis, the Soviets, and the Japanese. So we were not unique."

- Edwin O. Reischauer, Harvard professor and former U.S. ambassador to Japan, in *Science* magazine

FOREWORD

The historical footnotes are meant to enhance the reader's reading experience. They are meant to be unobtrusive, and can be skipped over if one does not wish to interrupt the story.

The following story is fictional, although it does incorporate declassified historical facts pertaining to Japan's atomic bomb projects during the Second World War. The story is inspired by actual historical events.

PROLOGUE

December 1937. Tokyo, Japan

A calloused hand held the magnum revolver, visible against the background of the stained glass window of the church office.

The bearded man holding the revolver was disturbingly dressed in a priest's black cassock with white clerical tab collar. He had hard creases on his weathered face, world-weary lines around his mouth and eyes though he was only thirty-seven years of age. His short, chestnut hair had touches of premature gray at the temples. Lockwood tucked the Smith & Wesson Model 27 into the right pocket slit of his cassock. To those who knew firearms, his was a first-run .357 Magnum with 3.5-inch barrel, customized with a deep blue luster.

Nearby, bound and gagged in a wooden chair, was a disheveled priest, similarly dressed. The pale man's Germanic features were stricken with dread but otherwise he was unharmed.

The bound priest eyed his captor with great trepidation. The holy man knew little about firearms; he had been too sickly with asthma as a youth to fight in the Great War[1]. But as a priest, he knew people. And the man in front of him had haunted, hardened eyes. It was the look of a man who had seen too much conflict and bloodshed in his life. Back in his homeland, the priest saw the same look on men in the confessional - haunted, violent men who had fought in the trenches, just some twenty-odd years ago.

The priest watched as the similarly-attired man loaded twin pistols, and tucked them into hidden slit pockets near his rear waistband. Interesting. No conventional priest cassock he knew of had such pockets. The man's clothes had been specially prepared for his task.

The holy man didn't know it, but the pistols were Browning Hi-Power models, renowned throughout the world for high-capacity magazines. His dual pistols tucked away, Lockwood went behind the desk. He pulled out what seemed to be two charcoal-black violin cases, setting them on the ground before him.

The bound priest's eyes went wide. He had seen enough American gangster movies to know that there probably weren't violins inside.

The priest's fear turned to curiosity. Whatever the man was planning, it required a massive amount of firepower. His captor's stony-faced expression was intent and focused. The priest's eyes flicked down, focusing on the other man's hands attentively.

With practiced ease, Lockwood's rough but deft fingers twisted open what looked like an elegant, burnished brass fountain pen, complete with gold clip.

The priest craned his neck, peering at it.

Lockwood's hands loaded a shell cartridge into the pen's barrel. He twisted the pen back together. The priest guessed it was single-shot pen gun. Unknown to the bound priest, it was actually a concealed tear gas gun called a "Faultless." It had a cocking mechanism using a ball bearing, activated by pulling the knurled knob at the end. Depressing

---

[1] Prior to the onset of World War II, many people referred to World War I as "The Great War."

the same knob as a plunger would fire the .38 tear gas shell at short range through the choked barrel.

The enigmatic man tucked the pen into his pocket. Approaching the prisoner priest, he stooped to speak to his captive eye-to-eye. Lockwood pulled down the man's gag to throat level.

Stern, Lockwood pulled a black-and-white photograph of a rather mousy-looking Japanese man in his mid-40s, dressed in an European-style overcoat and bowler hat. Circular black-rimmed glasses gave him an erudite appearance.

The captive priest's eyes widened in pained recognition. Lockwood spoke curtly in perfect German. "This man. You know him. He comes to confession at this church, this day of the week, every week, yes?"

The priest nodded slowly.

Lockwood pulled out a second photograph, that of a leather briefcase. "And he carries this briefcase, yes?"

The priest nodded again.

Lockwood did similarly in acknowledgement. "*Sehr gut.*" Very good. Lockwood turned his attention away to the desk.

Looking up at his captor curiously, the bound priest spoke. "You. You're not really German, are you?" he asked in the same tongue.

Hesitant, Lockwood stopped for a moment. Then he spoke over his shoulder, still speaking in German. "No. Forgive me Father. This is necessary."

Lockwood stuffed the gag back into the man's mouth. He went to the chair behind the desk and picked up its deep blue, square couch pillow.

Lockwood picked up the twin violin cases on the ground, preparing to leave.

Lockwood strode down the church's back hallway with stained glass windows. He carried his burdens in either hand, with the chair pillow tucked under one arm. Shafts of chromatic light streamed in from the windows, illuminating his passage. From down the hall he heard strains of the young girls' choir singing, soft angelic voices singing in Japanese.

The air was slightly musty. The Kanda church was the second oldest Catholic church in Tokyo, and had been established in 1874. It had been built and rebuilt several times over the past few decades due to various earthquakes and fires. Lockwood guessed the faint scent of ash was the result of those events, still discernible after all these years.

Violin cases in hand, Lockwood left the confines of the hallway. He walked into the main room with elegant stained glass windows along the walls. Rainbow-hued beams of light streamed in, illuminating the room in an awe-inspiring prismatic glow. The girls' singing became louder and distinct.

Up on the risers, about two dozen teenage Japanese girls dressed in pure white choir robes sang in unison. Their voices filled the air with an ethereal, reverently haunting melody that reverberated throughout the chamber. He recognized it as "Allegri Miserere." Their eyes occasionally flicked down to the choir books in their hands, before glancing up at the matronly conductor.

Lockwood walked past the choir risers just as the song ended.

The choir members began to disperse. Few of them paid him heed. One of the girls, about twelve, piped up curiously when she saw him, speaking in Japanese. "Where is Father Wagner?" she asked.

Lockwood managed a warm smile. "Father Wagner has taken ill," he replied in fluent Japanese. "I am Father Hoffman."

Lockwood excused himself, carrying the two violin cases with him. He walked down the aisle between the rows of wooden pews, towards the front door.

Quietly anxious, the choirgirl glanced over her shoulder at the receding man.

Concerned, she went to the back exit, squinting as she burst out into the bright midday sun. She half-walked, half-ran down the street.

Out on the street the choirgirl saw a *kempei*, a member of the military's secret police. She recognized this particular man. For some reason, he had been making patrols up and down this street the last few days. She guessed there were some military precautions he was watching out for, but she dared not ask.

She saw him strolling casually down the street, hands clasped behind his back. For reasons she didn't know, the man's nickname was "Rain." At least, that's what she heard from the other girls he had stopped and casually questioned. He was attired in his dark green military uniform with cap, indicative of his status as an MP as well as a distinctive white armband stating the same in Japanese.

She hesitated for a moment, finding him intimidating. He was unusually tall for a Japanese man, six-feet even, and walked with a regal bearing. He had a shaved head under his officer's cap, a neatly trimmed, short black beard, and his black eyebrows were furrowed into a near-permanent scowl.

She summoned what courage she could. As she approached him, he turned to her curiously. She stood up on tiptoe and cupped her hand to his ear, whispering. The policeman leaned to his side, listening intently, his brow furrowing with concern.

Carrying a violin case in each hand, Lockwood exited the door of the stone-facade church, squinting momentarily against the midday sun. He set the cases and chair pillow down near the rear entrance.

He checked his watch, growing tense. The convoy would be here within fifteen minutes.

He lit up a cigarette, puffing on it as he glanced down the street.

A stern-faced, uniformed Japanese man strode towards him, alone. He was dressed as a member of the *kempeitai*, the Japanese military's secret police. Possible trouble.

Lockwood hoped it was just an idle inspection. Foreigners tended to draw attention in Japan, unfortunately.

Staying casual, Lockwood snubbed out his cigarette underfoot. He pulled a second one from his pack of Lucky Strikes, lighting it.

Approaching the priest, Rain pulled a half-empty pack of Golden Bat cigarettes from his pocket and tucked one in his mouth. It was a popular Japanese brand.

Inwardly, Rain scowled. Unfortunately, he had orders to be polite to the *hakujin*, the foreigners, especially the Germans. He hated foreigners. Aside from their technological advancements, he found them to be a backwards and decadent people.

Standing in front of the priest, Rain spoke with forced courtesy, addressing him in Japanese. "Excuse me, may I borrow a light?"

Lockwood assented, saying nothing. He cupped his hands together around his Alkomet lighter as the policeman lit his cigarette.

Rain took a few puffs then spoke casually. "So, where are you from, Father?"

Lockwood responded in Japanese. "Germany. Munich."

Ah. Rain nodded politely. Yes, the man had a German accent when speaking Japanese, and his body language was appropriately subdued. Americans would have called the average German's body language rigid. However, to Rain's Japanese sensibilities it was reasonably appropriate.

Rain glanced down at Lockwood's right hand. There was a pale band of skin about the right ring finger. Rain frowned. He knew from his investigative training that Germans often wore wedding rings on the right hand. This was unlike Americans, who wore them on the left. For a German priest to have a ring mark there implied that he had been married, at least up until recently. Yet this man was supposed to be a celibate Catholic priest. Unusual, although it was plausible that the reason he had taken up the cloth was due to a failed marriage.

Rain glanced down at the crumpled dark green cigarette pack in the priest's hands.[2] Hmm. There was the answer.

Lockwood froze as Rain spoke to him - in surprisingly passable English.

"No you are not." Rain smiled patronizingly. "Your cigarettes. Lucky Strikes. They are American."

Recovering quickly from the shock of hearing the comment in English, Lockwood suppressed a wry smile. He responded in his native New Jersey tinged accent. "They sure are."

Lockwood let out a sudden puff into his cigarette.

A tiny fur-fletched dart shot out of the end of the cigarette and embedded itself in Rain's throat.

Face frozen in a grimace, Rain's hand flew to his neck. But it was too late. The curare in the dart acted quickly. Going rigid, Rain collapsed to the grass, muscles mostly paralyzed.

Lockwood quickly hunched over his prone form as the man's body twitched. From within a hidden pocket of his cassock he pulled a nasty-looking Mark I trench knife with knuckleduster grip, ready to finish the man off. Damn bastard was good. As soon as Lockwood had seen the man coming, he had pulled out the special cigarette from within the pack, which had been turned upside down to distinguish it. It had been safe to smoke. Curare was safe to inhale or ingest; it was only dangerous if it entered the bloodstream directly. If it wasn't for his little cigarette blowgun, it would have been all over for him.

Oh no. Lockwood looked up in consternation. From down the street came the revving of approaching motorcycles and the rumble of an automobile. The convoy was early and it was already here.

---

[2] Lucky Strike cigarette packs were changed to white in 1942. In 1937, they were still the famous dark green.

On the street outside the church, the motorized convoy rumbled towards their destination. Armed riders on military model Sankyo Type 97 motorcycles[3] guarded their charge. Some of the motorcycles had tire chains peeking out the crankcases from some earlier trip. Slung over the shoulders of the riders were German-imported submachine guns, the Bergmann MP18.

In the center of the formation of was an imported Mercedes-Benz W10, Type Mannheim 350. Its suspension ran low, heavy from the retrofitted three-thousand-pound armor plating. Through the bulletproof windows an indistinct silhouette could be seen, that of a man with a bowler hat.

Leaving the now-parked convoy behind, the suited man entered the double doors of the Kanda church.

He walked down between the rows of pews towards the confessional booth, lit by streams of subdued polychrome light from the stained glass windows. Somberly serious, the soon-to-be-confessor was the one from the photo. He was a Japanese man with circular black-rimmed glasses, dressed in an expensive European-style business suit and matching bowler hat.

The sole visible occupant of the room, he stepped into the confessional, drawing the curtain closed behind him.

Inside the cramped confessional, the little window drew back with the sound of wood sliding on wood.

The unexpected response was abrupt and harsh. Through the grating the confessor saw the muzzle of a pistol and the stern eyes of a white man he didn't recognize.

"Where is the briefcase?" Lockwood snapped in Japanese.

Taken aback, raising his hands, the confessor ~~stammered a response. "I left it o~~utside in the armored car."

[3] The Sankyo company later became the Rikuo Nainen Company.

19

"What!" Lockwood exclaimed. This would complicate matters exponentially.

The confessor rambled a response. "My superior told me not to take it with me like that anymore. He said it was unsecure."

Through the grating, the confessor saw the white man's eyes narrow. "Fine. So be it."

The confessor saw the man slap a blue couch pillow against his side of the window grating.

Six muffled gunshots rang out, tearing instant holes through the pillow and sending tufts of cotton drifting in the dark booth.

The Japanese man slammed back against the wall, a half-dozen crimson stains spreading on his white shirt. The confessor slumped back in his seat, glasses askew on his face, laying still.

Back outside behind the church where he stashed his violin cases, Lockwood simultaneously unclasped the latches and flipped open the lids. Nestled inside were two disassembled M1928 Thompson submachine guns, commonly called "Tommy" guns, along with 100-round drum magazines[4].

The convoy members milled about the church exterior. Some smoked cigarettes, sitting on parked motorcycles. Others glanced around warily.

Suddenly, a thunderous boom from a massive explosion erupted across the street and a gaseous fireball roared into the sky.

The mounted guards whirled in that direction, instantly on alert, grabbing their submachine guns and aiming all around. Pedestrians stopped and gaped at the blast, murmuring in dismay.

But it was just a diversion.

That moment, a paradoxical, alarming sight emerged

---

[4] A relatively rare C-type magazine for Thompson submachine guns.

from within the church's courtyard walls, behind the convoy escorts.

Like something from a nightmare, face cold and impassive, a priest wielding a Tommy gun in each hand stepped onto the street.

The bearded man opened fire, unleashing a blistering fusillade of hot lead, both barrels blazing out thunder and fury.

Caught completely by surprise, there was little the motorcycle sentries could do against the storm of lead. The majority died before they could even turn. The bomb was prepared beforehand for just such a distraction, which was partly why Lockwood had checked his watch. The barrage from the Tommy guns pockmarked their backs, ripping out spatters of scarlet and tufts of uniform. They twitched and spasmed in place like demented marionettes as bullets inundated their bodies. The men toppled off motorbikes or fell with them under the blistering fire.

The half-dozen remaining soldiers whirled. Most fired out of reflex. A few were caught for fatal milliseconds gaping at the sight of a grim-faced preacher wielding blazing submachine guns.

Lockwood's Tommy guns had been loaded with the 100-round drum magazines which afforded a withering amount of firepower. The man in the cassock hosed down the guards with bullets, being careful to avoid shooting the Mercedes. No reason to depend on its armor. It was the whole reason he set up a pre-timed explosion as a distraction, following the confessional assassination. He couldn't attack the convoy directly with a bomb, or he'd or risk damaging the suitcase and its contents.

Advancing, face stone cold, Lockwood let out a spray of chattering fire, hosing down the guards and advancing with every step. Most of them were barely able to return fire, letting out stray rounds into the air as their bodies were riddled and they collapsed.

A torrent of brass shell casings sailed out from his chattering firearms, clinking, littering the pavement at his feet.

The carnage was nearly finished. The guards lay sprawled on the street, a few of them twitching. The passerbys had already run off, leaving the street largely deserted. The occupants of the church were huddled inside, peeking through the windows at the spectacle.

Encased in black leather shoes, Lockwood's feet walked through the carnage of bullet-riddled bodies, towards the armored car.

Wounded, blood trickling from his mouth, the last remaining guard wheezed as he lay sprawled on the hood of the car. He craned his head to look at his attacker. His lips quivered and pink froth bubbled from the corner of his mouth as he struggled to breathe. He managed to draw his sidearm with a shaking hand and aim it at his assailant -

Loosing a bark from a Tommy gun, Lockwood plugged him in the chest and the guard thudded back, sliding off the hood to the ground. The driver inside the car cringed at the sight.

Setting one Tommy gun on the roof, Lockwood frisked a dead guard one-handed and fished a car key from his pocket.

Almost casual, Lockwood unlocked the side door and tore it open. He immediately shot the driver aiming his pistol[5], spattering the windshield with crimson as the driver slumped onto the wheel.

Lockwood grabbed the leather briefcase sitting in the back seat.

Briefcase in hand, Lockwood made to leave when he heard the roar of newly approaching engines. Damn. They had already sent people to investigate the explosion.

He glanced down the street. There were three scout cars[6], essentially jeeps, each loaded with three people.

He set down the briefcase and took cover behind the

---

[5] Nambu Type 14 pistol.

[6] Kurogane Type 95 scout cars.

armored car's bulk. He snatched the other gun off the roof. Both Tommy guns blazing, he blasted out the front of the first car, shooting the driver through the windshield and the soldier beside him. The windshield cracked and spattered with an obscuring crimson mess.

Speeding uncontrolled, the car careened to the sidewalk and smashed head-on into a telegraph pole, crumpling like a tin can. The driver slumped over the wheel, the car's horn blaring incessantly. The passenger side door contorted and the dead passenger's arm flopped out the window.

The other two cars screeched to a halt as their occupants dismounted. The men hid behind the V-shaped enclosures of their open car doors. The soldiers opened fire with submachine guns and pistols.

Magazines expended, clicking on empty, the Tommy gun barrels stopped spewing fire and went silent. Lockwood dropped the empty, smoking Tommy guns to the pavement.

His hands immediately went to his rear, drawing his twin Browning pistols in each hand.

Grim, he returned fire, fingers pumping, dual firing in rapid succession, like an old-time gunslinger from the Wild West.

Several of them went down, leaving two men.

Clips empty, he also let go of the Browning pistols and drew his magnum revolver. It had more stopping power than the Browning pistols, but held only six shots. He needed to end this fast and get the hell out of Dodge.

He landed three shots on each man's torso and they flopped back, sprawled on the street. His revolver clicked on empty.

Flanked from behind, boots treading almost silently, a hand held a bayonet blade[7] down by his side.

Rain rushed forward.

Hearing rapid footfalls, Lockwood pivoted. No time to reload. His cap gone, Rain's shaved head gleamed in the

---

[7] Type 30 bayonets were common from 1897-1945.

midday sun as he charged, expression malevolent, blade in hand.

Lockwood drew his trench knife, taking up a fighting stance and lunged out -

Rain grabbed a tire chain from the back of an overturned motorcycle and whipped the end around Lockwood's blade. He yanked, tearing the weapon away and sending it across the street.

Barehanded, Lockwood counter-rushed, charging to meet him. Lockwood trapped Rain's arm under his own, forcing him to drop the chain. Lockwood wrenched the blade away, using the knife as his own -

Rain lashed out, striking Lockwood's inner wrist. Lockwood gasped as a paralyzing tremor ran through his forearm and he dropped the knife. Lockwood lashed out with bare fists, sending out a series of knee and elbow strikes-

Moving deftly, smoothly, practically flowing around Lockwood, Rain let out a series of dodges, sidesteps, and evades...

And after several long seconds, Lockwood was unable to land a single blow. Panting, exhausted, he was absolutely stunned. He reached into his robe for his tear gas pen -

Rain retaliated before Lockwood could do so, unleashing a flurry of blows that were fast and furious, his hands and arms nearly a blur.

Cringing, Lockwood managed to block only a scant few of Rain's blows. Despite his years of experience undercover and in the final years of the Great War, there was little he could do against the onslaught.

Lockwood struggled. Rain was just too fast, most of his blows impacting -

His knuckle hit Lockwood under the armpit. Lockwood let out a gasp of pain -

His knuckle struck Lockwood's temple, and he grimaced -

A knuckle struck Lockwood under the chin and he reeled backwards -

A flurry of knuckle strikes battered him. Sternum. Back of his hand. Crook of his arm. Middle of his thigh. His calf. Between the eyes. Shoulder, just below the collarbone.

Pummeled, skidding backwards, backpedaling, in excruciating pain, his priest's cassock torn and dirty in places, Lockwood finally bought some space between him and his opponent.

He reached inside his pocket and pulled out the tear gas pen gun, depressing the plunger and firing.

There was a hiss of gas and the air was pervaded with a cloud of choking, suffocating chemicals. Rain raised his arm to his face, letting out a series of racking coughs.

Taking advantage of the momentary confusion, his own eyes stinging, Lockwood dashed away in a zigzag to evade fire. He sprinted towards one of the nearby overturned motorcycles.

Eyes tearing, coughing profusely, Rain grabbed a discarded pistol from the ground. He aimed in a double-handed grip, firing in rapid succession.

Bullets whizzed and cracked past Lockwood's ear. Several impacts thudded into his back and pain racked his body. He grimaced, stumbling. He didn't think anything vital had been hit but he wasn't sure.

Suddenly with another gunshot, blood spurted from the back of Lockwood's knee as it splintered with shooting agony.

Lockwood let out a tormented holler and grimaced, trying to block out the pain. He hobbled to the bike, trailing blood on the gray pavement.

The slide on Rain's pistol locked back, gun empty. Rain fast-reloaded, grabbing a fresh clip from his belt as Lockwood mounted the bike, speeding off.

Rain let out a few shots that spanged and sparked off the speeding motorcycle's rear just as it rounded the corner. Determined, Rain ran to another overturned bike and raced after him.

Engine revving, Lockwood's motorbike raced through the streets of downtown Tokyo. Panicked pedestrians in Lockwood's path screamed and dove out of the way.

Lockwood risked a glance at his wristwatch - and gritted his teeth behind his trimmed beard. Almost out of time. He had to get out of the city.

Bracing his arm against the handlebars as he sped through the streets, he reloaded his revolver with a speedloader, inserting bullets simultaneously with the little cylinder.

His motorcycle engine roaring, Lockwood sped through downtown, squinting against the wind, chestnut hair ruffled by his passage. With the urgent ding-ding of the bell, Lockwood narrowly missed the oncoming trolley car by inches, seeing the wide-eyed shock of the operator.

At the sound of approaching engines, Lockwood glanced at the motorcycle's side mirror. In its reflection, a trio of military motorcycles careened around the corner of an office building, racing after him, Rain in the lead.

Lockwood aimed his revolver over his shoulder, firing.

Rain ducked low as bullets sparked and ricocheted off his handlebars. He aimed his pistol and returned fire, the other two riders firing submachine guns in blazing unison.

Lockwood hunkered down as the volley of gunshots cracked by his head. He swerved into a narrow alley and hightailed it to the other side. The docks weren't too far ahead. Just a little bit further, he told himself.

Gunning the engine, Lockwood raced past the guardhouse at the entrance to the docks and smashed through the barricade, to the dismay of the uniformed guard who waved wildly, yelling over the wind.

Going full throttle, the motorcycle rattled as Lockwood rumbled over the wooden planks of the docks. He glanced ahead. There was a ramp used for moving heavy crates without a crane.

Determined, face set in stone, he hunkered down and

aimed straight for it. Hopefully it would give him enough of a lead.

Like a toy soldier astride another toy, the rider and the motorcycle sailed into the air, then arced down in a giant splash, sending up a massive white plume.

Immediately soaked, hair sopping wet, he shook off the disorientation. He took in a deep breath, swimming out to sea as fast as he could with one crippled leg. He noticed the motorcycle sink beneath his feet. It had served its purpose. He desperately hoped his stunt on the docks had gotten him far out enough to be useful, otherwise the water would be too shallow.

The saltwater sent throbbing pain through his injured leg. Gritting his teeth, he fought through it. The pursuing Japanese soldiers would arrive soon. He paddled onward, swimming hand-over-hand.

Out on the pier, soldiers armed with rifles[8] shot at him, racking the bolt and chambering a round each time. One took a kneeling position, firing over and over like a machine, racking the bolt with practiced speed.

Lockwood glared over his shoulder as a bullet zinged past his ear.

He dove under the surface, using the depth of the water to mitigate the energy of the bullets. In the murky blue, his movements were protracted and sound came through muffled. A bullet cut a sizzling path through the water, shattering his collarbone and he let out a gurgled yelp.

He involuntarily surfaced, unable to move his arm or bad leg to propel back down. He couldn't afford to drop the suitcase either. He hadn't come this far for nothing. Desperate, he waded on, paddling with one hand.

The soldier on the pier drew in a deep breath, face expressionless, zeroing in on the bobbing man. Timing the

---

[8] Type 38 Arisaka rifles were used from 1905-1945. As war commenced, newer models were put into production.

movement of the waves to compensate, he aimed the iron sights over the back of the man's head -

Out at sea, Lockwood suddenly heard a welcome sound off to the side. With a great roaring of water, the American *Porpoise*-class submarine rose like some beast of the sea, emerging from the depths of Tokyo Bay. It was the *USS Pollack*. Officially, it was currently on maneuvers on the western United States seaboard with Submarine Division 13, following its shakedown cruise. But of course, its unscheduled trip to Tokyo was known only to a select few. While underwater Lockwood had not even seen it; he had been facing the wrong direction and was preoccupied with not getting shot.

With a great metallic lowing, the submarine surfaced, frothing water streaming from every surface and cascading down the sides.

The top hatch swung open and twelve men rushed out onto the deck. Three men quickly manned the 3-inch deck gun as others sprinted to the six machine guns.

One crewman aimed a Springfield rifle[9] at the Japanese troops on shore, racking the bolt and firing shot after shot with precision. The deck gun boomed, blasting artillery at the troops, sending them diving for cover as geysers of dirt and sand erupted around them. The sub's machine guns sent chattering hail at the few Japanese troops in the water who had swam out after Lockwood. The barrage stitched lines in the rippling waves, sending them diving to the depths to escape.

Two crewmen on deck threw Lockwood a line. They hauled him aboard hand-over-hand, then propped him up on either side like human crutches. They helped him hobble down below decks, even as he clutched the leather suitcase in a blood-slicked hand.

It was hours later, below decks of the submarine. Shirt off, Lockwood lay on his belly, splayed on the table in the cramped mess hall.

---

[9] A M1903 Springfield bolt-action rifle.

Lockwood winced as the sub's *de facto* medic used metal pincers to dig around the wound with an audible wet squelch. He felt every movement inside his flesh as the pincers[10] fumbled around. The medic fished out a crumpled bullet, extracting the first of many from the crimson wounds dotting his back.

The medic dropped the round into the nearby pan of water, and a tiny plume of red swirled within.

Lockwood cringed as the man continued with his pain-inducing task.

The submarine captain stood in attendance nearby. He was a grizzled man with a trimmed silvery beard. He spoke to distract Lockwood from the pain and hopefully boost his morale. "Here Major. Here's your class ring back. We kept it safe."

Lockwood nodded in appreciation. The captain pressed it into Lockwood's hand. Lockwood slipped it onto his right ring finger. It was a distinctive, square-set sapphire class ring from his time as a West Point Graduate. He served in the Army prior to his temporarily assignment to the Division of Naval Intelligence.[11]

Nearby, the submarine captain took a claw hammer and knocked off the clasps of the suitcase Lockwood had retrieved. He opened up the suitcase. Inside was a stack of manila folders.

He picked one up, perused its contents, then handed it to Lockwood.

Expression focused, Lockwood thumbed through the papers. Pages of documents in Japanese. Physics equations. Schematics of a large cylindrical machine.

The last was most disturbing. Accompanied by

[10] By some accounts, bent spoons were used for such surgery where proper equipment was not always available.

[11] The United States naval intelligence organization would not be known as the Office of Naval Intelligence (ONI) until it was renamed in April 1945.

scrawled Japanese footnotes, it was a detailed hand-drawn illustration of a massive mushroom cloud, dwarfing trees nearby.

Staring at the picture, Lockwood felt a wave of trepidation. So the rumors were true. It had been three years since Tohoku University professor Hikosaka Tadayoshi had released his theory of "atomic physics theory" to the world. In the 1934 paper, he had pointed out that both nuclear power generation - and weapons - could be created.

Lockwood stared at the hand-drawn mushroom cloud, disconcerted. Even if the Japanese had not started developing such a weapon in earnest, they were looking into the possibility. Its potential yield was incredible, and could change the balance of power across the globe.

The sub captain spoke as the medic continued surgery. Lockwood cringed in pain.

"What happened out there?" the skipper asked.

Terse, Lockwood kept his answer to the point. "Cover got blown."

The old salt rolled his eyes. "You're a six-foot tall white man running around Tokyo! Sure you blend in!" he added with a touch of sarcasm.

Lockwood gave a wry smile.

Nearby, the medic peered at the wound in his knee, scrutinizing it. He shook his head in consternation. "Your knee. You'll never run again. Your days as a field agent are over."

Lockwood grimaced. He had figured as much. He decided to be the first to say it. "We'll need a replacement eventually."

Fighting through the pain and discomfort, Lockwood bit his lip as the medic dug inside his back. He sought to distract himself, focusing on the ideal qualities his replacement would have.

"It would have to be someone stealthy," he mused. "Subtle. With a lot of resolve. Someone innocent-looking who can blend in." He thought about it for a moment. "Maybe a girl."

The submarine captain stroked his beard. "Hmm. Yes. But where could we find such a person?"

1 KAPPA

Across the Pacific, at the same time. Honolulu, Hawaii. December 1937

The first thing Mina realized was the darkness. The sound of surf on the shore. The cry of seagulls. Heavy breathing and grunting borne of desperate concern.

It was a cloudy, overcast day. The gloomy gray skies were just beginning to shift towards sunset, cotton clouds suffusing with hues of orange and deep violet.

In his strong arms, lying prone on her back in a one-piece pink swimsuit was a young girl, small and frail. Her raven hair was tied in innocent pigtails. She had just turned ten years old scant weeks prior.

A discarded surfboard protruded from the sand next to her, a second larger surfboard nearby.

At the shoreline, with the waves coming in, her father continued the chest compressions, desperate. Never before had she seemed so fragile in his arms.

He urged her on in his native Japanese. "C'mon Mina! Breathe, damnit, breathe!"

He paused to pinch her nose and breathe into her chest. He pressed down on her chest again several times -

Suddenly, she was brought back to life in a coughing

fit. For long seconds, Mina turned her head to the side, retching as she choked, spitting out gobs of water.

Relieved, Mina's father comfortingly rubbed her back as she sat up wearily. He spoke to her in Japanese, tone gentle as always. "It's ok. Even *kappas* drown."

Mina's voice was subdued and weak. "*Kappa tte nani?*" she managed. What's a kappa?

"A Japanese water spirit," he answered.

Mina's expression barely registered the statement. Numbly, all she remembered was the undertow dragging her beneath the waves, flailing to no avail as she tried to claw her way to the surface.

He stood up and tucked his large surfboard under his arm, pointing back out to sea. He figured the best way to get her to recover was to get her right back on the horse, so to speak. "C'mon. Let's go on back while the waves are good."

Exasperated, petulant, Mina yelled back at him in English. It was her native language anyway. "Aww, screw that! I'm never going in the water again!"

Fuming, with balled fists and arms held ram-rod straight down at her sides, she stalked off.

2   ONE UNMISSED CALL

FOUR YEARS LATER
Saturday, 10:00 AM

Lazy, soothing Hawaiian luau music on the radio floated down main street of Honolulu. It was Saturday morning. The early morning breeze rustled the palm trees, carrying refreshing ocean air with it. The tang of sea salt filled the air.

A pair of roller-skate encased feet glided casually down the pavement, a feminine, pigtailed shadow angled alongside them.

Now fourteen, Mina Sakamoto had grown into quite a pretty young Japanese-American girl. She had big beautiful doe eyes, and naturally long eyelashes. She still retained some of the fat on her cheeks from early childhood, giving her a wide-eyed, baby-faced appearance of innocent youth.

The petite girl let out a little kick to propel herself forward, letting herself glide down the gentle slope without further effort.

With her usual vivaciousness, she skated down the street, cheerfully greeting people at the market stalls setting up for the day.

"Aloha, Mrs. Nanahara!" she said brightly, waving.

Grinning, the old lady Mina addressed crinkled her suntanned leathery skin around her mouth in a smile as she waved back.

Mina recognized a dark-haired German vendor and his son, who was about her age. They had recently moved into town. The son had asthma, and often needed new medications. Mina greeted them. *"Guten tag, Herr Schmidt! Wie geht se dir?"* Hi there Mr. Schmidt! How goes it?

They waved hello. The son called out. *"Hallo Mina! Wo ist die Apotheke?"* Where's the pharmacy?

Mina   gestured. *"Gehen Sie geradeaus! Dann links abbiegen!"* Go straight! Then turn left!

"Danke!" Thanks!

Mina glanced to the side of the street. There was a Russian businessman she recognized. He waved at her and said something she had trouble understanding. Ulp.

Mina did her best. *"Ya plokha gavaryoo pa rooskee. Gavareetye pazhalooysta myedleeney?"* My Russian is bad. Could you speak more slowly?

Chuckling, the businessman just smiled and gave a dismissive wave. Mina made a mental note to work on her Russian language skills.

Still smiles-and-sunshine, Mina glided along. Beaming, the French baker near the end of the block saw her. He tossed her something wrapped in wax paper.

Mina caught it one-handed. It was a soft, flaky, buttery croissant, still steaming hot. Mina called out, grateful. *"Merci pour le croissant!"*

He grinned back at her. *"Je t'en prie!"* My pleasure, don't mention it.

Munching on the croissant, Mina skated down the street, toward her father's clinic.

Flanked by swaying palm trees, the clinic was framed in the early morning sunrise. The peach-and-scarlet of the sun rose in the east next to it, bathing the building in a welcome glow.

Inside the clinic's patient room, her father adjusted his glasses by pushing them upwards with a middle finger. It was a mannerism of his Mina found endearing.

Gentle, mild-mannered, Mr. Sakamoto tended to the little boy sitting on the examination table. He gave the tyke a gentle pat on the head and pulled out a cherry-red lollipop from within his white lab coat, holding it out.

Gleeful, the little boy took it. The boy's mother gave Mr. Sakamoto a warm smile as they left the examination room.

A moment later, Mina ushered in a wizened, little Korean lady. She jabbered on as she sat on the examination bed.

Mina's father squinted, struggling to keep up. He cupped his hand and whispered aside to Mina in Japanese.

"Sorry Mina, my Korean is terrible. What did she say?"

Mina listened to the woman intently for a moment then turned to her father. "She says that her ear hurts."

Her father continued, asking diagnostic questions as Mina translated. Ever since her father had established his practice on the island, he had developed a good reputation among the international community. Russians, Germans, French, Koreans, etc., often came to see him. Over the years Mina had gradually picked up the languages of her father's patients.

Later, in the adjoining patient room, Mina tended to a little girl in a flower print dress. The adorable moppet had a haircut styled with bouncing Shirley Temple curls. Gentle, wearing rubber gloves, Mina stitched up a nasty three-inch laceration on her arm. The girl sat quietly, blinking occasionally as Mina threaded the needle through her skin.

Walking in, holding a manila folder, Mina's father quizzed her, speaking in Japanese. "Alright Mina. Pop quiz. What is mercurochrome?"

Multi-tasking, still focused on the patient, Mina

answered in Japanese. She spoke as she snipped off the last thread of the stitches with sterile scissors and bandaged the wound. "Topical antiseptic used for cuts, scrapes, and sometimes burns."

Mina's father adjusted his glasses, nodding. "Okay, good. Sulfa drugs[12]?"

"Antibacterial, infection prevention."

"Okay. Bleeding arm. Where do you hold it?"

Mina rolled her eyes, switching to English for her reply. "Dad, all too easy. Tell the patient to raise it above the level of the heart."

Mr. Sakamoto beamed at her, proud. "Good, good," he said in English. Meet me in my office, I want to give you something."

Inside her father's spacious office, the radio on the shelf droned on, an Atwater Kent Model 84. The male announcer made a running commentary on the ongoing fighting in Europe. The United Kingdom had just declared war on Finland.[13]

Her father sat behind the large mahogany desk, finishing up some paperwork. He scribbled a few notes down in a patient file.

Sitting semi-bored on a nearby high-backed chair, Mina swung her legs back-and-forth. Listening to the radio, a disquieting thought came to Mina, manifesting as a perturbed expression.

She spoke up. "Dad, if Japan goes to war with the U.S., what would you do?"

Looking up, Mina's father didn't even hesitate. To Mina, it was clear the topic was something he had thought of before. He deliberately responded in lightly-accented English.

[12] These drugs Mina's father mention were used at the time, but are generally obsolete today, with the advent of better antiseptics and antibiotics like penicillin.

[13] The UK declared war on Finland on December 6, 1941.

"Well honey, I love Hawaii and I love this country. If war breaks out, I will be with Uncle Sam."

Mina nodded. She had guessed he would respond as such. "There are many opportunities in this country that are not available elsewhere," he added.

He came out from behind his desk and strolled over to her, voice taking on a reflective tone. "It's complicated, but because of the law, I cannot become a citizen. Hopefully that will change someday." He gave her a tight squeeze. "You are very lucky you were born here."

His demeanor turned slightly serious. "Japan has a cultural context that does not pertain to you. Are you familiar with the concept of submission to the Emperor?"

Mina nodded. She was vaguely aware of the idea, given what she knew of Japanese society from her parents and some of her family friends. "I've heard of it, sure. Unlike the way some other Asian countries treat their people's descendants, if you're not born and raised in Japan, the Japanese do not consider you to be one of them. You are an outsider. I may look like them, talk like them, even act like them - but they will never truly accept me."

Mina's father nodded. "It's good that you understand. You have no other country than the United States, Mina. No matter what happens."

Mr. Sakamoto changed the subject, taking on a lighthearted tone. "Now, let's talk about more pleasant matters."

Going behind his desk, he pulled out a white, gift-wrapped box. It was slightly larger than a loaf of bread, tied with a pink ribbon.

"Happy birthday Mina!" he said. "Sorry for the late gift. It didn't arrive from the mainland until yesterday."

Mina's eyes fairly sparkled with anticipation. Her fourteenth birthday had been a month ago but she hadn't really expected any new gifts since that day.

She took the box encased in cream wrapping paper. She shook it gently, putting it to her ear. There was a faint rattling. She gingerly pulled off the ribbon and opened the lid, peering inside.

Nestled inside was a shiny new pair of Winchester Repeating Arms roller skates, laid end-to-end. Interestingly, they were made by the manufacturer of the firearms of the same name.

Bursting with joy, Mina wrapped her arms around him in a great big hug, looking up at him with her doe eyes. "New skates! Awww, daddy! You're the best!"

He just chuckled and ruffled her hair. "Alright. Best get ready to go home. Mother has dinner ready."

The rotary phone on the desk rang. Mina let him go as he went to answer. He picked up the receiver and listened intently, the speech on the other end indistinct to her.

Sitting down on the couch, Mina kept herself occupied. She pulled on the new roller skates, testing them out.

She got to her feet and took an experimental glide around the large hardwood floor, going in a circle. She kicked up a leg, circling about on one foot like a figure skater on ice.

Done testing her skates out, a pleased Mina sat back on the couch and pulled them off. She donned her shoes as her father hung up the phone. "Honey, we'll be making a house call for Mr. Miller first thing tomorrow morning."

Tying her shoelaces, the announcement caught Mina off guard. "Oh! Mr. Miller is sick?" she asked, concerned.

Her father gave her a dismissive wave, not wanting her to be upset. "Don't worry, I'm sure he'll be fine, it doesn't sound serious. He just wants a second opinion."

Going to the oak hat rack near the door, her father retrieved his white Panama hat with the black band around the brim and put it on. It was an elegant hat, made from high-quality toquilla straw and bought from a rather expensive haberdasher. Mina always thought he looked rather dashing with it, especially when he wore his matching cream-white suit as he did now.

Under the hat rack was a black leather doctor's bag with the red cross inside a white circle. Sitting next to the bag was an identical one. He picked up the first and opened the door.

Eager, Mina grabbed her own black medical bag, tagging along faithfully. She held it in front of her with both hands.

"Sure. Where's he at?"

"Pearl Harbor."

3   OPERATION Z

December 7, 1941

Glorious dawn. Golden rays of the sun peeked through the clouds. Emerald-sapphire waters glittered in the morning light.

On the east side of Ford Island, on what was called Battleship Row, sun-dappled ships, painted gray, fairly sparkled silver in the morning light against the fiery orange sunrise.

Palm trees swayed in the cool morning breeze near the barracks, the fronds of the trees rustling in the wind. Walking out ahead of her father and his friend, Mina marveled at the surroundings. Most of the nearby buildings looked brand new, having been built only six years earlier.

Walking out, attired in his cream-white suit with matching Panama hat, her father put his hand comfortingly on Mr. Miller's shoulder. "Get some bed rest and chicken soup," he advised. "You'll be fine. Just a stomach bug."

Miller nodded. Unlike many others around them, Miller was one of the few Army members stationed on base, compared to the number of servicemen from the Navy and Marines. Having expected to receive visitors this morning, he was snappily dressed in khaki-colored dress uniform, complete with matching tie and officer's cap. His attire made him stand out somewhat from the mass of men lounging about in tank tops and sailor suits.

"Thanks, Mr. Sakamoto," said Miller.

7:48 AM

Out in the skies north of Hawaii, in formation, nearly two hundred warplanes marked with the Rising Sun soared toward the island of Oahu.[14]

In tense anticipation of battle, strict radio silence was maintained. They had been detected by radar approximately an hour earlier, but had been dismissed as a flight of B-17 bombers expected to pass by Pearl Harbor.

The swarm of planes soared on towards an unsuspecting populace ignorant that war would soon be upon them.

Mina, her father, and Mr. Miller continued strolling near the docks along Battleship Row. Miller grumbled at the droning of approaching aircraft. He glanced at his wristwatch.

"Damn swabbies," Miller said, annoyed. "Running drills this early?"

Mina looked upwards and let out a little gasp, astounded by the sight of what was well over a hundred planes.[15] A multitude of passing shadows crossed her upturned face. She had never seen so many planes all at once in her entire life. It was an impressive display.

Her wide-eyed gaze fixated on something unexpected.

On the wings of the planes was the red sun of the Japanese *hinomaru*. At the sight of the emblems, she felt the hair rise on the back of her neck. No. No, it couldn't be. For a brief moment she convinced herself there was a chance the

---

[14] Operation Z was the Japanese name for the attack on Pearl Harbor.

[15] There were 183 Japanese planes in the first wave.

Navy was painting some of their planes with the insignia for war exercises - then immediately realized it was unlikely. Oh no. Oh, nonono. This just couldn't be possible. The air around her seemed to have dropped ten degrees. Dread filled her stomach and she felt her mouth go dry.

Flanked by its comrades, one "Kate" type torpedo plane dropped its payload and something streaked the surface of the water, heading towards one of the gray battleships anchored at dock-

There was a deafening boom. Every single person in the area gawked and gaped at the rising fireball over the battleship and the swarming planes overhead. Rising to their feet, roused from the indolence of their lazy Sunday morning, sailors, marines and everyone else looked to the flaming ship and skyward in disbelief and astonishment. This just couldn't be happening.

More planes swooped in, "Val"-type dive bombers, more "Kate" multipurpose torpedo bombers, and "Zeke" fighter planes, more commonly called the Zero. The planes dove in, swooping or weaving in-and-out depending on their roles. The Zeroes swarmed in like insects, strafing, providing air cover for the attack, spitting out dual-lines of flaming fury at people on the ground and onboard ships.

Air raid sirens started to wail, calling sailors and marines to general quarters. Without being told, sailors ran to their posts. Alarms blared.

One sailor hollered out to his compatriots. "The Japs! The goddamn Japs are bombing us! Wake the fuck up, this ain't no damn drill!" he yelled.

Down below decks, a handful of sailors still in their underwear scrambled out of their bunks, all traces of sleep gone from their eyes.

Outdoors, a voice blared over the loudspeaker. "Air raid Pearl Harbor. This is no drill!" the voice yelled over the sirens.

Standing lost amidst the throng of rushing servicemen, Mina looked every which way in bewilderment, not sure what to do.

A firm leathery hand grabbed her soft one. She looked up as Miller dragged her away, his face a mask of grim determination. He had to protect her; she was his friend's daughter.

As he dragged her through the bustle of sprinting servicemen in various states of dress, Mina had to half-run to keep her arm from being pulled out of its socket. Hopefully heading towards greater safety, they threaded their way through the grounds. Panicking, fear pulsing in her stomach, she looked every which way. Her father was nowhere to be seen.

Miller suddenly looked upwards. Mina followed his gaze.

High overhead the harbor, a flight of five Val dive-bombers swooped down, releasing armor-piercing bombs over the moored ships.

Massive fireballs erupted on the decks, and sailors screamed as the concussive force of the blasts flung them overboard.

She heard the chatter of machine gun fire. A half-dozen gray-painted Zeroes flew in low between buildings, cutting down swaths of sailors in a hail of gunfire even as they dove for cover and hit the ground.

Nearby, the sky over the gray ships lit up with streaking bolts of light, tracer bullets from numerous antiaircraft guns. Crewmen up on deck manned the turrets, some of them shirtless or in undershirts from their impromptu call to arms. The flak burst high up in the air, creating black cloud-like puffs as the shells exploded with resounding booms.

Overhead, there was a sudden flare of brightness as a Zero caught fire. Mina looked skyward, following the trail of sable smoke as the flaming Zero hit the ground nose first, mere feet away from sailors running for their lives. The plane flipped upwards at an awkward angle, keeled, rolled end-over-end, then skidded to a stop, a burning hulk of metal and fuel.

Still running, breathing fast, fear pounding in her

heart, her legs grew shaky. Adrenaline coursed through her as the enormity of what was happening sunk in. She was caught in the middle of an air raid. War had finally reached the United States.

The thunderous noise wasn't helping. For a moment she was reminded of thunderstorms from her childhood, hiding under her bed with her stuffed bunny, cowering from flashes of lightning and booms of thunder.

Out in the docks, tremendous explosions boomed onboard the ships. The blasts were so strong she could feel the shockwave on her skin from here, even as they sent tremors through the concrete beneath her feet. Black smoke billowed out in great plumes from the burning ships, great gouts of ebon gas. The smoke, black from burning petrochemicals, created a fog of war about the harbor.

Swooping down, a Val dive bomber dropped its payload on running sailors and Mina saw them enveloped in a roaring orange fireball. Their dismembered limbs joined the shower of dirt and debris, hitting the ground with wet smacks.

Over at a .50 cal sandbagged position, a sailor dove over the barrier amidst chattering machine gun fire, barely escaping the strafing of a passing Zero.

Over at one of the battleships, Mina saw a black man in a cook's uniform up on deck. From afar, she saw him drop the handful of laundry he carried and run to a set of dual-mounted heavy machine guns[16].

Swiveling in his turret, he screamed fury at the passing Japanese Zeroes and unloosed a firestorm into the sky, peppering the planes with a fusillade of machine gun fire.

A few incoming Zeroes strafed a handful of sailors on the ground, kicking up dust and chips of concrete at their heels as the men ran for their lives.

An elongated indistinct shadow streaked over Mina. Someone hollered out a warning at her.

---

[16] The famous Dorie Miller used Browning M2HB heavy machine guns here.

"Look out!"

Aflame, spinning out of control and trailing black smoke, the Zero screamed in directly towards Mina at two hundred miles per hour.

Frozen in fear, Mina let out an involuntary scream of sheer terror as the specter of death rushed closer and closer-

Her father dove towards her, shoving her to the ground and covering her with his body as the doomed Zero roared overhead just inches away, so close the stench of burning fuel suffused her nostrils and the spinning prop cut off a lock of her hair.

Aflame, smoking, the Zero smashed into a nearby sandbagged position, erupting in a gaseous, petrol-fueled fireball. Screaming sailors within the enclosure were literally blown to scarlet smithereens by the impact and disembodied limbs, raw red at the joints, flew through the air.

Ohmygodohmygod-that-coulda-been-me. For a moment, part of Mina's mind reeled in nightmarish hyperfocus. She was inexorably drawn into the image as if it were a vortex. It felt as if everything was happening to someone else. She had heard of such phenomenon in books and magazines, but never in her life did she think she'd experience it herself. For her innocent sensibilities, it was a harrowing image that would stay with her the rest of her days. Seeing patients' wounds in the clinic was one thing. Seeing what could have happened to herself like this was beyond anything she ever imagined.

Gasping with haggard disbelief, hair partially obscuring her face, Mina barely noticed her father get up. "Go, go!" he yelled.

Struggling to her feet, Mina distantly noticed her father run off. He rejoined Miller, who attended to a sailor sprawled at a smoking and slagged anti-aircraft gun. Uniform scorched, cap blown off, the sailor gasped for air, bloody foam bubbling out of his blue-tinged lips. He kept one hand clamped to his belly to keep his intestines from leaking out from a gaping wound. Mina saw her father rush to help.

Mina bit her lip, faintly registering the bloody foam at the wounded man's mouth, the cyanotic lips and wheezing. Punctured lung. Even if they patched up his belly, given their circumstances, he probably wouldn't make it.

There was a thunderous boom off to her left and Mina whirled.

From the harbor came the roaring screech of groaning metal as something massive started overturning. Half-obscured by smoke, out among the burning ships, the gray giant of a battleship overturned like a dying whale.

Looking like toy figurines, sailors and crew aboard desperately clung to railings, to ropes, to each other as the ship starting rolling over onto its side, their legs and arms flailing. She dimly noticed the stenciled ship's name on the hull. *USS Oklahoma*.

Through the smoky haze, sailors floundered in the waters below. They struggled through the churning froth, trying to escape the undertow created by the sinking ship. Black oil fires floated atop the water like flaming, ebon lily pads. In the firelit water, coated in oil and soot, sable-slicked sailors paddled to shore.

Aflame, a handful of sailors screamed, clamoring as they climbed ashore. Some sank to hands and knees. Some stumbled forward, then collapsed, going still, bodies still consumed by flame.

Sailors wielding M1903 Springfield bolt-action rifles[17] behind sandbagged positions shot at Zeroes streaking overhead, momentarily darkened by shadows of the planes.

Not too far from Mina, at the next building over, an overhead Val bomber dropped its payload onto another nearby sandbagged position. The fiery blast hurled its occupants into the air, most of them missing limbs, and Mina threw up a hand over her face to protect herself as concrete chips, flaming bits, and sand rained upon her.

---

[17] The famed, M1 Garand rotating-bolt rifles used by American forces would not come into widespread use until later.

The smoke cleared somewhat. Mina saw one sailor, still alive. He lay sprawled against the sandbags, screaming incoherently in agony, leg a gory mess. No one was close enough to help, and his compatriots were too busy fighting.

Momentarily, Mina looked down at her hand. In all the commotion, she didn't realize she was still clutching her black leather bag with the red cross on a white circle.

She glanced back at her father, attending to a sailor with a rag in his mouth to stifle the pain. Her father gripped the sailor's elbow and wrist, setting the bone with a sickening crunch as the sailor let out a muffled groan.

Mina bit her lip, emboldened by his example - then ran towards the wounded sailor at the bomb-blasted sandbags. This, at least, she knew how to do.

Reaching his side, she set her medical bag next to him. Fires still lapped at the smoldering sandbags scattered around them. Tongues of flame licked at his sleeves and pants. She quickly patted the fires out and tore open the char-dotted cloth around his leg wound, to gain better access.

She grabbed a sterile towel from the bag and applied pressure to the wound, staunching the bleeding. The soldier looked around deliriously, eyes unfocused, not really seeing her.

Mina took a deep breath, momentarily closing her eyes, willing herself to pretend she was at her father's clinic. She told herself it was just a farming accident. She lifted the towel off and inspected the wound, scanning it with a practiced eye.

There was a foot-long laceration running along his thigh, but the bleeding was not as profuse as it could have been. She peered at the raw flesh, angling her head to get a better look. Not too deep; femoral artery seemed ok. She had to be careful not to nick it or he could die within minutes. No embedded debris, clean cut. Alright, next step. Sterilize and clean the wound, dress it.

She tore open a palm-sized paper packet of sulfanilamide.[18] She sprinkled the yellow powder onto the raw wound then hastily swabbed around the gash from a brown bottle of iodine.

Bleary-eyed, dazed, his eyes focused on her – and angered alarm and recognition crossed his face.

He flailed at her, batting her away. "You dirty Jap bitch!" he cursed. "Get the fuck away from me!"

Mina turned indignant. "I'm an American, damn you!"

She struggled against his protests, warding off his flailing blows with her arms, trying to keep him from accidentally moving and opening his wound even further.

A few dozen yards away, her father's friend Miller and several harried sailors looked over at the outburst. Miller yelled over to Mina and her charge. "It's ok, they're with us!"

The wounded sailor hesitated for a split second, then relented, biting his lip, laying back.

Mina tore off a length of gauze with her teeth and bandaged his wound with a compress. Not exactly sanitary, but there was no time for niceties.

Several Zeroes screamed by overhead, strafing dual lines onto the ships and onto escaping sailors ashore. The planes weaved their way through, cutting them down as if they were rag dolls.

One of the sailors in the anti-aircraft guns onboard ship swiveled the double-gun turret, tracking the plane as it swooped in, firing.

Exploding flak formed puffs of black smoke surrounding the attacking planes, sending resounding booms throughout the skies. One perforated Zero caught fire, spinning towards the water. Frantically trying to swim away, a sailor treading water was too slow and the Zero slammed into him in a giant roar of water and a plume of spray. A cloud of seeming red ink spread in the water around the burning

---

[18] Sulfanilamide and other sulfa drugs were gradually phased out and replaced with penicillin over the course of the war as penicillin became mass-produced. However, Mina's use of the powder is consistent with the time period during Pearl Harbor.

wreckage.

Ashore, overhead where Mina tended to the wounded sailor, a Val dive bomber started swooping down on her.

Mina saw the plane release its payload. The one-hundred-and-thirty-two pound bomb arced, whistling...heading down...down...down...

For a moment, like a deer caught in the headlights, Mina stared in wide-eyed disbelief, gaping at the ovoid shape coming towards her as it grew larger and larger, blotting out the sun.

She heard Miller's voice yelling off to her side. "Mina! Run run run!"

Coming to her senses, determined, she hauled the wounded sailor to his feet and looped his arm around her shoulder, human-stilt walking. They limped away, trying to get as much distance between them and the impact-

The bomb detonated just a dozen paces away in an eruption of flame and debris, only partially contained by the few remaining sandbags, shock wave knocking them off their feet.

Mina felt her stomach drop and she knew she was flying. She momentarily saw the ground below her as she sailed through the air, legs and arms pinwheeling. The ground rushed up to meet her, knocking the wind out of her.

Groaning, she shakily got to her feet, face smudged with soot and dirt. Concrete gravel was embedded in her cheek, her raven hair was loose about her shoulders, and her ponytail was undone.

Her medical training kicked in and she instinctively patted herself down in a cursory self-evaluation. Gears of her mind whirred. No sharp shooting pains. Good sign. No major bleeding. Just aches and bruises, cuts and scratches. Okay.

She looked around. Then she saw it.

Lying on the concrete, amongst flaming debris and bits of scorched metal, was the sailor's head, decapitated by the bomb blast. Hair askew, face smudged with soot, raw flesh at the open throat. Whitish bone protruded from the ragged flesh, remnants of the man's spinal column. Transfixed, the sight was the sort she wished she could tear her gaze away from but her body wouldn't allow.

Mina remembered the eye. The sailor's aqua-blue eye in the disembodied head still darted about wildly in fear. Mina felt a chill as the man's piercing eye fixated at her pleadingly and the light faded away, growing dull. His expression fixed in an open-mouthed stare she would remember for years to come.

She was in such a state of shock from the sight she barely registered Miller's voice screaming at her. There was another odd sound, coming closer and closer.

The roar of an engine, belonging to a strafing Zero overhead. Mina looked skyward.

For a brief moment as the pilot streaked by Mina could see his face, right down to the fur lining of his cap and flight goggles. His gear momentarily reminded Mina of an Eskimo.

They made eye contact.

In the cockpit, the pilot gazed down, eyes within his goggles fixating on something. He saw the roll of bandage dressing in her hand.

The plane swooshed past her. Then she saw the Zero banking around...circling back, making another pass - straight for her.

Heart pounding in her chest, mouth dry, Mina took off at a dead run, arms and legs pumping. She wasn't used to such exertion. Panting, she put in a burst of speed, faster than she had ever run in her life.

Inside the cockpit, the Japanese pilot lined up the back of the pigtailed girl in his sights with a practiced, clinical eye. Target sighted. Deny medical aid to the enemy. His black-gloved fingers pulled the trigger -

The dual machine guns on the wings spat out tongues of flame, stitching bullets just three feet behind her. The fusillade kicked up chips of concrete, dust, and smoke, impacts sparking in a dotted line barely visible through the gray smoke-

Mina gasped as she was suddenly engulfed by a thick gray dust cloud, rapid-fire cracking of bullets whizzing by her ears. The ground impacts were so close she could feel hot chips of broken concrete stinging her ankles and the back of her knees. Barreling forward, heart pounding in her throat, she braced herself for the harrowing impact of bullets sure to shatter her spine and reduce her heart and lungs to mincemeat-

Suddenly, the bullets stopped as she heard staccato bullets pierce metal overhead and the whoosh of igniting flame.

Startled, she snapped her head upwards.

Intercepting the Zero, an American P-40 Warhawk, dual machine guns blazing, riddled the Zero's flank, perforating the metal chassis.

Trailing fire, the smoking Zero crashed onto the corner of a nearby building, sending up flame and powdered brick as its gas tank exploded, engulfing the wreck in a blazing conflagration.

Mina looked upwards to her savior as he flew overhead.

Visible within the cockpit, the Caucasian pilot in the American P-40 grinned and gave her a thumbs up. Mina waved at him just as a second P-40 veered off to join him in a wingman position, the American air insignia[19] a welcome sight.

Both swooped out of view around a smoking building.

A moment later, she heard her father call out.

"Mina! Hurry! More are coming!"

She whirled around. Running towards her, Miller carried a wounded marine on his back, accompanied by her medical bag-toting father. Mina sprinted in the same direction they were, towards a small overhang near a blasted building.

Still running amidst the chatter of gunfire and booms

---

[19] In the years prior to Pearl Harbor, US aircraft were marked with a white star with red circle all set in a blue disc. However, in the months after Pearl Harbor it was realized that the red dot could be construed as a Japanese *Hinomaru* from a distance or in poor visibility. In May 1942 the red dot was eliminated.

of explosions, Mina heard a croaking male voice call out for help.

Momentarily surprised, Mina's steps faltered. She glanced over her shoulder just as she made it to the overhang. The cries came from the corner of a collapsed burning building.

Leg pinned under a girder, surrounded by encroaching flames, a wounded sailor grimaced in pain and effort as he struggled to lift it off. It wasn't all that heavy but he didn't have leverage to move it.

Sprinting, Miller and her father joined her under the overhang. Miller set down his wounded charge as her father took a quick look outside and saw the trapped sailor. A flight of approaching Zeroes started strafing the area, coming in close.

Setting down his bag, grimly determined, her father dashed out towards the pinned man, running zigzag, dodging anticipated fire. He shouted over his shoulder.

"Mina, stay there!"

Watching anxiously, Mina saw him reach the pinned sailor. If her father hurried he'd have just enough time to get back before the Zeroes got too close. Straining, he lifted the girder off the sailor. The sailor grimaced at his mangled legs, twisted at an impossible angle. Broken. Mr. Sakamoto lifted the injured man onto his back in a fireman's lift, running back to cover.

Then, nightmarishly, Mina saw a Zero emerge through the gray smoke above a nearby ruined building, bearing down on her father and the wounded sailor.

Frantic, screaming, Mina pointed and yelled out an unheard warning, jumping up and down.

Inside the Zero's cockpit, the pilot's finger pulled the trigger.

The plane loomed behind her father as twin muzzles spat out fire and fury, kicking up a cloud of dust and chipped concrete all around him. Mina let out an involuntary scream as they disappeared in the smoke and debris.

Still screaming, face contorted in anguish, Mina was hauled backwards from under her arms by Miller as she struggled to run out. She flailed, kicked, and scratched wildly at him, desperate. No. Not like this. Not him, not her father, she prayed in what she knew to be a futile effort.

The smoke cleared.

Amazingly, amidst the debris, her father still stood on his feet. His glasses were blown off and he struggled with the weight of the sailor on his back, but both of them were alive.

Stunned, Mina and Miller stared. Slack-jawed, Mina blurted a question in wide-eyed astonishment.

"How!?"

Almost as surprised, Miller gave a relieved smile. "Got damn lucky. Bullets stitched a line on either side of 'em. Any more to either side, they'd be dead[20]."

Mina and Miller rushed out to them, helping them stagger towards the cover of the overhang. Mina glanced down. There really were twin stitched bullet holes on either side of her father's shoeprints, parallel like a railroad track.

The small group reached the overhang. Mina rummaged through her father's bag and grabbed bandages and sulfa envelopes. Miller set the patient down and attended to his leg.

"Mina, quick, get me the compress or he'll bleed out," her father instructed.

Suddenly, her father spat out a mouthful of blood, crimson droplets dribbling down his chin.

Mina stared at him in shock. His expression faltered with the realization of the inevitable. With the adrenaline and the shock of injury, he hadn't even realized he had been hit.

"Mina..." he said haltingly.

He looked down at his chest as a large crimson stain blossomed over his heart, spreading through his white dress shirt. The horrifying realization dawned on Mina and time

---

[20] This fortunate happenstance really happened to a survivor at Pearl Harbor.

seemed to slow. There was a miniscule shrapnel wound that pierced his heart from behind, but the flesh had closed around it to an extent; his motions aggravated it and tore it wide open. His body had been in shock and hadn't even registered it.

He teetered slightly, sank to his knees, and collapsed onto the debris-strewn ground, his grime-streaked white suit blossoming with scarlet. Mina rushed to his side. No, no, not after all that. How could fate be so cruel?

Sitting down on her knees, she cradled his head in her lap and stifled a sob, tears streaming down her cheeks. "No, no. Dad, you can't."

Swallowing the lump in her throat, she pressed both hands down on his chest wound in a futile attempt to staunch the bleeding. She could feel his hot lifeblood seep out between her fingers, and heaving sobs rose in her throat that she couldn't and didn't want to quell.

She tried her best to will him to live, lying through her teeth. She forced herself to smile gently and her tone to be as comforting as possible.

"Dad, no no. It's not as bad as it looks."

He gave her a wan smile, speaking to her in English. He only did that when he was serious. With a trembling hand he caressed her cheek in muted affection.

"Sorry, Mina-chan. We both know better."

His face turned ashen, bloody foam trickling from the corner of his mouth. The rise and fall of his chest slowed, then ceased. With a deep, quiet gurgling in the back of his throat, his head lolled to one side as his eyes closed.

His hand slid from her grasp and fell to his side, limp.

In a near stupor of abject shock and denial, Mina stared off into the distance. She sat listlessly silent, her father's warm body still cradled in her arms. Numb, the sound around her seemed to fade away as she stared out to sea in haunted disbelief.

Several nearby servicemen, faces smudged with soot and ash, looked away, evading eye contact in pained sympathy.

Amidst the carnage of the harbor, one little girl

cradled her father's body in a small overhang of a ruined building. Outside over the harbor, was the somber realization of total devastation of what had once been Battleship Row. High overhead, the Japanese planes flew back to sea, the second wave over, their task finished. Where the proud fleet of America's navy once stood, the attacking planes left burning, smoking, or sunken devastated hulks of vessels in their wake.

Further out over Battleship Row, the ships moored at anchor were aflame, sinking, overturning, or all three. Cries and pleas wafted towards shore. Each man and woman there, as well as an entire nation - and one particular little girl - was only beginning to realize how their lives would be completely, inevitably changed, forever.

4   THE AMERICAN NIGHTMARE

The ensuing days and weeks following Pearl Harbor were a whirlwind of nightmares and turmoil. Standing in the community center room, Mina numbly watched Roosevelt's announcement in the black-and-white newsreels and the declaration of war. Her mother came up from behind and held her close, trying to console her.

Then came the round-ups. One of Mina's best friends she had known since childhood came running to their house tearfully. The girl's father had been rounded up and questioned by the police, along with other local men from families of Japanese descent. A curfew was instated, and Mina had to be home by 6:00 PM. Most of their activities and social gatherings were heavily curtailed. Gone were the days when her only concerns were what shade of lipstick to wear or whether that cute quarterback would ask her to homecoming. It was a different world.

Those were her exact thoughts as she bid farewell to her father, standing atop the cliff's edge near the shoreline.

Gray ash seeped out from between her loose fingers, sailing from within her fist as Mina scattered the ashes to the wind and out to sea.

Standing at the cliff's edge at sunset, Mina sighed, her

expression morose. Her ebon hair flowed out in front of her, the wind at her back. She wore a formal, solid-black western style dress, with a single strand of pearls about her neck. Due to the hubbub and chaos since that fateful Sunday morning, the funeral was nearly two weeks after that day.

Done bidding her father farewell, Mina carried the empty urn under her arm towards the waiting car at the side of the road. Somberly quiet, her mother stood outside the car's open door, dressed in *mofuku*, a black mourning kimono.

Head down, Mina approached and whispered to her mother in English. "Mom, I just really want to be alone right now. I'll be back home later."

Understanding, her mother nodded assent. With that, Mina watched her climb inside the car. It drove off, pulling away down the parkway, leaving Mina alone at the side of the palm tree lined road.

In the waning light of day, a single coffee-colored eye peeked out between blades of tall grass. Mina had crept through the underbrush, slingshot in hand. She felt she needed the distraction.

The wind rustled the field of tall grass, sending a rippling wave through the stems.

Up ahead, a rabbit nibbled on weeds, its nose twitching.

In hushed anticipation, Mina stayed prone and raised her Y-shaped slingshot up to eye level. She had given it the moniker "Lucky Charm."

Mina pulled the elastic band of the slingshot back as far as it would go and let fly, flinging the marble-sized rock out in a blur.

Alone, hair loose about her shoulders, Mina sat sideways on the beach as the sun dipped below the horizon, knees drawn up to her chest. In silent rumination, she huddled near the small cooking fire, her petite form silhouetted against the rippling silvery-orange waves. She waited for the skewered rabbit meat on the makeshift spit to roast.

Quietly morose, she sat in solemn contemplation, lost in memory. Happier days gone by flitted across her mind's eye.

As a little girl, lounging around the soda fountain, her father would put a few cents into the jukebox. She'd dance atop his feet, giddy and carefree, thinking she could cut a rug.

The day he brought a phonograph home and she'd lie on the carpet, swinging her legs in the air lazily as she listened to Frank Sinatra.

Watching Saturday afternoon serials on the black-and-white screen of the theater, sharing a big tub of buttery popcorn with her father; she would see Clark Gable on the screen and swoon into her father's arms, her hand to her forehead, and he'd chuckle at her antics.

That one afternoon they went to the bookmart and he dropped a whole dollar on Doc Savage *and* Flash Gordon *comics for her; she sat on the carpet for hours, engrossed in the fantasy of faraway lands, a mesmerized expression on her face.*

Going with her father to the local jazz club and listening to the big band play swing music; riding atop his shoulders she'd clap and cheer with the crowd.

Sitting on the sand, Mina sighed resignedly, shaking herself out of her reverie.

She muttered to herself. "So much for the good ol' days."

Gazing up at the clouds, Mina thought she saw two clouds shaped like surfboards go by, one larger, one smaller. Mina recalled the fateful day at the beach she had nearly drowned.

Mina sighed to herself. She might as well go into town and do something else before curfew.

Mina glanced around as she strolled down Honolulu's main street. The reactions of the passerbys were very different than the day she had skated gaily down the road not so long ago. One boy wearing a newscap leaned casually against a lamppost outside the drugstore. He shot her a distrustful look as she passed by.

Mina did her best to ignore it, avoiding eye contact.

She perked up slightly when she recognized one of the neighbors, a housewife dressed in a fur coat. She waved at her.

"Hi Mrs. Jones!" Mina said merrily.

Mrs. Jones stiffened and turned away, pretending not to know her, and continued down the street with her head down.

Mina's smile faded and her hand faltered mid-wave. Damn. She had hoped that at least Mrs. Jones would be more understanding.

Several passerbys shot baleful glares at her. One woman spoke something aside to her companion and pointed at her. At this distance, Mina barely made out the words.

"Who's the Japanese girl? She shouldn't be here," the woman said.

She wasn't the only one with the sentiment. Across the street, a fried shrimp vendor Mina didn't recognize glowered at her over his steaming food cart.

A few other lounging people turned from their private conversations, shooting occasional hostile glances in Mina's direction.

Swallowing hard, Mina piped up, her expression innocent. "Uhh...erhm, I'm Chinese. *Ni-hao!*" she said, giving a polite little wave.

The hostile pedestrians relented, moving on.

Head down, Mina grumbled to herself as she walked down the street. Time to head on home.

Mina's father having been a physician, the Sakamoto family was relatively well off. Mina generally considered herself fortunate for a kid growing up in the middle of the Great Depression. They resided in a modest Colonial Revival style house constructed a little over ten years ago, just about a mile off the main road. It was one-and-a-half stories high, and elegantly asymmetrical. It even had a sunroom, with large sliding windows, and an enclosed lanai in the back.

When Mina arrived home, still in her black formal dress, she was greeted with an unpleasant surprise.

5 G-MEN

Mina was shocked to see several sable-colored 1939 Ford Deluxes parked outside the house, their curved surfaces gleaming with fresh coats of wax. Through the lit window she could see the silhouette of a man with a trenchcoat and fedora, speaking to someone out of view.

Mina grumbled to herself under her breath. Ah, hell. G-men.[21]

A black-gloved hand ran along the centuries-old *katana* sword on the stand of the shrine in the corner of the living room. Coated in layers of polished lacquer, the ornate scabbard was inlaid with gold in traditional designs. There was almost no dust; Mina's mother made sure to take care of it regularly.

Standing in front of it, one of the half-dozen G-men wearing trenchcoats and fedoras turned to his supervisor. "Hey boss, look. Another one of those samurai sabers."

The agent picked it up. Mina protested.

---

[21] G-men is a slang term originating in the 1920s to refer to "government men," particularly agents of the Federal Bureau of Investigation.

"Hey, that's a family heirloom! Put that back!" Standing nearby in an apron, hair tied in a bun, Mina's mother wrung her hands, powerless to do anything.

Ignoring her, the G-man tossed the katana into the nearby cardboard box of household items as if it was yesterday's newspaper.

Over in the kitchen, a similarly-attired agent sat on his haunches over by the large wooden cabinet. The cabinet doors were flung open. Inside were little bottles, individually labeled and meticulously arranged. He called out.

"Look, sir. Drugs. Maybe toxins they could use to poison the water supply."

Mina exclaimed with indignation. "Those are medicines to treat patients! My dad was a doctor!"

Ignoring her, the man grabbed the bottles and dumped them into the cardboard box.

One of the other agents spoke up, noticing her use of the past tense. "What do you mean, 'was'? He die in a car accident or something?"

Mina clutched her father's Panama hat to her chest like a lifeline. There was still a bullet hole through its crown. "Hey, my dad died at Pearl Harbor!" she protested indignantly.

The man snorted in derision. "What, was he an Imperial fighter pilot?"

Gritting her teeth, Mina suppressed a groan of exasperation. Getting all riled up was not going to help right now. "No, he was a doctor. He died saving a Navy sailor."

His back to the front door, a dark-suited man in a Homburg[22] hat stepped into the hallway leading to the kitchen. Gripping an oak cane in his calloused right hand, his ring finger had a square-set sapphire ring. His left leg had a steel leg brace.

In the kitchen, Mina argued heatedly with one of the junior agents, their voices rising.

Out in the hallway, the arguing voices were indistinct.

---

[22] Like a fedora, but slightly more formal.

With more lines on his face and gray at his temples since his last mission in Tokyo, Colonel James Lockwood observed the exchange curiously. He stroked his chestnut-toned beard. Who was this young female firebrand?

A few moments later the arguing stopped. The junior agent walked up to Lockwood[23] in the hallway, leaving Mina in a huff, arms crossed over her chest.

"What did she want?" Lockwood inquired.

The young G-man looked glum. "She wants to help the war effort. Too young, right?"

Expressionless, Lockwood mulled the statement, glancing at Mina. She stood sullenly in the kitchen, arms still crossed over her chest, lost in thought.

Standing in the hallway, Lockwood and his subordinate whispered as the other G-men in the adjoining room watched the exchange uncomfortably, awaiting instructions.

Finally, Lockwood sullenly shook his head. It probably wasn't a good idea. He turned to Mina and her mother. "We'll be off. Goodbye, missus and Miss Sakamoto. Sorry for your loss."

He gave her a tip of his hat and turned to leave. With that, Mina watched as the man who called himself Lockwood exited with the G-men through the front door. She heard car engines turn over.

Standing at the front door, Mina peeked through its side window. She heard the rumble of thunder outside and the sudden pitter-patter of commencing rain as the cars pulled away. They drove off the property and down the dirt road. She glanced down.

Next to the door was the rug where footwear was laid out, pair-by-pair. At the end was the pair of shiny new roller skates her father had given her that Saturday morning.

They were the last gift he ever gave her.

---

[23] Members of the military often worked in conjunction with the FBI, especially following Pearl Harbor.

Mina pressed her lips in a thin line. Deliberating, she took a moment to make a decision - then swung open the front door, running out after them, out into the pouring rain.

6   CHASING THE MAN WITH THE BLUE SAPPHIRE RING

Sprinting through the downpour, Mina ran through the woods, ebony shoulder-length hair unbound, sopping wet. There was a shortcut through the woods she knew. If she hurried she could get ahead of them, assuming they weren't going off-road.

Putting on a burst of speed, legs a blur, she raced through the winding woodland. Running through the trees, she heard the rumble of engines through the grove of loblolly pines ahead and knew she was in the right place.

Through his front windshield, the driver saw a blurry form streak out of the treeline, a soaked teenage girl dashing out into the middle of the road, caught in the glare of headlights-

Horn blaring, the car screeched to a halt barely an inch in front of her, lurching back onto its suspension. She slammed both hands onto the hood. She stood there, braced against the front of the car.

There was the sound of a car door opening. Concerned, a fedora-wearing G-man stepped out of the driver's seat, whipping out a Tommy gun from within the folds of his trenchcoat and leveling it at her.

Almost simultaneously, other agents in the two jet-black cars behind them emerged, pulling out pistols and training them at her in double-handed grips.

For a moment, in the pouring rain, everyone stock-still.

Bathed in the harsh beams of the headlights, the illumination bleached the color from the front of her body, giving Mina a near surreal appearance. Still braced against the hood of the car, Mina stood like a statue in her black dress, sopping ebon hair hanging to her shoulders, bangs obscuring her eyes in an uncanny fashion, almost like the Japanese ghosts of old. Droplets of water ran down her face onto the hood of the car. For a wary moment everyone just watched her, unsure what she was going to do.

The words caught in her throat as she felt the wellspring of sadness, loss, and anguish rise up inside her all over again. The grief manifested as pained tightness in her throat and chest as she finally spoke in a small voice.

"Please. Please. I want to do this. Hell. I need it."

Her fist trembled on the hood of the car as she spoke. Breaking down, she started sobbing. "Please. Just let me fight," she pleaded.

Mina tilted her head up, looking through the front windshield. On the seat next to Lockwood sat cardboard boxes of manila folders, with a few folders piled on top.

He plucked out one in particular and perused it, licking his finger and turning a few pages. He beckoned to her.

She went around to the side of the car. He swung the door open to speak with her, but was unable to give her a seat because of the boxes.

Lockwood examined her curiously, looking the sopping girl up and down. It was rare to see such determination. "What are you? Fifteen? Sixteen?"

Mina was indignant. "Sixteen," she lied.

He raised a disbelieving brow and held out an official looking document. It was a copy of a birth certificate for the state of Hawaii. "I have files on all your family members here," he chided. "According to your birth certificate, you were born on November 6, 1927. You're fourteen years old."

Caught in the lie, Mina swallowed hard. "Sir. Please. Let me do something."

Lockwood scoffed. "Like what, fight? You're just a pipsqueak."

Then, his expression softened as sympathy crossed his face. "Miss, I'm sorry, but you're too young. Come back when you're seventeen."

Mina felt her chances slipping away. She exclaimed in protest. "The war could be over by then!"

"God willing. You're too young to die."

Mina snorted in derision. "Oh please! We both know for enlistment you're only as young as you look."

Lockwood was quiet as he pondered the situation. Something came to mind. "You might be able to translate, though," he mused. "Or maybe be a nurse."

Anxiously hopeful, Mina looked to Lockwood.

Solemn silence ensued save for the pitter-patter of the rain. In the downpour, fedoras sopping wet, the trenchcoated G-Men exchanged looks.

Mina said nothing to the man inside the open door of the car, remaining silent.

Finally, he reached a conclusion. "Very well, Miss Sakamoto. I admire your persistence."

He pulled a Mont Blanc pen from his shirt pocket and scribbled onto the sheet of paper in his lap, ending with a flourish.

He handed the birth certificate back to her. Scrawled in his penmanship, the birth year had been changed to 1924.

"Today, you're seventeen," he declared.

Mina breathed a sigh of relief. "Oh, thank you sir."

"Don't thank me yet. You're just being given a chance to prove yourself. Meet me at Honolulu Harbor tomorrow morning, eight A.M. sharp. You're coming with me to San Francisco for defense language training[24], pending a background check. We'll take care of the other red tape later."

With that, Lockwood gave her a polite tip of his hat. The agent with the Tommy gun shut Lockwood's door and the agents boarded their respective vehicles.

Within moments, the small convoy drove off, leaving Mina standing out in the middle of the muddy dirt road, clutching a wet sheet of paper, alone in the pouring rain.

---

[24] Lockwood is referring to the Military Intelligence Service (MIS) school, whose members were largely second-generation Japanese-Americans like Mina. Mina is shipping out to San Francisco instead of Minnesota, since this is within a few weeks after Pearl Harbor. MIS didn't move to Savage, Minnesota until a few months later, in March 1942.

7   WILD BILL

OSS Headquarters Complex

2430 E Street in Washington, D.C. Operational Group HQ unit "Q Building"

Months later

Rather unassuming, just northwest of the Lincoln Memorial, the campus-style buildings housed the United States' fledgling wartime intelligence agency. The set of pillared buildings enclosed a courtyard, with trees out in the grassy lawn. It was a rather tranquil setting for such cloak-and-dagger work. The perimeter was enclosed by a chain-link fence and a guard post, the few indicators of its importance.

On top of the desk in the director's office was an open file folder. Paper-clipped to the sheaf of papers within was Mina's black-and-white headshot, her hair in a side braid trailing down her shoulder. The photo captured her looking into the camera with a serious expression. Various stats were listed in the attached form. Height: 4'11". Weight: 96 pounds, etc.

William "Wild Bill" Donovan sat behind the desk, dressed in a severe suit. This war hero was the director of the Office of Strategic Services, the agency for coordinating espionage activities behind enemy lines. Approaching fifty, the older Caucasian gentleman was about ten year's Lockwood's senior, and had a craggy face, weathered from time in the field.

Lockwood sat in the chair in front of the desk as Donovan posed a question. "She cleared the background check? I only care about loyalty and skills."

"Double checked, triple checked, and checked in ways that are just plain crazy," said Lockwood affirmatively.

Satisfied, Donovan gave a curt nod. "Gimme the rundown."

"Her father was a doctor," Lockwood stated. "Died at Pearl Harbor while trying to save an American sailor. She's out for blood. She risked her life too, doing the same."

Donovan nodded in acknowledgement. "Ah. Accomplishments?"

"She earned the Soldier's Medal for her translation work. Currently at naval intelligence in Maryland working on battlefield documents."

Donovon perused the file, nodding as he flipped pages. "According to this, she's a good translator. Why doesn't she want to continue doing it?"

"She wants to fight," said Lockwood.

Donovan perused the file for a few more moments then nodded casually. He looked to Lockwood.

"Alright," he said to Lockwood. "We have a number of women behind enemy lines, no problem. Any combat experience?"

"Unofficially, yes. She helped out during the Great Los Angeles Air Raid fighting the Japanese spies. Among other, um, 'incidents' that never occurred."

Considering it, Donovan nodded.

"Alright. Bring her in, see what she can do."

Naval Intelligence Headquarters - Suitland, MD.

In the translators' room, the man with the cane and square-set sapphire ring walked down the rows of desks filling the room. Most of the operators were of Japanese descent, with a handful being of other ethnicities.

At one particular desk in the row, Mina sat in her chair, headset on, giving a running translation in Japanese. *"Kochira ko taicho kara daitai e, teisatsu-ki o yosei shimasu. Dozo!"*

It was a recorded battlefield radio intercept. Platoon commander to battalion. Requesting air reconnaissance. Over.

Mina glanced up as the man with the neatly trimmed chestnut beard approached her desk. Attentively curious, Mina pulled off her headphones, letting them rest about her neck.

"Congratulations Mina. You passed the OSS interview. Your day has come."

He handed her a fat manila folder. "You've been accepted into training," he said. "You ship out for Area F in Potomac, Maryland in the morning."

8   OH SO SECRET

Prior to the onset of the war, Congressional Country Club was a luxurious, verdant golf course in Potomac, Maryland, USA. It was located along the back roads among rolling green hills and upper-middle-class suburbs.

With the war effort, most of the grounds had been repurposed into an OSS[25] training facility for future spies, saboteurs, and commandos operating behind enemy lines.

Riding in the back of the canvas-walled truck with six other recruits, Mina bounced and jostled as the truck creaked along. Seated shoulder-to-shoulder, Mina found the ride uncomfortable and tense. It was dim; the walls were covered with thick olive-drab canvas that made it impossible to see outside. The only source of illumination was from stray rays of light from tiny tears in the cloth.

Mina wondered with nervous anticipation what their destination would be like. Would it be like stories she'd heard about boot camp? There probably wouldn't be as many classrooms as there had been in the MIS defense language

---

[25] "Oh So Secret" was a droll nickname for the Office of Strategic Services.

school.

She glanced at the other recruits. None of them spoke. There were five Caucasian men with European features. They didn't seem to know each other.

One recruit was an Asian man. Mina guessed he was Chinese based on facial bone structure and the weave of his clothing, which didn't seem to be of American design. Mina postulated he could be a Chinese Commando here for training.

Another passenger was a flaxen-haired, Caucasian teenage girl. She was maybe a year or two older than Mina, with blonde curls, rather pretty. Mina would have struck up a conversation with her if it wasn't for the fact they were generally discouraged from doing so.

The truck came to a rolling stop and the brakes let out a slight metallic squeal.

She heard a sharp rap on the back of the truck. The tarp pulled back and Mina winced, squinting at the sudden flood of sunlight. Even though it was late afternoon, the sudden light felt harsh.

Standing at the back of the truck, wearing his Army colonel's uniform, Lockwood rapped his cane against the side of the exit. "Everybody out!" he shouted.

With her pack on her back, Mina climbed out. Of the few personal items she had been allowed to bring, Mina had packed along her roller skates. It was the last gift her father had ever given her, and she didn't want to leave them back home.

The other trucks were lined up alongside the curb. Looking out onto the grounds, Mina jaw dropped at the sight, stunned by the scope of the endeavor.

Up on the hill, like a looming castle, was the massive Mediterranean-style clubhouse overlooking 400 acres of verdant hills and grassy fields.

Mina noticed the smell, an odd juxtaposition of cut grass and freshly overturned earth, all mingled with the stench of gunpowder and cooked food.

Mina stood near the railing at the edge of the hills,

looking out onto the fields below.

Men jogged in formation through the yard, shouting cadence. Up on an elevated platform, a mock aircraft fuselage had been set up. Mina saw several men practice jumping out, their dome-shaped white parachutes billowing out as they leapt one after the other.

The practice hole had been turned into a shooting range. Blindfolded men fired pistols[26] one-handed at bullseye targets, lowering their hand to their side then snapping back up, loosing a shot. It was a test for memory combined with eye-hand coordination.

The fairway had been turned into a live-fire exercise zone. Mina watched men crawl forward on their bellies with rifles in their hands, as chattering machine gun fire kicked up tufts of dirt and grass all around them.

Down on the other side of the grounds was a tent city arrayed in an efficient grid.

Standing near the entranceway to the clubhouse, an uniformed officer with a cap waved them in.

Walking through the clubhouse, Mina noticed candidates from all walks of life. According to Lockwood, there were professions ranging from psychiatrists to gangsters and even accountants. She saw some stunningly beautiful women. Mina guessed those were the ones meant as seductress arm-candy for enemy officers.

Mina heard there were even crossword puzzle addicts. She guessed that had more to do with cryptanalysis than anything else.

She glanced to her side and noticed a few rough-looking fellows with brawny arms. Mina noticed some had prison tattoos, not done professionally, with faded bluish ink. Such tattoos were a tradition in Europe that stretched back centuries, she recalled from an old magazine. Lockwood had

---

[26] Common pistols were the Colt M1911A1. The British had some specific techniques regarding it they taught to American OSS forces.

spoken of ex-convicts here. Unique skills made them useful in the war effort. During her time doing translation work, Lockwood mentioned some of the OSS's expert forgers were former criminals.

For a moment, Mina wondered to herself. What the hell had she gotten herself into? Prior to her interview in Washington D.C., she had a rough idea of what this life entailed.

During dinner in the mess hall, Mina introduced herself with her training code name. They didn't use real names here, not even their first names. Lockwood had overseen her Japanese defense language exam a few months back and remarked that it had gone "smooth as silk" afterwards.

And so the name stuck.

Mina introduced herself to the other recruits simply as "Silk."

9   WEAVING SILK

The bugle trumpeted a morning call of reveille, rousing Mina from a deep slumber.

Bleary-eyed, Mina swung her legs over the side of the cot. Her eyelids each weighed a ton. The other five recruits in the tent did similarly, stirring, yawning or stumbling to their feet. Groggy, hiding her face in her hands wearily, Mina internally braced herself.

It was gonna be a long day.

A pair of boots strode down the line of recruits assembled in the grassy yard. Standing next to Mina, the blonde girl from the truck ride Mina knew only as "Goldilocks" whispered aside in a proper English accent. "Oh, what do you know, a fellow Brit," she said, glancing at their drill instructor.

Mina whispered out of the corner of her mouth. "I had heard about that, wasn't expecting to get him."

Mina's instructor was actually American, although there were other instructors who were. The newly-formed OSS was modeled after Britain's Special Operations Executive, and this particular consultant had arrived from across the pond.

In his British Commando uniform, the stony-faced

Briton with the green beret[27] strode down the lines of raw recruits, hands clasped behind his back. Raven hair in a ponytail, Mina stood at rigid attention in the middle of the line, eyes forward.

Loud and blustery, Ravencroft roared at them with London-accented thunder and gusto.

"Alright, you sodding lot! Let me be clear. Despite how things may look, you are not soldiers. You are soldier-*spies*.

"You will not usually be fighting on the front lines. You will be *behind* enemy lines, gathering intel, causing havoc, stirring up trouble, or just plain blowin' shite up! Hell, I'm gonna teach you how to castrate a man with your bare hands![28] Do you bloody get me!"

Mina and the others yelled in unison.

"Sir yes sir!"

So it was, each and every morning for three months. At the crack of dawn, it was bugle reveille, bunk making and other hurried morning preparations. Straightaways after, the bunch of them arrayed in the yard, silhouetted against the rising sun doing jumping jacks.

Mina and the other OSS recruits had only four weeks accelerated training for basic combat, much shorter than in the Army. The main purpose of their training was to prepare them for the unexpected, due to the unusual nature of their duties.

For the first month Mina and her class ran through manual-of-arms and basic soldiering. She learned how to use and maintain both Allied and Axis weapons.

---

[27] In modern days the green beret is associated with America's Special Forces soldiers of the same name, but its use originated with the British Commandos during World War II.

[28] Castrating a man with one's bare hands was a real technique taught to OSS recruits. Ouch!

Next to the mock aircraft fuselage platform, Mina learned hand-to-hand combat from Ravencroft.[29] Lockwood was no longer able to fight in such a manner, at least not effectively, but he was still a good manager and supervisor. He stood nearby, observing the activities.

Fighting with knees-and-elbows, Ravencroft pummeled Mina, driving her back in a flurry of blows almost too fast to follow. Unable to block that quickly, Mina backpedaled, stumbled, and Ravencroft used a sweeping kick to knock Mina's legs out from under her and jabbed his fist an inch away from her face. Had it been for real, Mina realized she would be unconscious or dead.

He extended a hand to help her to her feet. Mina struggled to fight the sinking dismay within her. She knew she still had a ways to go.

Most of the classrooms were outdoors. They covered numerous topics. Knots. Camouflage usage, including war paint and ghillie suits. Tracking. Map reading and navigation. Patrolling. Chemical warfare preparedness, a.k.a. gas mask use. Mirror and other signaling. All manner of communications, including radio, Morse code, and more covert methods, such as using a coded one-time-pad to encrypt messages. Reconnaissance, both day-and-night, and how to properly report intelligence.

Due to her pending duties, she was given specialized training with demolitions. (To which her response was a chipper "Yay! Fireworks!")

The caddie shacks and the rain shelters on the golf course had been turned into makeshift targets for mortar practice. Aside from the green hills, the country club had wooded areas perfect for nighttime commando exercises, practicing hit-and-run tactics and ambushes. With woodland-

---

[29] Historically, the actual hand-to-hand combat training area at the Potomac, Maryland country club training site.

style camouflage paint on her face, Mina would crawl through the bushes with a stiletto knife and pounce on the poor milkman making deliveries. Poor fellow, it scared the hell out of him.

Out at the banks of the Potomac River[30], dressed in a black two-piece swimsuit with flippers on her feet, Mina kneeled at the edge of the deep water. With great trepidation, she gingerly touched a toe into the water. Other recruits were already in the river, splashing and horsing around.

Nearby, Goldilocks swam in the water as if she had been born in it, taking in great gulps of air before diving. She streaked beneath the surface of the water, fast and fluid, outdistancing the other recruits as they tried to keep up with her.

Nearby, Ravencroft ran up to Mina, bellowing an inch away from her face, using her training code name.

"Silk! Get in the sodding water!"

Mina stammered a reply. "But sir, I-I-"

The bereted man berated her, losing patience. "Get. In. Now!" he roared.

The big Briton shoved her head into the water as she splashed, struggled, gurgled and sputtered, her arms flailing wildly.

A few hours later, floundering in the middle of the river, Mina struggled to stay afloat with her heavy gear. Sputtering, she gulped down gobfuls of water, trying to spit it out.

Swimming like a fish, face determined, Goldilocks paddled over to Mina. The blonde grabbed her in a lifesaver's carry under her arms and towed Mina back to shore.

Near the shoreline, other recruits in black swimsuits worked in unison, pulling their rubber boats[31] onto the sandy

---

[30] A real-OSS training area for water operations.

banks of the Potomac River.

Tired, bedraggled, her hair sopping wet, Mina looked absolutely miserable. Mina trudged onto the sand as her teammate hauled her ashore. Mina's Lambertsen rebreather mask dangled limply in one hand, a pack of detcord and a limpet mine in her other.

Propping Mina up, Goldilocks helped her totter onto dry land.

Teeth chattering, Mina croaked out a curse. "Damn it to hell. I can do everything but swim."

Goldilocks tried to console her. "Chin up, mate. You'll get the hang of it," she remarked in her usual British manner.

Exhausted, Mina coughed, bending over and spewing a great heaving lungful of water onto the ground.

A few of the other recruits nearby exchanged concerned glances.

Stern, standing a few feet away with his arms crossed over his chest, Ravencroft bellowed at Mina. "Silk! You have three weeks to improve your marks, or you're out!"

With a haggard expression on her face, Mina nodded weakly.

After the first month of training, there were two months spent on more unconventional aspects of their work - espionage, sabotage, and all around skullduggery.

They were given instruction on how to conduct oneself unobtrusively in EnemiArea, a generic term for areas of operation behind enemy lines. Learning the local lingo, keeping talk to a minimum, and observing local customs were all included.

There were a bevy of other topics. Counterintelligence. Search evasion. Intrusion detection. One black-and-white film showed how to evade a body search. Ironically, she found there was actually no foolproof way. Most

---

[31] The rubber boat portrayed here is the LCRL (Landing Craft Rubber Large).

of the time, if one was under enough scrutiny to be arrested and strip-searched, they were doomed to be discovered. Cyanide was advised in such circumstances.

Standing on the paved parking lot, Lockwood pointed at a dozen target silhouettes set up around the area. It was a test for out-of-the-box thinking.

"Alright!" he yelled to the gathered trainees. He pointed as he spoke. "Find a way to cross this parking lot in less than five seconds and take out all the targets! You have five minutes to plan, and can use any item on the premises. Go!" He blew his whistle shrilly.

Some of the recruits had ingenious solutions. One burly, tattooed ex-con was a former mechanic. He jury-rigged one of the nearby cars to run on its own, with a piece of wood jamming down the accelerator pedal. Engine revving, the car rammed into the targets and exploded into a fireball in their midst.

The blonde girl, Goldilocks, had previous mountain climbing experience. She set up a zipline from the roof down to street level, firing her Tommy gun one-handed, gunning the targets down.

Mina's solution was to use the roller skates she had brought along in her bag from home. She zipped in amongst the targets, dodging and weaving as if evading fire, took cover behind the various vehicles, gunned down the silhouettes, and raced to the end of the zone.

Lockwood checked his pocket watch and nodded approvingly. "Good. Innovative. I like that!"

Mina grinned.

10 THE BIG KAHUNA

For special weapons training, Mina was pleased to see that a fellow Hawaiian was her instructor. Given that he had no Japanese accent, Mina surmised he grew up speaking English and was *nisei*[32] second-generation Japanese-American, same as her.

Mina stood assembled on the grass with the other recruits as the man they knew only as "Kahuna" addressed them. The term was Hawaiian for a shaman or a wise sage. Given his combat prowess, Mina thought it apt.

"Aloha recruits!" he bellowed. "You don't need to know my name. I don't wanna know your name! All you need to know is I've been using a katana sword since I was four years old and I'll be your special weapons instructor.

Mina watched him attentively. He continued speaking. "If you are in this special class, you will be heading to Asia or the Pacific. In the field, you will occasionally encounter Japanese officers who use swords. *Kendo* is a common sport in Japan. It's like fencing here in the West. Some of these men

[32] *Nisei* is a Japanese-language term used in countries in North America, South America and Australia to specify the second-generation children born to Japanese people in the new country.

have been using a sword since childhood.

"You may not always have a firearm when you encounter them. Hell, you might be out of ammo and need to use one yourself.

"You need to learn how to counter them without a gat," he finished.

Later, in the middle of sword practice on the grassy field, the other students watched as Mina sparred with instructor Kahuna.

Woefully pathetic with her bamboo training sword, Mina was unable to block or parry any blows, wincing in pain as he struck her all over her body.

Kahuna whacked her once with his bamboo sword, striking Mina on top of her head and she flinched.

Backing away, trying to block blows, Mina started hyperventilating.

Kahuna's sword whacked Mina across the face. - Ignoring Mina's cry of pain, he admonished her. "Tojo won't care if you're hurtin', Silk."

Kahuna whacked her behind the ankle. Cringing, Mina hobbled away.

"Hell, he wants that," he snarled.

Kahuna hit her across the buttocks and Mina yelped in pain.

"And they'll do awful things to you if you're captured!"

With a flourish he disarmed Mina, knocking the bamboo sword out of her hands, then knocking her down with the hilt of his sword.

Mina's head tilted up. Mina saw him standing over her imposingly, holding the tip of his sword at her throat.

"Better to die right then and there," he declared.

Mina slumped back onto the ground in resignation.

Near the knife-throwing range on the course, some candidates cowered and cringed behind the corner as a blindfolded Mina flung knives at the target. The blades bounced and sparked off every surface with a metallic ping, ricocheting wildly. The wide motion of her arm and centrifugal motion of her hips kept throwing off her aim.

Eyes wide with fear, Goldilocks gaped as a blade embedded into the wall near her ear, vibrating.

The nearby students gave Mina a wide berth.

Nearby, Kahuna unwrapped a leather bandolier holding what appeared to be metal stars a little larger than his palm.

Hearing the sound, Mina lifted her blindfold and looked at the stars curiously. She vaguely recalled the name from childhood stories she had heard her father tell. Little blades. "*Shuriken*? Like the kind *shinobi* use?" she asked.[33]

Kahuna nodded. "Yes. My family is descended from the Koga clan in Japan."

He picked up a handful of shuriken stars. "Not very conventional, but still useful. Very good for forcing your opponent to throw up an arm to cover their face. Buys time. Good distraction."

Mina turned a star around curiously in her hand and tried to fling it. It bounced off the target with a ping.

"No," Kahuna corrected. "Aim along your middle finger and follow through."

Standing behind her, he gently grasped her hand, guiding her hand with his own as she flung it.

This time the star zipped into the man-shaped silhouette target right between the eyes.

Encouraging, he clapped her on the back. "There you go! Keep practicing."

Many of them washed out. Some of them actually sped through training. Goldilocks was deployed to Europe

---

[33] Shuriken: Small blades meant to fit in the hand. Can include various throwing spikes, but in the West the term is often used to refer to throwing stars.

Shinobi: Another word for ninja. 'nuff said.

early, leaving Mina virtually companionless. Mina pressed on.

In the ensuing weeks, Mina got progressively better. She received fewer blows from Ravencroft, learning the counters. Soon, she was able to hold her own against Kahuna. She wasn't able to surpass him, but at least she could stand her ground without faltering. On the knife range, she was able to eventually fling the knife with near perfect precision into the head of the human silhouette. On top of that, she could toss a cluster of shuriken stars around the embedded blade. But the real exams came the final week of training.

The final week

The shrill sound of the whistle resounded within the large indoor swimming pool.

Wearing black one-piece swimsuits, Mina and a dozen other candidates, both male and female, dove into the water from kneeling positions.

Sweeping her arms in a front crawl stroke, Mina swam out as fast as she could. Despite the name, the front crawl was one of the fastest swim strokes. She had been practicing it for weeks, struggling to quell the fear inside her.

Standing at the edge of the pool, Ravencroft walked by, clipboard in hand, taking notes.

Inhaling to her side, Mina splashed and cut her way through the water. She glanced to either side to check out the others.

It didn't look good.

Swimming furiously, the other candidates streaked ahead, outpacing Mina by nearly a whole yard. Coughing and sputtering, heart pounding, Mina pressed on, trying to keep up. At least she didn't want to finish last.

Suddenly, the whistle blew, shrill and loud. Everyone stopped where they were and the sound of splashing faded. Ravencroft pointed an accusing finger at Mina.

Livid, he turned red as a tomato, jowls working up and down. "You! Silk! Out of the water!" he roared.

Coughing and sputtering, Mina climbed out to the edge of the pool, dripping wet.

"What the hell was that!" he screamed in her face. "You've had three sodding weeks to improve your swim marks!"

Mina shivered, and glanced up at the large rectangular window of the observation room. She could see a familiar male figure, both hands resting on his cane in front of him.

The look on his face broke her heart. Sternly gruff, Lockwood shook his head, a gravely disappointed look on his face. Mina felt her heart sink even lower.

Still red as a tomato, Ravencroft yelled in her face, his nose just an inch from hers.

"Lockwood's office. Now!"

Hair sopping wet, Mina stared at the ground dismally, not meeting his gaze.

She had failed.

11 RIDE OUT THE WAVE

A secretary with a stylish Lana Turner hairstyle ushered Mina quietly into Lockwood's office. The woman closed the door behind her, and the latch clicked shut.

Mina sat in the high-backed chair, swinging her legs back-and-forth the way she had done as a kid. She found it a nervous habit she needed to kick.

Agitated, Mina looked around dismally. It was actually the first time she was here. Other times she had met up with Lockwood during training it had mainly been in conference rooms or outdoor courses of the facility. She felt like a kid sent to the principal's office, intimidated and small. He even made her wait. Saying nothing, not even glancing from his papers, Lockwood scribbled something down.

Growing restless, Mina hopped to her feet and looked around at the framed black-and-white photos on the walls. One showed Lockwood as a teenage boy, his strong jaw prominent even then, growing up on a farm. The photo showed him standing next to an older man in dirt-streaked farmer's overalls, out in front of a barn. Lockwood bore a strong resemblance to the man and she guessed it was his father.

Going on, Mina stopped at a photo of a chestnut-haired girl with pigtails, perhaps nine-years old, riding atop Lockwood's shoulders at Coney Island. The crest of the landmark Cyclone roller coaster was behind them. Both of them mirthful, the little girl smiled gaily, caught in a moment of unabashed delight.

Mina's interest was piqued. "Oh! You have kids?" she asked.

Still scribbling, Lockwood didn't even look up to respond.

"Had. Died of tuberculosis[34] in '28."

"I'm sorry, sir," she said, genuinely remorseful.

She glanced at the second photo next to it. It showed Lockwood, a few years older than in the farm photo, on a wooden fishing boat with a gruff-looking fisherman. The two of them were frozen in a moment of glee, hauling in a massive catch of flopping fish in a net, with flung droplets of water frozen in time.

She moved on. Inquisitive, she looked at a nearby display stand, cocking her head.

Mounted on the frame was a revolver, which she recognized as a Smith & Wesson Model 27 revolver from her training sessions. It was a first-run .357 Magnum with 3.5 inch barrel, customized with a deep blue luster.

Curious, she reached for it. Before her hands even touched it, Lockwood spoke up without looking at her.

"Don't touch that. That's a family heirloom. My stepfather gave it to me ten years ago just before he died."

Mina immediately withdrew her hands and respectfully clasped them behind her back.

Still curious, Mina went over to the table in the middle of the room. On it was a map of the world, pre-war, with

[34] Tuberculosis was a major cause of death during the early part of the 20th century. A vaccine called Bacille de Calmette et Guérin or BCG had been available since 1921, however it was not widely used. This was largely due to a health scare caused by a spat of deaths caused by contaminated batches of the vaccine.

Japanese notations and markings. Mina guessed it had been captured from some Japanese official's office. It was more of a political oddity and had little strategic value.

She examined the map more closely. The expanding rays of the sun of the Japanese war emblem radiated outward from Japan, encompassing the globe. Furthermore, all the countries in Asia and surrounding areas were marked with little Japanese flag icons. Europe and half the United States were left ambiguously unmarked, though the expansive rays of the rising sun still swept through the actual country.

Lockwood's voice broke the silence.

"You know what water is, Mina?"

Mina looked uncertain. She glanced at the captured Japanese map on the table, with its scarlet rays crossing entire oceans.

"Water represents the Empire of Japan?" she ventured.

Lockwood shook his head. "More."

He pointed to the map. "You know what '*hakko ichiu*' is, I'm sure."

Mina nodded. "Yes. Japan's pre-war plan of expansion. Loosely translated, 'all eight corners of the world under one roof.' Basically, global domination."

Lockwood spoke to her admonishingly. "Mina, if we don't stop Japan and the other Axis powers, it's the end of America and her way of life. They are as irrepressible as the tide-" he gestured, "and will sweep across the earth like a tidal wave and wash us away."

Mina felt a lump form in her throat. She spoke in a small voice. "Sir, there is only so much one person can do. Sometimes there isn't much you can do against the tide, if the storm is too severe. You would drown."

Lockwood raised a finger in agreement. "Agreed. Some things are too much for anyone. But I never asked you to stay aboard your ship. It would be splintered against the shore or capsize. But there are other things you can do."

Mina looked at him curiously as he stood up from

behind his desk and went to the large window. It was a bright day outside, and oddly peaceful on the rolling emerald fields.

Contemplative, he stood with his hands clasped behind his back, speaking musingly. "My stepfather was a fisherman. He once told me he had to weather many storms in life."

Lockwood pulled out a Lucky Strike cigarette from inside his suit pocket and lit up, taking a puff before continuing.

"He once told me that water represents the elements in this world that are outside our control and near impossible to resist. It could be an army. It could be a storm. It could be life itself."

Mina nodded, trying to follow where he was going. "Yes. I've read of some scientists and philosophers who equate water with life itself."

Lockwood reminisced. "My stepfather was once caught in a squall. Boat capsized. Had to swim sixty miles to shore."

Mina nodded, impressed. Lockwood turned to her and looked her straight in the eye.

"This is what he told me: 'Don't be afraid of the water. Don't be afraid of life. Never stop swimming, and never give up.'"

Lockwood continued encouragingly. "If your ship is in a storm, head for port. If you can't head for port and start to sink, bail water. If you can't bail fast enough and your ship sinks, swim. If you can't swim, well-" At this, he grinned. "-then all your problems are over anyway."

Mina suppressed a laugh, the edges of her lips curling.

"Water might seep through crevices and get you where you think you're safe," said Lockwood. "It might soak you and make you miserable. It may even drown you. It's an unstoppable force. You may not be able to swim against it-"

Lockwood held up a finger as Mina opened her mouth in protest.

"-but you can ride it out," he finished. "Fight the

waves, fight the tide. Don't just give up."

Lockwood turned and sat back down behind his desk, focusing on some of his papers. "You're from Hawaii of all places, Mina."

He looked her straight in the eye.

"Ride out that wave, Mina," he instructed. "If you wipe out, get right back on."

At this, Mina turned somberly quiet, turning away from him. It was like hearing her father the day she had nearly drowned. Her words almost caught in her throat.

"I never did," she said abashedly.

"You'll have to someday," he admonished.

Somber, Mina sighed. She turned to leave, head lowered and shoulders slumped. She had literally and figuratively washed out.

She stopped in her tracks and perked up when Lockwood added something.

"But not today."

With a resounding thud, his hand clomped a big red "APPROVED" stamp in crimson ink across Mina's candidate file.

Turning to face him, Mina felt hope flutter in her heart.

He stood up from behind his desk and shook Mina's hand, their two silhouettes against the wall-length office window.

"Welcome to the OSS," he said.

12 SUICIDE PILL

Surgical mask on the lower half of his face, the dentist poked his little round mirror inside Mina's mouth. He tapped the end of the pick against the false molar.

"Alright agent," he said. "You're all set. Just don't bite down on it unless you need too. You'd release the cyanide. Avoid chewing with that side of your mouth."

Mina climbed out of the dentist's chair. She winced, rubbing her jaw.

Lockwood waited at the door. It had been a few days since their meeting in the office. She headed over to him, and the two strolled outside.

Walking side-by-side through the country club grounds, Lockwood gave her the rundown.

"Officially, you'll be part of the Army Nurse Corps. The women there are actually given commissions, so you'll have the rank of Second Lieutenant."

Mina looked surprised. "I'm an officer?"

He made a dismissive gesture with his cane. "Don't worry about the age issue. Only a few people know, and in this particular case they think it might actually help."

Mina nodded appreciatively.

Lockwood continued. "There are four main reasons why you're being chosen for this," he stated.

Mina nodded again, listening attentively.

"The first, obviously, is because you are Japanese American. Your proficiency in languages and work as a translator was admirable. You blend in. You can go where I couldn't."

Lockwood rapped his cane against his metal leg brace. Not blending in had almost gotten him killed. Mina gave a solemn nod.

"The second," he resumed. "You're a girl. Going undercover, boys tend to be questioned more closely than girls. More apt to be a potential combatant. Girls can go where guys cannot."

"And the third?" she asked.

"Ties into all the above. Your nurse training. Your cover will be as a high school student with some training as a nurse. Since Japan's medical system is based on Germany's, your training from working with your father is basically identical to Japanese nurse training. It's damn good cover. Good excuse to be near soldiers."

Mina pressed. "And the last?"

Lockwood tapped his fist over his chest, grinning at her.

"Heart," he stated. "Out in the pouring rain, when you begged me to let you sign up, you wouldn't take no for an answer. You never gave up. In other words, you're exactly the kind of men and women we need to win this war. Ride out the wave, Mina."

"Sir, yes sir!"

Inside the clubhouse radio room, Mina and Lockwood stood behind the radio operator, who sat in front of the device with his headphones on.

"Okay Mina," said Lockwood. "We're letting you choose your own callsign."

Mina considered it for a moment. She had an older

callsign from her time with MIS translation work. She had only used it once or twice before. It should still be available.

For a moment, home flitted across her mind as she thought of the name. Great pink coral reefs offshore, and her childhood hobbies hunting hares with a slingshot.

A tight smile creased her lips as she responded.

"Coral Hare."

13 JIM

Visible from outside, the lights of the greasy spoon diner were on. A paper-capped waitress stood by a table taking orders. The diner was down the street from the country club, just a few blocks away. Charming, it bespoke of everything from weary travelers, to lonesome nights, to fun-filled mirth with family and friends.

Inside, sitting in the booth across from Lockwood, the waitress took their menus after taking their orders.

Mina glanced around the surroundings, looking at the female soda jerk at the fountain and the round swivel seats at the bar. The air was filled with the aroma of flapjacks on the griddle and sizzling pork sausage, with just a hint of sweet soda syrup. With a pang, it reminded Mina of the last time she had gone to a diner.

"Wow. I haven't been to a diner since my fath-"

She caught herself. The favor Lockwood had done helping her pass the water proficiency exam notwithstanding, she wasn't sure how appropriate it was to drag personal matters into the conversation. Despite her catharsis in the pouring rain, she wasn't that comfortable with openly discussing it with him yet.

"Um...since Pearl Harbor," she finished instead. "Thank you, Colonel."

"Please. Call me Jim," he said pleasantly.

Something occurred to Mina. It wasn't secure here. By and large, Mina and the other recruits were rarely allowed off the training facility.

Uneasy, Mina glanced around then hunched toward Lockwood, voice hushed. "Can we talk here?"

"Actually, yes. Everyone here is actually one of our people."

Mina nodded, shoulders relaxing.

Lockwood brought up a bit of business. "There's something you need to remember when you're out in the field. Training is no substitute for experience. After you get a few notches on your belt, the real work begins."

Serious, Mina nodded.

Two hours later, leaving the diner, Mina walked with Lockwood side-by-side down the sidewalk. Crickets chirped pleasantly. The pair were alone along the country road, down the street from the training facility.

Mina polished off the last few bites of her burger, licking her fingers then dusting her hands off. "Man, that was a good Liberty Steak[35]," she marveled. After a moment, Mina poised a question.

"So, Jim, any last bits of advice for me?"

With his cane, he gestured down the road. The lights from the country club were visible a few blocks away.

"Just one," he said. "There's something I used to do before a mission. Before you ship out, take a nice, hot shower. It may be a while before you get another one."

Mina gave Lockwood a cutesy two-fingered salute.

---

[35] During World War II, hamburgers were called "Liberty Steak" due to anti-German sentiment. This is similar to the incident in 2003 where French fries were temporarily renamed "Freedom Fries" due to declining French support for the Iraq War.

"Will do."

Approaching the entrance to the golf course grounds, Lockwood bid her farewell in Japanese.

"*Ja matane*, Mina-chan." See you later.

"*Ja matane*," she said in kind, and the two parted.

The shower head turned on, spraying water, steam rising. The water was hot and inviting. Mina savored the moment, letting the welcome warmth wash over her face and run down her body. Lockwood was right. For all she knew it would be a while before she had a hot shower again. Best to make the best of it.

Standing in the shower, Mina let the heat sluice across her bare back, her skin baby-smooth and unblemished.

14 BECOMING TOO OLD, TOO YOUNG

THREE YEARS LATER

Mina stood in the same shower she had used prior to shipping out for the first time three years ago. She let the steaming hot water sluice down her bare back and over the mass of scars and damaged skin, her back no longer baby smooth. Several dozen healed bullet wounds over the years left her back pockmarked. Stab wounds left raised scars here and there. Raised vertical scars remained from a flogging with a whip. There were even bite marks, animal as well as human.

Like her body, her heart and soul bore scars as well. Losing her father had broken her heart, but the war had broken her soul.

Her doe eyes, normally wide and innocent, currently bore a haggard world-weary expression for one so young. Weary, she propped herself against the wall with her arm, leaning against it as steaming hot water sluiced down her back. Water dripped down the side of her face as it trailed from her sopping raven hair.

Forlorn, her eyes stared distantly downward as she lost herself in memory. The events of the last three years flitted across her mind.

Wearing a Japanese white nurse uniform and cap, she ambushed the Japanese general in his own office. Stabbing him in the back, the blade of a tanto *dagger sprouted from his chest. She had jammed it all the way to the hilt and could feel the grip twitch in time with his fading heartbeat, his hot lifeblood running between her fingers -*

He flailed, grabbing a heavy bronze paperweight shaped like a carp from his desk. He slammed it against her temple, leaving a jagged wound. Mina grimaced, blood streaming down her left cheek, tussling with him down to the floor -

Wet with shower droplets, there was a raised splotch of lighter skin on Mina's temple the size of a nickel, where the wound had healed over.

Strapped down nearly naked to the operation table, harsh lights flared on overhead as Mina wailed, flailing and struggling against her bonds. The "doctors" from Unit 731 gathered around her, starting their work. Enigmatic in their surgical masks and scrubs, they pulled out scalpels and bone saws. Mina let out a sob as one doctor started an incision at her shoulder, trailing a crimson line across her skin -

Two identical surgical scars shaped like crescents were on either side of her belly, glistening with moisture and steam from the shower.

At the Battle of Changde, Mina crawled on her hands and knees through the earthen trenches, wheezing. The choking, gasping Chinese troops around her fell to their knees as they were enshrouded in a fog of yellow-brown mist. The deceptively cloying scent of geraniums filled the air as lewisite-mustard gas permeated her surroundings. Frantic, fingers shaking, Mina heaved as she grabbed a gas mask off a dead Japanese soldier. She struggled to get the mask on over her face as Japanese battle cries floated towards her.

Surprising her, far from dead, the Japanese soldier jammed his knife into her shoulder and she let out a pained gasp -

Her left shoulder was marked with a ragged scar shaped like a sideways lightning bolt.

Inside the Japanese mess hall, uniformed officers keeled forward in their seats. They vomited, blood gushing from their mouths. Wearing a kitchen worker's bandanna and robe, Mina dashed out of the kitchen towards the doorway. The similarly-attired cook ran out after her, wielding a Nambu submachine gun. He let out a spray of chattering fire, and Mina lurched forward mid-run as several rounds thudded into her -

On her back, hot water streamed over the half-dozen pockmarks on her skin which marked the passage of the bullets.

In the smoke-shrouded forests of the Vosges Mountains in France, a silhouetted, pigtailed Mina wielded a blazing Tommy gun in each hand, gunning down Nazi soldiers.

Screaming a battle cry at the top of his lungs, the charging German trooper thrust his bayoneted-rifle into her side as if she were a stuck pig. Her face contorted in pain as she screamed, his blade twisting within her abdomen.

Gingerly, almost without thinking, Mina's hand went to the area next to her belly button. There was a whitish, star-shaped scar of raised flesh where the bayonet impaled her.

Exhausted, she turned off the water and stepped out of the shower, wrapping the beige towel around her chest.

Mina heaved out a weary sigh. It had been an arduously long three years.

She stepped out of the bathroom and flopped backwards onto the bed, staring up at the slowly rotating ceiling fan.

The last thing she wanted right now was other memories drudged to the surface. Still, the memory came back to her, uninvited as she stared at the spinning fan. *The burning Hellcat fighter plane crashed through the trees towards her as she hit the scorched dirt. Lurching, the plane caught partway in jungle vines and tree limbs, its whirring propeller held at bay mere inches from her face.*

Mina rubbed her eyes with the palms of her hands, then muttered to herself.

"Not what had I expected," she said softly under her breath.

There was a knock at the door. Mina tilted her head up to look as the door opened. The secretary with the stylish Lana Turner haircut glanced in. Over the last three years, the woman had gotten slightly older, bit by bit each time Mina saw her. She addressed Mina by rank.

"Captain. They're waiting for you in the briefing room."

The briefing room was a small auditorium with a projector screen. Comfortable, it was filled with burgundy-hued padded recliners. Seated, Mina looked up as Lockwood entered and made his way towards her. She wore her brown Army Nurse Corps dress uniform complete with tie and skirt.

"How much do you know about splitting atoms, munchkin?" he said affectionately.

Lockwood, as Mina had discovered in the last three years, was a fan of Judy Garland's *The Wizard of Oz*[36]. Mina's response was chipper. "I know it'd make a very big boom! That's about it!"

At this, Lockwood couldn't help but suppress a smile. He sat down next to her. "Alright Mina. We've known each other long enough to cut the bullshit. I'll get right down to it."

He took a deep breath, turning serious. "Your mission will be to stop the Japanese atomic weapons program by any and all means."

Mina looked mildly surprised. "I was under the impression the Japanese were devoting more resources to radar technology than atomic weapons," she said, interest piqued.

"Very true. It was initially thought their program wasn't much of a threat. Their own top researchers had concluded that their gadget wouldn't be completed until after the war."

He gestured to the silver screen. "I want to show you something."

With a click, the lights in the room shut off, leaving it in semi-darkness.

From the back of the room, there was whirring as the reel spun up and beams of light streamed out onto the screen.

With accompanying beeps, the screen showed the

---

[36] The film had come out just two years prior to America's entry into the war.

typical numeric countdown with the sweeping hand like a clock, and the film started.

Canned patriotic trumpet music blared over the speakers. An authoritative voice reminiscent of all the news and training reels Mina had watched started voicing over the footage. She waited through the usual "top secret information" warning she was accustomed to. Her mind raced, thinking of what awaited her. Would she be sent to Alamogordo? Work on the Manhattan Project? The possibilities sped through her mind.

Mina focused on the show. Up on the silver screen, leaning against an ornate wooden desk was a rather serious looking white man. The study behind him was filled with bookcases of leather-bound tomes. He wore a sweater vest over a dress shirt and tie, and seemed brooding and stressed.

"Who is this?" she asked curiously.

Lockwood whispered aside to her. "This is Robert J. Oppenheimer. Leader of the Manhattan project, and America's best hope for the atomic bomb. After the war, he'll probably be famous."

Ah. So this was the man. Mina had heard of the name but never met him. She scrutinized the man on screen. "He looks kinda like a college professor," she remarked.

"He used to be one."

The former college professor appeared lean and rather severe. Mina guessed the man must have the weight of the world on his shoulders. Now it seemed, he was about to pass some of that burden onto her. Dour, he puffed on a briar pipe and spoke to the camera in grim tones.

"Greetings agent," he said, his voice slightly staticky on the recording. "If you are watching this, you are about to embark on a mission that could have very dire consequences for America and her allies."

He prattled on for a few minutes. There was some vague history on Japan's atomic weapons project.[37] He

---

[37] The Japanese atomic weapons program officially commenced in

mentioned the founders, Nishina, and the history of atomic research.

There was a smattering of physics explanations and some cartoon animations of the mechanics behind an atomic blast. Mina admitted to herself that she didn't comprehend everything, but made a mental note to read up on it later.

One particular film segment caught her attention. It was footage recorded from an overhead plane of a particularly large blast cloud from a conventional explosion.

"The blast would have a projected yield of twenty kilotons of T.N.T," he stated.

Astounded, Mina whispered in awestruck aside to Lockwood. "That's twice the British Grand Slam!" Mina referred to the 22,000 pound bomb the limeys were developing.

Lockwood whispered. "Yes. Imagine what would happen if this were dropped on Los Angeles. Or New York. D.C. Or Honolulu. The city would be wiped off the face of the map."

Mina fell into somber silence. His mention of Honolulu, was of course, deliberate. The thought was sobering.

The film cut back to Oppenheimer in the study as the film concluded. "Best wishes agent. Good luck, and Godspeed."

A few moments later, the reel ended, the film flapped circularly within the reel, and the projector clicked off.

Mina was the first to speak.

"There's more you're not telling me Jim. What prompted us to do this now? What's the current problem? What changed?"

"The fresh blood they brought onboard. New major players."

He pressed a button on a corded control with a click.

Instead of another film, a slideshow commenced. The image shifted to a still image of a stern-faced Japanese officer.

April of 1941.

Sitting with regal bearing, he was posed for his official military photo in full dress uniform, bedecked with medals. Intimidating, he had a shaved head, a neatly-trimmed short black beard, and his eyebrows were furrowed into a near-permanent scowl.

"Colonel Tetsuo Matsui, of the Imperial Japanese Army," Lockwood narrated. "The program is under his command."

Mina was slightly taken aback, blinking once at the name. A sense of repulsed realization washed over her.

"Wait. I know that name," she exclaimed. "Rain! He was called 'Crimson Rain' back in China. We also called him the Butcher of Bataan[38]. The Iron Beast of Nanking. Among other things."

Solemn, Lockwood nodded. "So you've heard of him. Be careful. Rain is former *Kempeitai*."

A sour expression crossed Mina's face. The *Kempeitai* was Japan's equivalent of Nazi Germany's Gestapo. By some accounts, they were even more brutal and cruel. A combination of secret police and soldier-spies, they had a fearsome reputation.

Mina hid her apprehension. This would make her job tremendously more difficult.

Lockwood continued. "It gets worse. He was also a graduate of the *Rikugan Nakano Gakko*.[39]

---

[38] During World War II, there were actually several Japanese officers nicknamed "The Butcher of Bataan", including General Tomoyuki Yamashita and Lt. General Masaharu Homma. Rain is a fictional character but shares a similar moniker.

[39] The existence of the long-rumored *Rikugun Nakano Gakko*, the Imperial Japanese Army's secret military spy school, was finally confirmed in 2012 by the Japan Daily Press. For decades it was initially believed that all documents related to the school were destroyed prior to the end of World War II. However, newly discovered documents confirm its existence. Most famously, in addition to conventional military intelligence techniques, the school also taught ninjutsu - ninja techniques. Guess what folks, effectively

Stiffening straight in her padded chair, Mina blinked again. Whoa. Double whammy. She hadn't been expecting that.

"This man's a *shinobi*?[40] Jeez," she said.

Black-and-white footage played across the screen. Wearing black garb, Rain pulled a black mask over his face, leaving just a horizontal slit for his eyes, the only part of his face that remained exposed.

Mina watched him dash and roll through an obstacle course with impressive fluidity and speed.

Lockwood continued speaking. "According to his service records, no one has ever beaten him one-on-one."

The black-and-white footage cut to that of a training yard, a clearing in the middle of a bamboo forest.

Without any headgear, Rain stood in the middle of a sandy sparring circle, wearing a black *gi* martial arts robe. An uniformed attendant blindfolded him. Mina tilted her head curiously at the sight. The attendant proceeded to tie one hand behind Rain's back with a cord.

Working in concert, Rain's attackers assaulted the blindfolded and half-bound man. Dodging and weaving, Rain was completely unperturbed, untouched. Mina watched spellbound as he repelled each and every single one of his opponents with effortless one-handed blocks, flips, throws, and strikes. With bone-crunching efficiency he often used one assailant's blows and momentum against another, leaving all of them sprawled on the ground, writhing in pain in under a

---

speaking, ninjas fought in World War II! ;-)

[40] In 1945, few Americans knew what a ninja was unless he/she had knowledge of Japan and its people. Unlike today, knowledge of ninjas and its proliferation in Hollywood didn't occur until after the American occupation of Japan following World War II. Prior to the occupation, stealth fighters portrayed in Hollywood and other popular media were commonly Thuggee. These were Indian cult members who used yellow scarves to strangle their victims. They were featured in the 1984 film *Indiana Jones and the Temple of Doom*.

minute.

Mina looked over at Lockwood. He had a rather disturbed expression on his face he tried to suppress.

"You know this man," she said softly.

Mina glanced at Lockwood's leg encased in the metal brace.

"Yes. He gave me the leg," he said quietly.

Lockwood took a moment then added in a tidbit of advice. "Don't go toe-to-toe with this guy. If you have to fight him, shoot him."

Lost in thought, Mina put her fist to her mouth, pensive.

Lockwood continued. "I won't bother going into his service record in Southeast Asia. You've heard the stories. He's not called "Crimson Rain" for nothing."

Mina thought back to the last few years and memories flitted across her mind. *Piles of decapitated heads, swarming with buzzing flies, the stench overwhelming in the summer sun. A six-year old village boy being handed a Nambu pistol, then forced to shoot his parents, then himself, the trio of sprawled corpses rotting in the mud. A Japanese soldier, under orders, tossing a screaming infant swaddled in a blanket into a boiling cauldron.*

Yes, she had seen the aftereffects. But she never thought she would be put in a situation where she would see the commander in person.

Mina shook herself out of rumination. The past few years had been grimly unpleasant. War hadn't turned out as cut-and-dried she thought it would be.

"Never met the man, but I've seen his handiwork," she commented.

The slide clicked again. This time the screen showed a black-and-white photo of a rather creepy looking Japanese man in his mid-fifties. He had round thick-rimmed spectacles, like Hideki Tojo's and wore a white lab coat. Mina's looked at the screen with interest.

"Hey. Who's this old geezer?" she asked.

As Lockwood spoke, the screen shifted to black-and-white footage of the same man. Wearing a white lab coat, he worked in a laboratory, chalk in hand, gesturing at physics equations on a blackboard. There was no audio, but she saw him speaking to someone to his right.

Lockwood gestured to the man. "This is Doctor Satoshi Fujita. We've nicknamed him 'The Owl'."

The footage on the screen pulled out...and surprisingly, he was speaking with someone Mina recognized. She bolted upright in her chair.

The Owl's contemporary was a very familiar, rather kindly-looking white man in his mid-sixties. Smiling, he had a grandfatherly disposition and a bushy mustache. A receding hairline formed distinctive wild tufts of gray-white on either side of his head. Albert Einstein.

Mina exclaimed. "Holy Hannah! He knows Einstein? This bad guy's one smart cookie."

"Einstein met him at the conference you see here."

"What did Einstein say?"

Lockwood's tone turned wry. "Einstein's generally a nice old man. But he called the Owl, and I quote, 'a real lecherous, perverse old bastard.'"

Mina turned droll. "Wow. The Owl sounds like a real charmer," she said wryly. "So he's Japan's top atomic scientist?"

"No, that's Nishina," Lockwood corrected. "But he's basically unreachable. Not realistic to go after him. The Owl's the next best thing."

Mina glanced at the bookish man on screen. "So, in terms of importance, he's Robin, not Batman," she said, drawing out the analogy.[41]

"Basically. But both Robin and Batman can access Wayne Manor, so that's good enough for us," he said.

Lockwood continued. "The Owl's a genius though. Mastered calculus at age seven. Graduated from Todai[42] with a

---

[41] Batman first appeared in May 1939 in Detective Comics (DC) issue #27.

Ph.D. in physics at age fifteen."

Mina made a face. "Why'd you call him the Owl? Cuz he looks like one? Sounds apropos. Owls are familiars to witches."

"No. Rain always referred to him as 'his lucky charm'."

Mina remembered. "Ah. Yes yes. Owls are considered lucky in Japan, that's right."

Mina mulled it all over, quietly absorbing everything she had just seen. Passing through her mind, the mental image of palm trees arched in the gale of a firestorm, their fronds burning away to a crisp, nagged at her. It was worrying.

"Exactly how close are they to finishing?" she asked tentatively.

Lockwood seemed reluctant. "They're closer than we'd like to admit."

Mina nodded, processing the information. "So where am I going?"

The slide clicked over to show a geographical map of Japan and surrounding smaller islands. The capital was marked with a big star.

"Tokyo[43]," he stated. "Their main atomic research facilities are at the Riken Institute in the Komagome district of Tokyo. It's their main research and processing facility."

The slide clicked forward, now displaying an enlarged surveillance photo of a quaint looking building and a grassy quad area. Tranquil, it looked almost like a university campus.

"Your objective is to mark the facility for destruction during the upcoming B-29 firebombing mission of Operation Meetinghouse. Get in, mark the target, get out. Verify the destruction."

Mina nodded, mulling his words over. She stared at the black-and-white building on the projector screen until it

---

[42] Todai is the nickname for Tokyo University. It is still considered among one of the world's most prestigious universities.
[43] During World War II, Tokyo was often spelled "Tokio" with an "-I" instead of a "y". Also, sometimes Riken is spelled "Rikken" with an additional "k".

burned into her memory.
Destination: Tokyo.

15 APPLES TO APPLES

Amidst the hustle and bustle of the Japanese marketplace, Mina walked through the rows of vendor stalls. Customers haggled, chatted, or otherwise went about their business.

Standing near the corner, idly chatting with a patron, a uniformed Japanese police officer glanced in her direction.

Casual, Mina walked up to the apple vendor, a portly woman. Mina asked for three apples, requesting it in polite Japanese.

Suddenly, a loud buzzer sounded.

Mina looked up. From behind the balcony of one of the buildings, Lockwood stepped out onto the terrace, addressing the crowd.

"Alright everyone! Point out the agent!"

Every single person in the street pointed at Mina. She looked around. Damn. She didn't think it should have been so obvious. What went wrong?

Lockwood clapped his hands together once. "Okay! Reset to first positions!" he shouted.

The buzzer sounded again, and with quiet hubbub, the workers started taking apart the simulacrum. The entire square half-mile was a fake town, simulated to look like part of a real Japanese city, complete with cardboard backdrops to simulate the Tokyo skyline. The vendors started moving their stalls and setting up signs.

Mina went to the nearby stall and picked an apple up in her hands, turning it over curiously. The red apple was just a shiny wax fake. Everything around her was just a realistic, simulated enactment.

The apple vendor approached her. The portly woman was one of the few trusted first-generation Japanese immigrants that were part of the program. Her Japanese husband had fought for the United States during the Great War, and was thus one of the few Japanese eligible to apply to citizenship and earn it.

Mina sighed resignedly. "What gave me away?" she asked. The apple vendor spoke patiently in accented, somewhat fractured but understandable English.

"Your Japanese language, very good. But your mannerism too American. Dead giveaway."

Internally growing exasperated, Mina wanted to let some childlike insolence slip and stick out her tongue. Unfortunately that kind of sass would only reinforce the lady's point. She forced herself not to. If she was going to be trusted to go into the heart of Japan, she needed to be a more responsible and mature person, at least outwardly.

The portly woman pointed at the fake street. "Walk down the street and come back," she instructed.

Mina did so. The woman grew upset.

"No! The way you walk. Too American! More Japanese. Japanese society different. Should act more demure. Subservient. Your posture. The way you move your hips. Smaller motions."

The apple vendor gestured, walking down the street. Mina tried to imitate the more subdued motions.

"Good good. At least you fast learner."

The apple seller spoke to her imperatively. "Count to five."

Mina counted to five, extending her index finger first and then the others, with the thumb last.

The portly lady smacked her wrist and Mina cringed.

"No!" the vendor admonished. "Japanese count with closed fingers to tally, not open!"

The apple vendor closed her fingers, starting with the thumb and then the others. Thus, a closed fist would mean five, while a closed thumb would indicate one.

Mina nodded. This wasn't good. She didn't realize there was that much of a difference in body language and mannerisms. Mina had undergone cultural adaptation training before, for her missions in Burma and other parts of Asia, but never at this level of rigor.

The apple vendor gave it a moment of thought. "Hmm. Point to yourself," the portly woman ordered.

Mina instinctively pointed her index finger at her own chest.

The lady grew exasperated. "No, no! Point to your nose instead! Not your chest! You are using Western body language, not Japanese!"

She grabbed Mina's hand and pointed it at Mina's nose.

The apple vendor continued on, mild irritation marring her composure. "Beckon to me, as if you wanted me to come over to you."

Mina raised her hand, palm facing herself and fanned her hand towards her chest.

"No! Too American!"

The apple lady bonked her on the head with her fist. Mina winced and rubbed the sore spot.

"Beckon with the hand pointed down, not up, flapping at the wrist," the lady said, losing patience.

The lady demonstrated, doing so, then let out an exasperated sigh. "And be careful. Many things you used to, not allowed in Japan. Not as Western as you may think."

"I thought Japan became very westernized during the Meiji Restoration."

"Yes, except before the war Japan became very anti-Western. No coffee, no dancing, no Western movies. No hand-holding or kissing in public."

Mina was taken aback. The constrictive nature of Japanese civilian life was a little alien to her. She was only familiar with situations battlefield soldiers were accustomed to. Actually walking around a Japanese city would be very different.

"Eww!" Mina exclaimed. "So no lattes, no big band swing, no Flash Gordon, and no boys? What bluenoses[44]! What the hell do they do for fun?"

"Gossip with friends. Listen to radio. Like that." The lady's demeanor softened slightly. "Okay. Shoo. Go off. Talk later."

Mina left. As she departed, Lockwood hobbled up to the apple vendor.

"Do you think Mina would be okay, running around Tokyo?" he queried.

She clucked her tongue. "Yes! Run around like headless chicken, after secret police chop her head off with sword!"

Lockwood considered it for a moment, then spoke defensively. "Mina did fine in Burma and other places. No one really noticed any unusual behavior as far as I know, except one or two people."

The apple vendor scowled, raising her voice. "This not Burma! This Tokyo! *Kempeitai* secret police everywhere!"

Lockwood took a moment to weigh her words. There had been concern about sending agents into the Japanese main islands because the risk of capture was so high. Burma and other places in Southeast Asia where Mina had been were relatively safer. Such un-Japanese behavior could have been chalked up to battlefield conditions or a side effect of overseas training. Mina could have passed it off as her medical training, which sometimes involved interaction with consulting German physicians.

But in Tokyo, things were far more difficult. The

---

[44] "Bluenose" is 1940s slang for a prudish person.

kempeitai were not known for being forgiving. His leg ached with the memory.

Lockwood spoke, grimly concerned. "Do you think she can learn to fit in, with a little more time?"

The woman pondered it for a long moment. "Yes," she capitulated finally.

"Very well," Lockwood said affirmatively. "I'll send her to the Armorer to get ready."

16 "OOH, SHINY!"

Flanked by rows and rows of firearms and other assorted weapons, Mina stood in the armory room of the repurposed castle-like clubhouse.

Arrayed before her on the table was a wide assortment of gear, laid out in an orderly fashion. Mina's eyes fairly sparkled as she marveled at the variety. They were really going all out for this one.

"Ooh, shiny!" she said with a sense of wonder.

Standing on the opposite side of the table, Lockwood pointed to several fist-sized boxes and document pads. "Standard messaging gear. Microfilm and invisible ink kits."

He pointed to several firearms fitted with suppressors. "Silenced Mark VI Sten and silenced M3 grease guns."

He pointed to another gadget on the table. "Altimeter bombs. Detonates when the plane reaches a certain height."

Lockwood picked up what looked like a fountain pen. It was the same model he had used in Tokyo eight years ago. "Faultless-model tear gas pen gun, disguised as a fountain pen. Short range. Single-shot, specialized shell."

The next gadget was a miniature camera that fit in the palm of his hand. "Minox miniature camera. Fifty exposures. Works best for documents but also works for general photography."

Lockwood picked up a modified Colt M1911 pistol and a metal dart in his other hand. He slid the dart's shaft down the barrel, leaving the vicious-looking metal tip protruding. "This is a 'Bigot.' Modified Colt .45 pistol. Quiet. Good for underwater incursions."

Lockwood held up what appeared to be a gunmetal-gray tube of lipstick. "This is the 'firefly.' It's a heat-activated explosive charge you put in gas tanks of vehicles. Boom. Stops them dead in its tracks."

Lockwood took out two little vials of pills, one filled with blue pills and the other with red. "These are your 'K' knockout pills and 'L' lethal pills. Use them at your discretion."

Lockwood lifted an insectoid-looking rebreather mask of the kind she used during training. "Lambertsen rebreather for combat diving. Leaves no telltale air bubbles on the surface."

Lockwood pointed at a radio on the table the size of a loaf of bread. It was the standard Strategic Services Transmitter Receiver Number 1 used by OSS members. It operated on a 10.2 megacycle frequency and could be hidden in suitcases or carried under the arm as a package.

"Your standard SSTR1 Radio. Use it no more than five minutes at a time, no more than twenty minutes a day."

Lockwood picked up a small, rather bare-bones looking pistol. It looked inelegant but efficient. "Single-shot FP-45 Liberator pistol. Good holdout weapon."

He held up a small knife, about the size of a razor blade with a little tab as a grip. "Thumb knife. Hidden in a false callous made of latex then covered with skin-toned makeup."

Mina took it and turned it around in her hands curiously.

"Keep more than one on your person," he advised.

Mina nodded, paraphrasing a common commando adage in case of capture. "'One for them to find, one for me to keep.'"

Lockwood picked up a .22 semi-automatic pistol.

"Silenced High Standard HDM .22 caliber semi-automatic pistol, loaded with .22 LR. Very quiet, good for assassinations. After close penetration, the bullets tend to ricochet inside the skull, turning the brain to jelly."

Lockwood picked up an intimidatingly long knife. It was 16.5 inches from tip to grip's end, with a broad leaf-shaped blade. It was so large it was essentially a short sword, and coated with a matte finish to prevent reflections. "Fairbairn-Sykes fighting knife[45], sometimes called the 'smatchet.'"

Lockwood motioned with a fast stabbing downward thrust. "You can use it to sever a man's spinal cord at the base of the neck P.D.Q."

Lastly, Lockwood held up what looked like a saucer of green tea cookies, slightly stuck together. "Green tea *matcha* cookies, filled with 'Aunt Jemima' type powdered explosive."

"Aunt Jemima" was an explosive[46] made to look and smell like whole wheat flour. Mina had always wondered how the OSS scientists in the labs[47] made this stuff. Interestingly, the powder could actually be moistened, shaped, then baked in an oven into a loaf or other form of baked goods.

Mina nodded affirmatively. "Right. Not chocolate chip cookies cuz they're American."

"Use just one cookie for blowing locks. Use the whole plate for something bigger."

He made an additional comment. "They're actually edible. Just don't eat all of 'em."

Mina took a cautious nibble - and immediately regretted it. Incredibly bitter, the cookie also had an unpleasant

---

[45] This is not the Sykes-Fairbairn, which is a similarly named but altogether different knife.

[46] The modern name for this is "octogen" or HMX.

[47] The division that developed a number of such gadgets was the OSS Office of Science Research and Development. The British SOE also had their own labs.

grimy consistency. She made a face of disgust and spat it out onto the floor.

"They're horrible!"

"Well, if they tasted good, they would eat all your explosives. Just don't smoke after you eat them."

17 CIGAR

In the murky depths of Tokyo Bay, the dark silhouette of an American *Tench*-class submarine slinked its way through the blue waters, letting out intermittent sonar pings.

Torpedo Bay of the USS Torsk

Protesting vehemently, clad in a diver's dry suit and fins, Mina wedged herself into the portway with her arms and legs. She struggled to stay lodged within as if her life depended on it, while several crew members strained to manhandle her towards the launch bay.

She was only partially geared up. Her pack with her radio was strapped to her back, along with some infiltration gear. The rest of her equipment lay on the deck in a waterproof duffel bag.

Fearful, she clenched her white-knuckle grip on the portway even tighter, yelling in wide-eyed panic.

"No! No! I don't wanna be shot out of a torpedo tube!" she protested.

The crewman latched onto her arm hauled back uselessly. "Oh c'mon you'll be fine!" he said. "Someone tried it[48]

---

[48] On April 15, 1909, Ensign Kenneth Whiting, a future naval

about thirty years back!"

"He lost his rebreather and almost drowned! Surface and lemme out!"

"We're too close to shore!" The patrol will see us!"

One crewman struggling to pull her off the hatch let out a grunt, heaving against her vise-like grip. "I don't get it. You've faced down Nazi stormtroopers, been mauled by German Shepherds, tortured by Unit 731, and you're afraid of getting a little wet?"

"It's a long story!" she strained. "Plus I didn't have to swim much the last three years!" she added. The past few years she avoided swimming like the plague and did so only when absolutely necessary.

Suddenly, her protestations were interrupted as the lightning snapped to a crimson, combat red, and they all looked up. Muffled shouts came from above.

Frantic, a junior officer slid down the ladder behind them and ran to the skipper, breathless. "Captain! Incoming destroyer!" he reported.

Immediately on alert, all trace of humor gone, the sub captain bellowed an order. "Send her off before they find us!"

Taking advantage of her distraction, one crewman shoved a Lambertsen rebreather over her head. Gripped awkwardly by the crewmen, with full-face rebreather mask on her head and clad in a combat diver's dry suit, Mina looked like an abused humanoid insect.

"Alright Coral Hare, are you ready?" the submarine captain queried.

Mina jerked her thumb down vehemently over and over.

The captain just grinned and ignored her. "Alright then! Flood tube three!" he shouted to his crew.

The crewmen flanking Mina unceremoniously dragged

---

aviation pioneer, tried an experiment. Convinced that a man could leave a submarine launched through the torpedo tube, Whiting tested his theory with himself as a guinea pig. What a brave man.

her from the porthole and stuffed her inside the open torpedo tube, slamming the hatch shut.

On the deck next to bulkhead, lay the waterproof bag of gear, unnoticed in the commotion.

From inside the torpedo tube came muffled metallic banging of protest.

"Fire!" the captain ordered.

The nearby crewman yanked the waist-high lever next to the torpedo tube.

Outside the submarine, Mina blasted out in a gush of bubbles. The exit was so violent she could feel aching bruises already forming on her arms and legs.

Disoriented, Mina floundered for a moment in the heavy sluggishness of the water, then kicked her way upwards. Swimming, she swept her arms like a frog. The water was unpleasantly cold. Fortunately, she was equipped with the dry suit, which was warmer than a wet suit.

All she could hear was the sound of her breathing through the mask and rapid thudding of her heartbeat. Anxious to get out of the water, she kicked her way to the surface, barely slow enough to avoid the bends.[49]

Her masked head broke the surface and Mina immediately flipped her rebreather up, taking in a deep gasp of night air. She had been breathing too fast. Someone should really invent a regulator for that thing, she thought to herself.

She shivered inside her dry suit despite its insulation, teeth chattering with the cold. Out in the distance, she could see the jagged edge of Japan's shoreline, black against the dark blue sky. She turned her head every which way, looking for the signal.

There, she saw it. There was a fiery-red dot dancing in the misty darkness, the glowing tip of a lit cigar.

---

[49] The bends is a term for decompression sickness, which can be caused by too rapid an ascent in water.

Inconspicuous, the cigar was meant to act as a beacon in the damp night.

There was the fisherman she was supposed to contact.

She started paddling towards it. She heard the creaking of wood on the water before she actually saw the outline of the small fishing boat as it made its way towards her. Standing on deck was a grizzled fisherman. Jutting out the corner of his mouth was the big cigar, smoke curling from its red-hot tip.

He looked about sixty, with a scraggly short gray beard. Made sense. In wartime Japan, adult males younger than sixty were drafted into the military. He himself was too old to fight, so Mina and those like her did the actual dirty work. People like him were just there to provide material support. He was a dissident whose son had died in the second Sino-Japanese War.[50]

With a wooden oar in his hands, he paddled over as she tread water. He spoke in Japanese, voice gravelly hoarse from years of smoking. "What are you doing out here?" he asked, his tone deliberately curious.

"I was diving for sea urchins," Mina responded.

"Only eat them with wasabi."

Mina's teeth chattered as she responded with the countersign. Hurry up old man, she wanted to say, get me outta here.

"I prefer lemon," she said instead.

He nodded. The fisherman leaned out and extended a hand, helping Mina slosh out. Stern, he spoke in an urgent hiss as she clambered aboard. "Shh! Quiet! You're making too much noise."

Anxious and miserably cold, Mina sat. He tossed her a folded square of cloth. She quickly covered her head with the bandanna and tied it to hide the fact her hair was sopping wet. The fisherman sat and took up the first set of oars, starting to

---

[50] In the decades preceding World War II, loyalty to the emperor was drilled into members of Japanese society virtually since birth. Dissidents were rare.

row back to shore.

Desperate to leave, Mina took up the second oars. She paddled furiously, out of sync with him. Glaring, he hissed at her. "Careful with those oars! Slow down," he said, annoyed. "The shore patrol can tell if you don't row like a native."

Taking a deep breath, she felt her pounding heart calm somewhat. She forced herself to slow down.

Her stroke of the oars evened out, matching his, carefully avoiding telltale desynchronization as the two of them rowed to shore.

Out on the beach, near a thatched observation hut, a Japanese soldier in a khaki-colored uniform stood at the bamboo railing, binoculars to his eyes.

Through the double-lens view, he gazed at the small wooden rowboat, the fisherman, and his passenger curiously.

He noticed that the girl was wet, and even though she rowed proficiently, seemed nervous. He shrugged. Perhaps she had had an accident, had fallen overboard and was shaken.

The sentry shrugged. It might be worth checking out later.

The fisherman's hut was a simple austere abode, but serviceable. Traditional *tatami* straw mats were on the floor. The walls were unadorned save for a handful of traditional Japanese watercolor paintings and two calligraphy banners. The air was filled with the rich aroma of tobacco. The fisherman considered tobacco his sole luxury.

Mina toweled off her wet hair. He spoke to her sternly in Japanese. As per their training, they used casual Japanese, lest an observer see them in the streets later and think their behavior unusually distant for family.

"You can't avoid the water forever," he scolded. "If you could have, it wouldn't be a requirement during training."

The grizzled fisherman looked weary. "I'm getting too old to be a revolutionary," he said. "If you get caught I'll be the one to pay the penalty."

She set about unpacking her gear. "Don't fret. I'll be gone soon enough. I'll be checking out the Riken facility in the morning. We'll reconvene afterwards and be 'conveniently' out of town in Yokohama during the firebombing raid."

The fisherman sighed and agitatedly puffed on his cigar.

Mina tried to assuage him. "Don't worry. There isn't much water hereabouts anyway. I won't have to swim."

He gave her a glum look. "I hope you're right."

18 INFILTRATOR

Tokyo, Japan. March 9, 1945

As Mina walked down the streets of downtown Tokyo, she heard the ding-ding of the trolley bell as tram cars passed through. Since most of the men had gone off to war, these days trolley cars were mostly driven by teenage girls.

Mina strolled the streets, mildly curious. It was okay for her to look around a little like a nonlocal; her cover identity said she was a Japanese native from out of town visiting relatives. Even though Mina had run operations behind enemy lines, those were in China, Burma, India, and a few other places in Southeast Asia. This was her first time on honest-to-god real Japanese soil. The simulation couldn't compare to the real thing.

She glanced at the commercial buildings. By 1940s standards, Tokyo was a modern city. Paved streets, trolleys. Cars with flowing, curvaceous body shell lines. They drove down the left side of the road[51], the way the British did. Modern brick-and-mortar construction, at least downtown. No

---

[51] Japanese law stipulated driving on the left in 1924. This was due to a number of historic safety reasons.

skyscrapers though; she didn't notice many buildings higher than six-stories. Japan was too earthquake prone for that. Here and there she saw firebombing damage and burned-out buildings. If things went according to plan, tonight would be the biggest firebombing yet.

The weather was surprisingly pleasant. Just days prior the weather had been rainy and dismal, making a surprise change to mild temperatures, gusty winds, and clear skies.[52] Mina nodded to herself. Fortunately, the weather forecast was correct. This was ideal weather for a firebombing raid. There was little moisture to dampen the fires but plenty of wind to spread them.

Walking down the street, Mina wore a Japanese schoolgirl uniform of the sailor-suit variety called *seifuku*. On top of the uniform, she was outfitted with steel helmet and padded air raid hood on her head. She also had a first aid kit in a thin, beige cloth bag slung across her shoulder like a purse.

It was not the first time she had worn a school uniform disguise; she found it useful since it helped her blend in, given her age. However, in military areas she usually kept her guise as a nurse. Still, even out in the field, it was a good distraction and psychological warfare tactic. It drew attention away from her allies. Gun-toting schoolgirls were not a common sight on the battlefield.

Selected with care, the uniform had been handpicked; it was even particular to the school in Kobe she was supposedly from. Even her school transfer papers were in order. If anyone made inquiries to the receiving Tokyo school, they would find, correctly, that she was due to report in a few days.

Her sailor suit uniform was largely white, with navy blue touches here and there. It had a navy-blue broad collar

[52] This really was the weather the day of the Great Tokyo Air Raid, according to French reporter Robert Guillain, who was unable to leave Japan following the attack on Pearl Harbor and witnessed the firebombing of Tokyo.

with square flap across the back which tapered to a V in the front, with scarlet neckerchief. The pleated skirt was a modest ankle-length, navy-blue. White schoolgirl clogs. On her back was strapped a beige canvas backpack.

She checked her wristwatch. Mid-afternoon. Since 1944, Japan had issued the school student mobilization order. It was common for schoolgirls in high school to attend school half the day. The second half they usually took on a tram car or defense-related job, such as factory work. Her walking the streets at this time of day was still relatively inconspicuous.

Mina strolled by the Riken Institute, turning her head to look at the tranquil grassy quad and the buildings reminiscent of a university campus. She needed to do some quick reconnaissance of the area in advance of the bombers.

Then, she heard the rumble of engines as an entire convoy of Toyota KB/KC trucks rolled out the main gate, departing the grounds of the facility. There must have been at least twenty trucks she counted. They were all fully loaded based on how low their suspensions hung. The guard at the gate waved them through, gesturing down the road.

Mina felt worry tie a knot in her stomach. What the hell were they moving that required that many trucks? Most likely they were relocating everything. Growing anxious, Mina followed them.

It wasn't easy, but Mina trailed the trucks across town, hopping from taxi to trolley then running through the back alleys.

She jimmied the lock on a bicycle rack and stole some kid's Zebra-brand bike, hightailing down the street as fast as she could pedal. She raced along, trying not to attract any attention. Just a schoolgirl on a bicycle.

She sped through an alleyway and stopped, looking ahead across the road.

Finally, one of the trucks' brakes squealed as they pulled up to what looked like an office building in the commercial sector of Tokyo. So, Mina thought to herself. They really were picking up stakes and moving everything.

She craned her head to get a better look, but there was a food cart in the way. She stashed the bicycle behind a few trash cans. She headed out the alley, towards the food cart across the street from the facility.

The little steaming food cart was in disrepair and rather beat-up. It reminded Mina of the local economy.[53] Oftentimes there was little food or living necessities available in town stores.[54] Restaurants often had meat substitutes. Mina hadn't wanted to ask what it was made of, but she guessed it was a mix of tofu, scraped-together squid and mashed-up beans.

Then again, she had also heard it was made from dead rats.

She glanced at the handwritten sign on the cart. The only things for sale were tea and fried squid-on-a-stick. Sparse pickings; not too surprising.[55]

---

[53] For Japan, war had started about nine years ago, not at Pearl Harbor, as it was for the United States. For Japan, war started in the Imperial Japanese military's first forays into China in the late 1930s. As a result of rationing in support of the Japanese war effort, there was a continual severe shortage of food and clothes in the Japanese cities. Malnutrition among civilians was not an uncommon problem, but fortunately there were no (reported) cases of starvation. Rice rations were reduced to two-thirds of a bowl mornings and evenings.

[54] Most Japanese households were experiencing shortages of food and consumer goods, since most domestic food depended on imports which had been largely cut off by American submarine and bombing campaigns. Commodities such as matches, sugar, and rice were in short supply.

[55] For the past four years, deep sea fishing had all but stopped. People like the small-time fishermen Mina was staying with brought in only small amounts of fish. Most of the seafood available was squid caught just off the coast.

She gave the money to the vendor, a glum elderly man who looked too old to fight in the war. As she had expected, the price was exorbitant, but she bought it anyway so she would have an excuse to be around. She slowly nibbled on it. She was genuinely hungry, and didn't want to impose on the old fisherman more than her mission required.

Mina looked at the reflection of the nearby closed toy shop window. This way it wouldn't be too obvious she was observing the activities at the facility entrance behind her. Unfortunately, this was as close as she could get without arousing suspicion.

Inside the gates of the facility, workers started to unload crates[56] off the trucks.

Interestingly, she saw a worker in an MSA[57] hazmat suit carrying a boxy Geiger counter walk over to the truck. He waved the counter's cord-attached wand over an unloaded crate. Even from across the street she could hear the counter's fast clicking. So this was the uranium.

Oh no.

Something came to her. A map of the local area flitted across her mind. She mentally placed the target area and the bombing area.

No overlap. The bombers would miss it completely if she didn't warn them. Obviously, it was probably why the

---

[56] There was no radiation symbol marking at this time. The first international radiation symbol would not be around until 1946, after the war.

---

[57] The industrial firm MSA Auer was an early manufacturer of hazmat suits. The company, *Auergesellschaft* was founded in 1892 and headquartered in Berlin. Up until the end of the war, *Auergesellschaft* had research activities in the areas of gas mantles, luminescence, rare earths, radioactivity, and uranium and thorium compounds.

Japanese moved material to this new location this afternoon. She would bet dollars to doughnuts the transition had been taking place for a while. Most of the gear was likely already at this new facility.

Mina made to leave. She needed to warn the incoming planes.

Suddenly, a stern hand clamped down upon her shoulder. Stiffening, Mina turned around.

Her eyes widened when she recognized who it was.

19 FIRST ENCOUNTER

She saw the familiar neatly-trimmed short black beard, and eyebrows furrowed into a near-permanent scowl. Colonel Tetsuo "Crimson Rain" Matsui himself stood in front of her. Crimson Rain. The Butcher of Bataan. The Iron Beast of Nanking. Even though she had read his profile, he was much more imposing in person. Unusually tall for a Japanese man, he stood an intimidating six feet tall, and towered over her petite frame.

The smile faded from Mina's face when she saw him. She felt her resolve begin to falter. Fear pounded within her chest, rising into her throat. She knew he worked near the Riken building, but hadn't expected to run into him. Hell, why did he have to be here now? Did he already know who she was? Did the fisherman sell her out?

Stern, Rain looked down upon her with the scowl etched into his brow. Her appearance here had caught his eye. Being former *Kempeitai* secret police, he was cognizant of and at least familiar with the faces of the regular passerbys in the area, and he didn't recognize her.

Rain scrutinized her with a wary eye.

"I have not seen you around here before. What are you doing?"

Mina responded as calmly as she could. "Food is difficult to find in stores. This is the first vendor I've seen for blocks."

Out of habits instilled by exemplary training and experience, Mina was careful not to give out too much of her cover information too fast. Otherwise, it would sound rehearsed.

She saw his eyes flick over her. She could almost imagine the gears of his mind whirring as he automatically processed the information, judging her accent, posture, mannerisms, body language, memorizing every detail in case it somehow became important later.

Rain decided to make a casual inquiry. Her answer was reasonable enough, given the rationing. For civilians, food was not easy to come by. His tone shifted, speaking to her gently.

"What is your name?"

"Tanaka Ayano." She said her surname first and then her first name, conventional in most Asian countries.

Flattering her, he commented on her first name. "Ahh. Ayano. Beautiful name. 'Colorful woven silk'"

"Yes sir," she said demurely.

It was early afternoon. With the Japanese school student mobilization order it was common for students to work the second half of the day, after school. Following up on this, he gestured at her schoolgirl uniform.

"School just ended. Are you going to work?" he inquired.

"Yes sir, soon. I'm a nurse."

Rain frowned inwardly. He noticed during their discourse that her inflection lacked the pitch accent common to residents of Tokyo. However, that wasn't necessarily an issue; there were many nonresidents in town. He made his next phrasing intentionally misleading.

"So, you're from around here, I take it? Tokyo?"

"No sir, I'm from Kobe," she replied politely.

Although she spoke impeccable Japanese, Mina and her superiors at OSS knew she didn't have a local Tokyo accent. But Lockwood and her mentors had coached her well. Instead of trying to teach her the Tokyo dialect, which would have been too difficult to learn to the point where she could fool a local, they integrated part of her actual heritage into her cover. She naturally spoke Japanese with a bit of a Japanese western accent, since both of her parents were from Kobe.

Rain gave a slight nod of affirmation at her answer of "Kobe". The surname she mentioned, Tanaka, was very common in Hyogo, the prefecture where Kobe was located.

He took a split second to reflect on her words. Her Japanese was flawless; no tinge of Korean or Chinese inflections. That was fine then.

As for Kobe, could she back that up? And if so, why was she in town? He half-heartedly suspected her parents were dead from an air raid and a relative was taking care of her, but he needed her to confirm that.

"Ah, I see. Why are you here in Tokyo?"

"I live with my uncle."

"Really? Why are you living with your uncle? Where are your parents?"

Mina lowered her gaze, feeling a wave of melancholy wash over her as she recalled her father dying. She utilized the pain and injected the sorrow into her words.

"They died in the firebombing of Kobe last month."[58]

Genuine sympathy crossed Rain's face. "I am very sorry. But I must still ask to inspect your papers and belongings. Forgive the intrusion."

Mina dutifully handed over her beige canvas backpack. Almost everything incriminating had been left behind at the fisherman's hut, hidden under false panels, or buried.

Almost. There was still the tin of cookies. Argh. The

---

[58] The first Allied firebombing attack took place on February 3, 1945 on the Japanese city of Kobe. The day Mina meets Rain here is on March 9, 1945. By this point in the war, Japanese cities were susceptible to attack on their dwindling naval and air defenses. This was due to the encroaching American air bases established in the Marianas, closer to the Japanese home islands.

cookies. She had brought them with her in case she needed to blow locks. Damnit. Next time, she'd just stick with lockpicks.

As she handed him the bag, he focused on her hands, looking at them closely.

He saw some telltale, white rough ridges. He grabbed her wrist. Her bookbag dropped to the ground.

Mina winced.

"Please sir, that hurts!" she exclaimed. Most ordinary schoolgirls would probably say such a thing, though it really didn't hurt that badly.

Ignoring the comment, he examined her hands closely. He turned them over and looked for callouses, particularly on the forefinger and thumbs. They were possible indicators of frequent trigger pulling, and thus a regular firearms user.

It generally wasn't practical to soak off or cut off such telltale callouses. At least, not if the subject planned on going into combat. Otherwise prolonged firearms use would cause their hands to bleed.

His brow furrowed in concern. Her hands indeed had such callouses. He must ask.

"You said you were a nurse. Why are your hands so rough?"

Mina had a response ready the moment she saw him inspecting her hands. "I help out my uncle with fishing sometimes."

He hesitated for a moment, then nodded. His own hands had been scarred from handing cages and nets for many years prior to joining the military, helping his father. He let her hand go. "Sorry. Can't be too careful these days. You understand," he said with forced courtesy.

Shaken, Mina nodded. She didn't have to try very hard to pretend to be scared. Their verbal game of cat-and-mouse was starting to take its toll on her.

He picked the beige backpack off the ground and overturned it, shaking its contents out onto the sidewalk. There were some cosmetics, pieces of candy, paper money, what appeared to be a tin of cookies - and some identification papers.

He picked up the papers and began to scrutinize them.

Rain examined the documents with a critical eye. They were not overly fresh, and showed an appropriate amount of creasing and wear-and-tear. As was common with such documents, the OSS preparers had simply walked around with the papers strapped under their armpits to give it the proper amount of sweaty use. The papers attested to her registration as a transfer student. They also attested to her status as a freshly-trained nurse at the Tokyo Medical University Hospital, due to report in a few days.

Anxious, Mina awaited his response. Fortunately, she had an extremely good cover. Every fact of her backstory could be corroborated. Her identification papers weren't even entirely forged; they had been expertly modified from those of a girl who had died last month in an air raid. The girl's entire family had been wiped out. There were few surviving friends and no family to personally invalidate her. Her relationship with the fisherman was the only aspect that was forged. Even her birth certificate and other papers had been substituted at the highest level by other OSS operatives should the need arise to verify her story. Her mission was that critical.

After a moment, Rain finally handed the papers back to her, apparently satisfied with the documents for the moment.

Picking up her bookbag, he ran his hand along the interior of the bag and looked at the stitching. No hidden pockets or indicators of anything secreted within the lining. No conspicuous lumps or unusual stiffness in its flexibility. He handed the limp empty backpack to her.

Demeanor softening somewhat, he tilted her chin up with a finger, inspecting her face. She was unusually pretty. There was still a trace of wide-eyed childlike innocence about her. Big beautiful doe eyes, naturally long eyelashes and delicate facial features. The last caught his attention. Her facial bone structure bespoke of Japanese ancestry; if there was any non-Japanese, Asiatic blood in her, it wasn't apparent. The only real distinguishing mark was a coin-sized splotch scar on her temple. He looked a little closer at her face.

He frowned. The girl still had some baby fat on her cheeks. Her cheekbones weren't quite as exposed as it would be for someone living on rations. Hmm. Most countries in the war reserved the bulk of their food for their battlefield troops - and sometimes their spies. Without food, they'd be too weak to fight if the need arose.

"You look reasonably well-fed," he commented. "Most people are quite hungry."

Mina's response was polite. "My uncle is fortunate in his catches. He takes good care of me."

Rain raised a bemused eyebrow. "Oh? Why did you come here to buy food if your uncle provides for you so well?"

Uh-oh.

Caught in the lie, Mina fought down the split-second of panic. She smoothly covered the lie with another one that was actually half-true.

"Sometimes when I'm hungry, I go to a vendor just for a snack. That way I will not shame my uncle by making him think he's a bad caretaker."

Rain took a moment to mull that over. Then he nodded curtly, finding the answer satisfactory. Saving face was an integral part of Japanese society, and he understood the sentiment immediately. It was an honorable answer, and considerate of her. He let his finger drop from her chin.

He turned his attention to the scattered contents of her backpack on the sidewalk. He sat down on his haunches to look at them, picking them up one by one.

A hand mirror. A hair brush. A tube of lipstick. Some wrapped hard candy. About ten yen[59] in cash; pocket money of insignificant amount. Nothing of importance.

He turned his attention to the round tin of cookies. He stood up.

---

[59] Ten Japanese yen in 1945 is approximately $48.00 USD in modern currency.

"Open the tin," he commanded.

Cautious, he had given her the order to open it herself in case it was booby-trapped. Mina complied and held the open container out to him.

He peered inside. Inside were maybe two dozen *matcha*[60] green tea cookies, slightly melted and stuck together.

He plucked one out from the bottom of the tin, in case the top ones were fake, and took a bite.

A revolting bitterness spread over his tongue. He made a face, his expression contorting with disgust. He spat it out onto the sidewalk, wiping his mouth on his sleeve.

Mina bowed respectfully, apologizing. "Sorry, they are not very sweet. My sugar ration is small."

Gruff, he made a discontented grumbling and a dismissive gesture. Sugar was a rare commodity these days.

"Carry on. Scram, get out of here."

Mina stooped down to stuff her belongings into her pack. She shouldered the beige backpack and walked off. Once she had turned the corner out of sight she sagged in relief.

If he been any more suspicious and had decided to take her down to the station, she would have been strip-searched. Every inch of her possessions would have been taken apart and turned inside out, then inspected with a fine-tooth comb. Mina and her peers were taught in training that no one would be able to withstand that kind of scrutiny and still maintain their cover. The best protection was to avoid notice. If she had been arrested, that would have been it for her.

Walking as fast as possible without attracting attention, she headed down the street to the nearby rail station. She had already lost too much time. She had to get back to the fisherman's hut.

Now.

---

[60] Powdered green tea.

20 THEY'RE GOING TO THE WRONG PLACE

Outside the fisherman's hut, the sun had already sunk beneath the horizon.

The fisherman was in the kitchen. Working over a wooden chopping board with knife in hand, he gutted mackerel, preparing a simple dinner of fish and rice porridge. Nearby, two empty bowls rested on the counter.

He looked up as Mina rushed in breathlessly. "They're going to the wrong place!" she hissed urgently.

"What?"

"They transported everything out on trucks this afternoon! It's not at Riken anymore!"

The fisherman looked appalled. "Where at?"

"The building near the old toy shop."

"Then it's outside the bombing area!"

Mina looked grim. "We have to warn the incoming flight."

A consternated look crossed his face. "We'll have to make sure the bombers hit the new place tonight. Forget Riken for now. They can hit Riken in a few weeks when they can, just to be safe."[61]

Not saying anything else, he immediately went to a tatami mat in the middle of the room and tossed it aside. He lifted the edge of the floorboard, revealing a hidden compartment below.

Reaching in with both hands, he pulled out a boxy radio, about the size of a loaf of bread. It was a SSTR1, Strategic Services Transmitter Receiver Number 1.

Mina took it and placed it on the mat next to him, hurriedly setting it up. Power. Antenna. Twisting the dials, she adjusted the megacycles.

In the night skies over Tokyo, an intimidating, awe-inspiring flight of literally three-hundred B-29s Superfortress "Superfort" bombers approached, escorted by P-51 Mustang fighters. Visible from the exterior, their crews manned their posts in tense anticipation.

High above the city, the massive flight of aircraft soared over Tokyo Bay and the ships moored there. Plane after plane passed over the waters below, an indomitable procession of impeding death, towards the sleeping city.

Back inside the fisherman's hut, empty static-filled whistling and warbling emitted from the radio's speaker. Mina turned and twisted various dials. For some reason, the damn thing wasn't tuning in to the proscribed 10.2 megacycle frequency.

Mina spoke urgently as she fiddled with the dials, not looking over her shoulder. "Check the antenna."

The fisherman followed the wire antenna lined around picture frames, corners, and edges of walls, searching for the source of the problem - breaks in the line, corrosion, anything that could be the cause.

Anxious possibilities raced through Mina's mind as she twisted the knobs. Radio components tended to be vulnerable

---

[61] In April 1945 the US bombed Riken's laboratories in Komagome, Tokyo.

to shocks and vibrations. Was it the housing? A deformed housing could influence the frequency by changing stray capacitances.

She turned the radio around, looking for any obvious signs of damage. There were none. Was it a blown fuse? That was a common issue.

Scowling, brow furrowed, she opened up the casing and inspected the interior. She fixated on the fuses. No, the little finger-sized glass and metal tubes looked fine.

Oh fucking hell.

"The crystal oscillator is broken!" she exclaimed, her doe eyes wide with horror.

She stared at the tiny canteen-shaped component dismally. The quartz crystal oscillator inside the radio was an extremely high precision electronic component.[62] Not just that, the quartz crystal itself hadn't just rattled out of place; it had shattered into several pieces, most likely by the force of her ejection from the torpedo tube.

She spun around, turning to the fisherman. "I need your radio."

The fisherman was confounded. "Broken too! You were the one supposed to bring spare parts!" he exclaimed in consternation.

Her fearful antics onboard the submarine flitted across her memory. The little satchel of spare parts for the radio had lain in the corner of the torpedo room. With her protestations and the threat of the destroyer, she hadn't secured all of her gear. If it wasn't for her antics, they probably would have remembered before she disembarked the submarine. She cursed herself.

The room was silent save the quiet warbling and static of the radio. Mina stared at him in dismay. She swallowed hard, turning away from him abashedly.

"We were in a hurry," she said pathetically. "I left the

---

[62] During the World War II era, no mass production industry had ever been developed to produce this critical component.

spare parts aboard the submarine."

Disheartened, his face fell, growing haggard. He posited a question, although he already feared the answer. "The radio shop?"

Mina sat down heavily, head in her hands, daunted by the prospect. Her voice cracked, growing agitated. "I can't just rush out to the local radio shop and pick up new spares! Civilian radio parts have their military frequencies disabled."

Civilian radios couldn't access the military frequencies she needed because civilian radio crystals were commonly "swept", heated in such a way as to remove the capability to access certain frequencies.

There was a trace of bitterness in her voice. "Me and my goddamn self. It's all my fault."

She knew all too well it was her own fault, and now she'd have to pay for it. Hell, she had probably endangered the whole mission.

Anxious, she tried to think of alternatives. She had no available smoke grenades with which to mark the building. Even if she did, it wouldn't help much. When the city started lighting up like kindling, her signal would be lost in the smoke of the firestorm anyway.

Brow furrowed in thought, the fisherman chewed anxiously on his lit cigar. "The only working radio nearby I can think of that can communicate with the American planes would be inside the atomic facility itself," he said reflectively.

Mina gaped at him.

"Are you nuts? Into the lions' den!? she squawked. "You have any idea how many troops they have inside!? And - I'm supposed to run out there in the middle of an air raid!?"

Puffing on his cigar, the fisherman ignored her protests, pressing on. "I'll be waiting for you at the crossroads near the bank downtown, outside the facility. I hope you succeed."

Half-distracted, not looking at him, Mina nodded assent. Time was of the essence. All modesty dismissed, she hurriedly stripped out of her schoolgirl outfit, pulling it over her head and tossing it aside.

Mina grumbled to herself as she changed. "Goddamnit, I should have stuck with translating."

Standing unabashedly in her beige-pink bra and brief-style panties, she grabbed the folded Japanese nurse uniform in her pack and started donning it.

Picking the discarded sailor uniform off the ground, the fisherman went to the stove as Mina tugged on the white nurse gown. Using tongs, he picked up a hot coal and pressed it against the school uniform in spots. He started little flames and charred parts of the uniform, and singed the edges.

Patting out the licking flames, he quickly folded it and stuffed it into her nurse's first aid satchel. He grabbed a nearby padded air raid hood. The hood was a drab navy blue, dotted with patterns of small white flowers. The hood was of the sort that widened out in the rear to cover one's shoulders.

Nearby, done dressing, Mina brushed down her nurse's uniform and fitted the complementary white cap onto her head.

She grabbed the air raid gear ubiquitous in the Japanese cities: steel helmet, gaiters, and the padded hood. She left behind the first aid bag since she already had her nurse satchel.

Mina glanced at the rest of her available gear. There was an additional bandolier of dressings and bandages. She decided to leave those behind. Those were really only appropriate out in the field and they would look somewhat unusual in the cities. No need to look out of place.

Urgent, he handed her the nurse's brown leather satchel holding her gear. Mina spoke quickly.

"If I'm not at the bank crossroads in an hour, it means I'm dead."

They both looked up at the sound of air raid sirens spinning up from across town, building into a continual loud wail.

"You must hurry," the fisherman urged her. "Go, go! *Hayaku!*"

Mina rushed out the hut's doorway.

21 B-SAN

Up in the night skies over Japan, the massive flight of B-29 Superfortress bombers and their P-51 fighter escorts approached the city borders.

The bombers from the 20th Air Force had departed a few hours before, the night of March 9th. Taking off from air bases at Tinian, Saipan, and Guam, the bombers and their escorts encroached upon the city of Tokyo, at approximately 1 AM local time March 10th. This was the night of reckoning.

Awaiting up ahead, Japanese Zero fighter planes and Kate bombers circled. The planes swarmed in towards the approaching aircraft in a near-futile effort to defend the city.

Their efforts were largely in vain for a simple reason. The B-29 Superforts were too difficult for even the venerated Zero fighters to intercept. The Superforts' new engines were simply too fast, and the Zeroes, quick as they were, couldn't chase them down if the Superforts got ahead.

In the past, B-29 air raids on Tokyo were conducted at altitudes of 30,000 feet that insured immunity from Japanese anti-aircraft fire. Although their high altitude protected the bombers, it also decreased the accuracy and impact of their bomb runs. To amend this, Major-General Curtis Lemay ordered a dramatic change in tactics. The new bomber runs would be at low altitudes of five-to-eight thousand feet, delivering a payload of high explosive and incendiary bombs.

At this low altitude range, the B-29 bombers that were initially too high for the anti-aircraft shells were now too low; the fuses on the shells simply couldn't be cut that short to hit them.

Therefore, the Zeroes only hope of effectively attacking was to await the bombers far ahead of them. They would swoop in and attack the bombers from the front then weave through the oncoming planes, continuing to the next flight of B-29s towards the rear of the formation.

Screaming in amongst the B-29s, much smaller Japanese Kate bombers dropped phosphorus bombs in front of the planes.

The leather-capped and goggled crew within the B-29 threw their arms up over their faces at the blindingly white flash outside their cockpit window.

Outside, P-51 Mustangs swooped in to defend their charges, fending off the Zeroes and Kate bombers, their three pairs of machine guns blazing.

Engines screaming, one of the Zeroes made a suicidal run at a B-29, ramming into an engine in a fiery blast.

Remaining engines chugging in protest, ablaze and trailing smoke, the Superfort arced towards the city below.

Down in the streets of Tokyo, it was a tumultuous scene. The air was filled with the wailing of air sirens. Tense and anxious, Mina ran through the streets, dressed in her white nurse uniform and air raid protective gear, sans gaiters. She checked her Seikosha[63] wristwatch. It was approximately 1:00 AM Tokyo time.

Searchlight beams swept back and forth across the sky in a pivoting arc. The city's panicked denizens, similarly-attired

---

[63] Founded in the late 1800s, Seikosha was a branch of the Japanese company Seiko, known today for producing clocks, watches, computer printers and other devices.

in protective gear, rushed through the streets, some running to air raid shelters if available.

Standing atop a crate at the street corner, a boy about ten years old hollered at the top of his lungs. "B-san is coming! B-san is coming!" he shouted, using the colloquialism for the B-29 bombers staging air raids throughout Japan.

Mina continued running through the hectic streets and the throngs of fear-stricken people. Tense, she gritted her teeth, glancing upwards. The bombs would start dropping any moment. In the skies above, there was the multitudinous roaring of aircraft engines, screaming and swooping about. Occasionally one could make out black outlines of planes dogfighting against dark blue sky, amidst the indomitable procession of shadowy larger bombers.

Numerous searchlight beams pierced the heavens, sweeping the dark skies in an arc-like fan. The rays occasionally illuminated overhead planes in a splotch of painted colors against the night.

In the skies overhead, American fighter planes continued fending off attacks by Zeroes. Largely unscathed, the B-29 bombers descended low to begin carpet-bombing.

The bombers' main target was the industrial sector of the city that housed workers for the factories and docks - namely, the people who supplied the manpower for Japan's war industry.

That residential district was right next to Tokyo Bay. It was densely-packed with wooden homes haphazardly lined winding streets. With the dry weather and blustery winds, they were essentially giant piles of kindling for the perfect firestorm.

The B-29 bombers descended low over downtown, flying in between five and eight thousand feet.

Inside one of the B-29 bombers, the bay doors swung open. The bombs were almost cylindrical, save the tip and tail fins. Released, the shells receded into the distance below. A stream of bombs descended over the city from each Superfort, a seemingly incessant cascade of impending death.

In midair, the trajectory of the bombs straightened out and vents on the cylinders opened up, scattering into 38 individual bomblets filled with jellied gasoline and magnesium, sailing down, down down, onto the densely built - and wooden - metropolis of Tokyo.

In the streets below, amidst the piercing wail of air raid sirens, Mina heard the whistling of the first incoming bombs and she craned her head upwards. Incandescent streaks of light from dozens of fiery globules arced downwards through the night sky, like fiery trails of hair against a dark backdrop.

Awestruck, some of the running passerbys glanced upwards as the bomblets sowed the sky with fire, hailing down on the roofs of the houses, setting them alight with a whoosh of ignition.

Soaring above the city, the B-29s left behind a trail of fire and destruction in their wake, turning the rows of densely packed houses below into a roaring ocean of flame.

In the city below, cries of panicking people rose into the air. Tense but determined, running among the dozens of screaming civilians, Mina dashed through the streets. The earth trembled beneath her feet and nearby buildings shook from the explosions.

Mina looked ahead at the gated facility entrance where the trucks had passed, prominent against the backdrop of the night sky with the sweeping fan of searchlight beams.

Standing at the open, iron-barred gate, a yelling officer waved the panicked civilians through. He was rather young, with a thin mustache and beard. Frantic, he shouted over the wail of air raid sirens. "Hurry, hurry! Get inside!"

Mina sprinted on ahead, joining a handful of civilians as the officer herded them indoors.

Inside the auxiliary corridor, the wailing sirens and

muffled explosions were still audible. Hastily ushered along by the soldiers, Mina joined the fear-stricken civilians.

There was a clamor as two nurses bearing a stretcher rushed a wounded officer, a major by his insignia, down the hall. Caught in the onset of bombing, the major had a gaping abdominal wound. Mina could see blood-slicked coiled intestines in the wound where he clamped his hand.

Getting her out of the way, the young officer from the gate shoved Mina through the nearby door of a janitor's supply closet.

Mina shut the door. Inside the closet, there were shelves of cleaning supplies, a sink, and along the wall a row of lockers.

Anxious, the young officer looked at Mina as she brushed herself down and pulled off her air raid gear. His brow furrowed in pain. Mina glanced at his arm.

Blood trickled down his forearm and down his wrist. Shrapnel blast, probably.

"Here. Lemme take a look at that," she offered.

She set her leather nurse satchel onto the floor. She reached inside it -

-and pulled out her silenced .22 pistol.

Face cold and almost expressionless, she brutally jammed the barrel directly into his chest, shoving him against the lockers, clamping one hand over his mouth to stifle any screams.

She pumped six rounds into his rib cage, pistol letting out muffled *phuts* of baffled air accompanied by quiet clack-clack of the slide.

Eyes still wide in shocked surprise, he sagged to the ground limp. His officer's cap slid down, covering his eyes. He toppled onto his side, then sprawled onto his belly, limbs splayed onto the tiles.

Hurrying, Mina set her nurse's bag on top the sink and rummaged through. There would only be limited time to get downstairs to the radio room. According to the signs she had seen, it was probably downstairs, not upstairs, to better protect it from air raids. She hoped she was right.

Behind her, the guard stirred, almost noiseless. Hand trembling with stricken effort, his hand went to the flap of his sidearm holster. Struggling, he drew his pistol, aiming in her direction silently.

22   THE UNPLANNED RAID

There was the faint sound of cloth brushing against tile.

Mina looked up. Ahead in the mirror on the wall, slight motion behind her reflection caught her eye.

She whirled and stomped down on his wrist.

Still clutching the pistol, his hand spasmed but he didn't drop it. Hand trembling, he managed to squeeze off three rounds into the air, deafeningly loud in the enclosed space.

Alarmed shouts came from down the hall. Oh, not good. Tense anxiety flooded her body.

Down the hallway, alarms started blaring, voices yelled orders and the lighting snapped to flashing red.

Several pairs of boots pounded down the corridor amidst alarms and yelled orders. Hands grabbed rifles and submachine guns[64] off weapons racks.

At Mina's feet, the wounded soldier groaned, his twitching fingers fumbling with his pistol. He tried to angle his

---

[64] The Nambu Type 100 was a Japanese submachine gun used during World War II. It was the only submachine gun produced by Japan in any quantity at the time, and included several variants.

wrist upwards to shoot at her.

Coldly furious, Mina stood over him and plugged him in the back of his skull for good measure.

Blood spurted and his head impacted onto the floor as his entire body shuddered momentarily, the bullet inducing a final firing of neurons within his brain, and he lay still.

Angry, Mina kicked his corpse in the ribs almost petulantly. Damn bastard blew her cover.

Yelling voices outside in the hall grew closer, a mere yard away.

Dual-wielding Nambu submachine guns, Mina side-stepped into the hallway and loosed a blazing barrage at the onrushing soldiers.

The hail of lead cut them down in their tracks. Their bodies jerked spasmodically as they were riddled with bullets and they crumpled backwards. One soldier was knocked flat onto his back, involuntarily firing into the ceiling, and a shower of plaster and broken ceiling tiles rained down upon them.

More yells came from down the hall, just around the corner. Adrenaline coursed through her system. It was all going to hell way too fast. She reckoned they'd be upon her in seconds.

She flung a block of C2 plastique onto the ceiling and backpedaled down the hall, laying down a chattering stream of cover fire.

Strafing out and firing from behind the corner, oncoming soldiers at the end of the hall fired in an overlapping *crack-crack-crack* of rifles.

Loosing another stream of gunfire, Mina hoped they'd keep their heads down and stop advancing-

A second later, the block explosive adhered to the ceiling detonated in a great boom that echoed down the long corridor. The ceiling collapsed in a rain of broken ceiling tiles, plaster and dust, entombing the screaming soldiers underneath.

Buying a moment's respite in the midst of the alert, Mina sprinted down the corridor to the elevator at the end.

Lit by intermittent crimson light of the alarms, grimacing, Mina jammed her fingers into the seam of the double doors. Prying with bare hands, she started to wrench open the elevator. They had already locked down the elevator on this section of the floor. No power would be running to it. She had to get down the old-fashioned way.

Behind her, down the hall, there was the crumbling sound of shifting masonry. She heard bits of concrete rolling off the top of the rubble and muffled voices. Soldiers were already trying to make their way through, shoving aside debris.

Gritting her teeth, she finally forced open the elevator doors. She peered into the dark chasm. It was a long drop.

Behind her at the debris pile, a hand became visible, shoving aside a broken cinder block.

Slinging her submachine guns on her back, she slid down the elevator cable like a fireman down a pole, as soldiers emerged through the debris down the hall. She descended down, down, into the pitch blackness.

The door to the radio room slammed open as Mina kicked it down and burst into the room, submachine guns spewing fury.

Rifles still clutched in their hands, both guards inside the doorway collapsed, bodies riddled with bullets just as they lifted their rifles. Her clips empty, Mina dropped the submachine guns and pulled her .22 silenced pistol from behind her back in one smooth motion.

The radioman sitting at the desk whirled in his seat, reaching for his side holster-

Close to the door, a third guard near the file cabinet rushed in and grappled with her, trying to wrest the gun away. The radioman aimed down the wavering sights of his pistol at the struggling pair, unable to get a clear shot-

Mina twisted the guard into an armlock and shot him in the side of the head. As he sagged she grabbed his collar, holding his still-warm body as a human shield.

She peered around her meat shield, firing the pistol in

quick succession of *clack-clack-clack*. Red dots on the radioman's chest spurted blood. He flopped back onto the table, blood trickling from his mouth, pistol clattering out of his grasp.

Pushing with her back, Mina shoved file cabinets, tables, whatever heavy furniture was in the room against the door, barricading herself inside.

She ran to the boxy radio on the desk against the wall. She shoved aside the slumped radioman and snatched the headset off his ears before he even hit the floor. She donned it and immediately started tuning the knobs on the radio.

There was sudden rattling at the doorknob, barely visible through the piled furniture. She glanced behind her. It wouldn't hold for long.

The radio warbled as she tuned to the proper frequency. She spoke into the microphone in English.

"American flight Baker Seven, this is Coral Hare. Authentication   one-six-able-charlie-baker-five-king-sugar-niner.[65] Kitchen's in the wrong place and I'm at the stove."

She glanced at the map to double-check. Pinned to the wall was a map of Tokyo. The facility she was in was marked with a red thumbtack. Bingo.

She spoke again. "Shift your approach to zero-six-six, zero-eight-six, over."

Technically, the location she just gave was the pedestrian street outside. However, the underground facility extended beneath the city streets, unbeknownst to the city's populace.

Mina waited tensely, listening to empty static on the other end.

Out in the hallway, wielding a table from a nearby room, a handful of soldiers used it as a battering ram, smashing at the door.

---

[65] The World War II military phonetic alphabet is different from the modern NATO phonetic alphabet.

Inside the radio room, tremors rattled the floor and the walls. Shouts came from outside the door. The half-empty cup of tea next to Mina quivered on the desktop.

She glanced over her shoulder. Only partially obscured, the door behind the mass of furniture started to splinter, cracks appearing in the wooden frame.

Finally, the radio squawked.

"Code confirmed, Coral Hare," said the American pilot over the crackling speaker. "Adjusting our approach. Danger close, repeat, danger close. Get outta there!"

Finally, the door gave way, splintering open. The soldiers on the other side rammed it ajar, shoving enough furniture aside for a man-sized gap to appear.

A handful of grenades lobbed into the room, sailing through the air.

23 BOOM

The resounding explosions shrouded the radio room in dense smoke.

Guns at the ready, the soldiers burst in, sweeping the room.

But it was empty.

Crawling frantically through the cramped ventilation ducts, Mina's petite frame hurried along, nurse's bag strapped to her back.

Suddenly bullets spanged and sparked all around her as rounds ricocheted within the confined space. Flinching, she hurried on as coin-sized shafts of light burst into existence with the gunshots, peeking through holes perforating the metal.

Spurred on, breathing quickening, Mina scurried down the claustrophobic passage.

The ventilation grate flew out of the wall, kicked from within. Mina climbed out the vent and into the conference room, her nurse uniform ripped and spotted with blood that fortunately for the most part wasn't hers.

She pulled her bag through the vent, setting it atop the

table and started loading two submachine guns.

There was an electronic screech overhead. The loudspeaker blared to life and a male voice boomed out in Japanese.

"All personnel. There is a fire in the cyclotron chamber. Please assist immediately! Hurry!"

Mina mumbled under her breath. "Fast, fast," she said to herself.

Suddenly, it hit her and her eyes lit up. Did she pack it? She looked at the open bag.

Her roller skates were visible within.

Seconds later, she tore off the edge of the nurse's white skirt so it ended just four inches under her buttocks, turning it into...what? A miniature skirt?[66] Her mother would call it scandalous. Whatever. She needed the greater mobility and freedom of movement.

She racked back the bolt on the submachine gun in her hand.

Zipping along, a pair of rollerskate-encased feet rounded the corner into the large lab.

Caught by surprise, the handful of soldiers and lab-coated scientists gawked at the unexpected sight. A grim-faced nurse on roller skates in a makeshift short skirt, dual-wielding submachine guns in each hand. Mirthless, face cold and impassive, she skated in, gunning down troops in her path as they came to their senses and fired back.

Muffled, rumbling explosions from outside echoed throughout the spacious chamber. Skating from cover to cover behind the lab benches, Mina fought her way through, gunning down remaining soldiers within seconds. One of the scientists made a dash for the alarm panel on the wall.

In a chattering storm of fire, the man slammed against

---

[66] The modern miniskirt wouldn't be invented until five to ten years after World War II, and didn't become popular until the 1960s.

the wall and slid down, leaving a crimson trail on the drywall, glasses broken and askew on his face.

Her rollerskate-encased feet glided through the carnage of mangled bodies and sprawled limbs on the tiles. She approached the lab bench.

On top of the workstation, splotched with blood spatter, was a set of blueprints the scientist had been working on. Her eyes scanned the white wireframe on the blue material. It looked like a detonator, possibly for the atomic device. Nearby was a sheaf of important looking documents - shipping manifests, purchase orders. Lying askew on the table were several brown leather messenger canisters with carry straps.

She grabbed all the papers, stuffed them into a canister and slung it across her back.

Mina skated into the main cyclotron chamber. The chamber was about the size of her high school gym or maybe an aircraft hangar. There were railings on the upper floors where soldiers patrolled.

Up ahead were the cyclotrons, two large particle accelerators vital for conducting research for processing uranium into weapons-grade material. They were massive circular machines, one twice the size of the other.[67] The larger one was roughly a hundred feet in diameter and forty feet high, encased in a vault of six foot-thick concrete.

Two technicians in coveralls and hardhats crouched in front of the first machine. They looked up at Mina in surprise and bolted, running off. The scientists ran for cover as the soldiers rushed to defend them.

Mina reached behind her back and pulled out a grenade[68], pulling the pin and cap with her teeth and tossing it onto the upper floor. Her submachine gun chattered in her other hand as she hurriedly shot the soldiers above, as they had

[67] The real-life Tokyo facility at Riken had two such cyclotrons.

[68] A Japanese Type 91 grenade. The arming mechanism, is not quite the same as the American style.

the vantage point. One screamed as he fell over the railing, plummeting to the chamber floor.

Hunched behind the low wall, the soldiers on the upper floor aimed from behind cover, firing at the speeding form below. One by one they fell, shot or blown apart by grenades she hurled into their midst.

The vaults on the still-spinning cyclotrons were open for maintenance. They were usually closed while in operation, but Mina guessed the technicians had been running tests. She tossed two timed blocks of C2 onto the cyclotrons.

Two successive fiery blasts rocked the room, shaking the tiles beneath her feet. With a screech of tearing metal and a groan of ripping steel, the whirring machinery within the cyclotrons ground to a smoking halt, sparking occasionally.

Face smeared with soot, uniform peppered with debris, one soldier was still alive, lying on his back, blood trickling from his mouth. Wheezing from punctured lungs, he looked up at her.

There was the droning of aircraft engines overhead. With a series of rumbling explosions from above, the roof partially caved in.

He saw the nurse loom above him in a domineering stance, her expression cold. A deafening cascade of burning debris, ceiling tiles, concrete, and plaster rained down behind her in a shower of fire, exposing burning scaffolding of wooden beams. The dim silhouettes of B-29 bombers were visible in the night sky.

Face impassive, the nurse extended her submachine gun directly at him, the barrel looming in his field of vision. There was a bright muzzle flash but he heard no gunshot, as light traveled faster than sound, and everything went white.

Having finished off her opponent, Mina looked around the room. All around her, the crackling fires spread, snaking over burning machinery and making their way towards her.

Up on the second-floor railings, near the huddled scientists, stood a single surviving officer. Lit by the orange glow of nearby flames, the man slammed his hand on the large button panel on the wall. Alarms blared, echoing throughout the chamber and the loudspeaker blared a warning over the din.

"*Ka sai ga hassei shimashita. Hinan shite kudasai.*"[69]

Evacuate, evacuate. Tense, the remaining scientists in white lab coats dashed through the exits, desperate to escape the spreading flames.

The building was about to collapse.

---

[69] "There's a fire! Please leave the building."

24 INFERNO

In the cyclotron chamber, there was another resounding explosion and even more burning debris rained down. The building was collapsing in on itself.

Running, a scientist looked upwards and screamed as a falling beam collapsed onto him, cutting him off mid-scream.

Following the fleeing staff, Mina made for the exit in a mad dash, zipping through the burning rubble into the corridor.

Passing by a sprinting soldier who paid her little heed, Mina glanced over her shoulder. A raging fireball started to fill the hallway, consuming everything and everyone in its path. The reflected glow on her face intensified from the approaching flames -

Gritting her teeth, she put in a last-ditch burst of effort, arms and legs pumping faster and faster.

She outpaced the soldiers running for their lives. In moments the soldiers were engulfed in flames and pitched forward, screaming, too slow to escape the raging inferno consuming the chamber behind them. The heat at her back was intensifying, becoming nearly unbearable.

Finally there was a roar and a blast wave, knocking her off her feet, launching her into the air -

She landed on the debris-littered tiles, wind knocked out of her. Catching her breath, she got to her feet and looked behind her. The corridor had collapsed where she had been scant seconds before.

Panting, wheezing, Mina skated down the remnants of the burning hall, towards the door. The sign above the doorframe read "Emergency Exit" in Japanese characters. She dashed inside, hoping it would lead to safety.

From within a pile of burning rubble, a lone figure arose. Panting, khaki uniform scorched, soot streaking his face, Rain's visage was a mask of baleful anger.

In his field of vision, through the haze of heat and smoke, he saw what seemed to be a female figure in a white nurse uniform, skating away, receding into the distance.

In the underground corridor, Mina saw the stairs at the end of the tunnel, a faint orange glow emanating from outside.

She climbed the stairs to the entranceway, feet still enclosed in roller skates, taking the steps one at a time.

Mina emerged outside - hoping for a breath of fresh air –

And was instead met by stifling, searing heat and the continual wail of air raid sirens.

Live sparks and red-hot embers swept by gale force winds filled the air. Burning bits of wood and paper rained upon her, scorching her disheveled nurse's uniform in spots.

She raised her arm to her face, not expecting the incandescent ferocity of the flames nor the suffocating heat. Even here, it was like standing before a blast furnace, and she could feel the heat on her face. Her nostrils were suffused with the odor of burning wood and choking smoke.

Out in the distance she could hear the clamor of panicked voices, indistinct over the roar of flames. On top of that was the whistling of falling bombs and ongoing explosions.

The building she had been in was built on a hilltop. At the fringes of the property she could have a decent view of the city. She raced out onto the street corner - and stopped, staring out in awe of the devastation.

The city was ablaze.

Out across the Tokyo metropolis, waves of flames twisted in the wind across blackened scaffolding of roofs. Dark debris swirled in the air above the rooftops, silhouetted against the orange-yellow flames, all against the midnight sky.

Air raid searchlight beams swept the skies from horizon to horizon, occasionally punctuated by crimson streaks, futile bursts of anti-aircraft fire. In the skies, the outlines of mammoth bombers soared unhindered.

Further out in the skies, through the columns of smoke, Mina saw the looming silhouettes of even more bombers intermittently glint golden from reflected firelight. Other planes passed through sweeping searchlight beams, underbellies glittering then darkening as they passed out of sight.

As the planes passed overhead, clusters of bomblets exploded over the buildings, arcing down in a fountain of liquid flame. Wavy streaks streamed in a dome shape, looking like tendrils of flaming hair cascading upon the city.

Tokyo was in an utter firestorm, complete with the hurricane force winds that came with it. It was a fearsome juxtaposition of gale wind and searing flame.[70] The overhead bombers had succeeded in their objective, turning the closely-packed, wooden buildings prevalent in Japanese cities into this devastating freak of science.

In such phenomena, the bombing ignited numerous fires that soon united into a single uncontrollable mass of flame, so hot it generated its own self-sustaining, gale force

---

[70] The Allies first encountered the phenomenon of the firestorm earlier in the war, in August of 1943, when the British bombed the German city of Hamburg.

winds. The winds carried flaming debris aloft and spread the flames even further. Sometimes, it would literally suck the oxygen out of the air, suffocating people in the vicinity. The end result was a raging, self-perpetuating sea of fire that would consume the city.[71]

Making her way to the city streets, Mina hastily found a desolate alley. Down the street, the flames began to spread. One building was engulfed in flames, with the adjoining one starting to burn.

She set down her nurse's pack and unclasped it. As glowing embers blew about her, Mina stripped her nurse's uniform over her head and pulled out the purposely-scorched schoolgirl uniform from earlier, donning it quickly.

She let down her bun of nurse-style hair and shook it loose about her shoulders. From within the bag she pulled out a folded, beige school backpack and the navy blue air raid hood.

She quickly changed the roller skates out for white schoolgirl shoes then stuffed the nurse's bag inside the backpack, concealing it from the eyes of any soldiers that might have been in the facility earlier.

Mina quickly tied the padded air raid hood about her head, knotting the ties at her chin. With the hood and the scorch-spotted schoolgirl uniform, she looked like any one of the fleeing civilians in the area. Not too far from the truth at this point; getting out of this alive would be messy.

She pushed the sobering realization out of mind. Unlike most exfiltrations, this one was even more uncertain than most. Even surviving the night would be difficult.

There was no real safe area within the city tonight, and the anarchy downtown would make things worse. Due to the unplanned nature of her one-woman raid, in terms of survival,

---

[71] In terms of brightness, the fires were so fierce that even people in distant towns miles away could read newspapers by the light of the Tokyo fires.

she was now stuck in the same situation as the rest of the city's denizens.

Not to mention the living hell she would find herself in if she were discovered and captured.

She took a moment to gather her bearings. She needed to get to the crossroads near the bank and rendezvous with the fisherman. It was a landmark location, and despite the chaos in the city, he would hopefully be easier to find. After that, she figured they would try and get to an air raid shelter or find some way out of the bombing area.

Grimly resolute, she grabbed a Nambu semiautomatic pistol from her pack and tucked it into her back waistband. She shouldered her beige backpack, making to leave.

Mina ran out onto the streets of Tokyo, lost among the mass of fear-stricken, luggage-toting, fleeing civilians.

She looked up ahead. A family of four ran through the streets in quiet anxiety, trying to escape the blazing fires and suffocating smoke. The father, tensely anxious, held his handkerchief over his nose and dragged his approximately eight-year old son along. The beleaguered-looking mother, face tense with worry, had a screaming baby strapped to her back, his little arms flailing as he wailed incessantly.

For a moment, Mina considered offering to help carry something, to better blend in. Then she dismissed the thought. Not this time. Her training had drilled into her the need to keep her hands free, in case she suddenly needed to fight.

In scorched schoolgirl outfit, a hooded Mina caught up to them, trailing a few feet behind. She jogged along. Hopefully, she'd be close enough to be mistaken as a member of the family from passerbys, but not so close as to draw the family's attention.

Suddenly, she heard men yelling behind her, at the end of the street. She glanced back.

Turning the corner, a squad of soldiers armed with rifles ran down the burning street, boots pounding the pavement. They pushed aside the already harried civilians behind her. The lead sergeant led out a holler. "She's dressed as a nurse! Find her!"

Still running, Mina tensed, her hand gripping the pistol tucked in her waistband.

Mina and the family ahead of her rushed aside as the yelling soldiers raced past.

One soldier glanced back at her - then ran onwards, none of the squad giving her a second thought. Just a schoolgirl.

Mina let out a breath of relief and loosened her grip on the pistol's handle, letting her hand drop to her side. She ran on.

The city was in absolute pandemonium. One of the objectives of Operation Meetinghouse was to attack the workers who worked at the war factories. It was working. Reaching the nearby crossroads, Mina rushed out, joining the throngs of inhabitants as they fled.

She looked around. She had made it to an area of office buildings, ranging from two to six stories high. There. The bank. The fisherman was supposed to be around here somewhere, but if he was here, there was no way to pick him out from amongst the crowd. The din of the mob, explosions, roar of engines, and whistling bombs combined into an indecipherable cacophony. Everyone wore air raid hoods, and faces tended to be smudged with soot and ash. Damnit.

As she ran out onto the wide crossroads, she was met by the clamor of people desperate to escape the flames. Fires lit up the night sky, suffusing the horizon with an orange glow. Throngs of civilians ran through the streets in a panic, padded hoods on their heads, first aid pouches slung across their chests.

Mina saw parents hauling children through the streets. Some people clutched precious household items to their chests, others hauled luggage. One housewife carried a stack of love letters tied with twine. Mina saw one teenage girl about her age carrying an armful of cookware. Another, possibly her sister, carried a stack of folded silk kimonos, probably exorbitantly expensive given the embroidery Mina glimpsed. The mob rushed in a panic through the streets as bits of burning debris drifted down upon them.

Looking overhead, the procession of death continued. The bright light of the fires flared in the skies, occasionally revealing bomber-plane shapes here-and-there against the dark blue heavens. Occasional bolts of scarlet, salvos of ineffectual anti-aircraft fire, overshot the silhouettes of the bombers that flew on.

Lost in the crowd, Mina kept her head down, rushing through. The heat was stifling. She had been near bonfires before, had escaped from burning buildings, but this heat and devastation was on a scale she had rarely seen. Given her short stature, Mina craned her head over the shoulders of the crowd. She struggled to peer through the throng, the orange glow of nearby flames reflected on her face.

The wind gusted, sweeping up a flurry of burning debris from the inflamed sky and sending it elsewhere to birth new fires. There was a mass outcry as a shower of sparks landed on their heads, scorching their hoods in dark spots. Mina cringed with the rest of them. A few people's hoods were set alight and they tore them off, patting out the flames.

Suddenly, off to her left, she heard a woman's bloodcurdling scream. A murmur of dismay and alarm swept through the crowd. Mina snapped her head in her direction.

There was one mother who carried her baby strapped to her back, Japanese style. Her entire back was aflame from the shower of flaming debris; the padding enveloping her infant had caught fire.

But it was too late to save her. Several people in the dense crowd had also been set afire. The conflagration spread person-to-person, like an incendiary contagion. Their hoods flamed under another shower of sparks, and even more people were set alight.[72]

---

[72] This was a real occurrence. Refugees clutching their belongings

Fortunately or unfortunately, proper air raid gear as recommended by the government included the padded hood that was intended to protect people's ears from explosive blasts.

However, for months Tokyo had mostly been bombed with incendiaries, not with concussive fragmentation blasts the hoods were initially designed to protect against.

Now the hoods turned into more fuel for the fire, even as surrounding people hastily struggled to pat out the flames. Panic ensued as people realized they were going to be immolated. It turned into a free-for-all, a desperate mob of people trying to clamber out.

In the middle of the crowd, face grimly determined, Mina found herself one of the people pushing, shoving, and climbing over one other to get out of the spreading inferno. People who did not burn from the head down from falling flaming debris, found themselves burned from the feet up from flaming debris they had stepped over. Trampling over the teenage girl holding the crockery, Mina ran forth from the flaming human stampede.

She felt intense heat on her arm and searing pain. She looked to her side. Her forearm was on fire. She hastily patted it out and ran to the street corner, next to a man who had collapsed and sprawled in the gutter.

Having barely escaped the fiery deathtrap of the crowd, she stood with her hands to her knees. She panted as if she had run a mile, glowing cinders floating down all around her. A few yards behind her, she still heard the clamor of people caught in the human bonfire, unable to get out. Standing in the sweltering heat, heaving, sweat poured down her face. Her hair was sopping wet beneath her hood as if she had just emerged from a bath.

---

crowded into the rare clear spaces unobstructed by the city's infrastructure - crossroads, gardens and parks, etc. Unfortunately, their bundles caught fire even faster than their clothing and the entire mob would be set aflame from the inside out.

Suddenly, a stern hand clamped down on her shoulder from behind. Mina let out a started gasp and stiffened. She turned around.

She looked up into the dark folds of the hood...and saw the red-orange dot of a lit cigar, plume of smoke curling upwards. She caught a whiff of rich tobacco.

Relief flooded her body and her shoulders sagged. The fisherman wore a dark red, almost burgundy hood, embroidered with stylized fish.

He spoke urgently. "Come on! Let's get outta here!"

Mina nodded assent. The pair threaded their way quickly through the streets, just another two refugees escaping the funeral pyre of the city sector.

Air raid shelter

The underground shelter was dimly lit. The single bare bulb buzzed sporadically as its light flickered in and out of existence with the distant booms outside.

Crowded. The air raid shelter's occupants huddled on the dirt floor, quietly anxious. Some of the occupants sat nearly shoulder to shoulder. Some stood, some crouched, some were wounded and lying down, attended to by friends and family. Some sat leaning against the bare wooden support beams lining the walls.

There was the reverberating impact of an explosion outside. The room's occupants glanced upwards, then hunched their heads as a shower of fine dust rained upon them. Notably, a spiderweb of cracks started to form on the concrete ceiling, spreading outward.

Running in between the buildings, Mina and the fisherman dashed into the marketplace. The stalls had been emptied, packed up, and were now reduced to flaming kindling.

Up ahead, Mina saw a staircase leading underground. She noticed the sign next to it and a wellspring of hope rose within her.

Growing excited, she pointed her arm through the blowing red-hot cinders. "There! The air raid shelter!"

She made to run for the entrance. But having been the survivor of several months of fire raids, the fisherman yanked her back by the shoulder. "No! Not in fires like this! You'll be roasted alive!"

Just then there was the whistling of an incoming bomb, uncomfortably loud and close.

Mina yelled. "Under the stall!"

She and the fisherman sprinted for the overhang of the nearby fish stall. Up in the dark sky, a fount of fiery trails streamed down from the falling cylinder, spattering liquid flame that skittered along the roofs, setting fire to everything it contacted -

Several flaming globules rolled onto the shelter doorway - spreading a wash of dancing flames in front of the entrance.

Inside the air raid shelter, the roof caved in. The world became a cascade of dirt, rubble - and liquid flame. Shrieks of alarm and yelps of pain rose as flaming gasoline washed atop the mass of people, setting occupants alight even as they bolted to their feet.

Screaming in a wild panic, the crowd surged outside even as the flames spread within the mob -

Outside, Mina watched in horror as dozens of occupants ran out of the underground entrance, screaming in agony, clothes aflame, padded gear becoming a liability. They ran out, slowed in their steps, then pitched forward, immolated, just a few feet away from Mina.

She knew better than to touch these particular victims to try and help them. Their bodies were doused in jellied gasoline, the stench of petrol so strong it suffused her nostrils. If she tried to pat out the flames she's probably end up like them.

Grim, Mina gazed down at the prone, blackening

bodies, still awash with flame. One man's burning face was already blackened beyond recognition. His lips peeled back with the heat and his eyes sunk in. Mina was momentarily reminded of the Hawaiian *imu* fire pits used for barbecuing whole roast pigs underground, and one particular summer where the pig had been left unattended for too long. The occupants of the shelters were similarly being reduced to charred flesh and bone, as if incinerated on a pyre.

Amidst the blowing red-hot embers, Mina turned to the fisherman, shouting over the wind. She tried to quell the grim sense of fatalism welling inside her. In this situation, she would defer to his experience. "Where to now?" she asked loudly.

He put a hand to his hood against a gust of superheated wind, hollering over the bedlam of surrounding turmoil.

"The bridge! Safest place from the flames! That's where I used to go!"

The two of them took off at a brisk run downtown.

Running through the market, Mina yelled over the clamor of screaming voices and crackle of flames. She flinched at the sound of nearby shattering glass coming from a nearby two-story building, its windows blowing out from overheated air within.

The neighborhood air warden, attired in his scorched khaki uniform, waved the fleeing crowds through the grounds in exigent gestures, channeling them towards relative safety.

Nearby, the loudspeakers hooked up to the radio droned on, making pre-recorded pronouncements to the city's refugees.

Suddenly, a live radio announcement interrupted the feed, crackling to life. "Incoming wave! All residents please be advised..."

The announcer's last words drowned out with the droning of aircraft engines from the skies above.

Scowling, Mina gritted her teeth, her face lit by the

orange glow of nearby fires. This would make life even more difficult. With broad hand gestures, several police officers ushered them through the alley, funneling refugees through the residential area. There was a fire break dug near one of the houses, but despite it, fires spread due to the heavy winds hurtling burning debris.[73] The debris started new fires which spread through the largely wooden metropolis at the breakneck speed of a forest fire.

Following the horde of civilians, Mina and the fisherman ran through the smoke and spark-filled residential areas of the city, civilian homes aflame nearby.

A few feet away, Mina saw firefighter crews hosing down a burning house, struggling to contain the flames.

Mina knew their efforts were in vain, considering how far the fires had already spread. Most homes in the target area were two-story wood structures floored with straw tatami mats. In a fire test conducted by the U.S. military, a typical Japanese home burned to the ground in a mere twelve minutes. Trying to douse the flames now would be futile.

Some of the firemen hand-pumped jets of water at the fires. Some tossed wet mats and sand onto the licking flames. Useless.

Outside one of the houses, a man hopped into the water barrel[74] that stood outside the house, soaking himself and then setting off down the street. Mina grasped the lip of the barrel, about to do the same but then –

There was an incoming whistling sound.

---

[73] According to interviews from the B-29 bomber crews, from their cockpit windows they could see pieces of houses, windows and doors, floating in the air outside the plane. The debris was carried by updrafts up to elevations of eight thousand feet.

[74] Such water barrels stood in front of each house.

25 INCOMING

Mina yelled out a warning. "*Kuru zo!*" Incoming.

Scrambling, Mina, the fisherman, and the handful of civilians they were with dashed through the drifting cinders to the end of the road. Behind them, there was the crash of breaking wooden boards and ceiling tiles as a flower-burst of fire streamers fell directly atop a house.

The roof collapsed with the force of the bomb impact. The earth trembled beneath Mina's feet as the wooden panels of the house rattled.

In moments the flimsy house of wood and paper was ablaze, ignited like a paper lantern during a festival gone wrong.

Hurrying onward, they reached a crowd of refugees that had gathered at the end of the street for some reason. Mina stood on tiptoe, craning her head over people's shoulders, searching for the holdup.

Holy Hannah. Up ahead was a wall of flame blocking the street, extending from one side of the road to the other.

A team of firefighters with hoses tried to douse the flames, but all they could do was prevent it from spreading further. It was not a promising sight. Oftentimes, the hoses wouldn't work at all. In the rare instances where they did, water was in short supply and the pressure was low in most of the city's mains.

Suddenly, there was a gust of wind coupled with a shower of sparks and glowing cinders.

The fisherman's hood went up in a blaze of smoke. The flames spread to his shoulders even as he frantically struggled to smother them. Alarmed, Mina desperately tried to pat out the flames with her hands.

Flailing, the fisherman dropped to the ground and rolled back and forth, trying to smother the fire spreading to his back and legs[75] -

A sudden torrent of water jetted out and doused the flames. Mina looked up.

A nearby fireman held the end of his hose onto the fisherman, the nozzle dripping water.

Mina raised a hand in acknowledged gratitude. She proffered a hand to the fisherman to help him to his feet. He answered her unspoken question before she could say it. "I'm fine. Just a little singed."

Nearby, the fireman turned on his hose, drenching Mina and the fisherman as well as the people around them. Mina turned around in the cooling spray, making sure her entire body was saturated. Now soaking wet, droplets of water dripped from her navy-blue skirt onto the steaming earth at her feet.

Done soaking the crowd, the fireman urgently waved them through the wall of flame. "Go, go!"

A family of five ran ahead. Mina put a soaked handkerchief to her nose and mouth and clasped hands with the fisherman.

Holding hands, sopping wet, the two of them ran in side-by-side into the blaze, leaping through the wall of flame. She momentarily felt the heat on her skirt and clothes, the cool

---

[75] This was a common occurrence during the Great Tokyo Air Raid. However, it was often the clothing on the ankles that caught fire first then spread to the rest of the body.

dampness replaced by instant warmth. But there was no searing heat, thankfully. They landed on the other side, alive and relatively well. Mina gestured thrice. Move move move.

Huddled together, the pair dashed down the street of burning houses, the sweltering air filled with blowing sparks. Within minutes the water from the fireman's hose had already evaporated, leaving Mina's sailor uniform dry. To make matters worse, the smoke grew so thick she could barely see five feet in front of her. She raised an arm to her face, squinting through. Progress slowed to a trudge. The heat intensified even more, almost unbearable on any exposed skin. Not a good sign.

Up ahead, through the dense smoke and searing heat, Mina saw a father and child collapse forward, wheezing, gasping for air. Mina's doe eyes squinted as she peered through the smoky haze. A few yards ahead there were prone, crumpled forms of other people, asphyxiated by the hot air and smoke.

Heads hunched down, Mina and the fisherman pressed on through the corpses laying about. She blinked rapidly, eyes stinging from the acrid smoke.

A spark-filled gust of wind swept over them, unbelievably hot. But this wind, created by the firestorm, would not extinguish any flames. It would cause the opposite.

Squinting through the blistering heat, Mina saw a handful of hooded people struggle onward, probably a family. Suddenly, their clothes started to smoke and steam, plumes of gray rising from their shoulders and back.

Wide-eyed realization crossed Mina's face. She recognized the signs and threw an arm up over her face. "No, no! It's too hot! They're gonna-"

Mina was interrupted as the people ahead of them burst into flames where they stood. Screaming as they suddenly ignited into human torches, they crumpled to the ground. One man struggled forth on his hands-and-knees for a few feet, then faltered, collapsed, still burning.[76]

---

[76] Incidents of spontaneous human combustion (or rather, their

Mina gestured frantically for them to go down a side path. "Other way, other way!"

Arms over their faces, the two scrambled back down through a side alley.

Piles of refuse littered the streets, forming walls of burning junk that blocked their way; fallen telegraph poles and overhead trolley wires that were ubiquitous in Tokyo fell in tangles across roads. There were burning, overturned automobiles. Nearby flames consumed a derailed trolley car.

"Back, back!" Mina urged.

Then, above them, blazing rubble collapsed as the nearby building caved in, closing off the route they came.

Biting her lip, Mina looked every which way in the encroaching inferno. In every direction, they were surrounded by flame.

"There's no way out!" she yelled.

---

clothing) due to the proximity of the heat were eyewitnessed during the Great Tokyo Air Raid. In addition to jellied gasoline, the bomblets that were dropped contained magnesium, which can burn as high as 5610 degrees Fahrenheit. The additional pyrodynamics of the firestorm only made matters more severe.

26 TRAPPED

Feeling the dual-burning sensation in her chest, she put the back of her hand to her mouth in a coughing fit. The heat was searing her lungs and the smoke around them was getting thicker and denser. Already anxious, she started to feel panic rise within her throat. She looked around for some kind of exit.

There. The alleyway. Mina saw a smaller pile of junk where the debris wasn't piled as high, clearable by two people. A way through.

She pointed. "There! Over by the trolley! We can clear that!"

Mina grabbed a car fender off the ground next to the burning trolley. Using the fender, she pried aside a fallen telegraph pole laying atop the junk pile. The fisherman snatched up a scorched plank of wood and started on a mound of concrete rubble. Together, the two of them levered debris out the alleyway with their makeshift crowbars.

Sweat beading her brow, Mina glanced behind them. The fire was spreading, just a few yards away now. "Hurry, the fire is getting closer!"

Spurred on, Mina and the fisherman redoubled their efforts. With a grunt, Mina shoved aside the remnants of a smoldering, wooden cabinet.

Suddenly, from the other side of the debris pile, they heard a man yell out. "Over here! Over here!"

Instantly on alert, the fisherman's hand whipped to his rear waistband, ready to draw.

Mina peered at the debris pile. Through a tiny gap in the junk, she saw the bobbing edge of what looked like a police officer's cap, not military headgear. Police, she mouthed to the fisherman.

He nodded warily and in one fluid motion, the fisherman pressed his back against the corner, pistol held down with both hands, ready to whip around and shoot.

There was no telling if the people on the other side were there to capture her or just aiding civilians. She took a deep breath, letting out a plaintive plea. "Help! We're over here!"

She immediately ducked behind the other corner and braced herself, expecting gunfire.

She heard the voice yell in response and a clatter of shifting debris.

"Hang in there! We're coming!"

Okay. They were probably trying to help. Hopefully. Mina made a hand signal to the fisherman. Stay there. He nodded cautiously.

Mina continued prying away debris with the car fender.

Sure enough, a moment later as the debris cleared, she saw two Japanese police officers in olive green uniforms emerge atop the shrinking debris pile. Braving the flames, their attire was scorched and soot-smeared. They had handkerchiefs wrapped about their lower faces like bandits from a Western, as smoke protection.

One police officer reached out, grabbing Mina's hand and pulling her over the smoking pile of now-navigable debris. Mina yelled out to the fisherman. "Uncle! This way!"

If she they had been in trouble, Mina's innocuous prearranged phrase was to be "It's ok, they're alright" and the fisherman would have opened fire on them. With the all-clear given, the fisherman emerged from his hiding spot, pistol tucked out of sight. He stepped onto the debris pile and the second police officer lent him a helping hand, pulling him over.

The first police officer urged them on. "Hurry! Get to the Azumabashi Bridge!"

"There is a path where the fire has already burned out," the second officer added. "Go!" He pointed down the blackened alleyway where earlier fires had carved safe passage.

She gave them a wave of acknowledged thanks. Mina and the fisherman rushed down the alley, burning buildings visible in the skyline ahead of them.

Sprinting, panting breathlessly, Mina and the fisherman approached the last burning city block. Almost there. Just a little bit more until they got to the Azumabashi Bridge overlooking the Sumida river. As they got closer, she heard a mass hubbub of anxious voices.

The two of them rounded the corner -

And Mina stared out at the parks and gardens lining their side of the riverbank. A teeming throng of literally thousands jammed the grassy areas like human ants, desperate to find a refuge against the inferno that had become the city.

Another teeming mass of people already struggled to stay within the boundaries of the bridge and away from approaching flames. Mina and the fisherman ran to the edge of the bridge, at the edge of the mob. The fires had already spread and the air was suffocating from the searing flames, smoke, and heavy odor of perspiring bodies.

Then, several dozen people from the gardens outside the bridge rushed to join them, trapping Mina in the middle. The fires were getting too close, and they had retreated to the bridge for sanctuary. Soon, Mina found herself lost in the pressing throng of humanity.

Pushed and jostled about, she could feel the vise of people compressing her chest, making it difficult to breathe amidst the crushing mass of bodies. She craned her head in every direction. She had lost sight of the fisherman and had no idea where he was. Squirming, she tried to edge and shimmy sideways, but even her petite form couldn't squeeze through.

The oppressive throng of humanity seethed and shifted about her like a thing alive with a mob mentality of desperate survival.

People forced to the edge of the bridge started jumping into the river, desperately trying to escape the flames. Some people were pushed over, sometimes intentionally.

Suddenly, she heard a gravelly voice call out over the din of clamoring voices.

"Mina! Mina! Over here!"

She looked at the direction of the hollering. The fisherman sat over the edge of the railing, ready to jump. "Into the water!" he called out. "It's safer!"

Mina watched as the fisherman clasped his hands and dove in an arc, aiming for a spot devoid of bobbling people.

He splashed underwater for a moment, then surfaced, hood sopping wet. He wiped his face off with both hands and looked upwards to her, beckoning urgently.

Feeling a quiver of trepidation, she took a deep breath, gained a few feet of clearance and ran -

She skidded to a stop at the edge of the bridge. Grasping a nearby handrail, she leaned out, looking out over the water.

Down below, people splashed. They churned the area around them into a froth, bobbing up and down and treading water. A clamor rose from people who had already jumped down or were unwillingly pushed.

A few yards away beneath the railings, a twisted steel girder formed a metal outcropping. Someone had either tried to wrench out a makeshift ledge for safety, or repair work had been done. A man in coveralls sat on the ledge, looking down, surveying the scene.

She looked downriver. At the shallower ends, people stood, half sunken into mud.

Down the way, the crowd let out a roar of horror as a

crushing mass of bodies forced a line of dozens over the railing. Some fell into the water, others clung to railings in last-ditch efforts. The man in coveralls on the outcropping was knocked over the side by a falling person and both splashed into the water below.

Down the way, out of Mina's reach, Mina saw that one of the people clinging to the railing was a doe-eyed teenage girl about her age, dressed in a sailor schoolgirl uniform not unlike her own. Scrabbling, face contorted with effort, the girl strained to maintain her grip on the bottom railing, legs flailing.

Their eyes met.

In that instant, there was a mass outcry as the flailing girl's hands slipped. She let out a bloodcurdling scream, limbs pinwheeling as she plummeted down -

- her acceleration was momentarily interrupted as her head gored upon the steel outcropping. There was a harrowing wet *thunk* as jagged steel tore off a third of her skull and she tumbled end-over-end before plunging into the water below. Her limp body surfaced, bobbing up and down like a ragdoll's, a spreading pool of vermillion visible on the shimmering firelit water.

Swallowing hard, Mina grimaced. She'd rather take her chances with the mob up here. She clenched the handrails with both hands, trying to think of alternatives.

She suddenly yelped and tore her hands away from the rail. She stared down at her palms.

Puffy white blisters started to form. She looked at the railing she had been holding. It started to glow white-hot.

She looked around. The steel girders and spans of the bridge's framework all about them started to glow white-hot from encroaching flames. The surrounding fires were that intense.[77]

Clusters of people who had fallen over the side still clung desperately to the bridge's railings. Steam rose from their

---

[77] Eyewitness survivor accounts and newspapers reported that the bridge truly was white-hot.

hands as flesh sizzled, their faces a mask of anguish. Their limits surpassed, they finally let go, falling into the water. The current carried them downstream.

The fires surrounding the bridge grew ever closer. As more people witnessed the sight of glowing-white girders around them, panic spread like the wildfires downtown. More and more waves of people pressed onto the narrow stretches of the bridge, pushing the people at the edges irresistibly toward the brink.

Prodded on by the heat, suddenly a whole wall of screaming humanity at the fringes toppled and plunged down, down, down, splashing into the depths below, some never surfacing.[78]

In the waters below, the fisherman's voice filled with urgency as he beckoned to Mina. "Mina! Damn you, jump!"

Up on the bridge, there was a roaring whoosh and unbeknownst to Mina, flickering orange light lit up the back of her hood. She whirled around -

And Mina's doe eyes went even larger as she saw a massive wall of fire race down the street to the bridge, consuming screaming civilians in its path and engulfing its surroundings in flame.

"Hurry!" the fisherman screamed, frantic.

Taking a deep breath, even as frantic civilians around her leapt into the water, she pinched her nose and closed her legs tightly in the prescribed way of diving. She clenched the muscles of her anus shut to prevent internal tearing by the incoming rush of water.

Ramrod straight, she stepped off the railing, plummeting as flames overtook where she had been a split-second earlier.

There was a momentary sense of weightlessness just before she plunged into the water and she sank down, its liquid heaviness enveloping her. It was uncomfortably hot, almost

---

[78] Thousands of drowned bodies were later recovered from the Sumida estuary.

scalding.[79]

Beneath the surface, holding her breath, Mina looked up. By the peach-hued light of the fires, she could see silhouettes of the flailing throng bobbing-up-and-down on the rippling surface.

Sweeping aside the water with both hands like a frog, she swam upwards.

She drew in a deep gasp as her head broke the surface, her shoulder-length raven hair dripping about her.

The fisherman paddled over to her and held her close, like the protective uncle he was supposed to be. Her sopping wet bangs nearly hung over her eyes, giving her a rather timid appearance. Her voice quavered despite the heat.

"I hate the water."

"It's okay, it's okay. We're safe," he said reassuringly. Mina leaned against his chest, taking solace in the steady beating of his heart and the strong firmness of his arms.

Lost in the throng of civilians treading water, the two of them stayed huddled together. With the skyline of buildings around the bridge aflame, the procession of planes overhead continued their razing of the city throughout the night.

---

[79] Mina, the fisherman, and the civilians in the water with them are relatively lucky. According to newspaper accounts of the incident, some parts of the river were so hot the people there were simply boiled alive.

27 GINGKO

For Rain, it had been a sleepless night. The carpet-bombing procession of death had lasted until dawn. The bombing kept the denizens of the city on the run with its raid-by-raid unrolling over the metropolis. The air raid sirens hadn't sounded the all clear until around 5 AM. Now in the untouched half of the city, the city's denizens went to work. For the less fortunate half, their part of the city continued to burn for twelve hours more.[80]

Bleary-eyed, his army uniform torn and smudged with ash, Rain rode a Zebra bicycle through the streets of downtown Tokyo. He surveyed the scene which he knew of, quite simply, as home.

Everywhere, the burned-out hulks of buildings stood, if they hadn't been outright burned to the ground. Occasionally

---

[80] The night air raid of Operation Meetinghouse was of the most devastating air raids in history. It was conducted by no less than 300 B-29 bombers, which dropped over 2,000 tons of fire bombs onto downtown Tokyo. By dawn, more than 100,000 people were dead, a million were homeless, and 40 square kilometers of Tokyo were burned to the ground.

he saw a firefighting crew trying to snuff out fires, but the damage had already been done. Lying on the rubble-strewn streets were incinerated victims. Sprawled figures of ash were fixed in their death throes. Gnarled fingers grasped thin air, reaching for the sky.

Respectful, he weaved his bicycle's tires through the charred corpses strewn about the street. The absolute worst part for him was when the number of corpses grew too dense for him to navigate through. He got off his bike and walked it through the bodies, trying not to step on any of them.

There was a light wind blowing. Grimly, he noticed some of the bodies reduced to ashes simply scattered like sand to the wind. Drawn off by the breeze, little remained save vaguely human-shaped lumps on the pavement.[81]

Walking the bike along, Rain turned the corner, attempting to go down a side street in an accustomed shortcut.

He stopped in his tracks when he saw the passage blocked by an entire crowd of incinerated bodies. Like twisted mannequins of ash, the bodies were piled as if they had tried to crawl over each other to get out.

Grimacing, he turned the other way and headed down the street.

Quietly solemn, reaching the other road, he rode the bicycle down the street and passed Sensohji Temple Hospital[82].

---

[81] Survivors described the morning's aftermath as being gruesome because of these scattering-ash-bodies situations and the like. Ironically, more people were killed in the Great Tokyo Air Raid of March 9-10 than in the atomic bombings of Hiroshima and Nagasaki five months later. If it weren't for the astounding level of destruction from the atomic bombs, and the fact that those few bombs constituted the final chapter of the war, this Tokyo firebombing would probably be one of the better-known actions of the Second World War.

[82] Approximately 2,000 burn victims were received at this particular hospital for care.

Packed shoulder-to shoulder, victims waited outside the overflowing facility, lying on sheets, attended to by friends and family. Even with his hardened constitution, Rain could only bear to look at them for so long. He saw numerous people with burned clothes melted into their skin and bandaged arms extended like mannequins.

Biting his lip, he got rode on, continuing into a residential area. Constructed out of wood, the houses had burned to the ground, leaving nothing but rubble, ash and bits of foundation.

Suddenly, there was the massive boom of a reverberating explosion and the earth trembled beneath his feet, rattling the nearby houses that still stood.

Rain whirled around, hand on his holstered pistol. His soldier's mind raced. A new attack, a new attack. Adrenaline surged through him.

No wait, it wasn't. One of the nearby firefighters apologized. "Very sorry," he called out. "One of the Americans' time-delay bombs from last night."

Rain relaxed slightly as he saw smoke rising from a nearby rooftop. It was just a delayed fuse bomb that had landed among the incendiaries. They were designed to cause shock and confusion even days after the initial bombing.

Adrenaline still surging through him, Rain wilted. Nodding somberly, he continued his way on the bicycle.

Passing the Azumabashi Bridge, he saw numerous wrecked bicycle trailers. Overturned hand-drawn carts spilled out household belongings. Cooking pots and pans littered the Azumabashi Bridge. People had carried their valuables out with them, or had tried to. Charred corpses lay stacked like cordwood, piled atop each other. It was a sobering sight.

He rode onwards. The Matsuya Department Store was still on fire. Firefighters attempted to hose the blaze down, as flames billowed from cracked and broken windows. The scene wasn't all that different on Nakamise Shopping Street. The air was still uncomfortably hot from the smoldering fire, with glowing embers drifting through the air. He turned back.

He went near the park, where the encroaching fires had incinerated scores of people. Trucks were gathered on the scorched earth. Soldiers irreverently tossed bodies of the dead into the back of trucks for transport to mass graves. Some of the soldiers used fire hooks. Unfortunately, some of the charcoal-like bodies came apart during the rough handling, leaving a pile of uncollected broken hands and feet on the ground.

Grimacing, Rain turned away as he saw the sight of a charbroiled infant lying on the ground, about a foot away from the incinerated mother, like statues made of ash. She lay on her belly on the ground, her arm outstretched toward her child.

Swallowing hard, his face flushed with emotion. Tears actually started to stream down his cheeks as Rain rode onwards on his bicycle. He rounded the corner -

- and his face fell. He scrambled off the bicycle, letting it topple over. He sprinted down the street, leaving the overturned bicycle's wheels spinning in his wake.

The atomic facility lay in smoking ruins before him. Soot-smeared weary soldiers and rescue workers were busy, carrying out limp victims from the wreckage. Pristine just the day before, the building that had been his charge was now a pile of rubble, its foundation laid bare. Little remained but a pile of charred bricks and crumbled ash, still so warm the air above it shimmered and wavered.

The sight of the building's destruction was too much. He fell to his knees and sobbed, bawling like a child.

The nearby soldiers exchanged heartbroken glances.

Rain sat on his knees in a quiet spot in the burned-out park. The hulks of charred tree trunks lay about him, twisted and blackened, leaves and most branches stripped bare. The hushed stillness felt oddly serene.

In front of him, laid out on the pure white rectangle of

silk, was his ritual *tanto* dagger, polished to a gleaming shine.

He whispered to himself solemnly. "I have failed my country and my Emperor. The safety of the facility was my responsibility. It is now but ash. My Imperial majesty, I apologize."

Quietly subdued, he unbuttoned his shirt, exposing his bare muscled chest. Stoic, he ran his left hand down his abdomen. With his other hand he picked up the *tanto* dagger, preparing to make the fatal thrust into the side of his belly and draw it left to right -

Suddenly, he heard a mature woman's voice, almost melodious. Warm and inviting, the voice had just a touch of authority as it called to him.

"*Taisa-dono*. Stop, please."

He turned to see a Japanese woman in her mid-twenties, dressed in a Shinto priestess outfit. Her clothes consisted of red *hakama* pleated pants and a pure white kimono jacket. She must have only just put it on, because the clothing was unblemished without a trace of ash, giving her the appropriate appearance of a god's herald amongst troubled villagers. She was stunningly beautiful, with unusually pale alabaster skin, long raven hair, and a regal bearing.

Gentle, she gestured, bidding him to rise. "Come with me please," she asked melodiously. "I wish to show you something."

Somewhat perturbed, Rain got to his feet and sheathed his dagger. Buttoning his shirt, he followed the mysterious woman through the burned-out park.

He saw nothing of interest except charred surroundings until she turned the corner, to a spot near the riverbank.

Ah. In front of him stood a pair of great ginkgo trees, towering above. He guessed they must have been centuries old. Despite serious burn damage, with their weathered bark blackened and branches stripped bare of leaves, the trees had mysteriously survived last night's inferno.[83]

The woman spoke. "Over a third of the city burned to the ground last night. The radio puts the death toll at 100,000.

The woman spoke to him comfortingly, pointing at the abiding specimens.

"Despite the fires of last night, these gingko trees have survived. Their leaves have burned away. Their branches are broken. Their bark is scorched.

She smiled at him. "But they still live. Their roots run deep and they are resistant to the wind, the snow, and flame.

She approached the tree and gently touched one of the newly-formed buds. Her ruby red lips creased in a grin.

"New buds bloomed just this morning. It is a miracle. She turned to him with a gentle smile. "They live. And so shall we.

Rain stared at the incredulous sight, gingerly touching the budding flower with a curled finger. He gazed upon the miracle, drawing some measure of solace from both her words and the sight. For him, the image would forever be burned into his memory as a symbol for resilience, and he made a point to remember it for the rest of his life.

The enigmatic woman continued. "In ancient times, the samurai would commit *seppuku* with their short sword or *tanto*, if they failed their master."

She stretched out her hand.

"Give me your *tanto*, for you will no longer need it."

Almost without thinking, Rain complied, handing it over slowly, eyes faintly distant. The woman took it and flung it away, sending it spinning into the river.

"Remember the proverb. 'After the rain, the ground becomes firmer.' We will survive." The proverb was *Ame futte ji katamaru*. It was a common proverb for "adversity builds character."

With that, she gave a courteous bow of her head and bid him farewell, addressing him by his rank.

---

[83] Gingko trees such as the ones mentioned here were mentioned in survivor accounts of those who were in the Great Tokyo Air Raid.

"Live well, *Taisa-dono*. If you must die, take the enemy with you."

Rain nodded in acknowledgement and bowed to her. "Thank you. What is your name, if I may ask?"

She just gave a slight shake of her head. "My name is unimportant. But if you wish to do so, you may call me Autumn."

Rain nodded in acknowledgement. "In that case, thank you Autumn. *Sayonara*." He bid her goodbye, using the long-term form. He did not expect to see her again.

The woman allowed herself a tight smile. "Not quite. Until we meet again, *Taisa-dono*. Perhaps we shall meet again in another life."

And with that, Rain departed, leaving the silhouette of the mysterious woman as she kneeled before the shadowy outlines of the trees. Her head bowed as she began to pray silently, hands clasped.

28 THE GIFT

Mina's hands presented Lockwood with the gift-wrapped box. It was a little over a foot long on all sides. She had asked the submarine captain to keep it for her until she returned.

"Happy birthday, Jim," she said sincerely.

The two of them stood inside Lockwood's cramped quarters onboard the American submarine. Following the harrowing night, the fisherman took Mina back out to sea on his fishing boat, whereupon she dove into the water to rendezvous with the sub. Fortunately, nothing occurred in regards to the shore patrol possibly noting her initial arrival. No one had come to the fisherman's hut to make inquiries.

Accepting the gift graciously, Lockwood pulled loose the pink bow ribbon and tore open the festive paper.

Inside was a white Panama hat with a black band around the brim. It was an elegant hat, made from high-quality toquilla straw. The sweatband had been replaced, and the hat had been cleaned, refurbished with care, steamed, and reshaped.

Lockwood beamed. "Ah! A Panama hat! I've always wanted one of these!"

Looking at it curiously, he held it up to the light. The hat looked brand new, save one detail.

Lockwood stuck a finger through a hole in the crown that went from one end all the way to the other.

"There's a bullet hole in this," he remarked.

"It belonged to my father. I thought you would look good in it," she said sincerely.

Lockwood donned the hat and wrapped his arms around her in a warm embrace. "Thanks, Mina-chan[84]."

They stepped apart. "C'mon, let's go," said Lockwood. "Time for shore leave."

Mina brightened. "Ice cream and mail call, here we come!"

US Pacific naval base
Two weeks later

A black-and-white photo was tossed onto the desk. Mina had taken it just before leaving Tokyo. She gathered with Lockwood and the submarine captain in the conference room, doing a post-operation assessment after data had been collected and analyzed from naval intercepts.

The photo on the desk displayed the burned-out atomic facility Mina had escaped from.

Lockwood was pleased. "The damage done was considerable. Their cyclotrons are offline. Good work."

The submarine captain chimed in. "Next month we'll send in another air raid over the other facility at Riken, just in case."[85]

Still wearing the white Panama hat, Lockwood pointed to the blueprints from the facility on the table, weighed down at opposite corners with a stapler and a Lambertsen rebreather mask. "Problem is those blueprints you brought back," he stated.

Mina perked up, pointed to the blueprints. "Ok, so

---

[84] In Japanese, the "-chan" following a name is a diminutive suffix. It denotes affection for someone the speaker finds endearing.

[85] As mentioned earlier, the Riken facility really was destroyed in a subsequent air raid in April of 1945.

their recipe is ready. But where's the filling? Do they already have the tin and crust?"

Lockwood shook his head. "Unfortunately, more than that. The pie is already baking in the oven."

At this, Mina's smile faded, replaced with concern. They were that far?

The projected slide on the wall screen clicked over to an overhead aerial map. It showed a coastal town in the south of Asia, the buildings tiny like toy models.

"Since the air raid on Tokyo you facilitated, Tojo's moved their base of operations. They've been working on a prototype at an existing facility in Konan, in occupied Korea," Lockwood commented. "The facility used to focus on uranium mining, heavy water production, and atomic research, but now assembly has been added to the mix."

He clicked the control and the slide shifted over to an impressively large facility built into a mountainside cave. Frozen on the image, workers went in and out, heavy bulldozers and other machinery labored outside the entrance. "It's a cave leading to a secret laboratory and underground bunker. Heavily guarded.[86]

Lockwood continued, voice taking on an authoritative tone. "Your objective is to infiltrate the facility, report on their progress, and sabotage their efforts any way you can."

The slide clicked again, showing an aerial view of a fenced enclosure with guard towers. "There's a Japanese P.O.W. camp nearby with American prisoners."

"Am I supposed to rescue them?" Mina asked.

"No, not part of your mission. I'm actually telling you to avoid it. The Japanese would notice if prisoners went missing. No unwanted attention."

The slide flicked over to a downtown inn. Lockwood continued. "You are to meet with the local Korean resistance

---

[86] One of the Japanese atomic bomb projects really did have a James Bond style cave facility set up in modern-day North Korea, while it was under Japanese occupation.

leader. Called 'The Barber.'"

"I'm guessing he's the one who took these photos?" Mina inquired.

"Yes, at least his resistance cell did." Lockwood stroked his beard. "The man used to be an actual barber," he remarked. "A pacifist too. Then one day, a Japanese officer raped and beat his wife to death."

Mina wrinkled her nose. Ugh.

"The Barber killed the man during a shave and a haircut," said Lockwood. He mimicked the sound and motion of a blade slashing across the neck. "Slit his throat. Nowadays he uses a straight razor while fighting. Alright. That's all."

The lights came on and Mina stood up. The sub captain left. She approached Lockwood, lowering her voice.

"I wanna go by air this time."

Lockwood disagreed. "But Konan is a coastal city. Going by sea would be best."

Mina shifted uncomfortably, trying to come up with an excuse. "I'm better with airdropping in," she said lamely.

Lockwood sighed. He jabbed a finger at her. "Fine. Suit yourself. But after this, you'd better brush up on your water skills."

"Rabbits don't do well in the water."

Lockwood looked at her pointedly, adding a remark. "Marsh rabbits are actually strong swimmers, especially when the warren is flooded."

Mina blinked. She hadn't been expecting that.

"Sink or swim, Coral Hare," he said. "*Gambatte ne*! Good luck."

Konan, occupied Korea. March 28, 1945

Cold and rugged, Konan was a rather unassuming town in the northern part of Korea. It lay on the coast off the Sea of Japan. A mountain chain rose from the coastline, bordering China to the north. Like the rest of Korea, Konan[87]

---

[87] Konan is known as modern-day Hungnam, North Korea. Like its

had been occupied by Japanese military forces for the past few decades as part of Japan's policy of territorial expansion.

One of Konan's significant attributes was power production from its two hydro-electric plants some forty miles north of the city. The plants supplied over 400,000 kilowatts per day, powering Konan, Pyongyang, Seoul, and outlying areas. Other than that, it had a significant fertilizer and chemical complex, one of the largest in the Far East, as well as a POW camp[88] holding 350 Allied prisoners captured during the fall of Singapore. The prisoners were often sentenced to hard labor, packing lime fertilizer into bags.

Tonight, there was a new addition to Konan's significance on the map.

Up in the dark skies, there was the faint silhouette of a black-painted plane, an American B-24 Liberator, flying low at only 600 feet.

The lone outline of a petite human figure detached from the plane. A jellyfish-shaped parachute billowed out in full, small against the black sky. The solitary figure attached to the harness descended in a static-line jump, gripping the lines.

Down on the ground, a Japanese soldier with binoculars pointed upwards with a shout. The crew sitting nearby stopped smoking their cigarettes and sprang into action, grabbing their rifles[89]. Since the plane was flying too low for a flak gun, one of the soldiers grabbed the light machine gun[90] off his sandbagged mount.

---

role in World War II for the Japanese, it plays a major role in North Korea's nuclear weapons programs today due to local uranium deposits.

[88] The POW camp opened on September 14, 1943 and the prisoners were released in mid-September 1945, approximately a month after Japan surrendered.

[89] Arisaka Type 99 rifles were intended to replace the older Type 38.

[90] A Type 99 light machine gun.

Gnashing his teeth in tense urgency, he aimed it up at the receding plane in his sights. Letting out a chattering hail of lead, the gun muzzle flared a star-shape in the dark.

The pitch black skies were filled with white-hot bolts of tracer fire as the plane's fuselage was peppered and pelted with bullets.

Descending in the parachute, Mina glanced up at the resounding boom as the plane burst into flame. Arcing downwards, it trailed black smoke as it streaked to its demise. She saw no parachutes.

As she sank through the air, Mina felt a sudden pang of guilt. If she hadn't requested the airdrop, those men onboard might still be alive.

She pressed on. Time to mourn later. The air cold on her cheeks, breath steaming in front of her, Mina glanced downward vertiginously past her swaying feet at the little figures on the ground. They scurried around, aiming their rifles at her. There was the tiny blink of a muzzle flash and a shot cracked past her ear. Then another and another, and the chatter of a light machine gun entered the fracas, puncturing her parachute and leaving a dozen finger-sized rips in the fabric. She gritted her teeth. Again, if she hadn't requested the airdrop, she might not be in this situation. She looked down.

She descended upon the target area, the middle of a flat grassy field. Flat ground was a relative rarity in the mostly mountainous and hilly terrain of northern Korea. The ground wasn't too far away, and she braced for impact.

Even with the parachute slowing her decent, the thirteen mile-an-hour impact still knocked the wind of her. It felt like she had been tackled by a three hundred pound linebacker. Those uninitiated in parachute jumps generally didn't know the impact was so jarring.

In the distance, she heard what sounded like the baying of a hound and vicious barking. She snapped her head in its direction. The familiar rush of adrenaline coursed through her veins.

She knew she had to hurry. She quickly cut the

parachute off with a bayonet blade[91] and stuffed the voluminous fabric into her rucksack. Due to the clandestine nature of this mission, most of her gear except for a few weapons were of Japanese manufacture. She slung the pack of gear over her shoulder, taking off at a run.

Mina sprinted towards the treeline and into the woods.

---

[91] A Japanese Type 30 bayonet.

29 RUN MINA RUN

Running full tilt through the underbrush, Mina risked a glance over her shoulder. The beams of half a dozen flashlights cut through the darkness, probing the area. The not-too-distant baying of dogs echoed through the dark woods. Damn, they were already too close.

Breathing quickening, she suppressed a grunt as her ebon jumpsuit caught on some brambles, the thorns tearing off a swatch of her sleeve.

Mina's mind realized the implications as soon as it occurred. Damn, damn. It'd be easier for the dogs to track her. No time to try and recover the torn-off swatch in the darkness. The scent would give her away anyway. Without stopping, Mina rushed onwards.

Almost dragged along by the massive German Shepherd[92], the dog's handler struggled to keep up with his

---

[92] War dogs used by the Imperial Japanese military were often German Shepherds. Some reports suggest that such dogs were imported from Germany for the war effort. The Japanese military used them in all major fields of battle including China, Burma, the Solomon Islands, Luzon, and Okinawa.

furry companion. The flashlight in his hand cast a bouncing ray of light in the dark.

The dog suddenly stopped in front of a thicket of thorny bushes, nuzzling the branches. The handler, a young sergeant, shined his flashlight on the object caught on it.

The sergeant grabbed the scrap of bloodstained cloth and held to the dog's snout.

The German Shepherd sniffed it intently a few times, catching the scent - then arced its head upwards and bayed like a hound.

It bounded off, dragging its owner along through the underbrush at a frantic pace.

Running, Mina glanced over her shoulder.

She reached into a pouch on her belt and pulled something out. It was the tear gas pen she'd been issued, named the Faultless. She hoped the model lived up to its name.

She triggered the pen's release, ejecting the capsule behind her. With a hiss, the shell released its contents into the air.

In hot pursuit, the handler slowed and almost stopped in his tracks as he ran into the cloud of irritant. Coughing incessantly, he put his arm over his mouth, tears streaming down his face. Nearby, the other sentries let out racking, pained coughs. One man bent over, clutching his stomach, heaving and vomiting onto the ground.

Still on his leash, the dog winced, putting its paw to its snout and whimpered. Eyes tearing, the dog whined petulantly and nuzzled the ground.

Its delicate olfactory passages inflamed by the tear gas, it turned in a circle several times, tilting its head curiously. Confused but not losing the trail, it found a second wind and bounded onwards, yanking its owner along.

Mina sprinted through the underbrush. Up ahead, through the tree branches, its rippling surface glinting in the moonlight, was what she sought. On the map charts she had memorized, there was a small pond, surrounded by reeds, clumps of grass and stones.

Mina skidded to a halt at the banks of the small body of water. Hesitant, she looked down with a touch of fear. She grumbled to herself. "Damnit stupid water."

Excited barking came from the treeline. Mina glanced back.

No choice. Taking a deep breath, trying not to splash too loudly, Mina slipped beneath the surface.

Submerged, all sound came through the muted filter of the water, giving it an odd hollow quality.

Through the surface of the rippling water, she saw the distorted image of the dog and its handler standing at the shore of the pond, looking around.

The dog pawed at the shore of the pond. It whined, sniffing the dirt with its snout. Mina willed it to go away. Damn mutt.

Then the ray of a flashlight beam penetrated the watery depths. The dog handler shined his electric torch.[93]

Shying away from the probing beam, Mina let herself sink lower, letting her gear weigh her down. She curled into a ball near the seaweed-like algae, letting the bright beam pass over her.

She felt her heart pound in her ears. She had only been under for less than a minute and her lungs were already beginning to ache. Her body urged her to inhale. She was a poor swimmer indeed. Mina momentarily wished she had time to cut a hollow reed from the pond's banks beforehand, use it as a snorkel. Then again, it wouldn't do much good. She had to be too close to the surface to use it, and the probing flashlight beam would find her.

Mina strained, cheeks puffing out like a chipmunk's. Her head throbbed in time with her pounding heartbeat, seemingly loud underwater. Her hands went to her mouth,

---

[93] Older term for flashlight, also commonly used in Britain and Canada.

trying to suppress the few escaping bubbles that could pop on the surface and give her away.

How ironic. She had chosen the airborne insertion option instead of being shot out of a torpedo tube so she could avoid the water. Yet here she was, underwater, struggling to hold her breath, heart thudding so frantically it seemed like it was in her throat.

Her fear only made matters worse. Every fiber of her being screamed at her to get out of there, her training doing little to suppress this particular innate fear. Kicked into high gear, her body was burning up what little precious oxygen she had even faster, and she realized it. The fear of being discovered compounded the issue. Mina tried to stay as still as possible, not moving a muscle, conserving energy.

Lungs feeling like they were on fire, she risked letting just a few tiny bubbles out to relieve the ache in her chest. She could feel her diaphragm contract and shudder, her lungs screaming for air.

It didn't help enough. Mina glanced up through the rippling water, peering at the dark shapes of men and canine beyond. It didn't seem like they were ready to leave anytime soon. Hell, they might start poking the water, shoot in, or send someone in if they grew suspicious enough.

Lungs ready to burst, Mina knew she had few options left. One, she could climb up and surrender herself. But unless she could escape later, she'd probably be tortured to death.

Or two, she could slowly let out the little remaining air in her lungs and let herself drown.

Frankly, she'd rather be tortured to death.

Inevitably, that dismal, harrowing day on the beach with her father crossed her mind. She recalled the nightmarish heaviness in her chest. Furthermore, Mina remembered all the other stories she'd heard about drowning. Your lungs would fill. You'd struggle to breathe air where there was none. Your body would spasm so violently that you would break your own spine as you involuntarily tried to breathe, drinking in gasps of nothing but choking fluid.

Then Mina dimly remembered her L-pill, the cyanide capsule embedded inside a false molar. Option three. It was supposedly quick and painless.

Then again, she had heard substantiated rumors that it was all a lie designed to placate them. Your lips would turn blue as you struggled to breathe, your diaphragm froze with the poison, and you'd foam at the mouth as you *also* struggled for air. Not much better.

Starting to feel resigned, her tongue probed the edge of the false molar. All it would take was one strong chomp and the casing would break...

Up on the banks of the pond, the canine whined and whimpered, pawing at the ground.

One of the other searchers spoke to the dog handler. "Are you sure he's in there?" asked the young corporal. He didn't know that the airdropped person was a "she."

The dog handler shook his head. "No. The tear gas threw us off."

He considered other possibilities, then shouted to the others. "Check the nearby stream! Both sides! Up and down! Hurry!"

Suddenly, Mina saw blurry motion in the water above her. Finally, the rippling dark outlines of the dog and its handler turned to leave.

Letting out a tiny stream of bubbles to relieve her aching lungs, Mina waited long after the barking receded and the voices fell out of earshot.

Cautious, Mina peeked her head out of the surface of the water and looked around. The coast was clear.

She sloshed quietly out of the water, climbing onto the banks of the pond.

Gasping for air, she flopped onto her back, haggard and tired, still shaking with adrenaline. Her hair was sopping wet about her shoulders and she was soaked to the skin. The breeze picked up and Mina immediately shivered with the damp cold, teeth starting to chatter. Alone, panting breathlessly, she stared up at the night sky, taking a moment to recuperate. She wondered for the umpteenth time over the years what it was exactly she had gotten herself into.

After evading the patrol, navigating by starlight, Mina made her way to the foot a grassy hill. There was a second airdrop with parachuted crates of supplies.

She stomped her boot down onto the entrenching tool's blade, digging a hole. She buried some of her gear, caching it for later. The crates contained a small arsenal of firearms, explosives, flight gear, and extraction equipment, and she tamped earth over the watertight pile.

Finished, she dressed in local garb only after she was done, to avoid getting dirt on her clothes. In this case, local Korean garb actually meant wearing modern 1940s western fashion. Western clothing was a common sight in Korea. The modernized version of the traditional Korean *kaeryang hanbok* dress had been falling out of fashion over the last decade. Mina chose a dark-colored western dress and headed into town on foot.

The next day, wearing the dress, Mina entered the town square. Curious, she looked out at the assembled crowd. There was a male voice from up on stage, a booming tone making an announcement in Japanese.

She looked up at the stage - and froze. Cringing, she turned her head away from the speaker.

Dressed in his Imperial Japanese Army uniform, Rain stood on stage, voice booming as he spoke to the assembled Korean locals. "There was a paradrop here last night on the outskirts of town. If anyone is found harboring or aiding the enemy, you will be shot."

She dare not let him see her, lest he recognize her. Mina bet he was damn good with remembering faces.

Careful to face away from the stage, Mina made her

way down the street. The local resistance cell supposedly had some members who worked some of the street stalls.

Walking by, Mina glanced around.

Nearby, a trio of soldiers questioned civilians. She overheard a snatch of conversation as she walked by.

"There was a paradrop in the vicinity last night. Have you seen anything?" one soldier queried a suited man.

The Korean businessman with a fedora responded politely in Japanese that no he hadn't. Having been under Japanese occupation for the last thirty-some years, a great number of Koreans had grown up speaking Japanese as well as Korean.

Up ahead was a street vendor selling *soondae* blood sausage. She glanced at his stall. One of the decorations hanging from the sign was a dried lotus flower. Mina nodded to herself. The lotus grew from muddy water and often represented the purity that could be achieved even in trying circumstances. As a combatant for the Allies, Mina found it to be an apt symbol for this cell's resistance against Japanese occupation. As far as she knew, its hidden meaning was not yet known to the Japanese.

She approached the sausage stand and spoke to the vendor casually in Korean. "One *soondae* with vegetables please."

The jowly man in the newsboy cap nodded, tending to the steaming cart. Mina posited a question. "Do you know where the fish vendor is?"

"Second stall to the left, a few buildings down," he said, pointing.

"Does he sell salmon?"

"Only on Tuesdays, when his brother is in town."

"That's too bad," she said, sounding mildly disappointed. "I don't like the brother."

Recognizing the countersign, the man nodded assent, eyes glinting.

Mina whispered to him, leaning in close. "Where's the Barber?"

He shook his head with a note of concern and replied in hushed tones. "He's been missing since last Tuesday. The *Kempeitai* probably took him."

Disconcerted, Mina made a face. This was not good. She hissed at him. "Get me what you can."

Suddenly Mina heard barking from down the street and she looked off to her side.

30 HOT ON THE TRAIL

Down the road, the massive German Shepherd sniffed the air and barked, agitatedly scampering in a circle.

Uncertain, the uniformed dog handler hunched down and scratched the dog behind its ears. "Hey, boy, what's wrong?"

Whining, the dog nuzzled its owner's leg, trying to get him to understand.

The sausage vendor noticed Mina stiffen. Urgently, he handed her the *soondae*. Wrapped in wax paper, the steaming sausage was stuffed with rice cakes and vegetables, and would have looked scrumptious if it wasn't for the sudden circumstances.

Mina paid for it and left, threading her way through the crowd down the street. She walked as quickly as she could without arousing suspicion, not looking back.

Straining on his leash, growling, the German Shepherd fairly dragged his owner through the crowd. Alarmed, people parted, making a way for the canine handler and his charge.

Running now, the handler followed the scampering hound as he rounded the corner into the alley -

The handler saw only a piece of broken-off sausage lying on the ground. The German Shepherd went over, sniffed it, then gulped it down, licking its chops. Panting with satisfaction, it looked up at its owner.

Sighing, the dog handler scratched his forehead under his khaki cap. Stupid dog.

Alone in a quiet spot in the public park, Mina sat on the bench, the remainder of the sausage in her hand.

Taking it in both hands, she broke it in half. Protruding within the steaming meat, vegetables, and rice was a roll of rice paper.

She pulled it out and unrolled it. On it was a hand-drawn but reasonably detailed floorprint of the Japanese cave facility. She grinned.

Jackpot.

Standing in her beige underwear in the dingy, austere surroundings of the Korean hotel room, Mina dressed in worn worker's coveralls with a bandanna tied about her head.

She also put on a little dosimeter badge necklace. It was basically just a paper packet of dental film attached to a lanyard. This type would be standard issue at the facility, according to intel.

Mina affixed the miniature Minox camera from her gear to the inside of her coveralls. The camera fit in the palm of her hand, and was comfortably light.

The lens was barely visible through the tiny hole in the coveralls' chest. The camera controls were attached to a cable that ran inside her sleeve and down her arm. The cable was linked to a little remote control she could surreptitiously access by clicking a little button held in her palm.

Mina pinned a cheap, tin flower brooch over the hole in the clothing, disguising the lens in the center of the flower. There. Ready.

Konan cave facility

Later, standing outside the cave entrance, Mina joined the line of similarly dressed men and woman reporting for their shift inside the cave. They were the group of specialized Japanese workers that were part of the project.

Mina recalled what she knew of the area from the report Lockwood gave her. One scientist was master director of the entire project. Six others, all eminent Japanese scientists, were in charge of six different phases of the bomb's production. Each of these six men were kept in ignorance of the work of the other five.

Intelligence gathered by the Barber's men stated that the entire atomic project was staffed by about 40,000 Japanese workers. Of these, approximately 25,000 were engineers and scientists. Although the numbers seemed significant, the project wasn't deemed a major threat until now, which is why Mina was sent to investigate.

However, those staff members were located in a plant near town. Mina wasn't interested in that. Besides, the organization of the plant was designed so workers were restricted to their areas. Furthermore, their tasks weren't that vital, at least according to Allied intelligence.

What Mina really needed was access to the inner sanctum of the project, hidden deep in the cave in front of her. Here only 400 specialists worked, and she needed to masquerade as one of them.[94]

Standing on tiptoe, Mina craned her head over the shoulders of the workers ahead. One by one the uniformed guards at the fence checked their papers.

It was Mina's turn. She approached the guard and handed her forged papers to him. He glanced at them, then looked into her face curiously. Mina gave him a polite smile.

He handed her papers back to her and waved her though.

Walking among the group of workers, Mina glanced up as she approached the cave entrance looming before her. The hand-drawn map of the facility Mina committed to

[94] The distribution of labor described here were the real labor figures of Japan's atomic bomb project at the Korean facility.

memory didn't do the thing justice. The entrance to the cave was daunting, a gaping maw carved out of the side of the mountain. It had once been a normal cave formation, but was expanded and bored into by mechanical means. Armed guards stood nearby. Mina saw work crews move equipment in and out on mining carts.

She walked with the procession of workers into the cave facility. The sunlight faded as she walked in deeper. There was a damp, earthen smell. Their surroundings were lit by humming, overhead lamps, with bare power cables running along the ceiling rocks. Not all the pipe casings had been laid yet.

The group of workers walked past a set of double blast doors. As a general rule, the doors of any kind of bunker needed to be as strong as its walls, otherwise the bunker would be useless. Mina caught a brief glimpse at the blast doors as she walked by. She guessed they were roughly two dozen tons of steel each. Holy Hannah.

Mina looked ahead. There were two entrances to the depths of the cave that she could see. Flanked by guards, up ahead was a large freight-style elevator, essentially a metal cage. Nearby was an alternative entrance, a spiral minecart ramp leading down to the cave's depths. The rail track led to the other carts she had seen outside.

Silently, the workers were ushered onto the elevator and a guard pressed the button. With a mechanical whir, the elevator cage started its descent.

Going down, light from the shaft's bulbs played across their faces, chain-link elongated shadows crossing their features. Slightly tense, Mina and the assembled workers remained silent. Her hearing went muffled and she could feel her ears pop as they descended. Mina guessed they were going ten or twelve stories underground, maybe more. The air filled with damp coldness, and her skin felt clammy.

Reaching the bottom of the shaft, the chain-link elevator door slid open. Mina and her fellow passengers disembarked. She noticed the wooden plank flooring felt hollow. She guessed there was a crawlspace beneath the floor for maintenance purposes.

Mina made a few educated guesses based on what she saw and the limited intelligence from the Barber's resistance cell. The underground complex consisted of excavated chambers and tunnels in the bedrock. It was a steel network of subterranean enclosures, essentially buildings on steel frames, mounted on springs for earthquake resistance. They were joined by flexible vestibule connections that acted as corridors.

Most of the facility had been hewn out of the bedrock by heavy machinery. The interior looked relatively new, and no internal blast doors had been installed yet that Mina could see. Good for her. It might make her life easier.

She glanced at the air vents. Hmm. All air ran on a filtration system. It was almost certainly meant to prevent gas attacks.

As Mina followed her group to their workstation, she broke off into a side corridor. Unfortunately, her intel didn't include the facility's workschedule, and she needed to look as inconspicuous as possible. Ideally, she would have had it, but there was no time to procure it. She had needed to enter the facility as soon as possible. This was risky; she knew there were assigned workstations here. Anyone outside of their assigned areas without good reason would be questioned. As was usual in such places, workers from each area were kept in the dark on each other's work.

Mina grabbed a nearby handcart of lab gear and bomb parts. She ferried it through the different rooms, trying to look busy as if she were moving equipment.

Rolling the cart along, she entered a massive assembly area the size of an aircraft hangar. Its walls were hewn out of the bedrock and the chamber was lit with a large array of overhead electrical lamps. Various support columns ran throughout the room, at equidistant spaces.

At one of the workstations was a partially assembled

bomb, its casing open. Its internal mechanisms were visible, and several tools lay haphazardly around it. Mina guessed the bomb was probably an atomic one, given its overall design.

Near it, Mina noticed a worker in a hazmat suit. He walked up to several crates. He held a boxy Geiger counter in one hand, the cord-attached wand in the other. The device emitted several fast clicking sounds.

With a similarly-suited companion nearby, the man unpacked the crate, tossing out straw stuffing.

Rolling the cart by casually, Mina surreptitiously clicked the remote in her hand, flash-freezing images of the partially assembled bomb. The negatives would be stored in the brooch-obscured camera affixed to her coveralls.

She kept on rolling the cart, taking pictures of other nearby activities as she passed. Bomb components in various state of assembly. Chalkboards with jotted notes. Maps.

Nearby, one of the bandanna-headed factory workers, a woman, looked up from her work, eyeing Mina suspiciously.

Looking worried, she rushed up to Mina, speaking in Japanese. "Hey, this is my area. What are you doing here?"

Mina lied as smoothly as she could. "Sorry, I was told you were off sick today and I took over your shift."

The female worker nodded understandingly. "Sorry, you must have misheard. Who told you I was gone?"

"Sato-san told me this morning." Mina guessed the best she could. It was a very common surname and Mina hoped one of the workers was named such.

Uh-oh. The woman suddenly narrowed her eyes. "Sato-san died in childbirth last week. Everyone here knows that."

The factory worker let out a warning shout and pointed at Mina. "Hey! She's not one of us!" she yelled.

Dismayed, everyone in the room stopped and stared at Mina.

Mina bolted.

31 RAIN

The klaxon blared and the assembly chamber suffused with intermittent, harsh scarlet light. Everyone let out murmurs of consternation, staring after the lone running figure.

In a dead run, mentally cursing, Mina raced down the hallway, shoving a junior officer carrying a tray of tea in a shattering of broken porcelain and steaming liquid, leaving the shocked man sprawled against the wall. Damn damn.

Back in the cave's assembly area, the canine handler removed the leash about the German Shepherd's neck. Baying like a hound, it scampered off, racing down the hall on all fours.

Heart pounding, Mina heard alarmed yells - and a dog's angry barking.

The German Shepherd from her airdrop encounter bounded down the corridor, growling.

Mina glanced over her shoulder as it leapt into the air, its razor-sharp teeth chomping down on her forearm in a vise-like grip.

Mina let out a yell. Grimacing against the sharp pain,

she slugged the dog in the balls. The dog let out a surprised yelp, stiffening as if from an electric shock and released her arm.

She grabbed the dog by the head and twisted, snapping its neck in a crunch of bone as it let out a surprised whimper. Hurrying on, she ran off down the hall as yelling soldiers closed in on her.

Mina ducked inside a near-empty storage room. She glanced around. Aside from openly empty crates nearby, there wasn't much else. There were splotches of sand on the gray concrete floor, fist-sized piles tracked in by workers.

She looked every which way for an exit. Window. Maintenance hatch. Air grate.

There was no way out.

She heard Rain's voice yell from down the hall. "No guns! Take her alive!"

Mina grabbed a fistful of sand from the floor. Flanking the entrance, Mina pressed her back to the wall near the door. The sound of a single pair of boots, pounding down the concrete, closed in -

It was an officer wielding a *gunto*[95] sword. The man cringed as Mina flung the sand into the man's face. She grasped the man's head, snapping his neck with a crackling pop and his sword clanged to the ground.

Meg let the still-twitching body sag to the floor, his neck twisted at an impossible angle. She reached down and grabbed his sidearm[96] from his hip holster with one hand and snatched up his sword with the other.

A multitude of pounding footsteps came down the

---

[95] A *gunto* is a military version of the Japanese katana produced for the Japanese armed forces. They were often mass-produced, although a few of them were refurbished, traditionally-made katana, crafted by swordsmiths.

[96] Imperial Japanese officers generally had Nambu pistols for sidearms.

hall. Mina backed into the corner flanking the entrance. She shifted her grip on the sword warily.

Three men rushed in simultaneously, bayonet-affixed rifles poised to strike. She shot them down, sending them sprawling, emptying the pistol and its slide locked back. More running footsteps echoed down the hall. No time to scavenge their gear.

She tossed aside the empty pistol. Taking up a two-handed stance with the *gunto* sword, she braced herself. She judged herself to be capable with the sword, although not as proficient as those who had practiced since early childhood. Still, her level of skill was more than enough for most circumstances. She hoped Rain's men followed orders about not shooting.

The footsteps were almost upon her. Mina guessed there were maybe three or four of them. There was no way she could hold out forever, she realized. She was as trapped as one of the rats in the room.

But she might as well go down fighting.

Four helmeted soldiers burst in, lunging and yelling at the top of their lungs as they charged with bayoneted rifles.

She fended them off with the *gunto*, sword against bayonets, twisting and turning, parrying each and every single thrust and jab.

Slashing out gracefully, she utilized circular motions to accelerate her slashes, leading into arcing follow-up strikes.

One man screamed as she sliced his hands off at the wrists, his rifle still clutched in severed hands on the floor. Another's man's screams cut off as the blade slashed his throat and he collapsed while gurgling, hands trying to stem the gush of blood.

Mina cleaved downward in a strike like lightning, the slash so forceful it split the third man's helmet and body down to his shoulders. Kicking his chest, she pushed him away.

The final man let out a war cry, thrusting his bayoneted-rifle like a spear. Mina narrowly side-stepped the charge, his bayonet tearing out a swatch of cloth from her side, exposing pale skin. Mina thrust her sword into his chest and withdrew it, the gore-slicked blade emitting a sucking sound as it exited. The man crumpled to the ground.

The soldier with severed hands was on his knees, bawling, bloody stumps in the air, face twisted with agony. Silent, standing at his side, Mina raised her sword overhead and brought her blade crashing down, decapitating the man with one swift stroke. The man's helmeted head rolled away, coming to a stop.

Blade still in hand, stony-faced Mina flicked her wrist in a *shiburi* cleansing move, sending the crimson droplets on the blade flying.

A tall shadow fell over the doorway.

Flanked by armed troops, Rain stood in the entrance, arms crossed over his chest. Despite her disguise, Rain recognized her immediately. He nodded somberly.

"So, so. Not just a schoolgirl," he commented grimly.

Scowling, he rolled up his sleeves. Seemingly ignoring the blade in her hand, without a word, he charged her.

Focusing on him, Mina braced herself, raising her blade for an overhead slash. She brought the blade crashing down just as he neared her -

Rain's hands clapped together in a sound like thunder. He caught the blade between the palms of his hands using a bare-handed technique known as *shinken shirahadori*. Mina gritted her teeth. She had only heard of the technique, but this was the first she had seen it in practice. The technique was ordinarily used to prevent someone from drawing a sword, not stopping a strike bare-handed. He was either supremely confident or damn good.

With an annoyed grunt, Rain twisted his arms and wrenched the sword from her grasp, sending it flying across the room in a clattering clang.

He slammed his palm into her chest in a shove that sent her reeling.

Mina backslid a few feet, kicking up a cloud of dirt as she braced her foot for traction and skidded to a halt. She took up a fighting stance.

One of the nearby men drew a bead on Mina, letting out a murmur of concern. *"Taisa-dono-"* he started, politely addressing his commander.

Rain cut off his protest. "You all. Stay out of this."

The man immediately shut up. The other men kept their rifles trained on Mina, warily watching the altercation.

Still facing Mina, Rain took up a combat stance, fists at the ready, his middle knuckles protruding from his other fingers -

Alarmed, Mina shifted her own stance, instantly on guard. Her mind raced, recalling what she knew of his formidable combat skills. His file mentioned he specialized in nerve and pressure point strikes. Supposedly, no man had ever beat him in one-on-one combat.

She mentally gauged his stance, his balance. His sense of resolute confidence was disheartening. Mina recognized his stance as *kempo* karate, a style of fighting she had only a passing familiarity with.

Not good.

Hesitant, she decided the best defense was a good offense. She rushed at him, closing the distance -

Mina let out a rapid-fire flurry of punches and kicks -

Moving deftly, smoothly, practically flowing around her, Rain let out a series of dodges, sidesteps, and evades...

And after several long seconds, Mina was unable to land a single punch. Panting, exhausted, she looked stunned.

Rain gave her a patronizing smile.

With that, he retaliated, unleashing a flurry of blows that were fast and furious, his hands and arms nearly a blur.

Cringing, Mina managed to block only a scant few of Rain's blows. She tried every technique, every down-and-dirty tactic she had picked up fighting in Asia for the last three years, all to no avail. In the midst of the fighting, her worker's bandanna torn off, leaving her raven hair flying.

She struggled. He was just too fast, most of his blows impacting -

His knuckle hit her under her armpit. She let out a gasp of pain -

His knuckle struck her temple, and she grimaced -

A knuckle struck her under the chin and she reeled backwards -

A flurry of knuckle strikes battered her. Sternum. Back of her hand. Crook of her arm. Middle of her thigh. Her calf. Between the eyes. Shoulder, just below the collarbone.

Pummeled, skidding backwards, backpedaling, in excruciating pain, her worker's outfit torn and dirty, Mina grew desperate. Every inch of her body felt as if it were on fire. The nerve strikes were designed to blast calculated spasms of overlapping and self-perpetuating pain. Completely on the defensive, she raised her arms in a flurry of blocks in a futile effort to curb the onslaught.

Rain kicked sand from the floor into her face then slammed his hands to her head in a double ear clap, leaving her ears ringing in an incessant high-pitched whine. She staggered back, disoriented -

Deaf, blinded, in absolute agony, Mina stumbled away from him, staggering to the far end of the room. The ear clap had left her without equilibrium, and she collapsed to her hands and knees, gasping for breath.

In her field of view, she blinked desperately, trying to see - and saw a hazy shadow loom over her.

Viciously grabbing her by the hair, Rain smashed a hammer fist into the back of her skull, sending her sprawling to the ground with an impact that trembled the concrete floor.

Barely conscious, bedraggled, senses dulled by pain, Mina let out a series of involuntary moans, a pathetic figure twitching on the ground.

Baleful, the nearby guards surrounded her and proceeded to beat her with rifle stocks and kicked her with their boots. She curled up into a ball, desperately trying to shield her head with her arms, unable to do anything but endure the inundation of blows.

One of the guards reared the stock of his rifle back, its

shadow looming large in her sight for the briefest instant. He slammed it into her face with the crunch of bone and everything went black.

32 DARKEST NIGHTS

In a side office within the cave facility, rough hands tore apart the Minox camera, ripping out the roll of film. One guard handed it to another, who left. The film would be taken to a lab so they could check what she had been looking for.

Naked, Mina stood cold and shivering during the strip search. The underground facility wasn't big on warmth.

Not leering, more analytical than anything else, Rain scrutinized the mass of scars on her back.

His tone was wry. "Some schoolgirl. Those textbooks fight back hard, don't they?"

The strip search uncovered one suicide pill in a false molar. The nearby medic yanked it out with a pair of pliers and Mina winced. She was fortunate; the OSS dentist had actually implanted a second, in a different tooth, that her captors had missed. As per the adage, one for them to find, one for her to keep.

Unfortunately, the strip search had discovered most of her thumbknives. On the bright side, she had one left, hidden in a false latex callous along her inner arm. So, a suicide pill and one thumbknife. She consoled herself with that fact as they took her away.

The heavy metal door swung open with a creak of unoiled steel. Struggling, Mina was manhandled into the interrogation room by two grim-faced soldiers on either side of her.

In the middle of the dingy room was a rust-spotted metal chair. A single overhead lamp hung from the ceiling. The dank room was suffused with the acrid, salty stench of urine.

Japanese language newspapers had been laid out in overlapping sheets around the chair like a mat. There were vermillion-colored spatters and splotches on the newspapers. Still wet, Mina noticed.

Walking behind her, hate simmering just under the surface, Rain spoke with contempt in his voice. "So. You were the nurse in Tokyo who marked the facility for destruction and killed three dozen of my men."

He grabbed her by the arm and threw her into the chair in the spotlight, leaving Mina panting and gasping for breath. Her head throbbed painfully in time with her racing pulse. The two soldiers shackled her wrists to the chair's armrests as Rain approached her.

Continuing his tirade in angry Japanese, he fairly spat out his next word.

"Bitch. You've set us back *months*."

With that, he gave her a vicious backhanded slap that left her reeling, ears ringing and blood trickling from the corner of her mouth. Face haggard, black hair partly hanging over her face, she stared back at him.

Rain taunted her. "If you had come in by sea, you probably would not have been detected."

An overwhelming sense of guilt washed over her as she was reminded of the plane shot down during her infiltration. She silently cursed herself. He was right. Her ineptitude with the water had already cost the lives of the Liberator's crew. Now her mission was in grave danger, not to mention her own life.

Rain peered at her curiously, scrutinizing her. "So. Who are you working for? The Americans? British? Chinese?"

Mina didn't respond. In regards to the rules of war, she could give him some basic identifying information about herself, but it didn't matter here. Spies weren't usually treated the same as soldiers.

Displeased with her silence, Rain snapped his fingers.

Two guards came in. One carried a lead pipe, the other a leather belt.

Oh hell. Mina braced herself.

They set to work on her. She let out a pained grunt as the pipe smashed down on her leg. The leather belt whipped across her face, leaving a stinging mark where the buckle pierced the skin. The lead pipe came crashing down on her thigh, and jarring shock hit her bones. Mina cringed. She didn't want to let them see her scream. Then they would have her.

The blows came, and Mina braced herself. She tried her best to think of Hawaii, the palm trees, the comic books she had read while younger. Saturday afternoon matinees.

The lead pipe across her skull brought her back to reality and her thoughts grew woozy. She let out a yelp.

Too late. Seizing the moment, the pair pummeled her. The pain grew to the point where she finally, mercifully, fell unconscious, and the world turned black.

33 K40 178 905

The harsh spotlight shone down on her head. Limp, Mina's head sagged to her chest. Her hands and feet were tied behind her back with rope.

Floating in the twilight haze between sleep and consciousness, her thoughts drifted back to Hawaii and home.

Spinning in her swivel seat playfully, she sat at the bar of the soda fountain. The fresh-faced soda jerk with the paper hat served her. He added an extra pump of cherry syrup into her Coke and winked.

Sitting in the darkened movie theater, the air was suffused with the warm smell of butter and freshly baked pretzels. She sat, almost ignoring the black-and-white moving images on the screen. She giggled as the cute boy next to her whispered sweet nothings into her ear.

Roosevelt High School. Its famous domed bell tower was built in a Spanish mission style she found quaint. The homecoming dance at the school gym. Go Rough Riders. She had worn a poodle skirt and rolled down her socks to the ankle.[97] Her mother didn't approve. Dancing in her socks to Frank Sinatra.[98] God, he was hot.

---

[97] In school dances of the 1940s, students often had to remove their shoes to avoid scratching the polished hardwood floors of the gym, and therefore dance in their bobby socks. (Hence the word "bobby soxer," a term for ardent fans of Swing music and their creators.)

Her thoughts drifted momentarily to her father.

It was her birthday, just a month before Pearl Harbor. Sitting at the dining room table with friends and family, a sliced birthday cake in front of them, she posed with her father. Her mother snapped a photo, catching Mina grinning from ear-to-ear.

Out in the interrogation room, she mumbled in English unconsciously, voice croaking in a dry whisper.

"Dad, I'm so sorry. I failed you."

A few feet away, sitting opposite her, Rain leaned forward in his seat, interest piqued. His face lit up at the phrase, recognizing the accent.

"Ahh! Yankee!" he declared.

He stood up and kicked her in the chest, sending her skidding backwards and she crashed to the floor. The back of her skull slammed against the cold concrete with a cracking sound and her vision swam. Spots of light flickered and danced in her field of vision as her head throbbed with pain.

Hands behind his back, he stared to circle her at a languid pace. He spoke in passable English. "I hate Americans. Such a vile and violent people. Fat and engorged on your own filth."

Mina winced. Fortunately the intense pain at the back of her head dulled to a throbbing ache and she could think more clearly. He continued.

"Your movies. So violent. Al Capone. Bootleggers. Chicago typewriter."

He mimed the recoil of a Tommy gun in his hands and mimicked machine gun sounds with his mouth.

Sullen, Mina didn't respond to the verbal prodding, remaining silent. She silently cursed herself for not being more conscientious of her environment. Hell, she was even conditioned to curse in Japanese instead of English, so even such inveterate behavior was consistent with her cover. Half-

---

[98] Frank Sinatra was the first singing teen idol. His popularity with American youth is comparable to the teen stars of today.

conscious, she had accidentally spoken in her native English. She had been trained to pretend to remain unconscious upon waking, garner information about her surroundings first, and if possible, ambush a nearby enemy. She wanted to kick herself.

In other circumstances, she could have blown her cover. Here, her cover was already blown so it mattered little.

Rain took a moment to sit on his haunches and looked down at her curiously, as if she were an oddity lying in the street.

"So. American," he stated. "What are you? Army Intelligence? Naval Intelligence? OSS?"

As he spoke the phrases, he scrutinized her body language and facial expressions. No substantial response during any phrase, no particular twitches, ticks, or blinks. Damn. Well-trained.

Probably very experienced as well, given the damage she had done both in Tokyo and here. He idly wondered how old she was; she seemed so young to be an operative behind enemy lines. Then again, at Bataan there were stories of a fourteen-year-old soldier fighting alongside those twice his senior.[99]

Rain snapped his fingers twice.

A Japanese nurse entered, dressed in white uniform and cap in much the same manner Mina had in Tokyo. Quietly solemn, she carried in her hands a steel tray. On it lay a little bottle of amber colored fluid. Scopolamine from their German friends, used as a truth serum. Syringes lay next to it, as well as a bottle of iodine and gauze pads.

The nurse swabbed her arm with iodine-soaked gauze, then prepped a syringe. She pulled back on the plunger, filling the syringe with amber fluid from the bottle.

She flicked the syringe and squirted it a little to get out the air bubbles, and jammed it into Mina's arm.

[99] This thought of Rain's refers to a real-life U.S Marine who was famous for his age, Joe Johnson, aptly nicknamed The Baby of Bataan.

The effects hit within seconds. Mina felt her mind cloud over. Her thoughts came swimmingly slow, as if through molasses. Mina desperately tried to think through the fog, but the drugs were making it difficult and started to sap her will.

Letting the drugs settle in, Rain asked her a question. His tone was almost gentle.

"So. Please tell me. Where are you from?"

Defiant, Mina answered through gritted teeth. "Name. Sakamoto, Mina. Rank, Captain.[100] Serial number. Kay-four-zero-one-seven-eight-niner-zero-five.[101]"

Technically, according to the instruction she had been given regarding capture, she could have told her name, rank and serial number earlier, but didn't want to give him the satisfaction. Not to mention she was trying to buy as much time as possible. It was unlikely, but perhaps the Korean resistance was trying to mount a rescue.

Doubtful. She summarily dismissed the thought. They didn't even try to rescue the Barber after he went missing. Why the hell would they help her? Besides, if she didn't report in soon, Lockwood and the submarine captain would leave her for dead.

Rain's voice took on a sympathetic tone. "Where are

[100] During World War II, generally speaking, captured American soldiers were instructed during training to give name, rank, and service number. In modern times, date of birth is also included. It's mentioned earlier that her birthdate is November 6, 1927. At this point in the story, she's seventeen years old.

[101] Mina's serial number, K40 178 905, although fictitious, has some meaning because the format generally follows World War II convention.

The "K" prefix was used by female reserve and specialist officers with service numbers 100 001 and higher. The 40 million series serial number indicated special duties. The digits after the forty represented the point of entry. In Mina's case, the "1", stood for Hawaii. Hence, Mina's serial number states that she's a woman who signed up in Hawaii and was assigned to special duties.

you from Mina? At least tell me what state you are from. That can't hurt, can it?"

It was a trick question. Besides, from her serial number they already knew she was probably from Hawaii. But if she started talking about the innocuous things, sooner or later a few important things might slip. Slippery slope.

At the edge of the light, a young officer stood with a clipboard, taking notes. Rain continued speaking. "How close are the Americans to completing the *genzai bakudan*?[102]"

Mina swallowed hard. She tried not to think of the things they were probably going to do to her very soon. She responded only with the stock response, trying not to let fear creep into her voice.

"I'm sorry sir, I can't answer that."

He responded with boisterous, almost mocking laughter. "So ridiculous. What makes you think you Americans can beat us, ehh?[103]"

Mina responded politely, but her voice was starting to slur as if she were drunk. She subconsciously took on a defeated tone. It was getting more and more difficult to resist.

"I'm sorry sir, I can't answer that."

Rain sighed. She was going to be a difficult one. Well,

---

[102] The term *genzai bakudan* was often used during the Japanese development of their own atomic weapons, loosely translated as "modern bomb." Later, after the war, the term *genshii bakudan* was often used, meaning "original child bomb", which is more accurate. The phrase "original child" is a literal term for "atomic", as in that from which all life has sprung.

[103] This was actually a common question used in interrogations in World War II. By putting the subject on the defensive and insulting their armed forces, the subject would often be goaded to retort with some affirmation of yes, they could defeat the captor's armed forces. However, in order to back up the said statement, the subject would have to offer a rational reason - possibly something of strategic or tactical value.

fine.

He went to the door and spoke quietly and indistinctly with someone in the hallway.

Mina took advantage of his distraction. Behind her back, Mina's manacled hands slid surreptitiously towards each other. Then she thought better of it. The thumbknife wasn't meant for picking locks. Chances were it wouldn't do any good here. Most likely she would be caught before she finished picking it. Besides, there were actually two locks she needed to worry about. There were the manacles themselves, and the chain binding the manacles to the chair.

Instead, she checked her molar. One tooth away from the gap of the old false molar, was another cyanide-filled tooth. An idea from her training came to her fog-addled mind.

Done speaking at the doorway, Rain left and a craggy-faced junior officer entered.

The uniformed man gave her a smarmy, lascivious grin. As the soldier approached her, she wiggled the false tooth free with her tongue and held it in her mouth.

Sitting down in the chair in front of her, grinning, the soldier ran his hands up and down her thighs, fondling her. Mina tried to remain stoic, enduring it. He leaned forward to kiss her on the mouth.

Mina let him. In a warm liplock, Mina passed the poison-filled tooth into his mouth with her tongue.

34 BITTER ALMONDS

Mina abruptly headbutted her captor in the jaw and he reeled back. There was a hiss of bubbling fluid as the cyanide released into his system.

Panicking, the man retched, trying to get the poison out. But his lips already turned blue as his chest heaved, and he took shuddering half-breaths as his respiratory system failed. The smell of bitter almonds filled the air and white froth dripped from the corner of his mouth.

Grabbing his throat, the soldier sank to his knees, taking great heaving gasps, writhing on the floor.

Alarmed shouts came from outside and two soldiers burst in.

Arms still bound to the chair, Mina bolted up and crouch-dashed at the nearest guard, bodyslamming him into the wall. The back of his skull cracked against the stone and he slumped unconscious to the floor.

The second guard ran at her. Spinning in a wild circle with the chair bound to her, Mina slammed the chair legs into the man's stomach and floored him.

She kicked her chair back and impaled the man's throat with the metal chair leg, pinning him down. His eyes bulged as he clawed at his throat and blood seeped out around the wound. His arms flailed, then faltered. Before he even stopped moving she strained downward at the twitching corpse, grabbing the keys at his belt. Frantic, she unclasped the lock tying her manacles to the metal chair, but had no time for the manacles themselves.

Nearby, the soldier Mina had knocked down came to his senses, shaking himself off. No time.

Free of the chair, Mina twisted about on the floor, sliding her looped arms under her bent-kneed legs. She swept her manacles to the front of her body just as the man charged her.

Using the metal chair as a weapon, she flung it across the room but the soldier dodged it and the chair crashed into the wall.

Piking to her feet, Mina smashed him in the face repeatedly with a double-fisted punch, the manacles adding extra heft to her blows. Loosing piledriver strikes, she drove the bones in his nose upward into his brain, killing him.

She ran towards the open door - and stopped in her tracks as three other soldiers ran in, grappling with her. Without the use of both hands, there was only so much she could do. Overpowering her through force of numbers, they shoved her to the floor.

Scowling, Rain entered and stood with his arms crossed over his chest, glaring at her.

Mina let out a yelp as one of the soldiers mounted her, straddling her hips and tearing off her coveralls. She grimaced, bracing herself. She knew what fate was going to befall her. Trying to console herself, she convinced herself this was a good thing. They would be too distracted to search her again and find the last thumbknife, at least right away. Angry, the soldier started to unbuckle his belt.

Suddenly, Rain clucked his tongue and held up a hand. Surprised, the soldier looked up to his superior.

"Hold it. I have other plans," Rain commanded in Japanese.

Approaching Mina, Rain stooped down and looked

her in the eye, speaking in English.

"I think I know why you chose the airdrop solution."

Hours later in the interrogation room, Mina sputtered and strained against her bonds as the streaming water soaked the swatch of black silk clinging to her face. She gasped for air where there was none to be had, panting. Choking, she let out a wheezing sputter as she accidentally breathed in the flow of water.

Mina was bound to an inclined wooden plank, about seven feet by four feet long, with her feet elevated in the air. She felt a pounding in her temples and a sense of vertigo as the blood rushed to her head. However, the sensation was grossly overpowered by the primal fear of drowning and the desperate sense of suffocation.[104]

Standing next to her head, Rain spoke to her. "You chose the airborne option instead of the safer water route. I *did* wonder why."

The water was poured onto the cloth from a pitcher held a foot above her covered face. The streaming water turned the saturated cloth on Mina's face into a suffocating shroud that turned her very existence into a terrifying struggle for air.

Mina struggled and flailed uselessly against her bonds. She gripped her armrests in a white-knuckle grip so tightly her fingers gauged crescent indentations in the wood.

The drowning sensation was terrifying. There was a tight fullness in her chest and the desperate need to breathe. All she could think of was the undertow near the beach that had dragged her under. Panic flooded her body. The edges of Mina's consciousness seemed to creep in about her, and she knew she was on the verge of passing out. For a moment,

---

[104] Waterboarding was a well-documented procedure used by the Japanese *Kempeitai*. One of the airmen who flew in the famed Doolittle Raid on Tokyo, Chase J. Nielsen, was subject to it following his capture.

Mina thought of Lockwood's stepfather. Here, she was inundated by a raging sea, but all she could do was endure.

After about a half minute, the cloth lifted, and Mina took in a long, ragged breath, coughing and sputtering. She drew in a few heaving breaths, tears streaming down her cheeks.

Mina slumped back against the wooden board, sobbing. The experience was far too close to her worst memories. And they had been doing it repeatedly for the last twenty minutes or so.

His face stony, Rain jabbed a baton into Mina's water-gorged, distended stomach. She vomited out a great gout of fluid. Water dripped from her nose and dribbled from her mouth as she turned her head to the side. Her chest and stomach ached and Mina could hold out no longer.

Eyes closed, Mina croaked a response.

"I'll talk."

If there had been anything of value that she had known, she would, unfortunately, have given it up. They were taught in training that regardless of any gung-ho stories they might have heard about resisting torture, it was essentially impossible to do so. Which is exactly why agents were given the bare amount of information necessary to carry out their mission. Fortunately, it was impossible to talk, because they didn't know anything to say. Most of the time, they didn't know much more than the enemy did about the mission subject.

Rain raised a bemused eyebrow. "I don't care," he responded.

He raised his hand and the soldiers placed the soaked cloth over her face. She let out a moaning wail as the water streamed out again.

Impassive, with his hands behind his back Rain stood over her, watching. After about ten seconds he raised his hand. The water stopped and the cloth was lifted.

Gasping in between life and death, Mina screamed at him in wailing protest. "I don't know anything! I'm just a field agent! They don't tell me jack shit!"

His tone was disconcertingly gentle. "I know you don't."

Mina glanced up at him. What, then?

The door swung open and an officer carrying a telegram on a slip of paper entered, handing it to Rain.

Rain scanned it then spoke to her. "During the Tokyo firebombing, there was a radio transmission to the American planes. The callsign of the agent was 'Coral Hare.'"

He shoved the paper in front of her face and her eyes flicked up-and-down as she scanned it.

"I take it that's you," he said.

He slapped her across the face and Mina winced, her cheek stinging and ear ringing.

"One third of the city destroyed," he snarled. "One hundred thousand people dead in one night. One million homeless!

He clenched a fist and socked her across the jaw. With crimson oozing from her mouth and dribbling down her chin, Mina managed a weak reply. "That wasn't all me. The planes did that. I don't know much else about it."

When he spoke to her again, he chose not to speak in English. "This isn't about information, Coral Hare. This is just revenge."[105]

Rain had told only a half-truth regarding his motivations for continuing this sort of physical questioning. There was no true need to do so in terms of intelligence. It was doubtful she had information of any real use. Like she herself said, she was just a field agent. His motivations were actually

---

[105] During the Great Tokyo Air Raid, the B-29 bombers targeted the downtown area by dropping fire bombs in a methodical manner as to encircle the war factory area within a "bomb cage" of sorts. Creeping inward from the edges, the fires would efficiently spread to engulf the contained area. However, the factories' workers were also trapped in the bombing perimeter where the fires spread. Thus, more than 100,000 people died. Depending on the point of view, they were either war effort factory workers or non-combatant civilians.

simpler, but not borne of cruelty or malice.

Rain was curious.

He was curious what kind of person she was and what made her tick. It was rare for anyone to fool him. For her to be able to do so was a rarity for him. His ego took insult to the wool being pulled over his eyes back in Tokyo. His superiors considered him to be very adept at reading people. After all, he had exposed the spy disguised as a priest in the Kanda church incident. It was part of the reason he had been assigned this post with the atomic project. In part it was because of his notable service record, and in part because of his astute powers of observation and attention to detail.

Not responding to Rain's comment about revenge, Mina kept silent. Anything she said in response would only make it worse for her.

Rain turned and made to leave. He spoke over his shoulder to the men in the room.

"Continue."

Mina let out a long shriek borne of hopelessness and despair as he departed and the soldiers resumed their work.

35 BROKEN

In between bouts of consciousness, beatings, and water torture, Mina lost track of time. It could have been days or weeks, she wasn't sure. There wasn't any way of telling in the dark, windowless room.

Her last cyanide pill gone, she was consigned to her fate. Kept under constant surveillance, she was unable to use her last thumbknife for anything useful. She didn't bother to take it out.

Hell, the close surveillance meant she couldn't even kill herself. Watching her like a hawk every moment, the sentries made sure she was unable to resort to other methods of suicide. She couldn't hang herself with strips of bedsheet or poison herself with her own feces. She couldn't even bite off her own tongue to bleed to death.

One day, head throbbing, she awoke in her chair to see Rain sitting in front of her. He spoke to her in English.

"Do you know what day it is, Mina?"

Weary, Mina shook her head. She was too exhausted to speak.

"It is the twenty-eighth day of the sixth month, of the year Showa 20," he stated, using the conventional Japanese calendar system. "You know it as June 28th, 1945."

Mina's mind reeled. She had lost an entire month? She couldn't tell if he was lying. It wasn't unlikely. Mina guessed Rain could have kept her under heavy anesthesia for a while, but she doubted it.

Then again...

Rain scrutinized her face, his eyes flicking side-to-side, seeing her moment of self-doubt. "Mina, I am sorry, but the war is over. Your people have lost. We are letting you go."

Mina let out a short barking laugh. Ha.

"Go fuck yourself," she said.

Rain's tone was gentle. "I am not joking. Our German brothers succeeded in a last ditch effort in developing their own *genzai bakudan*. They dropped it on Washington D.C. The war is over."

Groggy, disoriented, Mina wasn't sure. Her mind wasn't working properly, due to fatigue, exhaustion, and the multitude of drugs in her system.

Then she mumbled a half-hearted, defiant answer as the truth dawned on her. It took her several seconds to muster a reply.

"Bullshit. If the war had been over, you have no need for me anymore. You'd have killed me already."

"Not true. We want to know what you know. You can help us. You speak Japanese. We share the same blood of our ancestors. You will be treated well in the new order."

Mina's thoughts came to her slowly, and she struggled to manage even one simple answer. "Still bullshit. If you had won the war, you'd have captured the lead scientists. Besides, you have a bounty out on Japanese-American *nisei* like me who work with the American military. We would be treated worse than dogs."

Feeling her strength fail her, Mina slumped in her chair and passed out.

Whether the attending physician had ordered some measure of rest, or if Rain was preoccupied with other matters, Mina didn't know. She didn't see him again for an indeterminate amount of time.

The next thing Mina knew, it wasn't pain in her aching bones that woke her, nor a splash of cold water across her face - but gnawing hunger in her stomach.

She was greeted by the aroma of sizzling beef, sautéed onions and the down-to-earth aroma of homecooked French fries. For a moment, Mina thought she had been rescued and had awoken in an American military hospital because of the savory scents in her nostrils. She could feel her mouth water.

Sore from the beatings, she didn't want to move. Mina winced. One of her eyes had swollen shut and she could barely see out the other. She was absolutely famished. She could feel the gnawing ache in her stomach, and she was so hungry there was terrible weakness in her muscles. Guessing from how hungry she felt, Mina estimated it was probably several days since she had been imprisoned. Or was it? She didn't remember eating.

Laid out in front of her on the linen tablecloth, was a literal silver platter. On it was an American hamburger with lettuce, tomato, and onion. Next to it was a pile of freshly cut steaming fries. And to the side of the plate was an honest-to-god bottle of Coca-Cola, so cold it was dripping with moisture.

The heavy metal door creaked open and an uniformed officer whom she didn't recognize entered.

Mina glanced at the plate. She noticed there were no eating utensils. No surprise. Almost nothing that could obviously be squirreled away and used as a weapon. There were other options of course.

The officer spoke curtly. "In respect to your rank, I have an offer."

Stern, Mina looked at him, saying nothing.

"Become a double agent," he proposed. "Go back to Hawaii. Report in."

Sullenly quiet, after a brief moment, Mina gave a terse response. "Fine. Let's talk."

Nodding, the officer came behind her and unlocked

her wrists.

Bad move. Mina snatched the Coke bottle by the neck and smashed the end against the table in a shower of brown spray.

She jabbed the broken bottle over and over into his throat, then slashed across his carotid in a copious gush of blood. Gurgling, he clamped his hand to his throat, trying to staunch the flow.

There was the sound of a pair of running footsteps to the door. Rain looked in at the corpse slumped on the floor with scarlet staining his collar. Mina sat on her haunches next to the body, the bloody broken bottle in hand.

Rain glared at her. "Now you've done it. I'm leaving you with the Owl."

Rain walked towards the exit. Already waiting in the doorway, flanked by four guards was the Owl. He was dressed in a white lab coat and wore black round-rimmed glasses. He gave her a lascivious grin.

Mina screamed and struggled as the nearby soldiers held her down by the limbs and yanked the broken bottle away. Another soldier tore her worker's coveralls down to her ankles.

Leering at her, the Owl unbuckled his pants as he approached, climbing atop her writhing form.

Down the dim corridor outside her cell, the heavy metal door slammed shut with a note of resounding finality. Her screams echoed throughout the night.

36 RUDE AWAKENING

April 4, 1945

Darkness. There was...a sense of discorporeal weightlessness? No, not quite. There was some gravity. It felt almost as if she was adrift, but no, that wasn't quite right either.

Gradually, the disorientation started to lift. Numbly, she slowly became aware of pain throughout her body. Her ribs ached where she had been kicked. There was the unpleasant coppery taste of blood in the back of her mouth. One of her loose molars wiggled painfully as her tongue brushed by it. She could feel bruises forming all over her extremities.

There was a dull, throbbing pain in between her legs that she had experienced before and didn't care to feel again. A sense of heaviness was at her feet and a solid hardness ran along her back...she was propped upright from behind. A rough abrasive tightness encircled her wrists and ankles. Ropes, then.

She opened her eyes. Hazy, in her field of vision there was something dark looming above her. She faintly registered the sound of crickets. She was outdoors then.

Mina was tied to a wooden post, with a large, slanted

gridlike shadow across her face. Bleary-eyed, she blinked, clearing her vision. She looked up - and her eyes widened in shock.

Directly in front of her only a few yards away, impossible to miss, was a hundred foot steel-framework tower. The silhouette of its frame was outlined against the expanse of midnight blue. Dim moonlight glinted off the steel girders from the last quarter moon. She craned her head further upwards.

A trickling sense of trepidation and cold realization hit her as she saw the large, oblong metallic object sitting at the top, about ten feet long and two feet in diameter.

The daunting realization sent a chill through her spine and her heart began to pound. She let out a curse in Japanese. "*Shimatta!*" Oh no. Just wonderful.

She was strapped a few yards away from an atomic bomb.

37 DOOMED

Mina's heart pounded. Nearby, roused from a fitful sleep by her outburst, a few similarly bound prisoners stirred. They lifted their heads from their chests, looking up wearily.

She glanced around, trying to make sure no guards were watching her. She twisted her torso and head as far as the ropes around her chest allowed, trying to get a better view of her surroundings.

All around her, tied to wooden stakes at evenly spaced intervals, prisoners were set out in a particular fashion. They formed concentric circles in ever-increasing radii around the center steel tower. She idly noticed that each wooden post was painted with Japanese numbering in white over each prisoner's head, marking distance from center and location.

Amongst the prisoners at similarly distanced locations were abandoned vehicles, shacks, and furniture, to act as other damage indicators.

Just out of earshot, patrolling in and amongst the prisoners, armed Japanese soldiers walked through the circles of the condemned.

Mina peered out into the distant semi-darkness. Most of the terrain was flat as far as the eye could see. She knew it probably consisted of sand, gravel, patches of grass, and some shrubbery. Presumably, the Japanese had chosen the site for the blast test because it was flat, to better measure unimpeded effects.

Damnit. That meant even if she could break free and get away, there probably wouldn't be any hills to take cover behind for miles.

Mina squinted. Out in the distance she could see lights from the town of Konan. Going from the apparent size of the buildings, she estimated they were several miles away. She and the other prisoners were on the outskirts of town.

She looked off to either side, craning her head, looking for something, anything to help. Then she spotted it.

Jackpot.

One of the test vehicles nearby was a Type 95 Mini Truck that reminded Mina of a farmer's pickup truck, dilapidated and in poor repair. Its paint was peeling, its frame was dented and covered with rust spots, but with any luck she could make it serviceable. Hopefully the damn thing would start.

Approaching her, there was the quiet sound of a woman sobbing. Mina looked off to her right.

One of the prisoners was a pregnant woman. Her simple brown Korean peasant clothes stretched over her swollen, near-term belly.

Almost wailing, the woman sobbed as several soldiers tied her to the wooden post, binding her hands and feet.

Mina felt a rush of pity. She took a moment to look at the prisoners closest to her.

One of the prisoners was a man in a tattered U.S. Marine uniform. She guessed he was probably brought over from the Japanese POW base in Konan. Most likely an escape attempt had landed him here, and he was now awaiting execution.

Sardonic, the marine egged the sentry on in a Southern drawl that reminded Mina of Texas.

"Hey Tojo," he said to the guard. "Anyone ever tell you that you smell like week-old fish?"

Scowling at the half-understood smarmy comment, the soldier clubbed him across the jaw with the stock of his rifle. "No talking, Yankee!" the guard spat.

Glaring back defiantly, the marine spat out a tooth. Mina nicknamed him Dallas.

There were a few other prisoners. Mina haphazardly gave them labels based on whatever came to mind.

Chicago, because of the white man's accent and his baby-faced resemblance to Al Capone.

Hook. He had a prosthetic hook, not unlike a pirate's. Judging from the quality Mina guessed he couldn't afford a more mobile one. Going by his muttering, he was a bitter man. Mina wondered for a moment if his attitude was a result of their dire circumstances, his overall life, or both. She dismissed the thought and pressed on.

Scar. A Chinese-looking young man with a large, angry-looking violet scar running diagonally across his face from some years-old laceration. He wore a Chinese Nationalist uniform, complete with insignia of a twelve-pointed white sun within a blue background.

A bald man in a British uniform, whom she mentally nicknamed Chrome as in chrome-dome.

Oldtimer. A resigned-looking older Korean man with a gray beard and bushy eyebrows.

Hepburn. Because the Korean woman was beautiful.

The sobbing pregnant woman Mina mentally nicknamed "Scarlett" because her facial bone features made her think of Vivian Leigh, the actress from *Gone With the Wind.*

Mina turned her attention back to the truck. How to get to it? The last thumbknife she had saved would be useful.

One of the already awake prisoners took notice of her eying the vehicle, gauging her with a clinically practiced eye. He was tied to a post a dozen yards in front of her, within the innermost circle. He faced her almost directly.

Mina noticed him, a little off put by his scrutiny. There was a certain intelligence and defiance in his eyes the other prisoners didn't have. Even though he was tied and bound, he had a certain street-smart presence. From circumstances as well as his cheekbones, she guessed he was ethnic Korean. Was he the Barber? Was he a Japanese spy?

Alert, he scrutinized her from head-to-toe, analyzing every bit of information. Mina could imagine the gears of his mind whirring, processing the data. Her age, her clothing, her demeanor, her line of sight, her facial features, etc.

He glanced off to the side, making sure no guards were within earshot. Or was he just making a show of it?

He queried her, in perfect Japanese. No surprise considering Korea had been occupied by Japan for the last few decades. His expression was seemingly puzzled and curious.

"You. You look Japanese. Interesting. Why are you here?"

Mina glanced at him, but remained stoically silent.

She purposely didn't respond to the question, remembering her failure from earlier. She mentally weighed the risks. In this particular situation, she was probably among friendlies, being tied up and sentenced to die, but she didn't want to risk it, at least not yet.

Then again, for all she knew, the entire thing could be a ruse and he was working for the Japanese. The Japanese army had a number of conscripted Koreans working for them.

In all likelihood, the Barber was already dead, his broken-and-battered body rotting in some erstwhile shallow pit. Furthermore, there was no telling what he might have told them.

Ignoring him, Mina struggled and wriggled against her bonds, trying to loosen them. The hemp ropes were tight and bit deeply into her wrists and ankles, leaving bruised purple grooves. She strained against them, gritting her teeth against the pain.

She felt the bonds at her wrists loosen slightly, allowing her to turn the joints and wiggle her fingers more freely. Pins and needles coursed through her hands as circulation returned. Ah. Great. A small measure of relief.

Behind her back, Mina slid the edge of one chipped

fingernail along her inner arm where her last thumbknife was hidden in a false callous.

She pinched it out and started sawing away at the ropes binding her wrists, holding the blade awkwardly in her fingers.

There was a loud, industrial-sized click as floodlights came on. Harsh white light bleached the color from the prisoners' skin.

There was the approaching rumble of truck engines. A few seconds later, three Nissan 180 pickup-style trucks pulled up to the grounds. The lead truck rolled to a stop with a metallic squeak of the brakes and the other two followed suit.

Armed soldiers riding in the back dismounted, lifting off heavy furniture and a few bedraggled, bound prisoners.

Cautious, Mina continued sawing at her bonds. Almost free, just a few more cords to go. Tense, on the lookout for any guard who might be straying too close to her, Mina scanned the distance.

A few hundred yards away, looking like little toy soldiers, troops started binding the final prisoners to posts and emplacing test objects at the outer circumference of the area.

Mina glanced to the side. Her hands behind her back continued sawing at the last cord.

From behind, unbeknownst to Mina, a stern-faced Japanese soldier walked by, glancing over them with a watchful eye.

The prisoner that had spoken to Mina urgently hissed at her in Japanese. "The guard behind you is coming. Hide it."

Mina quickly slid the thumbknife in between her fingers, concealing it. She willed the guard to go away, praying that he wouldn't look too closely. Avoiding eye contact, she looked down at the ground. She tried to look sullen and resigned, which wasn't too far from the truth.

The guard glanced at her...then walked past.

A few moments after he passed, her shoulders wilted in relief.

She looked back up. The soldiers were done moving

the heavy test objects into place and were leaving, piled into the backs of their trucks. She heard shouted orders in Japanese. The truck's taillights flashed red, then receded into the darkness of the night. It wasn't a good sign if the soldiers were vacating the area.

Mina looked to the intelligent prisoner that had warned her. Well, he didn't call her out, so maybe there was some hope he was the real McCoy. Could it be...? She decided to venture a guess.

Mina forced a wistful, almost remorseful tone into her voice, like a condemned person wishing for a last meal. She spoke in Japanese; if she was wrong, maybe he'd believe she was a Japanese nurse who had gotten on the wrong side of a superior officer and was being executed. If anything, it would slow the enemy down.

"I wish I had a tin of Sakuma Drops[106]." As she spoke, behind her back she sawed away at the last bits of thread binding her wrists.

One of the other prisoners glared at her as he struggled against his bonds and scoffed. "Now? You're thinking of candy, *now*?" he said, annoyed.

But the prisoner with the intelligence in his eyes stiffened at her phrase. He looked to her with rapt attention. Ah. Good. He hadn't been expecting her to say the phrase. No tight smile of recognition here. If the Barber had talked, he probably would have leaked the challenge-response phrases to the Japanese and any imposter would be expecting it. Hopefully this guy was the real deal.

He gave her a cautious once-over and meted out a measured response. He was just as suspicious as she was.

---

[106] Sakuma Drops are a popular hard candy. Usually fruit-flavored, this particular brand has been available since 1908 and is prominently featured in the popular 1988 anime film *Grave of the Fireflies*. They are popular in Japan and other Asian countries even to the present day. Mentioning this type of candy to the prisoner is unlikely to attract attention. Good thing she didn't mention something like Mars M&Ms or Hershey bars.

"I like those too. The orange ones are the best," he said cautiously.

"But the grape ones rot your teeth," Mina answered.

"Only if you eat them with the lemon ones."

There was a brief pause. Mina and the prisoner allowed themselves tight smiles as recognition sunk in, both of their suspicions allayed. She spoke in English.

"Coral Hare," she identified herself. The Japanese already knew her code name so it didn't matter.

"The Barber," he said, confirming his identity. "Wish we met under better circumstances. How do we get outta here?" he said in passable, accented English.

Mina winced as she twisted her arms, sticking her tongue out of the corner of her mouth in a gauche expression. Behind her back, she bent her fingers awkwardly, trying to get a better angle at the ropes.

"Workin' on it," she told him.

With a final slice of her thumbknife, she cut the last few threads and the rope snapped. She bent down and sliced the bonds at her ankles.

Stretching a moment, she cringed at the soreness in her ribs. She approached the Barber and started cutting away the ropes at his wrists.

He glanced down. A trail of blood ran from between her legs and down her thigh. He gave her a concerned look.

"Are you ok?"

Mina bit her lip, her tone quietly subdued. The Owl hadn't exactly been gentle. She avoided meeting his gaze as she responded, still sawing through his bonds. "Not my first rodeo. But I hate being the bull."

He gave a sympathetic nod of comprehension. Mina figured his English was good enough to understand the reference.

Their brief discourse was interrupted by the rising wail of an air raid siren. The two exchanged looks.

One of the bound prisoners, the American with the Texas accent looked up at the steel tower before them in a panic. Lights on the ovoid shell at the top started flashing red, bathing the area in an intermittent crimson glow.

Panic rose in his voice. "Oh shit. Oh shit! They're going to test the bomb right now! Hurry!"

Mina tossed the Barber her thumbknife. He caught it mid-air and ran over to Dallas as she rushed towards the beat-up truck she saw earlier.

She glanced through the musty driver side window. The needle on the gas meter showed about a quarter tank left. Ok good.

She wrenched open the hood with both hands, giving it a cursory inspection, eyes flicking back and forth anxiously.

Ten miles away at a reinforced concrete bunker, visible through the horizontal port, the interior was a bustle of activity. Japanese soldiers and scientists made preparations, giving orders, setting up cameras, taking notes.

Scientists in white lab coats gave instructions to enlisted men who set up cameras. Other scientists with clipboards jotted down readings.

Rain stood by, a pair of binoculars hung about his neck. A subordinate with a clipboard consulted with him.

The Owl stood by, supervising, speaking into a phone in rapid-fire Japanese as another scientist did calculations with a slide rule. A third scientist stood by a chalkboard with numerous equations written on it.

By the long horizontal gun port, a soldier standing next to Rain squinted out into the distance. Sudden alarm crossed his face and he pointed outside.

"Sir! The prisoners are free!"

All conversation halted and everyone looked to him. Some of the officers went to the port, craning their heads to get a better look. Alert, Rain looked out through his binoculars.

Through the double lens view he saw Mina, standing at the open hood of an abandoned truck, desperately fiddling with something inside.

He shifted his view off to the right. The prisoner

known as the Barber freed several test subjects tied to stakes, cutting them free of their ropes with possibly a shiv or a piece of glass.

He lowered his binoculars and held up a hand, his face stern. "Don't pursue them," he ordered. "You'd be caught in the blast zone and so will they. Let them go. They're dead anyway."

Sitting in the driver's seat, with the bottom part of the dashboard torn open, Mina scrambled to hot-wire the truck. She hurriedly stripped the ends of two wires with her fingernails.

Holding a wire in each hand, she brought the ends together and they sparked.

The engine spewed out a ratcheting cough, refusing to turning over. Mina scowled. She tried again. Same deal.

Standing in front of the open hood, the Barber examined the interior. Spark plugs. Ok. Distributor cap. Ok. Air intake -

He saw what looked like a fleshy cord and something furry protruding from the valve. He shouted out.

"Got it! Jammed air intake!"

Grimacing, he dug around with his fingers...and fished out a dead rodent by the tail with a wet *thunk*.

Tense, Mina was still inside the truck. Wires in each hand, she touched them together, sparking the two ends.

The engine started ratcheting...then died.

Sweat beading for forehead, Mina scowled. "Godamnit. C'mon, c'mon!" she cursed.

She tried again. And again.

The engine spewed out another series of ratcheting coughs...and finally turned over, rumbling to life.

Mina leaned out the truck window and beckoned urgently. "Everybody onboard! Hurry!" she shouted.

The prisoners hurriedly clambered on. Scarlett the pregnant woman climbed into the passenger seat next to her as the Barber and the others got in the back.

Seeing this, the other prisoners bound to the posts nearby started to wail and clamor, begging to be cut loose.

Sticking her head out the window, Mina yelled an apology out in Korean. "Sorry you guys! There's no time and no room!"

Mina's foot floored the pedal.

The truck's tires spun, kicking up dirt and gravel momentarily, then the truck fishtailed as it sped out of the area.

They had been driving for a little over a minute. In the back of the truck, the other passengers sat, tense. Anxious faces. None of them spoke.

Mina glanced down at the dashboard's speedometer. The truck had a top speed of about 43 miles per hour. Her mind raced, doing rough calculations. Even at top speed, it would take them more than two minutes to get away to a survivable distance.

She glanced over at the Barber, who was apparently doing the same thing, counting silently on his fingers. He looked at her and shook his head, his expression somber.

One of the passengers in the back of the truck prayed silently in Korean. Amitaba. O Buddha, he mouthed fervently, eyes closed.

It was silent save the rumble of the engine and the creaking of the truck's suspension as they jostled up and down the backcountry road.

Swallowing hard, Mina squeezed down the pedal even harder, desperately willing the vehicle to go faster. Mina guessed they were roughly a mile, mile and a half away. Her grip on the wheel tightened. Not enough, not enough.

Suddenly, particles of light bounced around the cabin. Floating specks of golden light appeared in the air before her, then coalesced. Cold, hard panic rose in her throat and clenched her chest. A flood of adrenaline coursed through her veins and she gripped the steering wheel even tighter as a sense of horrified realization washed over her.

They were out of time.

38 OUT OF TIME

There was a double flash of light - first yellow, blindingly bright, then an even brighter flash tinged with blue, with the intensity of a thousand suns. The two flashes were so quick if she had blinked, it could have easily been mistaken for just one. The flashes were immediately followed by a deafening boom and Mina's ears filled with a thunderous roar.

Heat. Intense heat. Mina was suddenly acutely aware of the searing heat on the surface of her skin. It felt a million times worse than standing in front of a blast furnace. The temperature at the center of the explosion was seven thousand degrees Fahrenheit. Even a mile and a half away it was enough for their clothing to burst into flame.

The passengers in the back of the truck wailed as their hair was set afire. Dresses, shirts turned into blackening, crisping rags of orange-yellow flame, giving them the appearance of living human torches.

The back of Mina's shirt burst into flames, leaving a spreading swatch of exposed skin. She felt her back arch involuntarily in pain at the blaze and she grimaced.

Still alive, the passengers in the back of the truck screamed, clutching the sides of the truck's chassis, screaming from the inescapable heat. At their feet, the soles of their boots melted into the bed of the truck. At that moment, the Barber felt that he wanted nothing more than to be out of there, to be rid of the heat, even to die, but all he could do was scream and scream.

The skin on Mina's exposed back bubbled like water, hissing like a thing alive, forming into raised, bubbling blisters the size of golf balls as her blood flash-boiled underneath her skin.

The searing heat at her back was such that she had to struggle to maintain control of the wheel, hands and arms shaking with adrenaline. Tears welled in her eyes but were immediately flash-boiled away. Gritting her teeth, stifling sobs, pain welled up inside her until it grew too much, and it escaped her lungs in a long scream of excruciating agony as her back boiled.

In the back of the truck, aflame, blisters bubbling all over his body, one passenger fell off the truck, tumbling away in the truck's wake. The Barber saw him recede into the distance, limbs still moving.

Grimacing against the pain, Mina glanced over her shoulder behind them. For a split second she saw what seemed like a giant red sun simultaneously rising into the air and ballooning outwards behind them, expanding outward at impossible speed –

Like a radial wall of distorted air, a shock wave erupted from the center of the red fireball, overcoming them in an instant.

The truck lurched forward as the shock wave hit them, a wall of air so condensed it was tantamount to being hit by a sledgehammer. There was a thunderous roar and the sound of breaking glass as massive overpressure blew out the window behind Mina. She stifled a cry as hundreds of glass shards embedded into her blistering back, and she cringed over the wheel as the windshield exploded outwards.

The shock wave was so strong she could feel the core of her bones vibrate, her rib cage reverberate in her chest, and her teeth rattle. She could actually feel the tremors in her stomach and lungs within her chest cavity.

It had only been a few seconds since she saw the double flash until the shock wave hit.

Glancing up, she saw a terrifying sight in the askew and broken rearview mirror. She whirled around in her seat.

Directly behind them, shoved along by two hundred mile per hour blast winds, a massive wall of sand, dirt, rocks, debris, flying vehicles, and even people rushed towards them like an unstoppable tidal wave. Mina hunched over the wheel, bracing for impact. She screamed out a warning.

"Everybody hang on!"

The impact hit the truck from behind. Forces many times greater than the strongest hurricane rocked and jolted the vehicle. The momentum slammed Mina's head against the dashboard and she nearly blacked out, the world growing hazy.

The beyond-gale force winds overtook the truck. Struggling to stay conscious, blinking rapidly, all Mina could see was sand, dirt, and debris buffeting and whipping around them. Pebbles and grit pelted her from the broken side window. With a groaning of metal and the incessant squealing of tires, the truck teetered and swayed as Mina fought the wheel, desperately trying to keep the vehicle from overturning in the typhoon-force winds.

To make matters worse, the melting tires blew out, a resulting combination of the intense heat and exploding shrapnel from the blast winds. With the momentary flapping of deflated rubber, a moment later they were riding on rims. The truck's wheels sparked as if from an arc welder as they raced along the ground.

The truck winded a serpentine path through the manmade tempest, careening violently. Mina spun the wheel hand-over-hand, frantically going in the direction of the turn to avoid flipping over.

With the vehicle[107] veering side-to-side, the passengers

---

[107] In scientific tests, some modern cars with electronic ignitions or electronic fuel injection systems have experienced performance issues

in the back clung to the railings, to the chassis, to each other, desperately trying to hang on with blackened fingers, squinting through the hot grit whipping about.

One passenger fell off, then grabbed the edge of the truck. The Barber grabbed his wrist - then let out a shocked gasp as the skin sloughed off like a glove. The passenger slipped from his grasp and tumbled onto the road, disappearing into the sand-blasted winds.

Like the mother of all sandstorms, the devastating wall of gale winds and debris inundated the already battered vehicle with blasts of sand, rocks, glass, masonry, and roof tiles. The passenger next to the Barber let out a scream as a melting bottle embedded into his face. The Barber raised his arm to protect his head as blades of grass and twigs embedded into his charred forearm like darts.

Through the buffeting winds Mina saw a prisoner fly past overhead through the busted-out windshield, limbs splayed out like a ragdoll flung by some insolent child. A disembodied head, mouth agape in shock, flew past the driver side window. Next to Scarlett, a flying metal trash can sheared off the side mirror and she recoiled as it sailed past.

Racing along at top speed, the lone truck sped through the outback as the winds subsided. All around them, the area was littered with fallen trees, strewn debris, masonry, and occasional corpses from the test site.

Mina glanced out the busted driver's window. Some of the test subjects' bodies were blackened and steaming, limbs askew. They stared sightlessly upwards in a hauntingly appalled expression.

Suddenly, the winds shifted into a breeze coming towards them. Then it became a stiff wind. Mina shouted to the passengers.

"It's not over! Winds filling the vacuum coming our

---

when exposed to electromagnetic pulses (EMPs) from nuclear blasts. Mina's commandeered, 1940s non-electronic truck is safe from the effects.

way!"

As it was with most explosions, winds started to rush back in to fill the vacuum created by the initial blast. Only here it was on a much larger scale. The wind picked up gradually; light debris, leaves, grit started flying in through the broken windshield. Then pebbles, small stones, tree branches.

The approaching wind grew, becoming gale force, enough to slow the truck down. The blowing debris grew larger and heavier. Mina squinted against the wind and sand flying into her face. Then –

Mina's eyes widened in horror as an uprooted tree trunk, its branches broken, sailed directly at them.

39 ADRENALINE

"Duck!" Mina yelled.

The truck jolted backwards and shook with reverberating tremors as the tree trunk embedded itself in the seat cushion, smack dab in between Mina and Scarlett. She shot Mina an astonished look.

Momentum only momentarily interrupted, the truck started to pick up speed again, rumbling and creaking along the dirt road.

Gradually, the winds subsided. Passing through some areas, it looked like the aftermath of a tornado, everything laid to waste. Glowing, floating embers filled the darkness, like orange fireflies.

They were now out of the flat terrain of the bomb test area. Mina saw a relatively debris-free spot at the base of a hill and stopped. Despite being more than a mile out, most of the grass in the area still burned away, leaving a small clearing.

Chugging along, with the metallic rasp of rims on dirt, the battered truck slowed to a stop, brakes squeaking painfully.

The air was hazy, clouded with smoke. Floating red-hot cinders hung in the air, drifting to earth. Fires from shrubbery and trees lit up the night with a fiery orange glow.

The driver side door fell out onto the ground with a dull metallic clang when Mina reached for it. Exhausted, drained, Mina stumbled out, steam and smoke still rising off her back, her hair singed.

Surprisingly, the front of her body was largely unscathed, having been shielded from the worst of the blast by the truck's carriage and the passengers.

She turned around. In stark contrast, a sheet of whitish, golf-ball blisters covered her exposed back, surrounded by a crust of browned and blackened skin. Her worker's coveralls hung off of her, reduced to charred rags.

Those in the back of the truck, caught in the open, had taken the brunt of the heat flash and blast winds. Tired and bedraggled, they were seriously burned and wounded. Most of them wearily climbed off the back. Some of their shoes were stuck to the metal surface, leaving behind melted bootprints.

Shaking with adrenaline from their harrowing escape, Scarlett the pregnant women gingerly stepped out of the truck. Sobbing, she got down to her hands and knees and kissed the ground.

The Barber was still on the back of the truck. He tried to leave - only to find his hand stuck to the siding.

Grimacing, he grasped his left wrist with his free hand, pulling it free from the steaming surface where his skin had melted into the metal. He left behind a hand-shaped patch of charcoal-and-crimson skin.

Still in shock from their brush with death, the Oldtimer gingerly stepped off the back of the truck, helped by the Barber. The intensity of the fire had burned off his hair, beard, even his eyebrows, giving him a rather odd appearance.

The British man with the shaved head sat on the ground, curled up in a ball, rocking himself back and forth. The overpressure ruptured his eardrums leaving him with a ringing in his ears. He mumbled to himself.

"I can't hear. I can't hear. It's just the bloody ringing," he said in English-accented rambling.

Lungs hemorrhaging from the shock wave, Dallas the American had a coughing fit. Doubling over, he held a hand to his chest to suppress the ache and spat out a mouthful of blood onto the smoking ground.

A bedraggled and disheveled Mina glanced up at the top of the hill. There was a warm orange glow cresting the summit, coming from off in the distance.

Still winding down from the adrenaline, Mina's scrabbled upwards on her hands and knees, sending gravel and small rocks rolling down the hillside. She had to see for herself. She just had to. Fiery embers rose and drifted around her. The tang of ionized air filled her nostrils. Through the oven-like heat, the soot, the smoke, she climbed higher and higher, until she finally reached the summit.

The roiling mushroom cloud loomed over the horizon, reaching up to the heavens. In updrafts created by the blast, the after-winds sucked smoke, dirt, and debris high up into the sky with it. Mina could see dark spots of debris swirling about within the cloud. Like the throne of an angry god, the mushroom cloud dominated the skies, rising over twenty-thousand feet into the air. Burgundy-hued, the roiling cloud slowly turned white as water vapor condensed.

All of a sudden she felt tiny and insignificant, in awe of the devastation power of this monstrosity. Her face trembled with wide-eyed astonishment and fear.

Breathing quickening, she put her hand to her brow, visoring with her hand. She peered out into the distance in a mix of disbelief and shock.

Down on the plains below, the atomic blast had carved a swath of destruction a mile wide. Massive trees centuries old were laid low and aflame, torn from their roots by tremendous forces then propelled hundreds of yards, all branches stripped off. Fields of grass lay in glowing red embers, fiery patches against charcoaled earth.

She recognized some of the debris scattered about from the site. A washing machine lay on its side, half-melted into slag, its surface scorched brown from the intense heat.

There was a rustle of parched grass as the other survivors except the Barber approached her from behind. They stood by her, gaping at the destruction and murmuring in dismay as they crested the hill. She didn't bother to look at them, because she herself was still transfixed by the spectacle.

Solemnly quiet, the Barber quietly approached her right hand side. He proffered something in his hand, a dented pair of binoculars.

"Coral. I found these in the glove compartment," he said, addressing her by her code name.

Still stunned silent, Mina took them in a daze, barely registering his words. She brought the binoculars to her eyes.

Down below, faint movement caught Mina's eye. Through the smoke and floating embers, she saw odd lumps, vaguely bathed in an orange glow from nearby fires. Not prisoners; they were too misshapen. She should have been able to discern the bipedal nature of their movements, were they upright. Molten debris warping in the wind, she surmised.

No. The lumps actually *were* human, so disfigured at first Mina didn't recognize them as such. She thought they mustn't have been, or maybe part of her desperately wished they weren't. The ropes that bound them had burned away in the fires, and they now tottered about in a daze.

Mina drew in a sharp breath and felt a jolt run through her like an electric shock. She stiffened.

In the smoldering plains below, some prisoners who had survived the blast were covered from head-to-toe with massive white blisters formed by the flash heat, some as large as golf balls and melons.

Other prisoners stumbled about, skin blackened, arms held out, ghostlike. Their movements were stilted, reminding Mina of the zombie from the Bela Lugosi movie. Their flash-burned clothes hung off of them, reduced to burned rags, blackened and scorched.

Then, with a sickening realization in the pit of her stomach, Mina realized they weren't rags.

It was human skin.

The flash of intense heat had caused large areas of skin to be covered by blisters. The blisters would burst, causing the skin to hang. The black "rags" were burned, sloughed off human skin, wrinkled like the surface of a boiled tomato.

One particular prisoner was a man covered with fist-sized blisters that seemingly pulsated and stretched with his shuffling steps. The blisters burst like a water balloon with a single strained movement, and fluid ran down his body. Arching his back in pain, flinging his arms out, his face contorted in wide-eyed agony. He let out such a long scream of anguish that Mina and the others could hear him even at this distance. Sobbing, he collapsed onto his back, the deflated blisters collapsing into raglike sloughs of skin.

Even standing a few feet away, some of the survivors were so terribly burnt not even they themselves could distinguish if those among them were male or female. They couldn't tell if the person near them was facing front or back except when their arms moved - if they even still had arms.

There was one man stumbling about, so charred he seemed like an obsidian mannequin. His white eyeballs dangled from their sockets down to his mouth by their optic nerves, like white marbles strung against a blackboard.

One man clutched his stomach with both hands, his coiled intestines visibly bursting out from his body cavity.

A nearby woman held a hand to her hip. Her blouse had burned away completely, revealing her burned naked torso. On her right side, her bare breast swayed with her teetering movements, reddened by rays from the miniature sun. On her entire left side, white bones of her rib cage were exposed in a gaping hole; one could see the wheezing inflation and deflation of her lung like a balloon.

And the worst was yet to come.

Some of the victims who had been closer to the hypocenter arrived. Being even more severely injured, they took more time to reach the edge of the blast zone where conditions were marginally better.

A few more survivors tottered out of the smoke, like

ghosts.

Simply coated in blood from head-to-toe, one bedraggled man stumbled out, limping. Both of his arms were gone, bloody stumps staining his sleeves.

One woman crawled forward on her trembling hands and arms, one leg gone at the knee, trailing blood, the other leg completely missing. But the worst part was her face. Her lower jaw was completely gone, exposing her bleeding gums and upper teeth. Her scorched tongue wriggled about almost snakelike as she struggled forward.

Another prisoner, only a boy of perhaps nine years old, wailed incessantly. At the time of the blast he must have been bound near lamps or windows of vehicles, as shards of glass protruded all over his body. His body was just a mass of crimson, as if he had been dunked in red paint and allowed to wade out.

She saw one man, trailing behind, who had a stump of an arm and no legs, dragging himself along.

Looking out at the extent of the devastation, Mina swallowed hard as she realized the staggering implications. If the bomb were dropped on an American city...

She couldn't let it happen.

Inside the bunker near the test site, it was absolute exuberation. The faces of the soldiers and scientist filled with elation.

Ecstatic, Rain raised his arms in the air, leading them in a mass cheer. *"Ten'nouheika banzai!"* he shouted, unable to contain his glee.

While the phrase was also often used as a battle cry, it was also used as a victory shout. It literally meant 'May his Imperial majesty live ten thousand years!' Victory indeed. In this particular context, it was the Japanese equivalent of pumping one's fist in the air in celebration. Hooray, hooray, hooray.

Joyous, all the troops and scientists joined him, collectively raising their arms towards the sky in jubilation, shouting each time.

"*Banzai! Banzai! Banzai!*"

Sake cups were handed out, distributed by a grinning young officer.

Beaming, Rain and the Owl toasted each other, raising their porcelain cups to each other.

Back on the scorched hilltop, quietly somber, Mina beckoned to the ragtag group of survivors on either side of her.

"C'mon everyone. Let's get out of here."

They turned to make their way down the hill.

An entrenching tool bit into the ground, scooping up a shovelful of earth. The tool dumped its contents onto the small pile of dirt next to the growing hole.

Near the hill on the outskirts of town, the ragtag group dug up the rest of Mina's supplies cached earlier. Scarlett sat by on an unearthed crate and rested.

Sitting next to her, Mina tuned the handheld SSTC-502 radio.

Mina wondered about the date. How long had she really been in the facility? She turned to the pregnant woman.

"Hey. What's the date? Do you know?" Mina figured the woman would have a better idea if she hadn't been locked up for long.

"April fourth," the woman responded.

Mina's mind whirred. So, she'd lost only a week. It had felt so, so much longer. Fortunately, it wasn't the month she had feared. Maybe her allies were still around and hadn't given her up for dead.

Mina continued twiddling with the dials, speaking idly to the pregnant woman. "So. What's your story?"

The pregnant woman turned away from Mina abashedly. "I am pregnant with the Japanese colonel's child. He wanted to get rid of the problem, so he sent me to the bomb test site."

Mina swallowed the lump in her throat. She had heard similar stories about Nazi officers in Europe. It was a damn shame. Local girl tried to cozy up with the occupying forces to try and make a better life for herself but got the short end of the stick.

Mina twiddled with the dials on the static-emitting radio, agitated. She spoke into the microphone. "Coral Hare to Papa Bear, please come in!"

Unlike the system she had brought with her to Tokyo, this was a different radio system called the Joan-Eleanor system, or "J-E" for short. Its usefulness came in talking to aircraft while behind enemy lines. The system was comprised of a handheld SSTC-502 transceiver used by the field agent, while a SSTR-6 transceiver was carried on an overhead aircraft. The transceivers only had a short range. Both and the agent and the aircraft had to be in relatively close proximity.

The system was actually quite secure. While the two parties were in close proximity, they would transmit over the VHF band. The short range combined with the use of the VHF band made the communication very difficult to detect.[108] Unlike the intercepted communications Rain had spoken of in her interrogation, this would almost certainly be indiscernible to the enemy.

Trying again, Mina spoke urgently over the static-filled warbling. She desperately hoped the plane had stayed in the area. Otherwise, she'd be in a heapful of trouble. "Coral Hare to Papa Bear, Coral Hare to Papa Bear, please come in!"

She was answered by empty static. After a few seconds, the Barber approached her side, concerned. "What's wrong?" he inquired.

Mina responded without looking at him, radio still pressed to her ear. She strained for any sign that her allies were still out there. "I wasn't able to report in when I was supposed to. It's been a week. I think they gave me up for dead."

This was bad. She'd probably have to go into town

---

[108] This system was so valuable it was not declassified until 1976.

and leave a dead drop to contact her superiors. She might even have to go to port and hijack a fishing boat to make her way back to friendly territory. Sighing, Mina turned the dial to switch the radio -

Unexpectedly, the radio crackled to life. The familiar male voice was filled with relief. "Coral Hare, good to hear from you!" said Lockwood. "Over!"

Mina felt a weight lift from her shoulders. At least the overhead planes had kept coming in. Bless the man, Lockwood hadn't given up on her. She spoke urgently into the microphone.

"Tojo has The Gadget[109]! Theirs is working! The pie's out on the windowsill and it's hot hot hot! Over!"

There was momentarily static on the other end as the team deliberated. Mina waited in tense anticipation.

When the response finally came, Lockwood's voice was filled with agitated worry and resolve.

"Destroy their prototypes. Slow down progress any way you can. Keep them from making any more. Extract the chief scientist at the site - get the Owl. Over."

"Understood. Over and out."

The group members prepared to go their separate ways. The pregnant woman, the British prisoner, and the Oldtimer left for the relative safety of China.

After much well-wishing, Mina gave them a bundle of supplies, arming them with pistols and submachine guns and sending them on their way. Ships that pass in the night, so to speak. She never expected to see any of them again.

Mina bid them farewell. "Head north. The troops there will aid you."

The departing ragtag bunch waved their acknowledged thanks and Mina turned to those few that were left. These were the ones that would fight alongside her for the time being.

---

[109] For secrecy purposes, "The Gadget" is often how participants of the Manhattan Project referred to the atomic bomb.

There was the Chinese soldier she had haphazardly nicknamed Scar, Dallas the American marine, and of course, the Korean resistance leader the Barber.

Under the light of the moon, Mina and the three others deliberated around the crate that served as a makeshift table. The hand-drawn diagram of the cave facility was laid out on top of the crate. Next to the first crate was a second one, with a large rolled-up cloth bundle on top.

"No way we can sneak inside," the Barber concluded. "We are escaped prisoners and they know our faces."

Mina nodded assent. "We go in guns blazing."

Nearby, she unrolled the sheet on the adjacent crate. Doing so revealed a veritable arsenal of small arms and explosives, arrayed out in neat rows, snug inside cloth loops. Japanese firearms. Blocks of plastique, the newer C3, not C2. Assorted hand grenades and knives, both American and Japanese. A Model 99 antitank mine and a Type 4 20 cm rocket launcher, both Japanese. There were a handful of American weapons. Tommy guns, M3 grease guns, Colt M1911A1 pistols.

"Grab your toys boys," she said facetiously. The three men started arming themselves, picking up firearms, checking the actions and loading ammunition.

Mina pointed out one weapon amongst the others, addressing the Barber. "I was told to give that to you," she said.

Tucked among the various firearms and blades, was a worn but well-cared for straight razor. Mina guessed it was his own. Probably left over from some earlier mission and left in American hands.

The Barber grabbed it, then expertly twirled the blade around with mere flicks of his wrist as if it were a butterfly knife.

Not shy, Mina started changing her clothes, pulling off the burnt coveralls of her worker's disguise.

The others glanced away. The Barber politely turned

his back.

Gingerly, Mina peeled away the cloth melted into the skin on her back, stripping it over her head.

Cloth rustled. After a few moments, she called out. "Done."

There was mild surprise in the Barber's voice as he turned around and saw her attire. "Schoolgirl uniform?" he asked curiously.

Mina was dressed in a blue-white sailor suit uniform of the same type she wore in Tokyo. She spoke as she tied her hair into pigtails with powder pink bow ribbons. Fortunately, her hair was only slightly singed.

"It's on purpose," she explained. "I'll zip in and be the distraction. You guys take out the airstrip so we don't get strafed by Zeroes, then secure a getaway vehicle."

The Barber nodded. Mina grabbed a bandolier belt of shuriken stars from the assorted equipment, one of the more esoteric items Lockwood had packed. She also picked out a U.S. Ranger rocket-propelled grappling hook[110]. It looked useful.

She locked and loaded two Tommy guns, racking back the bolt. Given that her cover was already blown, using American hardware wasn't an issue anymore. Despite their formidable engineering in aircraft, Japanese small arms construction was inferior to their American counterparts.

Mina gripped the hem of the ankle-length skirt and tore the hem off, showing off quite a bit off leg. No matter, she wasn't really one for modesty. Besides, she needed the mobility.

Bemused, he raised an eyebrow. Miniature skirt. Scandalous.

She chirped a response. "Hey, maybe it'll catch on!

Her hands opened a little leather folding case like a

---

[110] These same type of rocket-propelled grappling hooks were famously used by the U.S. Rangers at Pointe du Hoc on D-Day to scale the cliffs at Normandy.

pocketbook. Nestled inside was a row of syringes. Mina pulled one out.

Concerned, the Barber glanced at her. "You've been through a lot. Can you still fight?"

Quietly sullen but dutiful, Mina didn't meet his gaze. She patted her arm to bring the veins to the surface and tapped the syringe to bring bubbles to the top.

"I have to," she said softly.

He eyed the clear fluid inside the syringe, apprehensive. "What is that?"

Mina thumbed down the syringe's plunger, letting out a spurt of fluid from the needle.

"Adrenaline," she answered.

Using both hands, she stabbed the syringe full of harvested epinephrine directly into her chest and depressed the plunger. She drew in a gasp as her back arched in pain.

Her pupil within the brown iris contracted, accompanied by the sound of a primal scream, more animal than human.

Cave facility entrance

Speeding along, a pair of roller skates zipped around the corner to the entrance where two sentries stood under the night sky.

Twin Tommy gun barrels erupted in fire and fury. The two guards collapsed to rocky earth as a pair of roller skates threaded their way past them.

Alarms blared and the twenty-four ton blast doors started to swing shut. Tossed from below, two blocks of C3 explosive adhered to the hinges of the blast doors. The double explosions resounded in the chamber, and with a whir of dying machinery and flying sparks, the giant doors ground to a halt. The facility could no longer be sealed in such a manner.

Running boots rushed out of the cave interior, only for their wearers to be met with a chattering fusillade from the Tommy guns and more khaki-uniformed bodies flopped lifeless to the ground.

The pair of roller skates glided along, weaving their way through the slew of sprawled, bullet-ridden corpses.

Boarding the cave facility's elevator, a gridwork of shadows from the elevator's scaffolding played across Mina's face as the elevator descended.

Locked and loaded, Mina was armed to the teeth. A pigtailed schoolgirl in sailor suit outfit, she had bandoliers of ammunition and American hand grenades[111] cross-strapped across her chest, along with a band of shuriken stars. Twin Colt M1911 pistols were tucked in her rear waistband. Two M3 grease guns were slung next to them. Two extra C-Type 100-round drum magazines for the Tommy guns were clipped to her belt. An M3 trench knife[112] was tucked at her waist. A U.S. Ranger grappling hook was strapped to her back.

She wielded a Tommy gun in each hand held down at her side.

Her doe eyes, normally so innocent-looking, went cold with battle-hardened resolution on her grim face.

Time to walk with the Reaper.

---

[111] Mark 2 hand grenade.

[112] Both certain grease guns and trench knives had the model "M3."

40 LOADED FOR BEAR

Alarm lights flashed. At the bottom of the elevator shaft inside the bowels of the cave facility, armed soldiers took up firing positions. Some crouched, some stood, all had firearms pointed at the elevator door.

The soldiers at the rear went to the hewn bedrock wall. Craning their necks up, they pointed firearms upwards, checking to make sure no one was rappelling down from the rear.

Suddenly, the chatter of automatic fire from beneath their feet perforated their bodies. The wooden planks they were standing on was pockmarked with bullet holes and the air filled with splinters and wood dust. The soldiers spasmed and jerked like demented marionettes as their bodies were riddled with bullets, and they sprawled to the ground. One soldier arched back, face a mask of pain, teetering backward on his feet. He let out an involuntarily burst from his submachine gun into the air before collapsing.

The manhole-sized wooden trapdoor in the floor flipped up and Mina poked her head out with a Tommy gun at the ready. She swept the area, checking that it was clear, then climbed out.

Going to one of the dead officers, she took off his

gunto sword and strapped it across her back ninja-style, instead of at her hip like the officers did.

She skated away down the hall, leaving the corpses strewn in her wake.

Up in the observation room overlooking the facility's assembly area, chaos ensued. The officer inside could hear muffled yells of soldiers baying orders. The Owl ran into the room, distressed.

"What's going on?" he asked.

The Japanese officer pointed to the rectangular observation window that dominated the wall. "There's a schoolgirl out there killing our men!" he exclaimed.

"You're kidding me," the Owl responded.

The echoing chatter of submachine gun fire out in the cavern below answered his question. The Owl went to the window - and his eyes went wide behind his black, round-rimmed glasses.

Mina was a sight to behold. If she had meant to be a distraction, calling the end result such was an understatement. Her outfit was a near-unbelievable juxtaposition of the innocent and the ferocious. Locked and loaded, she was positively loaded for bear, a pigtailed schoolgirl armed to the teeth with bandoliers strapped across her chest. Fighting, she glided about on roller skates, no less.

Down on the ground, soldiers in the area stared in near-disbelief, losing precious split-seconds in reacting. While the external blast doors had been installed, internal blast doors between chambers had not been, and Mina's rampage continued largely unimpeded.

Zipping in on roller skates, wielding a blazing Tommy gun in each hand, she gunned down everyone and anyone in her path in a chatter of automatic fire. Brass shell casings trailed in her wake.

Racing through, legs pumping, Mina hosed down several bomb prototypes, riddling the machinery with hot lead.

Soldiers armed with rifles and submachine guns

tracked her movements, trying to lead their target but Mina was too fast. Their bullets missed, sparking and ricocheting all around her, off rock walls and workbenches.

Mina crouch-dodged on her skates, making herself a smaller target. She sailed behind the cover of a workstation. Sheets of loose paper fluttered in the air, kicked up by flying rounds.

Still crouched with her back to the workstation, smoking Tommy guns empty, Mina dropped them and pulled out the M3 grease guns at her hips.

Skating into the fray, Mina dodged and weaved expertly on her roller skates, using whatever available cover she could find.

She yanked the pin on several grenades with her teeth, flinging them onto semi-constructed bomb prototypes at workstations.

Several soldiers dove for cover as secondary explosions rocked the room, the fiery blasts resounding in the chamber.

Airstrip

Topside, at the airstrip outdoors, sirens wailed. The Barber and other two survivors stormed the small airstrip from three directions simultaneously.

Emptying a pistol into one of the guards at the sandbagged position, the Barber reacted as the second guard raced to pivot his light machine gun in his direction.

Out of ammo, dashing into a flying kick, the Barber knocked the man into the sandbags and whipped out his razor, flicking out the blade.

In a flurry of *taekwondo*-style cuts and slashes, the Barber sliced the man's face to ribbons and finished him off with a slash to the throat. The guard sagged to the ground, crimson soaking through his khaki uniform.

The Barber ripped the machine gun off its mount. Firing it from the hip, he let out chattering fire, pockmarking the idling Zero fighters and shredding their wings in a stream of hot lead.

Nearby, Dallas and Scar lay down cover fire with submachine guns, cutting down a squad of Japanese soldiers.

Up at the guard tower, a searchlight focused on them, bleaching out the trio's features in harsh glare.

Squinting, the Barber loosed a stream of fire at the tower, blasting out the searchlight and plunging the area back into darkness. Scar fired a quick burst and the sentry let out a yelp as he fell flailing over the railing and plummeted to the ground.

Back inside the cave's assembly area, Mina dropped the smoking, empty M3 grease guns and they clattered to the ground. Making a beeline, she glide-weaved back towards the workstation. Her twin Tommy guns lay strewn on the brass-shell littered floor. She crouched and took cover.

Gunshots cracked over her head. Unperturbed, fingers nimble, she reloaded the Tommy guns with the 100-round magazines clipped to her belt. Nearby, the soldiers crept around workstations to flank her.

Fully loaded, adrenaline coursing through her veins, Mina dashed out of cover on her skates, dodging gunfire. Swerving, she evaded soldiers as they made wild grabs at her, but her dexterity on her skates was such they grasped empty air. A fluid specter of death, Mina weaved through the room. Twin Tommy guns chattering, she cut down ever more soldiers in her path as she cleared the chamber.

Gliding by, Mina tossed blocks of C3 onto the columns in the room, laying down cover fire with her other hand. Two soldiers ducked behind a desk, grimacing as .45 caliber bullets gauged out chunks of wood and splintered the surface. One of the soldiers had a shocked expression. "I've never seen anyone fight like that before," he said, dumbfounded.

Mina backpedaled, using the blazing Tommy guns' recoil to glide backwards on her skates with little effort on her own.

Magazines expended, the Tommy guns stopped spewing fire and went silent. Mina dropped the empty, smoking Tommy guns to the tiles.

Her hands immediately went to her rear, drawing her twin Colt pistols in each hand.

Grim, she returned fire, fingers pumping, dual firing in rapid succession, like an old-time gunslinger from the Wild West.

Zipping by, she flanked the two soldiers behind the desk. She gunned them down, their bodies jerking spasmodically against the perforated frame before slumping to the floor, firearms clattering out of their hands.

Back at the airstrip outside, the massive fuel tanks on the premises exploded in a roiling gaseous fireball. The nighttime surroundings momentarily lit up as brightly as if it were day.

Blocks of C3 affixed to remaining Zeroes on the airstrip detonated in a roaring explosion, adding to the inferno. The planes blew apart, broken wings sent spinning away. With fuselages engulfed in the conflagration, the warbirds were reduced to burning hulks of slag in the night.

Riding astride a commandeered motorcycle[113], the Barber fired a submachine gun over his shoulder as he made his escape.

Next to him, Dallas and Scar rode inside a sedan[114]. Leaning out of the passenger window, Scar loosed a withering hail of cover fire as the car burned rubber. The vehicle careened out of the gate, leaving the burning ruins of the airstrip behind them.

Deep inside the underground facility, Mina let the smoking dual pistols in her hand drop as they clicked on

---

[113] Type 97 Motorcycle.

[114] Meant to be a Type 98 Passenger Car.

empty.

Mina flung her trench knife into the throat of a nearby soldier. He let out a gurgling gasp and pitched forward, blood pooling around his prone form.

Completely out of ammunition, it was time for more unconventional methods. She grabbed a handful of shuriken stars at her belt in each hand.

Head down, Mina crossed her arms as if reaching behind her back, bracing herself, then -

Flinging her arms wide, she threw out a sweeping arc of shuriken stars upwards -

Zinging out, the metal stars busted out the overhead lamps almost simultaneously, leaving the chamber in total darkness save the intermittent crimson of the alarm -

Mina pulled the grappling hook from her back and aimed it up. With a boom of rocket propellant, the hook shot upwards and looped around one of the rafters.

Mina ascended, pulled into the darkness, melding with the shadows -

Suddenly, there was the sound of dozens of objects slicing through the air. From seemingly nowhere, the air filled with a barrage of ninja stars.

So fast they almost blurred, the stars *thunked* as they impacted, and a half-dozen stars embedded into a nearby workstation -

The hail of shuriken zipped and zinged thickly through the air -

Dozens of soldiers screamed as their faces and upper torsos embedded with razor-sharp stars, and they collapsed -

Cave facility side entrance

Outside an external, smaller side entrance, Rain bellowed orders, making wide gestures.

Parked at the rear of the entrance was a six-wheeled truck[115]. Next to it was a construction crane with a hook.

---

[115] Type 94 6-Wheeled Truck.

From the tunnel, soldiers wheeled out an ovoid metallic bomb shell on a dolly. The bomb casing was roughly ten feet long and two feet wide, painted dull olive.

Barking orders, the men used the crane to load the shell onto the truck. Soldiers climbed onto the back with it and closed the truck flaps.

Rain rapped his fist on the truck's back frame and the vehicle pulled away, rumbling down the dirt road.

Running in the dark, intermittently illuminated by flashing crimson of the alarm, the Owl sprinted through the cavern. He dashed through the ground floor of the assembly area in a wild panic, huffing and puffing.

There was the whisper of metal. Suddenly, he felt himself yanked back by the collar and cold steel pressed against his throat.

Behind him, eerily illuminated in the occasional red glow, Mina held the naked blade of her scavenged sword against his carotid artery.

She jammed a "K" knockout pill into his mouth and punched him in the stomach, forcing him to swallow as he tried to suck in air. Doubling over in pain, the man sagged and Mina caught him by the back of his collar. "Alright four-eyes. This way," she said.

Mina grabbed a submachine gun from one of the corpses on the floor. She checked the magazine clip and the action, then proceeded to leave.

Dragging the unconscious man along in one hand and aiming her submachine gun in the other, Mina exited. She emerged from the semi-darkness of the assembly cavern into the normal lighting of the elevator anteroom, still littered with corpses. The elevator area ran on a separate power system, in case of emergency.

From down the hall she suddenly heard whirring machinery and the rumble of an approaching elevator.

Damn. The doors opened and the squad of soldiers

inside immediately opened fire when they saw her.

Using the Owl as a human shield, Mina shot over his shoulder at the soldiers, who immediately ducked inside the elevator doors as bullets spanged and sparked about. She knew they wouldn't shoot at her, at least not yet. They still had some hope of rescuing the Owl.

Dragging him in front of her, Mina backpedaled into the adjoining mine cart shaft. As she had noticed in her initial visit, the shaft ran in a spiral to the surface. One track went up, the other down. It would be their ticket out.

She yanked the nearby lever and the minecart raced up along the rickety track. The soldiers in the elevator dashed out, the man in the lead yelling and pointing at Mina.

Sprinting, the soldiers climbed into another mine cart at the base of the rail and sped off, chasing after her. Mina guessed they were several seconds behind.

Checking behind, Mina peeked over the edge of the creaking, speeding mine cart. The wind whipped her pigtails in front of her and ruffled her sailor suit. Gambling that the Owl was safe at the bottom of the cart, the soldiers fired at her.

Mina ducked as rifle shots cracked past her ear and submachine gun chatter whizzed overhead. Racing upwards on the rumbling track, her ears popped with the ascent.

Raising her submachine gun over the edge of the cart, Mina blind-fired, letting out a chattering hail of gunfire. Her pursuers ducked as bullets pinged off their speeding cart.

She glanced upwards. Mingled with the stench of gunpowder and overturned loam was the scent of sea air. She must be getting close to the surface. Grabbing a block of C3 from her belt, she tossed it upwards onto the ceiling.

Scant seconds later, the block of C3 on the mineshaft roof... fizzled and let out a pathetic spark as the detonator short-circuited.

Bursting out laughing, the soldiers jeered at her. They let out potshots in her direction. Mina mumbled under her breath. "A dud? You gotta be kidding me."

However, back inside the cave facility's assembly area,

the ticking timer on the plastique affixed to support columns counted down to zero. The C3 blocks exploded in fiery conflagration and the entire chamber started to collapse in a deluge of earth and boulders.

On the rails, Mina's cart swayed and rocked as earthquake-like tremors jostled the cart. She peeked back at the pursuing men.

Screaming, they raised their arms in futile desperation as an avalanche of rocks and dirt buried their cart under a mound of rubble.

But it wasn't over yet. Mina glanced back down the tunnel as the rock barricade blasted apart, overwhelmed by great pressure from below. The blast revealed a roaring wall of flame that rushed up the mine shaft. Eyes widening in shock, Mina ducked as the inferno washed past above her head. After a few seconds, the flames ended.

The danger past, Mina's minecart raced alone out the cave entrance, out under the starry night sky.

Dead Japanese soldiers lay sprawled about the cave's topside entrance. Urgently, the Barber scrounged ammo clips from their pouches, stuffing them into his pockets.

Next to him, at his feet was a pile of weapons. Some were from Mina's cache, some scavenged from the airfield.

Also next to him, attached to a T-shaped detonator, a cord snaked its way along the ground. It branched out towards dynamite affixed to structural points around the entrance. This last device had been scavenged from the airfield.

There was the creaking of approaching wheels on the rail track and he snapped his submachine gun in the direction.

He saw Mina in the cart as it rolled to a stop a few yards outside the cave. Slinging his weapon over his shoulder, he rushed to help her drag the unconscious Japanese scientist out.

"Where's the other two guys?" she asked when she saw him approach.

"They went on ahead to clear the way."

"Did you get us transportation?"

The Barber grasped a beige canvas tarp next to the mine track and unveiled -

A Type 1 Kurogane motorcycle, also known by the name "Sanrinsha." It was a Japanese military "Trike", a three-wheeled motorcycle with an integrated cart in the back that could hold several people.

Mina was momentarily reminded of the little tricycle her father had given to her when she was eight. When she saw the Barber's procurement her eyes lit up with bright-eyed excitement, trembling fists bunched to her chest. "Ooh! A trikie!"

The Barber rolled his eyes. "God, you're such a kid."

Mina tossed the unconscious Owl into the back of the cart like a sack of potatoes. The Barber grabbed an armful of scavenged weapons and dumped them next to the kidnapped prisoner, then climbed into the back cart.

Suddenly, yells came from within the cave. Mina and her companion whirled in the direction. Either some of the surviving soldiers had dug themselves out, or had climbed out of the elevator shaft.

Hurrying, holding the T-shaped detonator in her hands, Mina shoved in the plunger.

The blast sent tremors through her feet. Soldiers that had only just escaped one cave-in screamed within the conflagration as a second cascade of rocks and dirt crushed them. Their screams cut off and a blast of dust and debris blew out from the collapsing entrance.

Mina allowed herself a moment of satisfaction. "There! If that doesn't slow them down, I don't know what will!"

She grabbed the goggles hanging off the handlebar by the strap and quickly donned them.

Mina throttled up the motorcycle and raced downhill on the dirt path. The orange-red glow of the sun crested the horizon, and soon it would be day.

41 TRIKIE

The three-wheeled motorcycle rumbled down the dirt road through the Korean countryside. The area crested into flat land, which in this part of the country constituted grassy plains dotted with copses of trees - a rare sight.

Unfortunately, their respite was short-lived.

There was the rumble of several truck engines coming their way. Mina looked behind them. In the growing light, their pursuers were clearly visible.

Over on the side path of a nearby hill, three military Nissan pickup-style trucks[116] came careening down. Soldiers were loaded onto the backs, armed with submachine guns and rifles. Several of them took aim at the girl in the driver's seat, firing.

Mina ducked as a shot narrowly missed her head, sparking as it pinged off the handlebars. Over the roar of the wind and thrumming engine, she yelled over her shoulder to the Barber. "Get them offa me!"

In the back cart, armed with a submachine gun, the Barber grimly took aim and let out a spray of fire at their pursuers.

---

[116] Nissan 180 pickup-style trucks.

The soldiers momentarily dodged behind the truck's siding as bullets sparked and ricocheted around them.

Mina looked back and fired her pistol over her shoulder, forcing them to keep their heads down as the Barber slapped a fresh clip home and resumed, his gun blazing.

Chased by soldiers in the three trucks, exchanging fire, Mina dodged and weaved the three-wheeled motorcycle, veering erratically. From afar they all looked like toys, mounted figurines complete with muzzle flashes in the early morning light.

Mina's ears perked up. There was the new rumble of a different engine and she heard the all-too-familiar grinding...of treads.

A Type 4 Ke-Nu tank burst forth from a nearby thicket in a flurry of twigs and flying splinters, crushing trees in its path. Leaves fluttering in its wake, it steamrolled towards them. The tank sided up next to the soldier-laden trucks, joining its compatriots.

Mina whirled in her seat in shock. "Holy shit!" she exclaimed.

"They have a tank!" the Barber shouted over the wind.

"Yes, yes, I can see that!"

Firing on the move, the tank's muzzle flared, booming.

The shell exploded, kicking up a shower of dirt and shredded grass that rained upon the cringing motorcycle's occupants. Mina swerved the motorcycle to evade the fresh crater and yelled behind her.

"Use the rocket launcher!"

"I gave it to the others!"

"Goddamnit! Switch!"

The Barber clambered into the driver's seat as Mina climbed into the back cart.

From the pile of gear lying next to the unconscious Owl, Mina grabbed a disc-shaped anti-tank mine. The mine was a Model 99 armor piercing, self-attaching magnetic mine, with fuse. Crouched in the back cart, fighting against the sway of the vehicle, Mina held the mine's fuse in her mouth in ad-hoc fashion. She screwed it into the mine's fuse hole, leaving the safety pin in and hurriedly strapped the mine to her back.

She also grabbed a Molotov cocktail from the pile. Like most Molotovs it was a glass bottle filled with a mix of oil and gasoline. Unlike many others, it was a good mass-produced Japanese-style Molotov. It had a mechanical fuse that would detonate it upon impact, not the improvised kind seen with flaming rag.

Concealment. She needed something to obscure their vision. She grabbed a smoke candle[117], basically a smoke grenade in a tube, and ripped out the self-launching mechanism.

She pulled the release. The canister started to spew gray smoke and she dropped it at the Owl's feet. She knew the fumes were somewhat toxic but damnit, she needed the smoke cover. Silently, she gave a fervent prayer that the winds wouldn't change and blow the smoke ahead of them.

Fortunately, Mother Nature was with them. The wind was steady, and blew the trailing gray smoke into the front of the tank, obscuring the vision ports.

Muffled yells and exclamations came from within the tank as it was enveloped by thick smoke. I can't see, I can't see.

As the motorcycle rushed along, Mina climbed onto the edge of the back cart as the wind whipped about her. Crouching on the lip of the cart, she gripped it with her hands, steadying against the swaying. The Barber temporarily straightened out their path so she wouldn't be thrown off. Tense, Mina gritted her teeth. She had to time this just right, or she'd be crushed to a bloody pulp under those treads.

Anticipating the motion of the tank, Mina tracked it with her eyes. She launched herself off, sailing through the air, landing onto the front of the tank -

Inside the tank, the crew looked up, startled at the muffled metallic clang.

Outside, with gray smoke billowing all around, Mina

---

[117] Japanese Type 94 smoke candle.

clambered onto the hand-railing near the top of the metal beast. Feet dangling, her foot slipped a few times as she clung on for dear life. A few inches from to the side of her head was the machine gun. It protruded off to the side and below the main turret.

Within the tank, the soldier manning the machine gun pulled the trigger, loosing a stream of automatic fire.

Mina cringed as the barrel spat out a chattering fusillade of flame inches away from her face, searing her cheek. Grimacing, she grabbed the hot muzzle with her bare hand. She shoved it out of her way as the machinery protested with the grinding of gears.

Suddenly, she heard grinding and clinking of metal of a tank shell being loaded. The main cannon shifted - aiming for the Barber and the Trike.

She kicked the tank turret, forcing it to swivel just as it boomed and the blast hit one of the trucks packed with soldiers. There was a mass of screams, a roar of flame, and flying dismembered limbs as the truck's momentum sent it crashing into a rock outcropping. Pieces of flaming bodies flung out even as the chassis crumpled into the rocks. The vehicle was reducing to a twisted fireball of flaming metal encasing burning flesh.

Approaching the tank's right side, engine revving as it shifted gears, the second truck pulled up. Yelling, the soldiers let out a hail of lead, spraying the tank's front surface with gunfire. They knew the tanks' armor plating could protect its occupants but that the girl would be riddled with bullets.

Scrabbling like a frantic monkey, bullets sparking and bouncing off the tank's plating all around her, Mina clambered to the opposite side of the tank, hanging off. Her legs dangled in the air as they flailed for a nonexistent foothold.

Racing along, the Barber glanced over his shoulder. Seeing Mina's plight, he throttled back the motorcycle. In the bike's rearview mirror, he saw the truck angling back, approaching her from behind so its soldiers could take potshots.

Leaning back, steering with one hand, he grabbed a Molotov from the rear cart. He yanked out the pin with his teeth and –

-hurled it directly into the throng of soldiers in the back of the truck.

There was the crash of breaking glass as the entire squad burst into flame, arms flailing wildly. Panicking, one flaming soldier jumped out - and was promptly run over. His limp body squashed like a discarded doll's as the tires of the following truck steamrolled him to jelly.

Still dangling by the tank's top handlebar, Mina reached up, swinging her leg up into a foothold. She climbed on top but stayed prone with her body against the tank's surface. No need to stand up and make herself a high-profile target.

Bullets cracked by her head as the troops on the nearby truck took shots at her. She flinched, keeping her head down. Damn. She had wanted to use the mine against the tank but couldn't do it now. If she did, she'd have to leap into the waiting arms of the truck's soldiers. The Barber was too far away.

She pulled the pin on the anti-tank mine and flung the two-pound disc directly into the path of the approaching vehicle. The panicked driver swerved but it was too close -

The deafening explosion roared as the truck rose several feet into the air, overturning while suspended. The force sent soldiers flying like pinwheeling rag dolls. Aflame, the truck chassis crashed back to earth, rolling over and crushing still-moving, burning passengers.

Finally, Mina thought. Now the tank.

Clambering up over the hatch, she stood atop the tank in a near-stylish pose, but she was just angling her legs to stabilize footing, not showboating. A soot-smeared, battle-seasoned schoolgirl riding atop a tank. She didn't bother trying to wrench the hatch open; she didn't have a crowbar and knew she didn't have the upper body strength to do so.

Instead, she crouched down and jammed the muzzle

of her submachine gun into the front vision port, blind-firing inside. She emptied the clip as brass casings arced into the air next to her. Pained screams and yelps came from within the metal beast, as well as the sound of ricochets. Then came a muffled *whoosh* of air.

A panicked muffled voice came from inside. "*Kaji da! Kaji da!*"

Fire, fire. Fires inside a tank were a nightmare. One of her rounds had hit the internal magazine. Inside, it was now worse than sitting on a powder keg. It was sitting on a powder keg while locked in a metal oven.

But Mina had to make sure. The crew was in a state of fear and panic. Time to seize the moment.

At her belt was the factory-made Molotov with mechanical fuse. Crouching, still atop the tank, she grabbed the Molotov. She yanked the pin with her teeth, leaned out, and flung it into the front vision port.

There was a *whoosh* of ignition and bloodcurdling screams as the tank's occupants were incinerated in the confined space.

Time for the *coup de grace*. She reached into a large pouch on her belt and pulled out a saucer of her explosive-filled cookies. The cookies artfully adhered to the plate were arranged in an optimal explosive configuration. In a jiffy, she could use it as an anti-tank mine. Hopefully it would pack enough of a punch.

Hanging over the side, she slapped the saucer of cookies onto the tank's treads. If anything, the tank would be immobilized. She had five seconds before they blew.

She heard someone yell incoherently over the wind. Up ahead she saw the Barber beckon to her frantically, the distance between them closing. Gauging distance, Mina jumped off the tank in a daredevil leap, arms flung wide.

She sailed through the air, sprawling unceremoniously into the motorcycle cart. Panting, she looked back over the edge of the cart.

A second later, the saucer of explosive-filled cookies

attached to the tank detonated. Combined with the fires raging within, the metal monster erupted into a raging fireball of too many munitions packed into too small a space. The blast left the tank a burning ruin, pluming ebon smoke. Its compatriot trucks were left in flaming wrecks not far behind.

Watching the ruined wrecks recede behind them, Mina felt the adrenaline start to drain from her system. She let out a small sigh of relief. From the bottom of the cart, she heard the gagged Owl let out a muffled moan.

Mina looked down. Having landed somewhat awkwardly, her foot was planted firmly into his groin. Not in much of a hurry, she lifted her foot off as he groaned in protest.

Stooping down, Mina patted his cheek condescendingly, speaking in English.

"You'll live."

The Owl let out a whimpering moan as the three-wheeled motorcycle raced on through the outback, unimpeded.

Now riding in front, Mina and the Trike's occupants raced through the outback.

There was the beep of a car horn. Mina instinctively swung her submachine gun in the direction - then snapped the barrel upwards as she saw who it was.

Dallas the marine and Scar, the Chinese soldier were riding inside a commandeered sedan. Grinning with camaraderie, they waved at Mina. She waved back.

Suddenly, off to the side was the rumble of another engine. Riding atop a military motorcycle, a Japanese soldier gazed in their direction, then veered off full throttle. A scout.

Mina yelled and pointed wildly at the escaping man. "Damnit. We've been spotted! Take him out before he gets help!"

42 SAPPHIRE

Mina revved the engine on the Trike, accelerating the motorcycle to top speed, the passenger car close behind her.

Scar leaned out the side of the car and fired bursts from his submachine gun. The Barber in the back cart of Mina's trike aimed a rifle, firing shot after shot.

Hunching down, the scout rider veered and weaved as bullets sparked off his motorcycle chassis. His gloved hand twisted the accelerator's grip, gunning the engine. He raced zigzag out of sight behind a hill, too far and too fast for Mina and her companions' more unwieldy vehicles to catch up to.

Sighing, Mina held up a fist above her shoulder, the military sign for stop. "Too late. He got away," she said dejectedly.

The Barber was grim. "We have to hurry. They'll be here soon. And there'll be a lot of them."

Mina pointed to a group of hills up ahead. "We'll make our stand up on that hill there!" she declared. "Elevated position, nice vantage point. Let's go."

Up on the hilltop the group dug in. They erected sandbagged positions and other defenses, preparing for the inevitable battle. The vehicles they used to escape formed a semi-enclosure around the hill, like covered wagons of the

American pioneers. Folded, empty sandbags had been packed in the airdrop gear. Mina sat on the ground with an entrenching tool, filling more bags with scoopfuls of sand and dirt. At already-erected sandbags, the Barber mounted a light machine gun[118].

Mina glanced over at Scar and Dallas as they set up the "knee mortar[119]". Alrighty. They'd be the stovepipe[120] boys then. Mina allowed herself a tight smile. She affectionately thought of them almost as Green Hornet and Kato from the black-and-white serials she once watched on weekends.

Near the base of the hill, the four of them set to work, planting hand grenades[121] into the ground as booby traps. The grenades were held upside down within tubes. When tripwires were pulled by a passing limb, the grenades would detonate.

Digging a hole in the hillside, Dallas buried a grenade. Turning to Mina, he inquired as to their situation in his Texan drawl. "So what exactly is the escape plan?"

Mina responded as she dug her own hole with an entrenching tool. "I have a plane on the way for pickup. We fashion additional harnesses out of rope. We holdout, the plane comes, and we take the Japanese egghead with us."

Dallas nodded. It wasn't the most solid of escape plans but it would have to do.

Back at the top of the hill, Mina opened up another crate of gear and started distributing them to the others. Bless the man's heart, Lockwood had thrown in a non-standard issue weapon - a sawed-off shotgun, a Winchester model 1912

---

[118] Type 99 light machine gun with the banana-shaped clip loaded on top of the gun.

[119] Also known as a Type 89 grenade discharger.

[120] Stovepipe was just a slang term for mortar.

[121] This tactic was commonly used with Japanese Model 91 hand grenades.

pump-action. She checked the action and started loading shells into the firearm.

There was an additional package wrapped in brown paper at the bottom of the crate.

Mina guessed it was plastique. She unwrapped the package. Inside the box, lying on a cushion of crumpled newspaper, was something Mina recognized.

It was Lockwood's personal Smith & Wesson Model 27 revolver, customized with a deep blue luster. There was a handwritten note next to it.

Mina picked it up and read it out loud, murmuring to herself. "'Thank you for the hat. As you know, this is my personal gat named 'Sapphire'. May she serve you well in your travels.' Papa Bear."

Mina grinned. This day was looking brighter already. She checked the revolver's action and loaded it[122], then tucked the revolver into her rear waistband.

Nearby, Dallas set up one of Mina's boxy radios on top of an ammo crate. He tuned the dials, and the speaker warbled with pitch shifts.

The Barber and Scar worked together, knotting coils of rope into makeshift harnesses. The Barber tried fitting one onto Scar, giving it a solid tug. Scar gave a thumbs up.

Unrolling another bundle of equipment, Mina began to tie the non-cooperative Owl into a factory-made harness. She was going to attempt a ground-to-air transfer, an Allied procedure of extracting people from behind enemy lines.

The process would entail donning heavy flight gear, helmet, and goggles. The extraction subject would unroll the harness, which was wrapped in a tarp, and strap themselves in. This preparation stage would take 5 minutes. After signaling the retrieving aircraft, the plane would swoop in with a pickup hook. The subject would lay on his/her back in a fetal position

---

[122] Flipping a cylinder shut on a revolver is a common trope in television and films (and looks cool), but generally damages the crane of the gun. Not recommended in real life.

to minimize the possibility of being hit by the plane passing overhead. The plane's hook would catch the balloon or pole attached to the subject's harness, and the plane would pull the subject up and away to safety...hopefully.[123]

In this particular case, she unfortunately only had one complete set of gear, but two regular harnesses and several makeshift ones. She quickly dressed the Owl into the heavy flight gear and the harness, trussing him up like a chicken.

Mina condescendingly patted his cheek. "There we go! All trussed up," she said.

Binoculars to his eyes, the Barber scanned the horizon below the dreary gray clouds.

Through the double lenses, he saw incoming dust clouds in the distance, kicked up with the passage of vehicles. The clouds heralded the arrival of the Japanese troops. He looked off behind them. Other vehicles approached. Some of the approaching elements had gone in a circuitous route, then doubled back so they would approach from all directions at the same time.

The Barber yelled out a warning in English. "They're here!"

No more time for preparation. All of them immediately hunkered down. The Barber manned the light machine gun at the sandbags, racking back the side lever. Scar and Dallas readied the mortar. Mina slotted a round into an Arisaka Type 99 sniper rifle and racked back the bolt.

The approaching rumble of engines grew louder. Then the engines combined with the sound of tires crunching on gravel.

Mina waited for the right moment, then yelled out to the others in English. "Let 'em have it!"

---

[123] This is an early version of the famous Fulton recovery system developed in the 1950s during the Cold War. Generally, early World War II versions of this process did not use a balloon to latch onto, but had a pair of poles. These were set in the ground on either side of the person to be retrieved, with a line running from the top of one pole to the other.

Manning the machine gun at the sandbags, the Barber let loose an unrelenting stream of fire and fury down towards the approaching vehicles.

Down the hill, the Japanese troops took cover behind their vehicles, hunkering down as bullets pinged, spanged, and sparked off the chassis. The fusillade from the Barber's machine gun was so withering none dared to stick their heads out to take a look.

Cautious, Mina stuck a mirror over the top of the sandbags at an angle, surveying the area through its reflection. She tallied a rough estimate of how many there were.

They were outnumbered almost twenty-to-one. Not good odds. Four people holding off a small army of troops. Wonderful, she thought wryly.

Scar and Dallas manned the mortar. They dropped a shell into the breech and stuck fingers in their ears, keeping their mouths open to better withstand the blast of air pressure. The mortar let out a pneumatic-sounding *thunk* with each round. Nearby, the Barber continued shooting the machine gun, hosing down the area with suppressing fire.

Suddenly, Mina whirled as massive explosions erupted and screams came from down the rear of the hill. Soldiers attempting to climb up had triggered the booby traps in the soil.

Rifle in her hands, Mina crouch-ran in that direction through smoke and gunfire. Lying low behind a gap in the sandbags, Mina aimed the sniper rifle through the opening.

She peered through the gap, keeping both eyes open while aiming. One eye maintained a wide view of the area, the other looked down the scope.

With her non-scoped eye, she searched for anyone yelling, shouting orders. Anyone with an officer cap or wearing a sword caught her attention. Cautiously, meticulously, she started picking them off one by one.

Holding her breath, she was careful to aim and fire before her diaphragm involuntarily spasmed and caused her to twitch, which would throw off her aim. Looking down the scope, she pulled the trigger. One yelling officer's head disappeared within a puff of red mist.

Suddenly, there was the *crack-crack* of rifle shots whizzing by her head and a shower of dirt rained down upon her. Riflemen below had marked her last location. She had to relocate.

Crawling on her hands and knees, rifle in her hands, she wormed her way towards a different spot.

At the bottom of the hill, the fighting was hectic. Infantrymen shot up the hill from behind the cover of vehicles, quickly chambering fresh rounds. The ground at their feet was littered with brass casings.

Furious, his sword in hand, Rain gestured up the hill and let out an almost bestial yell at his troops.

"*Minagoroshida!*" Kill them all. He wouldn't settle for anything less.

There was the impending scream of an incoming mortar.

"*Kuru zo!*" one soldier yelled.

Incoming. Soldiers ducked for cover. Some screamed as their truck was obliterated in a gaseous fireball, blowing them into scarlet smithereens.

At the top of the hill, Mina cringed as more explosions roared from the slope behind them. For a moment Mina thought the booby traps had caught more soldiers.

Then she heard the whine of shells and Mina realized the enemy mortar team below was deliberately targeting the rear of their position. They destroyed the buried booby traps, clearing a path for troops.

Mina yelled at Scar in Mandarin Chinese. "Hey, Chiang Kai-shek![124] Take out that mortar!"

He yelled a confirmation, rotating the mortar's

---

[124] Of course, Mina is just using the nickname of the Chinese Nationalist leader as a placeholder nickname.

direction.

Peering through gaps in the sandbags, Mina searched for the enemy mortar team. Where the hell were they?

There was the whistling scream of an incoming mortar. With a boom that was way too close, Scar and Dallas disappeared in a blast of dirt and disturbed earth.

As the smoke and dust cleared, Mina saw a blue-panted leg severed at the knee. Scar's dirt-speckled prone form lay slumped near Dallas', his leg gone, raw scarlet flesh at the wound. The stump's exposed arteries rhythmically gushed blood onto a growing puddle with each pulse of his still-beating heart.

Mina felt her heart sink. She yelled out to the Barber. "Dallas and Scar are down. Buy me a few minutes!"

Still manning the machine gun, he barely nodded in acknowledgement, loosing another barrage at encroaching troops.

Mina crawled over to the boxy radio on top of the ammo crate. She yelled into the microphone. "Baker Hawk, this is Coral Hare. Where the hell are you?"

After a few moments of static punctuated by gunfire, whistling mortars, and explosions, she heard the response. "Hang in there! Just a few minutes more!" the pilot crackled over the radio.

Mina cursed silently. This wasn't good.

Suddenly there was another mortar blast and clumps of earth rained down upon her.

Mina noticed the machine gun fire had stopped. She glanced over. The Barber lay askew on his back in front of the now unmanned machine gun. His lower jaw was reduced to a gory mass of crimson pulp, exposing his teeth in an ugly rictus of death. Mina felt her heart sink even further in dismay. Damnit.

Through the smoke and crack of gunfire, she crawled over to their pile of weapons and grabbed a Type 4 20 cm rocket launcher lying across a crate of ammo.

She raised it to her shoulder, aiming it at one of the

trucks downhill. With a lurch of recoil, the rocket streaked out.

The fiery impact dismembered bodies, blowing them into gory chunks. Limbs flew apart, and the blast lit up the surrounding area like a fleeting bonfire. For a moment Mina could see a gaping hole in one man's chest, red-coated outline of rib cage and lungs visible as he was blown to bits.

She cringed as a blast from a mortar came too close, showering her with clumps of earth and debris as she hunkered down. The explosion left her ears ringing with a high-pitched whine.

It wasn't until her hearing returned that she realized the bombardment stopped. She looked around at the sudden stillness.

The gears of her mind whirred. Then she realized why the mortars stopped. They were afraid of hitting the Owl. The man was curled into a ball nearby, whimpering. The Japanese soldiers must have changed their mind about killing everyone. Instead, they decided to try and mount a rescue attempt. But that would mean -

There was a metallic clatter at her feet.

Mina instinctively dove for cover behind some sandbags - then peeked over the edge as no explosion came, only a hissing sound.

It wasn't a fragmentation grenade. A canister from a smoke candle rolled around a few feet away, spewing gray plumes. She got to her feet.

A few voices called out from beyond the bottom of the hill. "*Hatsuento!*" Smoke. "*Hatsuento nageru zo!*" Throwing smoke!

Mina whirled. Then another canister, and another clanked at her feet. The canisters lobbed through the air and clinked to a stop around her, rolling slightly. The smoke grew thicker and heavier, and in moments her surroundings were shrouded in dense gray smoke. Visibility was reduced to just a few feet.

Momentary near-silence fell over the area. There was little sound save that of her heart pounding in her ears and her own heavy breathing, coupled with the hiss of emitting smoke.

Wary, her fingers shifted in her double-handed grip on her Colt pistol, with the palm of one hand cupped under her firing hand for support. Her fingers tensed. She tried to peer through the artificial fog but it was nearly impossible to make out anything except shapes.

Suddenly, a warlike cry broke the near-silence. "*Totsugeki!*" Charge! The sentiment was echoed a second later. Through the smoke rose a screaming clamor of angry voices.

"*Ten'nouheika banzai!*"

"*Banzai!*"

Holy god. Too many. Way too many. There were at least two dozen of them. Their little holdout hadn't thinned the enemy numbers enough. Breath quickening, she snap-pivoted her pistol in every direction. Sweat ran down her brow as the cold realization sank in.

She had to hold off a banzai charge all on her own.

43 BANZAI

Mina swallowed hard at the pained tightness in her throat. In the years since Pearl Harbor, fear was something she had come to know well but could never get used to. And where was the damn shotgun? It was meant for close quarters like this.

Screaming voices pierced the dense smoke, yelling at the top of their lungs. Filled with rage and bloodlust, the clamor built into a cacophony. "*Korose!*" Literally, kill. "*Shori ja!*" Victory. And of course, "b*anzai!*"

The infamous term *banzai* in this context was no longer used in celebration. Here, it meant "May my sacrifice ensure that the empire endures for ten thousand years."

With her need to defend the Owl, she might as well have been tethered to the spot. Hell, she couldn't even maneuver around them or she would have. Come hell or high water, they would take that goddamn hill and reclaim their prize, and her life with it.

With a mass roar, the swarm of shadow figures surged forth, growing seemingly larger through the obscuring smoke. Faint outlines of bayonets and swords became visible, as well as humanoid silhouettes behind them. The dark specters coalesced into charging soldiers.

Snap-looking around at the onrushing men, Mina

emptied her pistol into them. Blood spurted from their throats, their faces, their chests. Too many. She backpedaled towards her cache of weapons.

In the dense smoke, near the weapons in the midst of the sandbags, she saw the shotgun Lockwood packed. She grabbed it and put it to good use. Cutting down a half dozen soldiers rushing her, Mina pumped it after each shot, blasting them one after the other.

She let the empty, smoking shotgun drop to the ground and grabbed up two submachine guns in each hand.

Dual guns blazing, she shot down twelve soldiers as they rushed in. Through the gray swirling smoke, a white-hot tracer round streaked by her like a bolt from a ray gun, singeing her cheek.

For a moment, the streaks of light steaming through the smoke reminded Mina of the Flash Gordon serials she used to watch. The hero used a ray gun to fend off hordes of Emperor Ming's troops.

Her submachine guns clicked on empty. She dropped them and grabbed Lockwood's revolver from her rear waistband. Unfortunately, in the dense smoke she didn't know where the extra shells for the shotgun were.

All around her, dark shapes stormed her position, howling with bloodlust.

An officer wearing a cap instead of a netted steel helmet rushed at her with his sword raised high -

She emptied the revolver into his torso, aiming dead center of mass, the wheelgun booming with each shot. Incredibly, the man was barely fazed, running on adrenaline alone. He was dead before he even hit the ground. His lifeless body sank to his knees even as he pitched forward, sword clang-clattering away.

The nearby radio her allies had set up crackled. An urgent male voice yelled at her. "Coral Hare! Signal your position!"

Desperate, Mina reached down and grabbed a Very pistol bundled with the Owl's harness. It was a breech-loading, single-shot flare gun.

Suddenly, one soldier charged her, screaming wildly, bayoneted-rifle ready to gore her.

As a last resort, Mina shoved the bayonet aside, jammed the flare gun into the man's eye and pulled the trigger. He screamed and flailed at the flame sparking within his eye socket. He collapsed at her feet, the area around his eye blackening, charred from the heat.

Loading another flare into the muzzle, Mina aimed the gun upwards and fired. The flare sailed upwards into the air, a blazing beacon of light arcing in the overcast sky.

Rushing out of the smoke, more screaming shadows burst forth into soldiers, bayonets ready to run her through.

She quickly slammed home a speedloader into the revolver's cylinder. Last six rounds. She aimed every which way, making every shot count, cutting them down as they rushed forth.

As her gun clicked on empty, one soldier grabbed her from behind, wrestling her to the ground.

Struggling, Mina used a jujitsu grapple to get on top. Almost straddling him, she grabbed a rock from the ground and bashed in his face with repeated hammer strikes. Looking up at her, the soldier's thoughts instantly muddied and his vision hazed red with each blow.

Winding her arm back, Mina let out one final blow, caving in the man's skull. He went limp. Drained, she let the rock drop and stood up.

In the momentary silence, the smoke dissipated. Haggard, torso heaving with her panting, Mina stood amidst the carnage. Her sailor suit uniform was ripped and torn, spattered with blood that was fortunately for the most part not her own.

Flanked from behind, boots treading almost silently, a hand held a bayonet blade down by his side.

Rain rushed forward.

Hearing rapid footfalls, Mina kicked up a submachine gun from the ground and aimed, pulling the trigger. The gun jammed.

Desperate, Mina flung the soil-caked firearm away, grappling with him in brutal hand-to-hand combat. The two traded blows, using knee-and-elbow strikes. They went for each other's throat, groin, various nerve clusters.

But he was too strong. He grabbed her by the collar with both hands, bodily hauling her off her feet and slamming her against the sandbags.

She grabbed a netted helmet from the ground and tried to smash him across the face with it. Grunting, unfazed by the blows, he grabbed her hand and pounded it against the sandbag. The impacts forced her to drop it, and he proceeded to choke the life out of her.

Vision growing hazy, colored flashes of light appeared in the air above her as she struggled for breath. Mina looked around for something, anything. She saw a glint of steel of the corner of her eye.

The Barber's straight razor.

It protruded from the dead owner's pocket. Grimacing with effort, she reached out for it, hand trembling with the strain.

Her fingers caught hold. With a fluid motion she flicked out the blade and slashed Rain diagonally across the face -

Wild-eyed with blood streaming down his cheeks, Rain doubled-over and let out an inhuman howl, hands flying to his face.

A dozen or so soldiers came up behind Rain, reinforcing him. They trained firearms on her, advancing cautiously. Furious, visage streaked with gore and dirt, Rain charged her like a raging bull -

Suddenly, the soldiers were thrown back in a chatter of machine gun fire and Rain dove to the ground. The soldiers jerked and spasmed like twisted marionettes as bullets riddled their bodies.

Out in the distant sky, still on approach, the looming B-24 Liberator swooped in low. Blotting out the sun, it screamed towards Mina at over a hundred miles an hour[125].

A male voice screamed over the crackling radio. "Coral Hare, get that fucking loop in the air!"

The strafing having bought a moment's respite, Mina twisted the knob on the green helium tank affixed to the Owl's harness. With a hiss of compressed gas, the tank inflated the attached balloon. The man-height balloon went up into the air, its cord going taut.

Like a guardian angel, the plane streaked down, and the pickup hook...caught hold of the balloon.

The harness snapped taut above her head and she felt her feet lift off. The black-painted plane took off at a steep, near vertical climb to avoid dragging Mina and her unwilling passenger along the ground.

Lifting into the sky, her stomach dropped at the intense acceleration and she felt herself grow heavy. Swaying to-and-fro like a pendulum being hauled off, she felt vaguely sick to her stomach.

Aloft, she gazed down at the receding ground. Men rushed to help Rain, and they shrank to the size of toy soldiers.

Down on the ground, anger boiling inside him, Rain rose to his feet.

Running up behind Rain, four soldiers took up firing positions. Two in front took a knee, firing up at the air at the receding plane uselessly.

Rain shook his fist in the air at her. Livid, screaming obscenities, he tore off his officer's cap and flung it to the ground in intolerable frustration.

"Coral Hare! I will hunt you down and skin you alive! I will butcher and eat your children! I shall turn your ovaries into a fucking necklace!"

One of the sergeants tried to assuage him. "*Taisa-dono*. Please!"

Implacable, Rain let out a string of insults and curses

---

[125] 130-mph for Fulton extraction.

and punched the man in the face, sending him sprawling.

The surrounding men backed off and shied away, intimidated. Furious, Rain pulled his sidearm and shot one of his own men. Gasping, the soldiers turned and started running away.

Fearful, one young private ran off down the hill, glancing over his shoulder in fear of his own commanding officer who still seethed with rage.

Palm trees dotted the shoreline near the American base on the Pacific island. The stars-and-stripes flew overhead on the flag post, fluttering in the wind.

Palm trees dotted the flanks of the runway. As soon as the Liberator touched down, two burly Marines hauled the disheveled-looking Owl away.

Mina gingerly disembarked, descending the stairs. She suddenly teetered on her feet. Her head swam and the tropical sun seemed to spin above her.

She grabbed the hand railing – then promptly doubled over and vomited, gushing out a splashing brown puddle at her feet. Pitching forward, she collapsed like a deflating balloon and sprawled onto the tarmac.

44 SHRAPNEL

On the tarmac, several conversing medical staff in white lab coats saw Mina collapse and rushed to her side. Grimly urgent, they lifted her limp form onto a wheeled stretcher and rolled her away.

Nearly naked, Mina lay unconscious on her belly on the hospital bed. There was only ragged red skin on her bare back where the golf-ball-sized blisters had been. The white linen sheet barely covered her buttocks, pulled down to facilitate access by the medical staff.

Groggily, Mina stirred. She winced as the rubber-gloved nurse swabbed mercurochrome onto the burns. Bleary-eyed, Mina stared distantly out into space. After the adrenaline from the hilltop battle drained from her body, only the pain remained, and she ached all over.

Sighing, eyes flicking back with some semblance of life, Mina scratched her head -

And stared at the clump of ebon hair in her hand that fell out.

Hours later, Lockwood held Mina's hand in a tight comforting grip. Sitting in a chair by her bedside, Lockwood lent what support he could as doctors and nurses continued working on her bare back.

Mina winced. Using a pair of forceps, the doctor's rubber-gloved hands gingerly plucked out glass shrapnel.

Trying to keep her distracted from the pain, Lockwood spoke. "I went to visit your mother in Honolulu a little while back."

Mina was mildly surprised. He hadn't told her. "Is she okay?"

"Doing fine, but she misses you. She still thinks you're a nurse in a military hospital in the Philippines."[126]

Mina nodded. It was a necessary lie. But at least this way her mother wouldn't worry about her as much.

"I baked her some of that pineapple-upside down cake she loves so much," he said. One of the nice odd things she found about Lockwood over the years was his deftness with making pastries.

Mildly concerned at the comment, Mina was taken aback. "Where'd you get the sugar? It must have cost a small fortune, with the rationing."

Lockwood made a dismissive wave. "It's nothing, don't worry about it. You're practically family."

The windowed double doors off to the side opened. A balding, bespectacled doctor in a lab coat entered, a scholarly-looking white man.

Lockwood looked up at the physician, registering his arrival. "Mina, this doctor's been working with the Manhattan Project on radiation projections. You can tell him anything."

Feeling disoriented and lightheaded, Mina gave a faint nod.

Lockwood gave her a gentle double pat on the hand and stood up, hobbling away.

Looking up, Mina smiled wanly at the doctor. His disposition was so warm and gentle she nicknamed him "Hearth." Doctor Hearth approached. "Hello Captain. I hope

---

[126] Major fighting in the Philippines ceased around March 1945, about a month prior to when this scene takes place.

you - Good Lord!"

His eyes widened in shock, dismay crossing his face as he got closer to Mina. His eyes fixated on the multitude of scars on her back, still visible under the mass of newly reddened flesh. Bullet wounds, stab wounds, even bite marks. In particular, he saw a nasty star-shaped scar from an exit wound. A bayonet, he guessed, that pierced her front and all the way to her back.

"I've never seen anyone with such scars!" he exclaimed.

He perused her file, taking a moment to adjust his glasses, not sure if he was reading it right. His voice filled with quiet dismay. "It says here you've been beaten, shot, stabbed, flogged, bludgeoned, burned, blasted, bitten, poisoned, half-drowned, and just about everything else that's nasty under the sun. And then some," he said, rattling off a list of afflictions she had accrued over the last three years.

He turned the page. Peering at the file, he adjusted his glasses again, blinking in near-disbelief. "And it says here you just survived an atomic bomb! Good Lord, I thought Lockwood was joking!"

Mina let out a pained grumble. She flopped her head down on the bed and closed her eyes, too exhausted to speak.

In the mid-afternoon, Lockwood sat in a chair next to Mina's bed, maintaining his silent vigil since the doctor's visit.

The staff worked over Mina's unconscious form, treating her burns and multitude of other injuries. The bookish doctor glanced over at Lockwood.

"You don't have to stay, you know," he said to Lockwood. "I'll call you when she's awake."

Quietly concerned, Lockwood stubbed out another cigarette in the glass ashtray on the nightstand. "I prefer to stay. Make sure she's ok."

The doctor shrugged. "Suit yourself," the physician said.

Lockwood glanced over at Mina, worry creasing his

brow. With his hand, he brushed stray strands of hair from her face. He bent over her and placed a gentle kiss on her forehead. "Hang in there Mina-chan," he whispered softly

He sat back down and stubbed a second cigarette into the ashtray, its gray smoke curling towards the ceiling.

45 SILENT VIGIL

The ashtray was now lit by pale moonlight. Stubs from two dozen cigarettes littered the ash-coated bottom, smoke still curling from the most recent one.

Asleep, Lockwood sat in his chair next to Mina's bed, head resting on his chest.

The doctor placed a gentle hand on Lockwood's shoulder, rousing him. The physician beckoned and Lockwood got to his feet, hobbling out almost silently.

From out in the hallway, Mina was visible through the window in the door, face lit by pale moonlight.

Mina's physician silently exited into the hallway, trailed by Lockwood. The good doctor closed the door soundlessly, not wanting to interrupt Mina's rest.

The doctor and Lockwood walked down the hall, Lockwood tottering on his cane.

Lockwood finally spoke up. "Will she live?"

"Yes, but it will take time for her to recover."

Lockwood let out a small sigh of relief and his shoulders slumped slightly.

"How long until she can fight?"

The doctor suppressed a chuckle. "Are you kidding? She just survived an atomic bomb! Her fighting days are over!"

46 OVER

Lockwood wasn't sure how to respond. For a moment, his braced leg trembled. As an afterthought, he guessed it was a sympathetic response.

After a moment, Lockwood felt secretly pleased. Relief flooded his body. Mina could go home. She had more than done her duty and she was out of the fight. He wouldn't have to wait up at night, waiting anxiously for her to report in, wondering if she were still alive. Was she being shot at? Was she lying dead in a ditch? Was someone ripping out her fingernails? He could rest assured Mina spent the rest of the war recuperating, sitting on the porch, watching the tide come in at sunset.

On the other hand, she wouldn't be happy about this. Lockwood sighed. "Are you certain?" he asked glumly.

The doctor took a moment to construct a response, speaking slowly. "Colonel Lockwood, I'm sorry, but there is only so much medical science can do. We are only just beginning to understand the basics of radiation poisoning, mostly from X-Ray overexposure. This is something on a different scale."

Morose, Lockwood nodded.

"She will live, Colonel, but I doubt she will ever fight

again," said the doctor.

Lockwood sighed in resignation, his expression turning haggard and weary.

Dressed in a hospital gown, Mina stood in the military hospital's patient room. She wobbled unsteadily on the single crutch, using her left hand to prop herself up. Her right hand was in a sling. An X-Ray had revealed a hairline fracture and the doctor had thought it best to let it heal.

Mina winced at the throbbing ache in her skull. Her head was bandaged due to the multiple blows received during her trip to Korea. There were at least two serious ones she could remember; one from Rain's hammer fist that knocked her unconscious, then another from the interrogation room when her chair knocked over. The physician's examination said she would recover but needed time.

There was a gentle knock at the door.

"Come in," she called.

Not too surprisingly, Lockwood hobbled in. But he was accompanied by someone Mina didn't expect. There was a rather timid Japanese-looking girl about the same age as her that Mina didn't recognize.

Surprise crossed Mina's face a second time when she saw another figure stand in the doorway. A familiar, mustached British man wearing a green Royal Commando beret. It was Ravencroft, her old drill instructor. Mina recalled his cultured London accent and his tough but fair training.

Taken aback, Mina glanced at Lockwood. He shifted uncomfortably, fidgeting with his lighter. "Mina..." he started slowly, "This is Pearl." He rested a hand on the new girl's shoulder. "She's here to be your replacement. You've fought long and hard. You've earned your honorable discharge. Go home."

Mina had expected the conversation to be a simple morale-boosting maneuver, but she hadn't been expecting this. Not really. Sitting around, she would wither away and inwardly die. If she had wanted to sit at a desk for the rest of the war, she'd have stuck with translation.

Mina turned to Pearl, speaking in a low tone. "I need to talk with the Colonel in private. Could you please wait outside? I think Ravencroft could use a sparring partner."

Pearl nodded assent and left, closing the door behind her with a loud click.

Left alone with Lockwood, Mina's voice took on a resolute, hard edge. "Jim. Just gimme three weeks. I'll be fine."

"I don't think we have three weeks. We need someone in the field," responded Lockwood.

Mina grew sullen. "Is she even cut out for this?"

"Maybe, maybe not. Did you know she's a damn strong swimmer? She's descended from a family of Ama pearl divers."

Mina made a dismissive wave of her hand. "Yes yes. I know who they are. Can hold their breathe for an insanely long time and swim like a fish and all that. I know, I know."

Lockwood shrugged helplessly. "She passed all her marks. Did decently in combat training."

Mina looked out the window.

Outside, on the palm tree lined beach, Pearl sparred with Ravencroft hand-to-hand, using knee-and-elbow strikes, fast and furious.

Through the glass, Mina saw Ravencroft pummel her, driving her back in a flurry of blows almost too fast to follow. Unable to block that quickly, Pearl backpedaled, stumbled, and Ravencroft used a sweeping kick to knock Pearl's legs out from under her and jabbed his fist an inch away from her face. Had it been for real, Pearl would be unconscious or dead.

Turning from the window, Mina yelled at Lockwood in angry protest, pointing outside. "Look at her! She's too green! She'll get herself killed!"

At this Lockwood fell silent. After a moment, he spoke with quiet concern.

"I thought so too."

For a moment, Mina sat quietly on the edge of the bed in reflective deliberation.

Then, she pulled off the bandage on her head as well as the sling from her arm. She propped the single crutch against the wall. Shakily, she rose to her feet and shuffled her way towards the door.

Saying nothing, Lockwood watched her curiously. If there was anything about his little trooper, it was she never gave up.

Mina turned the knob and opened the door a crack before speaking over her shoulder.

"Two weeks. I'll be fine."

She staggered out of the room.

TWO WEEKS LATER

At the shoreline, Mina stood with her back to the beach. She shrugged off the towel draped about her shoulders, revealing a mass of circular white scars on her back just beginning to heal. Scars upon scars. After much cajoling, the doctor had cleared her for duty, with the caveat she avoid strenuous activity for the time being. Technically, she wasn't even healed yet; she was walking wounded.

She was attired in a black two-piece swimsuit. She stretched her arms up and grimaced at the twinge of pain. She clamped a hand to her shoulder. Her arm was painfully stiff. She gently rotated her arm.

Dipping her foot in the waves, Mina eased herself into the water.

Slowly, hesitantly, she swam out in a slow crawl. Her muscles ached and she feared she would tear something.

In mid-stroke, she felt a sudden twinge in her ankle and she stopped, inhaling a mouthful of water by mistake. She stood up in the shallow water and put her hands to her side, sputtering. Her ribs still ached. Damnit. But at least she was getting better. She started wading back to shore.

Mina glanced down the shoreline and saw a male figure in a Panama hat hobbling her way, cane in hand. She smiled at him, about to comment on her progress.

Lockwood looked preoccupied, and jabbed his cane in

the direction of her feet.

"Don't worry about swimming right now," he said.

The smile faded from Mina's face.

"What's wrong?"

47 A SPOT OF TEA

In the briefing room, there were photos taped to the chalkboard. Diagrams. Slightly-singed blueprints with bullet holes and a few spatters of blood. Japanese writing.

Dressed in a man's white tank top and olive drab military trousers, hair in ponytail, Mina walked in and approached the officials gathered around the chalkboard. Ravencroft glanced up. Sometime in the last few years he had gone from drill instructor back out into the field.

One of the other men was Hearth, the doctor from the Manhattan Project. He addressed Mina. "The good news is, the data you retrieved helped us make several major improvements to our trigger mechanism. Good work."

Lockwood spoke up. "The bad news is, we're not sure where Tojo is getting their uranium from. The test you err, 'witnessed' in Korea was not expected."

Mina wondered out loud, curiosity tingeing her voice. "I was wondering how the Japanese got so much uranium. They didn't process it all on their own."

Ravencroft spoke up. "The krauts are giving their uranium - I mean, err, 'apples' to Tojo because their own facilities are bombed out of commission. Figured the Japanese could make better use of it.

Lockwood nodded. "We get rid of the apples, no more apple pies to worry about."

Mina voiced her thoughts. "Ok, so Farmer Fritz is giving apples to Baker Tojo. But by what route? How?" she chirped.

Deep in thought, Ravencroft mulled it over for a moment. His eyes went cold. Speaking, his London-tinged inflection turned into steel.

"Let me talk to the Owl."

The interrogation cell on the American Pacific base was dingy and dimly lit, not unlike the one Mina had been locked in at Korea. Only this time, strapped to the chair was the Owl, bound and gagged.

His white lab coat was torn, grimy with dirt. His button-down dress shirt was rumpled. Exhausted, he sat limply in the chair, head slumped to his chest. His mouth and chin were coated with a greasy five-o'clock shadow.

On the table next to him was a wide metal tray with an array of implements. Pliers. A claw hammer. Pins and needles. Nails. A teapot, a pitcher of water, and a neatly folded square of black silk. Various vials filled with different truth serums. A few syringes.

There was a metallic creak as the door swung open. The noise roused him, and he looked up.

A pigtailed, petite feminine figure stood silhouetted against the yellow light of the doorway.

Fear coursed through his veins. Oh no no. He was hoping he would be questioned by more of the Allied atomic scientists, but this was far, far worse.

As Mina entered, the door swung shut behind her with a note of finality. Dressed in her sailor suit outfit, she stood before him, disconcertingly all bright-eyed and bushy-tailed.

Falsely coquettish, Mina put a hand to her mouth in a coy giggle. Lockwood and the others were quietly turning a blind eye to this little...intensive questioning session.

"My my, how the tables have turned," she remarked

coolly.

The Owl felt himself begin to sweat as she approached. Her tone and demeanor was disturbingly chipper.

"Sorry, our good friend the limey couldn't come see you today. *I'm* here instead!"

Facing him, she hopped onto his lap. Straddling his body with her legs, she ran her hands on his thighs like a licentious lover. She batted her long eyelashes at him with deliberately pretentious affection.

"And I owe you, so, so much!" she snickered, dropping the pretense for a moment. She picked up a pair of pliers from the table.

She pumped the handle of the pliers, mawing the jaws open-and-shut in front of his eyes.

"Let's see, what toys shall we play with? Perhaps, these?" she proposed.

She set the pliers aside, picking up a simple corkscrew used for opening wine bottles. Only here it had other uses.

He let out a series of muffled screams as he saw it, panic and fear overtaking his body. Mina could feel his muscles tense and cord beneath her. Good. Of the many things she learned during OSS training, interrogation and reading prisoner behavior was among them.

Her voice dripped with syrupy sarcasm. "Oh my gosh. Where are my manners? You must be thirsty after our long trip." She affected a false British accent. "Perhaps you'd care for a spot of tea?"

She slapped the black cloth over his face and poured a stream of yellow fluid over it, gripping him by the chin.

She glanced down. Glugging, choking, he twisted his head to either side, trying to break her grip as water soaked the cloth. The liquid splashed and spattered about them and she heard him gasp for air. His clenched fists strained at their bonds, trembling with effort.

Mina finally relented, taking the teapot and cloth away. He turned his head to the side, choking and coughing up gobs of fluid onto the floor. Mock disappointment filled her voice.

"Awww, no tea party? Okie okie, let's do something else."

The Owl let out a muffled sob. Mina glanced down. A dark wet stain spread from his groin.

Instead of showing disgust, her voice dripped with false sympathy as she ignored the warm dampness.

"Aww. Poor widdle evil genius pissed his pants."

She spoke brightly, tone chipper.

"It's ok. I don't mind golden showers."

He shook his head vehemently in near panic that looked almost comical. Mina adopted a cheerful tone.

"Hmm. Maybe these?"

On the table was a car battery with plier-like clamps attached by cable to either polar end.

Grinning, Mina picked up the two clamps in either hand, touching the ends together. Bright sparks flew accompanied by an intimidatingly loud *bzzaat.*

Gagged, the Owl let out a wide-eyed muffled yell of protest. Cold sweat beaded his forehead as his eyes flicked back and forth. He shook his head vehemently, eyes growing larger and larger.

Seemingly not noticing his distraught protests, Mina eagerly tore open the front of his dress shirt, popping off buttons. She ran her hands up and down his bare chest seductively.

Mina glanced at the table, her eyes sparkling with wide-eyed anticipation. "Ooh!" She gushed. "This is my favorite!"

Smiling with malicious glee, she held a floppy black dildo well over a foot long.

Down the hall, his screams echoed throughout the night.

Still dressed in her sailor suit outfit, Mina walked into the conference room with diagrams and maps pinned up. Half-asleep over a mug of cold coffee, a bleary-eyed Lockwood looked up.

"Did you get anything from the Owl?" he inquired.

Mina pointed to the map of the Pacific Ocean on the table. Her index finger traced a route. "There are several German U-Boats en route to deliver uranium to the Japanese. From there, the bomb will be assembled and be deployed to God knows where," she stated simply.

Lockwood was instantly on alert, his exhaustion forgotten.

"That route actually passes by not too far from here. We can intercept them ourselves. When will they be in the area?"

"Fourteen-hundred hours[127] tomorrow," Mina replied.

Consternated, Lockwood checked his watch - then braced his cane, rising to his feet. "That's only sixteen hours from now!"

Mina was already rushing out the door. "Well c'mon, let's go!"

---

[127] During World War II, U.S. forces near operating areas used local time for orders and reports. At the command level, Greenwich Mean Time was used because oftentimes operations spanned multiple time zones. Hawaii had its own special time zone due to its location. The Japanese military used Tokyo Time.

48 CARGO TO DIE FOR

April 24, 1945

Out in the waters of the Pacific Ocean, a massive geyser of foaming water erupted over the spot where the depth charge dropped.

The nearby Allied flotilla of four destroyers encroached on its position, swarming in for the kill.

The closest ship was the *USS Collett*, an Allen M. Sumner class destroyer. Sailing on, the racks at the ship's stern prepped another barrel-shaped charge. The charge rolled off the rails into the water.

Beneath the waves, the sinking charge exploded in a radial fiery blast, a spherical-shell of momentary flame and overpressure in the blue depths.

Tense, anxious, the German submarine crew inside the U-Boat looked up as another rumbling explosion rattled their surroundings. Two of the men on the bridge were not of Germanic descent. Wearing Imperial Japanese Navy uniforms, there were two Japanese envoys onboard, waiting in quiet agitation along with everyone else.

There was a distant rumble of explosions through the hull - then another one nerve-wrackingly close.

The cramped ship rocked to and fro and the crew braced themselves for impact, swaying on their feet as rumbling explosions sent tremors through the deck. Leaks burst into existence all around them, spraying water everywhere. The hanging overhead lamps swayed amidst the metallic creaking of the hull, and control panels emitted a shower of sparks from short-circuiting electronics. The lights flickered, died, then glowed back into existence.

An incessant spew of water from a leak overhead sprayed the captain in the face. He bellowed an order in German.

"Get to the escape hatch!"

Sopping wet from the overhead leaks, a crewman ran up through the narrow surroundings. He yelled over the rush of water and rumbling explosions. "We just tried! It's jammed! A depth charge must have warped the metal!"

The skipper scowled, trying to think of options. Nearby, one of the Japanese envoys spoke to him in terse German. "Jettison the uranium."

Nearby, the first mate made a plea to his skipper in plaintive German. "Captain. Please, just surrender to the Americans. Plead for clemency. The Russians are already in Berlin. The war is all but over for Germany."

The Japanese envoy who had spoken scowled. "But not for Japan," he said.

The other Japanese envoy, a man with a mustache, gave a hardliner's curt response.

"Just sink this fucking ship."

Nearby, the German submarine crew exchanged concerned glances. As had been said, the war was all but over for the Germans; all they wanted was to go home.

Musing it over for a tense moment, the captain responded. "I have a better idea."

Onboard the bridge of the American destroyer, Mina

stood tensely with Lockwood and the captain as they awaited the hydrophone operator's response. She wore her brown Army uniform, no headgear, raven hair tied in a practical ponytail.

The hydrophone operator with headphones on his head turned in his chair and spoke to them. "Sounds of decompression. They're surfacing."

Under the water, with torrents of giant bubbles rising about them, the U-Boat rose through the sea.

Some ten minutes later, the rubber boat[128] carrying Mina, Lockwood, the *Collett*'s first mate, and seven burly Marines headed their way towards the surfaced U-Boat.

Standing stiffly, the U-Boat crew stood assembled on the deck of their submarine. Disgruntled, the *Kriegsmarine* sailors muttered amongst themselves as Mina and the others boarded.

Glaring at the Americans, the two Japanese envoys stood next to the U-Boat skipper. Given that Mina spoke both German and Japanese, she jogged up to speak with them instead of the ship's first mate. This was simple translation work, not combat. Lockwood stayed a bit further back because of his bum leg.

As Mina approached the U-Boat captain, the Japanese envoys suddenly pulled grenades from behind their backs and yanked the pins.

"*Ten'nouheika banzai!*" one yelled, screaming the war cry as the German crew hit the deck.

Fierce determination on her face, Mina dashed up and shoved each of their chests at the same time -

Propelled from the deck of the U-Boat, the Japanese envoys arced into the water, arms and legs involuntarily pinwheeling -

The resounding explosion sent a frothy spray onto the

---

[128] A LCRL rubber raiding boat.

deck and the sailors cringed as scarlet-tinged water splashed onto them.

Everyone that hit the deck got shakily to their feet. Disturbed by what he had just seen, the grizzled German skipper peered over the water at the bloody ocean foam, muttering.

"*Mein Gott in Himmel.*" My God in Heaven. Mina glared at the captain, her tone accusatory as she spoke in German.

"You'd better not have known he was going to do that."

The weary-looking man shook his head vehemently. "*Nein nein.* But I am not surprised."

Mina pressed. "Are there any more U-Boats with orders like yours?"

The U-Boat captain protested, open hands outstretched. "How would I know? I know only *my* orders. I was to deliver my cargo to the Japanese."

"What was the cargo?"

The U-Boat skipper fell silent, not responding.

Glowering at the man, Mina chained the hatch open to keep the submarine from diving. She tugged it to make sure it would hold. Nice and sturdy.

"Alright *Mein Kapitan.* I've chained the hatch so you can't dive. Now we're gonna see for ourselves what your cargo is."

She and Lockwood climbed belowdecks, followed closely by the U-Boat captain.

The forms on the clipboard in Mina's hand were marked with Nazi Germany's eagle atop the swastika, the bird's wings swept to either side. Standing in the cargo hold of the U-Boat, Mina glanced at the wooden crates stacked before her.

Behind her, several of the *USS Collett's* marines carried out a few of the wooden crates stamped with Nazi insignia.

Going to the intercom at the bulkhead, Mina slammed her fist on the button and spoke to the bridge.

"Papa Bear, they got apples here."

Lockwood's voice crackled over the speaker. Nearby, the marines hauled off the last few crates.

"What kind of apples? That's important."

Mina spoke slowly and deliberately, trepidation in her voice. "The apples have already been cored. Looks like they're ready to bake. About thirteen kilos. We're carrying the last crate out now."

Up on the U-Boat bridge, a stunned expression crossed Lockwood's face. Thirteen kilograms was significant. It was roughly one-fifth the enriched uranium needed for a working atomic bomb, and could greatly accelerate Japan's timeline.

Standing nearby and listening to the conversation, the U-Boat captain yanked down on the dive lever. The ship's diving alarm sounded with a series of *ahoo-ga* sounds. Forcing the ship to dive while the hatch was chained open, the ship started to flood. With a sharp yank, the captain broke off the lever and tossed it aside, preventing others from surfacing the ship that way.

Lockwood shouted at him in disbelief and consternation. "That's insane! You'll kill us all!"

The U-Boat captain responded in guttural English. "My men wanted to go home. But my orders were to follow the Japanese who wanted to sink the ship. I am doing both."

Scrambling, the captain climbed up through the hatch, Lockwood following suit as best he could on his leg.

Up on the deck of the U-Boat, surprised and alarmed, the German sailors started to jump overboard into the waves as the ship started to sink right under their feet.

Mina was still belowdecks in the cargo hold. Suddenly, the deck lurched beneath her feet and she teetered back for a moment as she struggled to regain her balance. Back on solid footing, she whirled every which way as the lighting snapped to flashing crimson and the klaxon blared loud *ahoo-ga* wails.

From the entry to the next cabin, water started to flow in on the decks. It pooling around her feet, starting to fill the chamber. The water was already up to her ankles and continued gushing in. Through the bulkhead walls she could already hear the hull start to creak.

A sudden waist-high torrent of water gushed into the cabin, soaking her and leaving her hair sopping wet. Terror flooded her and Mina looked every which way in wide-eyed abject fear.

"No. No! Nonono! Not like this!"

It was her worst nightmare come to life. She was reminded of almost drowning all those years ago - the surf, the undertow dragging her under, desperately trying to surface but the current pulled her back underwater.

Desperate, she tried to wade her way towards the hatch to escape, but the torrent of incoming water was too strong, forcing her back. Pushing against the hatch door, her feet struggled for purchase on the wet slippery deck. She tried to swing the door shut, but the current tore her away.

Propelled backwards, she slammed into the opposite bulkhead and collapsed, floating facedown. Her prone form bobbed up and down as water continued to flood the sinking ship.

49 SINKING

Out in the seas where the U-Boat had been a mere minute before, the water churned to a froth as the multitude of German sailors clamored. They swam away from the doomed submarine, yelling for help. Nearby, ten rubber boats from the American destroyer sailed toward the stranded sailors, some of whom swam, others treaded water.

Nearby, onboard the initial rubber boat, a consternated Lockwood turned to the destroyer's first mate. Lockwood pointed to the receding, shadowy U-Boat beneath the waves.

"Mina's still in there!" he shouted.

Inside the U-Boat's flooding cargo hold, Mina floated facedown, bobbing.

She awakened with a gasp, choking, spitting out gobs of water, standing in the knee-high rising flood. She didn't know how long she had been unconscious but surmised it had been less than a minute, given the water level.

Frantic, her breathing quickened and she failed to subdue the panic welling deep inside her. She had to get out soon.

In a splashing run, she went down the corridor. In a

moment of opportunity she ducked into the captain's quarters. She hadn't had a chance to do so earlier. On the desk there were some documents in German and a marked map of the Pacific Ocean. The noncompliant crew hadn't bothered to help dispose of them before they were boarded. She hurriedly stuffed them into her pockets and waded out of the cabin.

The rising water was at her thighs, making progress difficult as she half-waded, half-ran through the empty ship's corridor. All around her, the deep shuddering groan of tormented steel resonated as the submarine's hull buckled under the stress of increasing water pressure. Already damaged by depth charges from earlier, deep moans of bending steel reverberated under her feet as the ship started to crumple like a tin can.

In the U-Boat's engine room, amidst the garish crimson lights, the water level rose. Leaks popped into existence on the overhead ceiling, some dripping, some spraying. Rows of boxy batteries lined either side of the narrow cabin, some of their casings cracked by the depth charge attack.

The rising seawater started seeping into the rows of batteries. Sparks erupted, and there was a fizzling sound. A pale, yellow-green gas spewed forth from the batteries, filling the air with a chartreuse haze.

A deck away, Mina choked as the air around her suffused with gas, encasing her in a lime-green fog that became denser and denser. She coughed at the corrosive burning in her lungs and doubled over, retching. Her eyes stung, welling with tears. Alarmed, her panic reached new heights as she realized what happened. Common on depth-charge stricken submarines, water seeped into the ship's batteries, forming toxic chlorine gas.

Heavier than air, the nyanza-toned gas accumulated on the deck. There was a groaning of metal as the entire deck started to list. Its angle tilted as one side of the ship started to flood faster than the other. Scrabbling, Mina climbed up the water-slicked slope, trying to escape the gas. Not only was the ship sinking, it was now filling with poison gas and sloping at an incline.

She coughed as the chlorine seared her lungs. The stinging pain in her eyes grew worse and they began to water. Mina remembered the same kind of gas was used during the Great War as a chemical weapon. More tears welled up and her vision became blurry, making it difficult to see more than a few feet ahead.

Through the haze, she looked around at the walls, the rushing water, to see if any Drager apparatuses were hung on hooks or floating by. Standard on German U-Boats, the rebreather looked like a beige life vest with attached mask. In the poisonous air and outside the sub, it could be a lifesaver. There were none in the vicinity she could see.

Desperately trying to quell her fear, she waded through the water, trying to find the escape hatch before she could be entombed in the metal shell.

Down the confines of the waterlogged ship, she found the escape hatch in an adjacent passage. She looked up. Protruding from the ceiling was giant tube, a cylindrical entrance with a ladder leading upwards. The U-Boat's lockout trunk accommodated four to five men and some gear. She pulled the nearby lever to flood the trunk and equalize the pressure so she could get out.

Hair sopping wet about her shoulders, water rising about her, Mina twisted the hatch wheel and pulled, straining. She tried again, gritting her teeth, hauling back with all her strength. Odd. The water pressure outside and here should be roughly equal because of the open hatch. She shouldn't have this much trouble opening it.

Then she realized it was probably damaged during the assault by the destroyers. Amidst the now waist-high rushing water, she peered up into the cylindrical tube. The metal around the hatch was twisted and warped. Cursing, she muttered to herself.

"Goddamn charges. Jammed the escape hatch."

She banged on the tube's ladder with her fist futilely. Her mind raced. She was no submariner but she knew U-Boats had a conning tower hatch and forward utility hatch, among other exits.

All around her, bulkheads shuddered, emitting a tremulous groaning of metal. There was another screech of warping steel as the submarine's hull buckled. There wasn't much time left.

She paddled back out into the corridor towards the conning tower. Water up to her shoulders now, Mina half-swam, half waded towards the conning tower.

By now, the combination of water pressure and hull damage started to take its toll. Nearby, the bulkheads bulged at the seams, letting out metallic moans. Rivets on the bulkheads popped off as panels burst and water gushed in. Seeing this, Mina hurried on, with fear on her face and a cold lump in her throat. To make matters worse, the increase in pressure caused the water to heat near boiling. With the heat on her skin, it was getting more and more difficult to paddle onwards.

The lime-green gas pervaded the corridor and Mina let out a hacking cough. Half swimming through the rising water, no longer able to wade, she swam higher to escape the suffocating gas.

Couldn't go that way. Even if she could reach the hatches there, the air wasn't pure enough for her to hold her breath long. As she passed through the ship she continually looked for a Drager breathing mask, but there were none in sight. They had probably been swept away by the current or stuck in other cabins.

Save for a few inches of air between the water and the ceiling, the compartments were almost completely flooded. She paused for a moment to breathe at the water's surface, sucking in air, her lips kissing distance from the ceiling.

There were few other options. Frantic, so tense her

heart felt like it pounded in her throat, she dove back underwater. She turned back, struggling to swim towards what she dreaded not too long ago - the torpedo bay.

She managed to swim to the starboard torpedo bay that was only partially flooded. Up here, given the tilt of the sinking ship, the water was only to her ankles. The whole room was canted.

Always on the lookout for a breathing mask, there were none found and no time to search for one. She knew she was a poor swimmer; there was no way she could delay further and still swim to the surface while holding her breath for that long. Her personal limit was only about two minutes; rather terrible considering human average was about 3 to 4. Not to mention she had barely passed the water exam back at training, and that was only because Lockwood fudged her paperwork for her. No choice. She had to leave now or die.

Suddenly, the lights in the cabin flickered and died, and the compartment was plunged into darkness. A moment later the lights resumed.

Hurrying, from the submerged deck she grabbed a chain used to secure equipment. She tied it to the firing lever of the torpedo tube and dragged the chain behind her.

Hands shaking with adrenaline, she tore open the breech of the torpedo tube and climbed inside, shutting it behind her.

Inside the claustrophobic, coffin-like confines, Mina frantically twisted the interior valve, manually flooding the enclosure. Completely submerged, she yanked the chain -

In the torpedo bay, the chain attached to the firing lever went taut as the lever flipped -

Outside the sinking, listing U-Boat, Mina blasted out in a torrent of bubbles, ejected out with such force it left her battered, bruised, and aching all over.

She swam upwards through the rising debris and oil bubbles. The silhouette of a petite girl with flowing hair swam among the murky blue waters and buoyant debris. A half-empty jar of sauerkraut floated by her as well as a tin of tobacco.

Soon came the dull ache in her lungs, the tickling desire to inhale, along with residual sting from the gas. She quelled them.

Doing a rough estimate, she guessed she ejected from the dying U-Boat at a depth of about 50 meters. In order to safely surface without experiencing decompression sickness, she could ascend no more than 10 meters per minute. In all, it meant she had to hold her breathe for about five minutes - well past her personal record.

Disoriented, she felt a sense of vertigo and glanced up. She followed the oily black globules floating towards the surface. She let a few tiny bubbles escape the corner of her mouth and she felt some relief in her chest as she expelled the spent air. She continued to ascend, careful not to exceed the speed of her bubbles, or she'd risk permanent injury.

Then came the dual burning sensation in her lungs, as if they were on fire. People usually don't feel the existence of their internal organs, unless they are ill or something else is wrong. Right now she was acutely aware of her lungs as they felt like twin coals in her chest, struggling to burst out.

The muscles in her chest and abdomen shuddered, starved for air. Frantic, Mina looked up. The water around her grew clearer and just oh-so brighter. She was closer to the surface. Just a little bit more, just a little more.

Her whole body trembled and quaked with effort and she felt her cheeks bulge with strain. Oh, screw the bends. Better to be permanently disabled than dead.

She kicked her legs and swept her arms upwards, accelerating her ascent dangerously. So close, oh so close. She could see floating debris ahead of her. There was a near-empty bottle of schnapps and a man's smoking pipe, the sun dappled waves not too far ahead. Her field of vision suddenly turned crimson as the capillaries in her eyes burst with the shift in pressure.

Suddenly, the muscles in her chest and abdomen

spasmed violently...and she simply couldn't hold it in anymore.

The muscles in her abdomen and throat gave way.

In her field of vision, a massive torrent of bubbles erupted forth, spewing from her mouth, her nose. What shocked her was that the large bubbles just wouldn't stop coming. They kept on gushing forth, almost incessantly, for a surprising number of seconds that she dimly thought would have stopped long ago. Instead of her past, her unfulfilled prospects flashed across her mind. She'd never go to high school prom. She's never see the palm trees of Hawaii again. She'd never walk down the aisle, or have kids.

Then, finally, the bubbles slowed. One final bubble escaped her lips and drifted upwards. A terrible, choking heaviness settled in her chest as seawater completely flooded her lungs.

Flailing wildly, her face a contorted mask of fierce desperation, Mina clawed at the water. She struggled to swim upwards, but with her lungs completely filled she was too heavy. A few moments later, the flailing slowed, and she sagged forward, growing limp. Her expression relaxed, turning serene, almost peaceful.

Slowly, she started to drift away, her petite form sinking among the rising oil bubbles and wreckage...and she descended down, down, down, into darkness.

50 SEEING THE WIZARD

Mired in the imbroglio of purgatory between sleep and consciousness, Mina was but a silent observer as images flitted across her mind's eye.

With a double flash and a massive boom, the roaring explosion engulfed the skyscraper skyline of New York City. Engulfed in flame, the Empire State Building blasted away, torn to bits by beyond-hurricane winds. People in the streets flash-burned to ash, collapsing to their knees even as the flesh was stripped from their bones. The hot gale wind left momentary skeletons in its wake, before those too were blown away as burning dust. Buildings flattened and turned to instant burning rubble as the great mushroom cloud rose over the ruins of the devastated city.

The Japanese army marched through the streets of Washington D.C. Lined up along the block, American businessmen in suits and fedoras, women in floral dresses, and children were held at gunpoint on their knees as soldiers marched by.

In front of the reflecting pool, the great ivory-white obelisk of the Washington monument was visible in the distance. A gallows was set up in front of the pool. Forced at gunpoint, several men were prodded up the steps to the nooses. Mina recognized the men. One was a suited older man, the second a glum general with sunglasses and his corncob pipe.

With a chop of the attendant officer's hand, the trapdoor fell out under their feet and the men dangled, legs twitching in their final moments.

Out in front of 1600 Pennsylvania Avenue, a trio of banners of the Rising Sun unfurled at the entrance of the White House. The banners' crimson rays radiated outwards, fluttering in the breeze.

Assembled in the front yard, the multitude of Japanese soldiers cheered in overjoyed merriment. Raucous exclamations burst forth in shouts of "*Banzai! Banzai! Banzai!*" May his Imperial Majesty live for ten thousand years!

Inwardly, as if from an emotional distance, Mina shivered. This was the fate that would befall her if she failed, she realized. Japanese troops would march through the streets of Washington D.C. and across the globe. Imperial Japan's dream of world domination would be realized. Her mind was a haze. Or did it already happen? Was she reliving her failure?

Suddenly, there was an odd sound, as if coming from a great distance, yet Mina knew it was close by. Oddly familiar, it was the sound of heavy, desperate panting, accompanied by the sound of lapping waves.

Choking, sputtering, Mina turned her head to her side, heaving out great gobs of water.

There was comforting warmth above her. She looked up. Lockwood's concerned face gazed down upon her.

Feeling weak, Mina sat up, coming back to her senses. Allied marines sat nearby in the rubber raft. All around them in the water, pools of black oil floated atop the waves, along with buoyant refuse. Debris from the U-Boat surfaced – bottles and cans bobbed up and down.

Lockwood rubbed her back comfortingly. "Easy there Mina, you'll be alright."

He wrapped a hot towel around her shoulders,

encasing her sopping form in welcome warmth.

Drained of all energy, Mina slumped back, letting Lockwood hold her in his arms as the marines paddled back to the destroyer.

Beyond the palm tree dotted shoreline of the American base, a single figure sped through the water. Mina swam in a fast forward-crawl type stroke.

Reaching shore, Mina splashed her way towards the familiar man with the cane and wiped the droplets from her face with both hands. It had been three days since the U-Boat incident.

Lockwood beamed at her and checked his stopwatch. "Excellent! You've been doing tremendously better since the U-Boat."

Panting, Mina bent over, hands on her knees, nodding as she caught her breath. "It showed me that you can still be revived even after almost drowning."

Lockwood looked mildly surprised. "Didn't you say your dad brought you back once when you were a kid?"

"It's different when you're a kid. Not really able to process it. At least, I wasn't. Just too scared."

He nodded at her approvingly. A thought came to him and he spoke musingly. "Maybe in the future the Navy can incorporate something similar into the U.D.T.[129] frogmen program."

Mina nodded and made a little affirmative sound. "For a moment, I felt like Dorothy in *The Wizard of Oz*. Weird dreamworld. I guess you could say I saw the wizard."[130]

---

[129] Underwater Demolition Team.

[130] Modern day Navy SEALS sometimes refer to the unusual experiences they undergo during drownproofing training as "seeing the wizard." This happens when they nearly drown and pass out during training and need to be resuscitated. Supposedly, this is not an uncommon occurrence. According to urban myths surrounding the SEAL training program, sometimes the drowning (or near-drowning)

Grinning, Lockwood ruffled her hair. "Welcome back to Kansas," he said.

Mina stretched. He jotted a few notes on his clipboard. "There's another problem. Since your cover is blown your nurse disguise won't be as useful. They know who you are now."

Mina pondered it for a moment, curled finger to her chin. "Maybe we can use that to our advantage," she suggested.

Lockwood gave her a facetious grin. "Hey, worse comes to worst, you can join the Navy."

Mina chuckled. Something came to mind and her smile faded. "Navy. Navy intercept."

Her eyes grew distant. Lockwood spoke, consternated. "Mina, what is it?" he asked.

Serious, Mina looked him in the eye.

"I need to talk to the skipper."

---

by instructors is intentional, although many sources dispute this. Ask a SEAL. ☺

51 INTO THE BRIAR PATCH

Dressed in uniform, Mina had a manila file folder tucked under her arm as she entered the conference room. She had hastily changed clothes, and now wore a limited-issue Experimental Tropical Uniform that was made of a cooling Egyptian cotton called Byrd cloth. She had been fortunate enough to be issued the item because of her OSS position.

The submarine captain from her Tokyo trip nodded in acknowledgement when he saw her. Mina mentally nicknamed Old Salt. Lockwood was already inside. With a half-dozen officers, they gathered around the central table. Upon it, a map of the Pacific spanned the table's length.

The sub captain spoke in affirmation. "Good work, agent. You cost Tojo a two month delay in deployment.

Lockwood spoke optimistically. "Additionally we can use the enriched uranium for our own. It's about a fifth of the amount needed for a full bomb. You've sped up our work greatly. We'll be conducting a test soon at Alamogordo.[131]"

Mina skipped the rest of the pleasantries. "Good to

---

[131] This refers to the Trinity test that took place at the present-day White Sands Missile Range in New Mexico, USA. It was the Allied test detonation of an implosion-design plutonium device.

hear. But there's a wrench in the works. There's something I figured out."

Mina opened up her folder and placed German documents from the U-Boat onto the table.

"I translated the documents from the U-Boat and cross-referenced the information from naval intercepts."

She took in a deep breath. "The skipper lied. There were at least two other U-Boats carrying uranium of some kind. According to navy intel, one of them, named U-234[132], is carrying a half ton of uranium oxide in ten cases."

The grizzled submarine captain looked over her shoulder, scrutinizing the document.

"That's not so bad. It'd still have to be processed."

"Yes, but the other is carrying enriched uranium," she said.

At this, the others in the room exchanged glances.

"Where is it?" Lockwood said sharply.

Mina smoothed out a map of the Pacific on the tabletop.

"They've already made it."

Murmurs of concern spread throughout the room like ripples in a pond.

Lockwood spoke in consternation. "That means their bomb is basically ready. They can launch any time."

Mina pointed at the map of the Pacific. "They're doing final assembly here-" her finger tapped a seaport city on the Indonesian island of Borneo, "-at Balikpapan. According to the documents there's a secret submarine pen there. That was their final destination. We'll have to storm the facility."

Lockwood nodded. "Our friends from down under are already planning an attack in the area. I suggest using the intervening time to properly recover and heal up. No use in going out half-cocked."

----

[132] A real-life incident. The U-Boat named U-234 (not referring to the isotope of the same name) was intercepted by the U.S. Navy on May 14, 1945.

Mina nodded. She needed to fully recuperate from her wounds.

Lockwood continued. "When the time comes, capture the Gadget if possible, destroy it if necessary," he said.

His finger stabbed the black-and-white photo of the jungle near the city. "We can airdrop you and a few Aussies behind enemy lines, here."

Mina shook her head and pointed at the shoreline.

"No. I can go in by sea. Head in with the Australian frogmen."

"Take rubber boats then swim in?" Lockwood asked. It was a common method of underwater demolition for frogmen teams.

"Naw," said Mina. "Let's be a little unorthodox. We take the underwater approach."

Mina glanced at Lockwood. Nodding approvingly, her mentor smiled at her, proud of his little protégé.

"Alright Coral Hare. Into the Briar Patch. Catch 'em by surprise."

52 BAPTISM

July 12, 1945

In the murky depths of the Pacific Ocean off the coast of Borneo, the dark silhouette of the *Tench*-class submarine slinked its way through dark blue waters.

In the prep cabin, Mina donned her outfit piece by piece. Combat diver's dry suit. Flippers. Belt pouches. Lockwood's magnum slipped into a waterproof holster. The Fairbairn-Sykes combat knife with the large blade slid into its sheath. She tucked her Y-shaped slingshot nicknamed "Lucky Charm" into her belt. All that was left was the Lambertsen rebreather, which she would don later.

Nearby, the similarly-attired leader of the frogmen whom she knew as "Boomer" tucked his namesake boomerang made out of submarine steel into his belt. Some rumors stated he was actually called "Boomer" or "Boomerang" because "he always came back," and was thus-far impossible to kill. Lockwood stood behind him, checking Boomer's gear.

Standing nearby were five other Australian frogmen. Clad in their diving gear, Mina and the others looked absolutely lethal and intimidating. The Australians were from the SRD.

Established in 1942 just three years ago, the Services Reconnaissance Department was the Australian special operations unit, modeled after the British SOE. The men and their unit had been fighting in Southeast Asia, largely behind enemy lines on reconnaissance and raiding missions.

Mina struck a dashing, almost heroic pose, one hand on her hip, geared-up frogmen arrayed on either side of her.

"Let's kick ass!" she announced.

Smiling, Lockwood snapped a photo with his camera[133], capturing the moment.

Fully geared, Mina stood in the submarine's pipe-lined torpedo bay. She was clad in a combat diver's dry suit with flippers, a full-face Lambertsen rebreather mask on her head. Standing ramrod straight, she looked like an intimidating humanoid insect. The six Australian frogmen stood nearby, performing final gear checks.

Lockwood spoke up. "The forward team already cached some supplies in a Davy Jones locker five hundred meters away."

Mina nodded. Several members of the U.S. Navy's elite U.D.T team had already gone ahead of them and cleared the way.[134]

The Old Salt sub captain turned to Mina. "Alright Coral Hare, are you ready?"

Eager and raring to go, Mina jerked her thumb up, over and over.

The captain grinned at her.

"Alright then! Flood tube three!

Mina climbed inside the open torpedo tube as her teammates did similarly. A crewman shut the hatch behind her. The sub captain banged twice on Mina's hatch with his

[133] Kodak 35.

[134] At the Battle of Balikpapan, several days prior to the actual landing, American frogmen went ahead to destroy obstacles planted by the Japanese to clear the way for landing troops.

fist. From inside the tube came two acknowledging metallic bangs. Ready.

The Old Salt let out a holler.

"Fire!"

The nearby crewman yanked the waist-high lever next to the torpedo tube.

Outside the submarine, Mina and her teammates ejected out in rapid-succession in multiple torrents of bubbles.

Gaining her bearings in the protracted slowness of the water, Mina beckoned to the others. She kicked ahead into the murky blue, propelling forward. All she could hear was the sound of her breathing within the confines of the mask, slow and steady, almost robotic[135]. She no longer feared the water, and her heart rate was actually lower than normal, borderline meditative. The frogmen followed her onwards.

After swimming for about ten minutes, they reached the Davy Jones' locker. It was essentially a submersible raft with crates of supplies held inside a net, anchored to the ocean floor. Except this time, four "Sleeping Beauty" canoes[136] were bundled with them. The canoes were motorized underwater vehicles that could help transport them to shore, saving them the swim.

Working quickly, with near-silent motions, Mina and the others freed the canoes from their netted moorings and departed. It was two men to a vehicle except for Mina, who had her own.

In the lead, Mina grasped her vehicle's handles as it propelled her the mile towards shore, and the group receded into the silent blue.

[135] Robots were already a known sci-fi staple by World War II. One popular film was the groundbreaking 1927 movie *Metropolis*.

[136] The Sleeping Beauty canoe was the forerunner of the modern Swimmer Delivery Vehicle, often seen in James Bond films and films featuring Navy SEALs.

53 TAKEDOWN

It was a quiet night along the shores of Balikpapan. There was the sound of lapping waves and chirping of insects. The reflection of the moon rippled on the surface of the water. Sentries patrolled the area around the pier.

In full-face rebreather mask, Mina's head rose out of the surface of the dark water, her companions doing similarly behind her. Intimidating, the masks gave them the appearance of malevolent insectoids. Unlike aqualung scuba gear, their rebreathers left no telltale bubbles on the surface of the water, and their approach had been undetected.

Mina's mask tilted upwards as she looked at the pier. A foot away, his back turned to her, a guard stood looking around casually.

Mina made a quick hand signal to her fellow frogmen. Creeping stealthily along the pier, they quickly got into position near the other sentries. Mina pulled out her Fairbairn-Sykes fighting knife, the one that was essentially a short sword. Adrenaline coursed through her veins as she gripped it, ready. She signaled the others, making a chopping motion with her free hand in the direction of the sentries.

Boomer's boomerang arced out, smashing a sentry in the back of the head and tearing out a chunk of his skull, the spray of blood near-black in the night. The guard collapsed as the boomerang whirred back toward the owner.

Almost at the same time, Mina rose out of the water, grasping her target's ankles and yanking him down with a splash. Her teammates did similarly with their own targets in a simultaneous takedown.

Underwater, motions slowed, Mina's target flailed wildly, bubbles streaming from his gurgling mouth. Grabbing him by the chin, with her other hand she drove her blade into the side of his neck. She shoved outward, tearing out the front of his throat, half-decapitating him. Crimson plumed into the water, like ink from an octopus except it was red. He sagged forth.

She let the guard's body go and he started to sink, weighed down by his gear. She swam the few feet upwards through the scarlet cloud and her head broke the surface.

Mina glanced around. The Australian frogmen had performed their task efficiently, setting down sagging bodies onto the sand or letting them sink beneath lapping waves.

With near-silent proficiency, Mina and the others dumped the bodies in the water with quiet splashes. No one was left around in the vicinity to hear it anyway.

With practiced speed, they planted blocks of C3 onto the moored patrol boats and piles of supply crates.

Standing with the others near the treeline of the jungle, Mina depressed the T-plunger.

The piles of supplies detonated in a roaring cascade of explosions, shaking the earth beneath her feet, heat felt on her cheeks even at this distance. Leaves rustled as animals behind them scampered or flew off, cawing. The explosion lit the night and the surrounding jungle, settling into a bonfire that would rage for hours.

Mina gestured over her shoulder to the others. Hurrying on, they raced into the jungle, disappearing into darkness.

Japanese Command Post

Tents were set up at the Japanese command post under the hot Pacific sun. Like most Pacific islands, Borneo was a sweltering jungle cesspool of mosquitoes and malaria, a muggy climate stifling beyond being simply humid. The air was filled with the sound of screeching animals and buzzing insects.

Sitting atop wooden supply crates, some of the younger Japanese soldiers engaged in banter.

A young private, rather emaciated, kept his shirt off. It was per orders to protect it from unnecessary wear-and-tear, as well as to mitigate the stifling heat. "I heard rumors. One spy dressed as a nurse took out some facility in Tokyo. She forced the project to move to Korea."

Sitting nearby, a corporal with a scar on his cheek scoffed. "Nah. I heard she wasn't even human."

Another soldier chimed in. "Oh, yes yes! I hear she is a *kappa* water spirit."

The corporal whispered. "I heard she can take human form. Become a schoolgirl."

Stern, Rain walked by and smacked him upside the head. "Quiet! Stop such talk. You're demoralizing the men. Get back to work!"

A pitched battle roared in the grassy hills just a few hours later. Down the hill, the Australian troops assaulted the position, but the Japanese were just too well dug in - and had turned the tables.

In the preceding weeks and months, entrenched positions had become concrete bunkers. Temporary lookout points had become machine gun nests. Naval bombardment from offshore hadn't done jack squat in terms of flushing them out or blasting them away. The Japanese just hunkered down and dug in deeper.

Every square inch was paid in blood. Like Okinawa just a month prior, it was a meat grinder of a battle for both the Allied forces and the Japanese. The Australians resorted to using "blowtorch and corkscrew" tactics established by their American allies on Okinawa - trying to burn out the Japanese and blast them out of hiding holes.

A chatter of machine gun fire kicked up tufts of grass and dirt. Nearby, a trio of troops from Australia's 7th Division dug in deep, praying they'd live to see another sunrise.

Inside the Japanese command tent, amidst the chaos and bustle of relayed orders, voices on the crackling radio were barely audible. There was additional din from whistling artillery and not-too-distant machine gun fire.

Standing at the map on the table, Rain pointed out a particular position with his finger, speaking to a Japanese major.

The man was reluctant. "But the high command has forbidden any more banzai charges. They are wasteful of manpower."

Scowling, Rain turned stern. "Their lines are broken. The time to strike is now."

Rain's finger tapped a conspicuous model on the map - a statuette of a Japanese submarine near the coast.

Rain's expression turned baleful. "No retreating. Or I'll cite you for disobedience of orders. We have to protect the submarine until it leaves."

Grudgingly, the officer complied and spoke into the microphone near the radio.

Out near the front lines, the radio near the bamboo-lined trenches squawked a message in Japanese. The nearby major yelled out an order.

"Prepare to charge!"

The nearby Japanese troops obeyed, affixing bayonets to their rifles. Officers drew their *gunto* swords.

Out in the grassy hills, artillery screamed in the skies above. Not too far from the battle raging below them, now dressed in jungle gear, Mina and her handful of companions crawled over the crest of a hill, firearms in their hands.

Reaching the top, Mina lifted out binoculars from her belt pouch. She peered downhill, careful to make sure she wouldn't catch the glint of the sun on the binocular's lenses and be spotted. They had a good vantage point of the battle from here.

There was the whine of a distant mortar and a resounding boom echoed throughout the hills.

Mina surveyed the area through the double-lens view of the binoculars. Below, a handful of Australian soldiers hunkered down, tense grimaces on their face. Some held their helmets to keep them from flying off. A chatter of machine gun fire kicked up tufts of dirt and grass about them.

She shifted her view to the other side of the engagement. Looking restless, the Japanese in the trenches affixed bayonets. An officer shouted indiscernibly, gesturing with his sword.

She gazed down the way, shifting her view again. She saw one of the Australian soldiers crawl towards a pillbox. He had an American-made M2 flamethrower strapped to his back, with its distinctive hourglass frame for double fuel tanks. Mina recalled it could let out a continuous stream of flame for about 7 seconds, effective out to around 20 to 40 meters.

Unfortunately, it didn't do him much good. A rifle shot hit one of the tanks, and the man exploded in a deafening blast that echoed throughout the hills. When the smoke cleared, all that was left was one leg, the rest of him spattered in burning chunks about the grass.

Engaged in a pitched firefight, nearby Australian troops looked like they were about to crack. Smudged faces were haggard and strained. They knew they were about to be overrun.

Mina lowered her binoculars, grim.

Crouched next to her, the Aussie frogman she knew as Boomer wielded a Winchester Model 1897 shotgun in his hands. He whispered urgently. "Oh my god. They're pinned down. We gotta help 'em!"

Mina spoke musingly. "There are too many of them."

Then an idea hit her. Her face lit up with a secretive smile. "I have an idea. Gimme those smoke grenades. Wait for my signal."

The Aussie balked. "You going out there by yourself? Who do you think you are? John Wayne?" he scoffed.

She pulled out Lockwood's cowboy-style six-shooter from her rear waistband and affected a Southern drawl. "Let's go, pilgrim."

Boomer let out a resigned sigh as she scampered off. "I'm gonna regret this."

54 PANTHER IN THE MIST

Downhill, the Australian soldiers cringed as a stream of machine gun fire stitched perilously close to their hastily-dug foxhole. One ricochet hit a private in the cheek, leaving a hole visible from one side of his face to the other.

Over on the other side, the Japanese trenches were lined with thick bamboo poles. Ramped up, the nearby Japanese troops were poised to run out, bayoneted-rifles at the ready.

The sergeant in the lead reared back his arm and threw a frangible smoke grenade, essentially a glass sphere filled with volatile titanium tetrachloride. He announced his intentions to fellow troops.

"*Hatsuento!*" Smoke.

"*Hatsuento nageru zo!*" Throwing smoke.

Nearby soldiers did similarly, flinging smoke grenades.

The glass spheres shattered in between the Japanese positions and the pinned-down Australians, and dense gray smoke spewed into the air.

Then another smoke grenade shattered on the rocky soil. And another and another, and dense smoke enshrouded the area. In seconds, the men were reduced to silhouettes in the gray haze.

Standing at the front of the bamboo-lined trenches, the officer in the lead drew his *gunto* sword and pointed it toward the Allied lines. He opened his mouth to shout the order to charge -

His eyes went wide as the blade of another sword sprouted from his chest, and a vermillion stain blossomed out.

Nearby, the wind shifted, and dense gray smoke started to blow back, enveloping the Japanese troops in the trenches. Confused, the waiting soldiers exchanged glances through the haze. Where was the order to charge?

Suddenly, there was a girlish laugh from within the smoke.

Instantly on alert, the men peered cautiously around the dense artificial fog, rifles leveled. One of the men that had been sitting on the crates snap-aimed his weapon at a nearby shadow -

- lifting the barrel as he recognized the man. It was just his sergeant.

Another girlish laugh drifted through. Behind the sergeant there was the brief silhouette of a pigtailed schoolgirl in the smoke.

Instantly alert, one of the men raised his rifle to his shoulder. He squinted, trying to peer through the dense haze.

Behind him, there were skipping footsteps and giggling laughter and he whirled around. But no one was there.

Suddenly, a petite hand clamped over his mouth as a wide blade jammed into his throat, and his wound gushed a torrent of crimson as he sagged to the dirt.

Tinkling child-like laughter resounded all around the remaining soldiers in the cinereous smoke, as elusive as a panther in the mist.

Looking every which way, the young private that had swapped stories earlier felt his breathing quicken. Cold sweat beading his forehead, he snapped his rifle in every direction, every snapping twig or rustle of cloth.

All around him, one after the other there was the

sickening sound of metal penetrating flesh, muffled groans, and ensuing wet thuds of bodies hitting earth.

Hands shaking, the man desperately tried to maintain his resolve. His mouth and facial muscles twitched, stoicism cracking. The stories were real. The stories were real. There was the *whish* of a blade slicing through the air -

With a wet thud, a decapitated head rolled about at his feet, bouncing once. He stared at it in shock. The disembodied head of his sergeant stared back at him, face frozen in a wide-eyed gaze of horror, mouth open in a silent scream.

That was enough. Fear overwhelming him, the young private threw his rifle to the ground and took off running through the smoke. Girlish laughter resounded all around, as the half dozen remaining troops in the vicinity took off after him.

55 KILLZONE

Sheer pandemonium in the trenches. Running in a wild panic, dozens of Japanese troops swarmed around Rain, who stood in the middle of the trench. He watched his men flee from the invisible menace in the smoke-shrouded killzone just yards away.

Livid, Rain stood sideways with his sidearm in his outstretched hand, firing at retreating soldiers around him. He screamed at them in a futile effort to regain control.

"No! No! No retreat! It's just one little girl!"

He shot down three of his men as they ran towards him, precise shots to the head that resulted in crimson spurts just before they pitched forward. Another panicking soldier ran past him.

"No it's not, it's a demon from hell!" he yelled.

Contemptuous, Rain dragged him by the back of his collar as if he were some insolent child and hauled him towards the fighting. "*Shiji suru n'ya! Okubyo mon ya uragiri mon ni wa yosha sen zo!*" I'll make it an order! I'll not forgive cowards and betrayers!

Rain drew his *gunto* sword and pointed, yelling the war cry at the top of his lungs. "*Ten'nouheika banzai!*" Rain shoved him towards the smoke where pained yelps and slicing metal could be heard. Shaking with fear, the soldier disappeared within the smoke.

Two gunshots boomed and his limp arm flopped out of the smoke.

Seeing this, more nearby soldiers turned and ran, their morale further broken. Routed soldiers fled through the trenches, every man for himself, yelling.

Seething with defeat, Rain stood in the middle of the chaos as his men fled around him. Chest heaving, pistol dangling in his hand at his side, he no longer bothered to try and contain the anarchy that had erupted.

Downhill, the emboldened Australian soldiers pushed forward. Troops climbed out of foxholes, reinvigorated, their compatriots already advancing up the path.

Joining the battle late, an Australian tank, a Murray FT tank[137] rumbled up the dirt path, armed with a mounted flamethrower.

A handful of Australian troops advanced, crouch-walking behind the cover of the tank. The terrain was far too rocky for massed armor assaults, so the occasional tank was a saving grace for the infantrymen.

The tank loosed a swath of flame across the few remaining Japanese soldiers in its path, setting them alight and sending them screaming as they combusted. They flailed wildly then crumpled to the ground, still aflame.

Up on the hill, Rain scowled at the sight. There was little he could do here. He turned and left.

Down in the trenches lined with bamboo trunks, a Japanese sergeant led his troops in full retreat. "Fall back! Fall back!"

They rushed through the trenches...into a choke point where the trench pathways met.

---

[137] A variant of the British Matilda II tank.

Eyes balefully cold, an imposing Mina rose to her feet from over the side of the trench, wielding a scavenged M2 flamethrower. The pilot tip of the wand flared with an ominous whoosh of ignition, glowing orange. Like a figure from some odd hallucination or a nightmare, she was a pigtailed powerhouse in sailor suit uniform with a flamethrower strapped to her back.

Wide-eyed, the soldiers stopped dead in their tracks, skidding to a halt. Nasty surprise.

"Aloha, bitches!" she yelled.

She loosed a geyser of flame into the packed throng of screaming troops just as they raised their weapons.

Expression stony, she sprayed the gun-shaped wand downwards across the crammed trench, setting all in the path of the flame alight. She loosed another gout of 40 meter flame across the human figures, igniting them.

Turned into human torches, the jam-packed troops let out bloodcurdling screams, flailing as they tried to escape the confines of the trench. Combusted, some tried to climb out. Others let out a series of gasping, stuttered yells of disbelieving agony as flames leeched the water from their bodies and turned flesh to black ash.

Howling, consumed by flames, those at the forefront turned to blackened crisps. Charred limbs twisted in the rictus of death from desiccated muscles. Gnarled, blackened fingers grasped for nonexistent aid.

Engulfed by flames, still moving, one soldier's charring form crawled along for a few feet before collapsing, orange flames still licking his body.

Surviving soldiers at the rear of the group tried to retreat, running the other way -

Only to be cut off by Boomer and his troops lying in ambush. They burst out of hiding positions flat against the earth over the trench. Grim-faced, they rose up. Some took one-kneed firing positions, some stood, submachine guns blazing. They cut down the running troops midstep. Boomer let out blast after blast with his shotgun, pumping it after each shot.

Running full-speed, determined, Rain sprinted along an adjacent trench. Pistol in hand, he glanced at the fracas nearby. That damn girl stood atop the trench, wielding the flamethrower as it sent torrents of flame into the mass of screaming bodies below.

He immediately grasped the tactics of what occured. The premise was simple. The Japanese troops initially had the Australian soldiers pinned down. Mina's antics caused a panic amongst the Japanese troops[138]. During the confusion, she escaped under the cover of the smoke and maneuvered back here. Demoralized, the routed Japanese troops retreated into a choke point, whereupon Mina now roasted them alive. Those trying to escape were caught in the crossfire from the Australians.

Sprinting onwards, Rain flanked her. A few yards away, her back turned to him, Mina continued hosing down troops with bursts of liquid flame. Rain leveled his pistol in a one-handed grip, firing in rapid succession at the fuel tanks strapped to her back.

Bullets plinked off of the flamethrower's frame, sparking as some of the bullets ricocheted.

Suddenly, a tongue of flame flared to life on the surface of one of the fuel tanks.

Boomer yelled out an incoherent warning, pointing at her back. Mina got it instantly. Frantic, she twisted and turned every which way, desperately trying to shoulder the pack off.

The flames on the back of the fuel-filled tank spread, ready to explode at any moment.

Nearby, two Japanese soldiers ran into a concrete pillbox, racking back the mounted machine gun, preparing to gun her down. They saw the petite flailing figure down the sights -

---

[138] Unhindered by the need to hold a particular position, such as Mina had done on the hill in Korea because of the presence of the Owl, Mina went on the full offensive here.

After an agonizing moment, Mina shrugged the rack loose and tossed it underhand into the pillbox as the flame on the fuel tank flared -

The thunderous boom within the confined space rattled her teeth even outside. Nearby, Rain threw an arm over his face to shield himself from falling debris. The two troops inside the pillbox ran out wailing, aflame. One let out a prolonged scream, sinking to his knees, crawling towards Mina as a horrendous freak of flame.

Mina quick-drew Lockwood's magnum from her rear waistband and shot him twice in the forehead, sending him sprawling with a spasmodic jerk, still burning.

A bullet zinged by her ear. Mina whirled, firing reflexively and emptying the cylinder.

She caught a glimpse of Rain just before he ducked behind the burned-out pillbox, dodging the shots. He ran off down the trench, sprinting zigzag to avoid fire.

Spurred on, Mina yelled to her Australian teammate. "Boomer! Trench gun!"

He tossed her the Winchester shotgun. She caught it midair, pumping it and raced after Rain, hot on his heels.

56 LUCKY CHARM

Running through the dusty haze, Mina swept through the bamboo-lined trenches with the Winchester shotgun. Gunfire echoed distantly and the air was suffused with the sulfuric stench of gunpowder.

About ten yards ahead, Rain sprinted around a corner. Grimly determined, his hands and legs pumped like a marathoner. Tracking him, Mina took aim, squeezing off booming shot after shot but he dodged and weaved. The blasts shredded bamboo trench lining, sending splintered wood into the air all around him.

Advancing quickly, Mina shot every soldier in her path who tried to stop her. They charged with bayonet-affixed rifles and shot pistols. Shooting rifles here was unwieldy and Mina was too close. Streaking in, Mina let out pumped blast after blast, cutting down the handful of soldiers as they approached. At these close-quarters, the shotgun was king, and booming blasts sent them sprawling into the dirt.

Out of ammo for the trench gun, she drew Lockwood's empty magnum and sped-loaded it. She had dropped the majority of her gear to wield the flamethrower and now the wheelgun was the only firearm she had left. She emptied the revolver at Rain but he zigzagged, evading every shot.

Rain yelled over his shoulder to nearby troops. "Stop her!" Armed with rifles and submachine guns, the soldiers took cover behind the corner, leveling weapons at her as Rain ran onwards.

Mina ducked and pressed her back to the corner as a withering fusillade tore out chunks of bamboo, sending tufts of wood fiber drifting through the air. She flinched at the flying splinters. Chasing Rain, she had gone too far behind enemy lines and now she was paying for it. Mina pressed her back to the corner as bullets whizzed over her head. Panting, she steeled herself. It sounded like there were three of them but she couldn't be sure.

Letting out a bestial scream, one soldier charged the ridge above her. Mina flung her trench knife and the blade embedded in the man's eye. Yelping, he teetered and collapsed like a felled tree. Momentum unstopped, he slid into the trench, staring slack-jawed with the knife protruding.

She saw the submachine gun clutched in his hands. She reached for it –

The submachine gunner at the other end of the trench saw her and let out a chatter of fire. Bullets kicked up clumps of dirt all around the dead man's weapon and Mina recoiled. No way she was getting to it.

Another screaming war cry grew louder, the voice of a second soldier rushing from behind.

Out of options, Mina grabbed her Lucky Charm slingshot from her belt and grabbed a rock off the ground. The screaming man zeroed in for the kill, bayonet poised to strike.

Aiming, she stretched the rubber tube on her slingshot as far as it would go. As soon as she saw his livid face crest the trench she let fly -

The rock hurtled through gelatinous flesh of his eye - and into his brain. He let out a tormented scream as he collapsed, still twitching.

There was the rack of a rifle bolt behind her. The submachine gunner had run out of ammo and changed weapons, flanking her.

Whirling, Mina hurled her slingshot into the man's face, throwing off his aim just enough as he discharged the shot into the air. Before he could recover, Mina grabbed the man by the boot and yanked him into the trench. Grappling, the man fought viciously, clawing and biting like a wild animal. Struggling, he got to his feet and kicked her in the ribs, knocking the air from her lungs.

Coughing, Mina swept his leg, bringing him down. Hurrying, she piked upright and stomped his throat and face repeatedly, crushing his windpipe and driving the facial bones into the man's brain, until he stopped moving.

She heard approaching footsteps. Mina hurriedly grabbed the man's sidearm and aimed it up the trench.

Weapons at the ready, Boomer and his compatriots emerged, looking down at her. They lowered their weapons as relief flooded her. Mina grabbed the discarded Winchester shotgun off the ground.

Boomer extended a hand to help Mina up. She took it gratefully. Boomer spoke as he handed her a handful of shotgun shells. "Where's Rain?" he asked.

Mina spoke as she loaded the shotgun, pumping it once. "Check the submarine pens! Go go go!"

57 SILENT GIANT VS. SLEEPING GIANT

July 31, 1945

Ominously imposing, the gargantuan Japanese submarine designated the I-403 rumbled to life inside the cavernous interior of the submarine pen. This massive monster of engineering was the brainchild of Admiral Isoroku Yamamoto, the Harvard-educated mastermind of the attack on Pearl Harbor. Fully 400 feet long, it was one hundred feet longer than the American *Tench* and *Porpoise* class submarines that Mina and Lockwood were accustomed to. Armed to the teeth and fitted with capricious fuel tanks, the I-400 series submarines had the capacity to traverse the globe one and a half times without needing to go to port - a stunning feat.

There were only a handful of these mammoth submarines in existence. Officially, the construction of this particular ship, the I-403, was canceled in October of 1943. However, the cancellation was a fabrication meant to allow its crew to carry out its secret mission.

Unknown to most, the submarine had new sonar-dampening anechoic coating. Based on German technology, this coating was a mixture of gum, asbestos, and adhesives applied to the hulls from the waterline. Enemy sonar pulses were diffused and the sounds of internal machinery muffled, making the giant submarine incredibly difficult to detect.

In essence, the vessel was a stealth supersub capable of a devastating first strike capability. A silent giant that skulked in the shadows, unseen and unheard.

Onboard the bridge of the behemoth submarine, the Japanese crew wore short-sleeved khaki uniforms and shorts. They had off-white caps with black anchor insignia, and light-colored shoes instead of boots.

Some of the bustling men wore brown jumpsuits, carrying on various assigned tasks. Some of the bridge crew sat at their stations, like the sonar operator with his headset on.

The captain bellowed out a command and the ship's lighting snapped to an amber-red hue.

The diving bell rang as the ship headed out underway.

Externally, the giant submarine sailed out of its berth and out to sea. Trawling atop the waves like a predatory shark, it sailed away from the palm tree dotted shoreline of Borneo. White foam outlined its massive form as it started to submerge beneath the waves, hidden from the world as it sailed towards its target destination.

Weapons at the ready, Mina and her companions swept into the cavernous submarine pen. The chamber was roughly cylindrical, with a flooded bottom that led out to sea and maintenance facilities on either side of the dock. The only thing docked nearby was a midget Japanese submarine, without any sign of its brethren.

Mina exclaimed in dismay as she saw the near-empty space. "We're too late! They already left!"

"But where are they going?" Boomer asked.

"I don't know!"

Boomer gestured towards the large empty berth that flooded the central channel. "What do you want to do? The stallion already left the stable."

Mina pointed to the midget sub still in dock, a

Type A Ko-hyoteki. "Then I'd better use the pony to catch up," she said.

Boomer balked. He didn't think it was a good idea.

"I'm going alone," said Mina firmly.

Boomer looked distinctly displeased. "Not letting you go alone. That thing can fit two of us."

"Yeah, but what happens after we get onboard? Sorry, you can't run around a Japanese-crewed submarine, my pasty-white Aussie friend."

Mina approached the submarine and popped the top sail. Pointing the shotgun down the hatch, she checked that it was empty and prepped the sub for launch.

Nearby, the other troops checked the guard house for gear Mina could use.

Boomer sat down on a nearby dolly, taking a moment to assess the situation. He spoke musingly, fingering his mustache. "We can't just send any ships to attack the Japanese sub. Most ships close enough to find and sink it would be caught in the blast. Tojo would just detonate it early and we'd lose our boys."

Mina climbed out of the little sub, grabbing some tools from a nearby toolbox.

Dressed in jungle gear, one of the other Australian frogmen looked around at the cavernous surroundings. "My god. Look at the size of this thing. What kind of submarine was in here? I've never seen a sub pen so massive."

Mina turned grim, not meeting his gaze. She feared the submarine was something only a select few of the navy brass and agents like her knew about. She knew about the giant behemoths of the I-400 series. If the submarine was what she thought it was, this wasn't gonna be pretty. One classified detail she couldn't tell her Australian companion was that the I-400 series had special sonar-nullifying anechoic coating that made it nearly undetectable. A silent giant. It was unlikely they could even find it in time before it pounced.

"Well, wherever it's headed, it can't be good," she remarked. "I'll have to get onboard and stop them. After I find out where they're going. I'll try and radio for help."

Mina did a quick metal calculation. The midget sub was actually faster than the I-403, but it had greatly inferior range. She could catch up to it, no problem, but only if she departed immediately.

"No time to grab gear," she said tersely. "If I wanna catch up, I have to go now with what I have."

Boomer handed her a folded Japanese submariner's uniform, a crowbar, and a submachine gun. He had retrieved them from the nearby guardhouse.

Mina nodded her thanks. The Aussie frogmen wished her good luck.

Settling into the driver's compartment, Mina closed the hatch and the midget sub departed, sailing out of the pen.

Standing up on the platform, Boomer bid her farewell, speaking more to himself than Mina.

"Good luck, Coral Hare."

58 DRAGONFLY

The interior of the Japanese midget submarine was cramped and stuffy. The close quarters were uncomfortable and damn near claustrophobic. Mina had taken the little sub out of the coastline and into the deep blue sea, towards the behemoth Japanese submarine. She took her best guess at their projected course. They hadn't been gone for that long, hopefully she could still catch up. Maybe she could get lucky and approach while the ship was surfaced and recharging its batteries, if it didn't have a snorkel.

Mina sat back for a moment and performed a quick mental assessment of her gear.

It wasn't much. Time had been of the essence, and the situation hadn't allowed her to bring everything she had wished. So be it. She was trained for situations like this.

Something occurred to her. How were the Japanese planning on launching the bomb? Was it mounted inside a torpedo? No that didn't make any sense. Underwater, the bomb wouldn't do nearly enough damage. The effects would still be devastating, but nowhere near the device's full potential. It would be a waste of the bomb's rare destructive power.

Mina mulled it over. Maybe they had a modified V2 rocket or something that could launch from a submarine.

Some kind of submarine-launched guided rocket. She pondered it for a moment, then decided to scratch the thought. Mina had heard the Germans had been developing such a weapon, but it was yet to be tested.[139] It was unlikely the Japanese had developed one first. So...

Then it dawned on her. A plane. It had to be a plane of some sort. Mina knew of several Japanese submarine types that could carry one or two seaplanes.

Then she did a few other mental calculations, and frowned. That still didn't seem right. Such seaplanes were small and couldn't handle the load of even a single atomic bomb, which was ponderously cumbersome, at least in theory.

So if a plane was the delivery vehicle, preferably she'd have one of the OSS's special altimeter-based bombs. She wouldn't even have to be anywhere near the plane bring it down, and she could walk away, dusting her hands.

Unfortunately she didn't have one with her. Oh well, she'd have to make-do. Better to focus on what she did have.

Her gear was arrayed on a blanket next to her. She started stuffing it into the pockets of the khaki-colored submariner's uniform laid out next to them. She had a small, single-shot FP-45 Liberator pistol intended for use as a holdout or insurgency weapon. It was easily concealable but didn't provide much firepower. The Nambu submachine gun she had brought with her from the island was too large to carry

---

[139] Germany was developing submarine-launched ballistic missiles (SLBM) but did not have time to test them prior to Germany's capitulation. The project codename was Prüfstand XII ("Test stand XII"), sometimes called the rocket U-Boat. If deployed, it would have allowed a U-Boat to launch V-2 missiles against United States cities, including New York, although only with limited efficacy. In 1944-45, Hitler and others in his regime alluded to the scheme in propaganda. The Americans nullified these plans coming to fruition with Operation Teardrop, meant to sink such submarines (no such subs were operational yet). The German engineers who worked for the program later worked for the USA and the USSR on their respective SLBM projects.

around the submarine undetected. It would look unusual. She'd have to leave it behind. Same deal with the shotgun.

She had a steel wire garrote, tied between two pieces of sturdy bamboo handles. Next to it were a few blocks of C3 explosive. Rather meager supplies but it was better than nothing.

She looked out through the transparent canopy.

"Whoa."

Up ahead, looming in the deep blue, was the shadowy outline of the largest submarine she had ever seen. It was a marvelous feat of engineering, and it took Mina a moment to compose herself.

Doing a last minute check, Mina started to gear up. Time to pay them a visit.

In full diving gear, Mina swam out from the midget sub towards the mammoth submarine looming ahead. Her breathing came slow and muffled, quiet in the murky blue depths.

Flippers kicking out behind her, she swam to the top of the giant submarine, towards the escape hatch.

From behind her back, movements protracted by the water, she pulled out a crowbar and wedged it under the hatch entrance.

On the bridge of the mammoth sub, a particular control panel for the indicator lights lit up a bright crimson, unnoticed by the crew. Hunched over a clipboard, the captain had his back to the panel, consulting with the first mate.

Inside the flooded escape hatch chamber, Mina floated through the water. There was a control panel on the wall. Moving as quickly as she could, fingers slowed in the saturation, she pulled off the panel. She twisted several wires together, flipping several switches. There was a momentary underwater spark -

The warning light up on the bridge died away just as the captain glanced over his shoulder, then resumed speaking to the first mate.

Inside the flooded escape hatch chamber, the water started draining away, receding to Mina's shoulders and continuing.

Entering the submarine proper, Mina climbed down the escape trunk's ladder into the side corridor. She paused for a moment, cocking her head side-to-side, listening intently.

She heard rousing sounds of a speech in Japanese echoing down the corridor. She recognized the authoritative male voice as Rain's. Aside from that, she heard no sign of nearby people.

She glanced around the corner at either end. The narrow corridor was empty.

Satisfied, Mina flipped her Lambertsen rebreather onto her forehead, taking in a breath of air. She quickly stripped off the diver's dry suit and donned the Japanese submariner's uniform. She tied her raven hair into a bun and tucked it under the off-white cap so she could better impersonate a boy.

The speech echoed on. She tread silently down the corridor and pressed herself against the entryway's side, peeking into the mess hall.

Dressed in his Imperial Japanese Army uniform, Rain stood at the front of the mess hall, speaking to the assembled crew. Rain's voice boomed, tone rousing and patriotic.

"Honored soldiers of the Emperor. The dragonfly is known throughout the empire as a symbol for triumph. Today is a great day for the I-403 Dragonfly, for today we earn the name for which it stands. Today, we earn victory. Today, we strike at the heart of the Allied fleet!"

Rain continued, pacing back and forth between the lines of the attentive crew, his hands laced behind his back.

"Our target is Ulithi Atoll, where the U.S. Pacific fleet is stationed," he declared. "Fifteen carriers are stationed there. The heart of their Pacific forces."

Murmurs of approval swept through the assembly.

Around the corner of the corridor, Mina looked as if she were about to be sick.

Rain's voice thundered on, rising with nationalistic pride. "It will be a great victory. Ships will burn in their docks. Sailors will burn where they stand. The back of their fleet will be broken. It shall be an even greater victory than Pearl Harbor!"

Mina swallowed hard.

Rain continued, his militaristic fervor rising to borderline fanaticism, building to a crescendo.

"Their fleet will be crippled! Within months our great empire shall make a great return to glory! We shall see New York and Washington D.C. lain to waste! We shall see the mushroom cloud of the *genzai bakudan* over the burning ruins of their once-great cities. The flag of the Rising Sun will fly over the skies of America's heartland, and the Empire shall reign for ten thousand years!"

The gathered sailors let out a roar of approval. Bursting with militaristic pride, Rain let out a cheer.

"Ten'nouheika, banzai!"

He raised his arms aloft in patriotic fervor. Responding, the assembled crew raised their arms and voices thrice in a thunderous chorus.

"Banzai! Banzai! Banzai!" they shouted in unison.

Mina felt her heart sink to the pit of her stomach as she realized the implications. If the Bomb was dropped on the Allied Pacific fleet, it would make the invasion of the Japanese home islands incredibly difficult. As Rain had mentioned, it might even buy Japan enough time to construct more atomic bombs and rescue them from the brink of defeat.

The images flitted across Mina's mind. Great ships aflame, pluming black smoke, lowed like metal beasts as they overturned in death throes. Sailors in the boiling water, slicked with burning oil, wailed for aid as their skin sloughed from heat a thousand times more intense than the sun. Palm trees burned away in a second to ash then tore away in a hot gale. Soldiers upon the sands screamed as the shore beneath their feet turned to glass. Their bodies bubbled with blisters the size of melons, and they sank to their knees in agony.

She couldn't let it happen.

Mina rushed around the corner. She sagged against the bulkhead, almost hyperventilating. She unconsciously whispered to herself, stammering. "Think, Mina, think. You gotta do something."

She ran down the hall as Rain's voice droned on and the occasional raucous cheer echoed through. Hopefully, with most of the crew attending Rain's speech the radio room would be unmanned and she could shoot off a quick message.

She dashed down the corridor, heart pounding in her chest.

Nearing the radio room, Mina was mildly surprised to hear a voice speaking in English.

Flanking the hatchway with her back to the bulkhead, she glanced around to sneak a look.

Inside was a seated Japanese radio operator, headphones about his head. He spoke in surprisingly perfect English, even adding in a touch of Southern twang.

"King's Castle, this is Zebra Baker 1. Authentication two-six-able-baker-three-king-sugar-one-niner. Captured Sally on approach, repainted in our colors. Do not fire. Please confirm. Over."

The slightly staticky reply was almost instantaneous. "Zebra Baker One, confirmed, we will not fire," said the American radio operator. "Welcome home. Over."

Mina sagged against the bulkhead in resigned consternation, thudding her head back and closing her eyes. Oh no, she mouthed silently.

With the bomber painted in American colors and the fake radio message forewarning their arrival, it was unlikely the troops at Ulithi would recognize the threat in time.

Mina considered her options. It was unlikely she could knock out the guard. Keeping him alive was not an option here. If she killed him and hid the body, people would notice him missing. Nor could she sneak in there while he was on break without being detected, at least not necessarily long enough for the base to authenticate her credentials.

Unlike her one-woman raid in Tokyo, there were only so many places one could hide onboard a submarine. If the crew thought their plans were revealed, most likely the submarine would launch their payload earlier.

Even if she were somehow able to send a message, there would not be enough to time for personnel to evacuate. Like Rain said, it would be a sneak attack inevitably worse than Pearl Harbor, with America's invaluable carriers sinking to the bottom of the ocean.

It was all up to her.

59 FALSE COLORS

Mina walked her way down to the hangar. She kept to the side corridor, trying to avoid contact with the crew. Despite her uniform and her hair tucked under the cap, it was unlikely she could pass muster as a crewman if they got too close. The crew would immediately recognize her as an outsider. Military men were aware of such things, and submarine crews were closer than most.

Cautious, she hid behind a pile of wooden supply crates. On top of a crate marked in Japanese, she saw an unattended roll of gray duct[140] tape. She stuffed it into her pocket. It could come in useful.

Mina peered around the corner of a crate.

Suddenly, there was a metallic rumbling as the massive hydraulic door in the hangar opened, letting in a sliver of daylight. The sudden illumination was harsh and she squinted. The door opened wider, letting bright sunlight flood in.

In the hangar, several mechanics rolled out what

[140] From the 1920s all the way through 1950, duct tape was called "duck" tape because it was made from cotton duck cloth. It was only after the tape started being used for ventilation ducts that it started being called by its modern name.

appeared to be dissembled pieces of plane, hauling them onto the forward deck. Mina felt a sense of affirmation. So it *was* a plane, as she had suspected. They weren't using a seaplane, although guessing from the interior of the hangar, the submarine had initially meant to carry them.[141] She deduced the crew's current plan was to use a deconstructed bomber plane, reassemble it, then launch it with the submarine's catapult.

Out on deck, she saw the crew of mechanics reassemble the plane quickly. She recognized the plane's profile. As the radio operator had mentioned, it was a Mitsubishi Ki-21 "Sally" (sometimes also called "Gwen") medium-heavy bomber.

Mina quickly did some mental calculations. The Ki-21 could just barely handle the weight of the atomic bomb, assuming it was similar to the one in Korea. The plane's overall carrying capacity was about five tons, just a smidge more than the weight of the atomic bomb.

The plane's normal bomb capacity was just over a ton. Mina guessed most of the plane's armaments and nonessential gear had been stripped out, then further modified to be lighter for this specific mission. The Ki-21 usually had a crew of five to seven men. She wondered how many people would be onboard.

Up on deck, Mina watched mechanics make modifications to the submarine's Type 4 No. 2 Model 10 compressed-air catapult system. To accommodate the Ki-21 bomber instead of seaplanes, the air tanks and pistons were replaced with larger, more powerful ones, and the 85-foot catapult was extended with temporary rails.

Hiding behind equipment crates, Mina surreptitiously

---

[141] During World War II, Allied intelligence was aware of the existence of the I-400 series of mammoth submarines. However, they did not know of the three seaplane bombers it could carry, the Aichi M6A Seiran. It was known that other submarines could carry seaplanes, but the triple bombers onboard the I-400 subs were a nasty surprise. Realizing the Japanese had this kind of strike capability must have come as a nasty shock.

observed the mechanics out on deck. Under Rain's watchful eye, they started to repaint the Japanese plane in American colors, complete with white star within the blue roundel.

Some of the work crew looked reluctant. One of the mechanics had a consternated expression. "Painting a plane in false colors is against the rules of war," he said.

The mechanic next to him looked even worse, bordering on ill. "This is dishonorable," he added.

Rain spoke to him soothingly. "Victory is everything. That is honor."

Resignedly, the men concurred with their superior. "Yes, *Taisa-dono*," they both said.

After they rigged the plane for flight, Mina watched the crew run a hose to the plane and start fueling. She calculated the weight of the fuel, gauging the amount by timing the duration with her wristwatch.

It was a one-way trip.

Mina noticed the hydraulic crane up on deck usually used to lift seaplanes back aboard. This time, it wouldn't be needed. No one would be coming back.

Time to make her move.

The plane was armed and the crew assembled on deck. With Rain among them, a flight crew of four men with helmets and fur-collared jackets walked out, amidst cheers of the crew.

With great ceremony, the four men tied on *hachimaki* headbands and took cups of sake from an attendant, drinking. An officer snapped a group photograph, and the four men boarded the bomber. The engine rumbled to life and the propeller props spun up.

The Ki-21 rammed down the catapult and launched into the air.

The assembled crew cheered as the plane flew off, waving their caps in jubilation. The Ki-21 bomber soared off into the sky, rising up towards the clouds like a bird of prey.

Unbeknownst to the crew, clinging onto the undercarriage, was the silhouette of a petite form against the orange-violet of the early morning sky.

60 ASCENSION

The fleet anchorage at Ulithi was a fat sitting duck.

Located some 260 miles southwest of Guam, Ulithi was once an average volcanic atoll with coral, white sand, and palm trees. Now, the Allied Pacific fleet had a considerable force stationed there.

The natives had been relocated to a nearby island, making way for the massive naval base with all the amenities of home. There were ship and aircraft facilities, mail service, and recreation on the island of Mogmog.

The giant reef of Ulithi enclosed a vast anchorage, running twenty miles north and ten miles south, with an average depth of 80 to 100 feet. The anchorage was ideal for accommodating every variety of ship. In preparation for the invasion of the Japanese main islands, vital carriers were still in dock, as Ulithi was a major refueling depot.

The stars-and-stripes of the American flag fluttered in the morning breeze, overlooking the peaceful anchorage. There were numerous warships in port, including fifteen carriers of the Allied Pacific fleet. The ships gleamed in the morning light, golden rays of the sun beaming down on their gray hulls.

Soldiers in mess tents ate breakfasts of savory bacon, scrambled eggs, and orange juice.

Relaxed, shirtless soldiers played beach volleyball in their trousers. They bumped the ball back and forth across the net, unaware the Japanese had plans to turn the whole area into a burning pyre.

Deceptively painted in American colors, the Mitsubishi Ki-21 heavy bomber soared through the morning skies towards its unsuspecting target.

Stowed away, clinging onto the undercarriage, Mina braced against the whipping wind as it buffeted her. Still dressed in the uniform of a Japanese submariner, the shorts and short-sleeves did little to protect against the growing cold of the increasing altitude. Her hands started to grow numb. If she didn't get inside the cabin or at least the bomb bay soon, it was likely she'd lose her grip and fall.

Working her way to the end, using the little maintenance hatch handholds, she climbed atop the plane, tension pulsing in her stomach.

Gritting her teeth, the gale flapping her clothes, she clambered on, crawling hand-over-hand against the howling wind. She had decided against trying to blow up the plane while on the sub. The numerous crewmen would make it too difficult to succeed. Better to do it up in the air.

Working her way up top, she reached the area directly overhead the fuel tanks. Unfortunately, the fuel tanks were behind and under the gunner's seat near the window.

She edged forward on her belly. Mina squinted against the wind at the window, making sure no one was in the gunner's seat that could see her.

The seat was empty. Mindful of the violent turbulence, she wrapped her legs around the framework and grasped a handhold so she could have one hand free.

Tense, she reached into her pocket and pulled out a block of C3 plastique.

A sudden jolt of turbulence knocked her off her feet.

The block of C3 flew out of her hand, receding into the plane's wake as she herself sailed back, torn by the wind -

Scrabbling on the mostly smooth surface of the plane, Mina panicked. The wind pulled her back and she flailed wildly -

Her fingers caught hold of a topside maintenance hatch and stopped her perilous backslide. The jolt wrenched her arm, nearly dislocating her shoulder in the process.

Panting, cringing with the pain in her shoulder, heart pounding in her chest, Mina took a moment to collect herself. Way too close a call. Fighting the wind, she climbed back towards the gunner's area and the fuel tanks under it.

Reaching the spot, she cautiously peered inside, scrunching her face and squinting against the biting wind.

She saw the back of the gunner in full flight gear complete with fur hood and goggles. His head moved up and down as he spoke indiscernibly.

Inside the warmer confines of the plane, the gunner felt the oppressive sensation of being watched. Out of instinct, he glanced over his shoulder just as Mina ducked out of sight.

With her hand shaking and breath misting as she panted from low oxygen, Mina reached inside her pocket for another block of C3. It was her second to last one.

Careful, with one hand grasping the top hatch for support, she leaned perilously over and slapped the timed C3 block against the side of the plane. She set it as far down towards the fuel tanks as she could reach. Any further, she'd probably lose her grip and fall. It'd have to do.

Reaching into her jacket, she pulled out the duct tape she'd absconded with and bit off a length. She reached down and pressed the strip of tape against the plastique block. There. That should hold it.

Task complete, she climbed back topside - and looked straight at the gawking face of the crewman through the gunner's window.

He pointed a gloved finger at her, shouting over his shoulder loudly enough he could be heard over the wind and window. Oh, hell.

Suddenly, her heart leapt to her throat as the plane started to veer and jink erratically side-to-side. Damn pilot was trying to shake her off. Her roll of duct tape flew away as she grabbed the nearest hatch grip with both hands, frantically trying not to get flung off. This high up, no way she would survive the fall.

Then the pilot, who must have been a madman, sent the plane into a barrel roll and she felt a sense of vertigo as the sky became the sea and the sea became the sky, over and over. Her vision became an indistinguishable swirl of white and blue, and she nearly lost her grip. The damn plane wasn't designed for such maneuvering. All around her was violent shaking and she barely clung on. The hull of the plane rattled and the metal groaned against the strain.

Dazed, Mina realized Rain was probably the pilot. He was the only one crazy enough to send a damn bomber plane spinning through the sky, which was generally prohibited since it put the crew at risk.

The plane continued wild aerial acrobatics as Mina clung to whatever handholds she could find for dear life. Over and over, she flopped back, banging into the hull like a ragdoll.

A gust of wind tore the cap off her head, exposing her hair bun. Mina gritted her teeth. There was no way in hell she'd last out here. Inevitably she'd tire or make a mistake, and she'd be flung into the ocean. She'd be better off inside taking her chances with the crew.

Clinging on, she slapped her last block of C3 onto the side of the plane.

From inside the bomber, a fiery blast blew a gaping hole in the fuselage. The crew threw their arms over their faces against the sudden torrent of wind tearing equipment and fluttering papers into the wild blue yonder.

Swinging in from outside, Mina landed inside the

cabin, legs splayed in an almost stylish pose.

Rain whirled around in the pilot's seat. So he really was the pilot. His face went livid when she saw her.

"You! Always you!" he screamed.

She wasted no time. Swaying slightly on her feet against the turbulence, face resolute and determined, Mina grabbed the nearest crewman, a gunner, and kneed him in the kidneys. He arched with the incapacitating pain. She jammed the single-shot Liberator pistol from her pocket against his temple, the part of the skull where the bone was thinnest, and fired, spattering the man's brains against the bulkhead.

One down, three to go. The dead crewman sagged in her arms and she grasped him as a human shield, crouching behind him.

The other gunner fast-drew his pistol, pumping a few shots into his former comrade's chest.

Holding the slumped figure upright by his collar, Mina grabbed the dead man's sidearm and aimed around his waist. She pulled the trigger rapidly, emptying the clip into her assailant's torso, dead center mass. The other gunner collapsed, sprawled onto the deck.

The co-pilot next to Rain bolted out of his seat in a flying tackle. The heavy impact sent both combatants and the dead corpse to the deck.

Grappling, struggling to get out from under him, Mina wrestled with the co-pilot. He apparently had some judo training, and with the dead man's added weight atop her, she struggled to break free. The co-pilot jammed his knee into her stomach[142], forcing the air from her lungs and she gasped for air.

He grabbed her hair and repeatedly slammed her head into the bulkhead, pulling her hair loose into a quasi-ponytail. Flickers of colored light swam in her sight.

On the verge of unconsciousness, darkness creeping in at the edge of her vision, Mina put in a last-ditch burst of

---

[142] The technique is called *uki-gatame*, or "floating hold."

strength.

Grimacing with effort, she let out a power kick with both legs, propelling the yelping co-pilot out the hole in the plane-

Outside the plane, pinwheeling midair, the co-pilot's scream cut off as he splattered into the spinning prop of the right-side engine in a massive burst of crimson spray and bits of gore. Scarlet dots bespeckled the hull. The engine emitted a grinding of machinery and dying whir of gears.

With a bang of combustion, the rattling engine burst into yellow-orange flames, trailing black smoke.

The Ki-21 bomber listed to its side and shuddered, engine wheezing and sputtering as the plane fought to maintain altitude. Ordinarily, one engine was enough to keep the plane aloft in an emergency. With the burdensome atomic cargo, it wasn't enough.

Inside the cockpit, the plane rocked to one side. Tense, gloved hands gripping the quaking yoke, Rain struggled to maintain control, face beading with sweat.

He reached one hand towards a particular button on the control panel, capped by a clear glass cover. In Japanese it read "Detonate." The mechanics had rigged up a control system for mid-air detonation, just in case.

Suddenly a wire garrote looped around his throat and hauled back. His hand whipped to his neck. Her face cold, Mina hauled back on the bamboo handles of the garrote.

Gasping, choking, Rain reached behind him with both hands and grabbed Mina under her shoulders. He bodily hauled her overhead and slammed her onto the console.

The impact jarred her to her core and she felt her internal organs quiver. She moaned, forcing herself to get up.

Gasping in gulps of air, Rain drew his sidearm.[143] Mina

---

[143] Pilots and officers sometimes carried Nambu Model 14 pistols

body-slammed him, trying to wrench the pistol from his grasp. The gun went off, deafeningly loud in the confined cockpit. There was searing hot pain at her ear. The gunshot had torn off a chunk of earlobe and blood trailed down her cheek.

Rain glowered, grabbing the pistol's grip, aiming it towards her.

Desperate, Mina jammed her finger behind the trigger, just barely keeping it from firing. Rain's gloved index finger squeezed against the trigger, and it edged back a hair's width-

Outside the bomber, the block of C3 explosive affixed to the fuselage detonated with a thunderous boom and fiery blast that rocked the airborne vessel and sent shudders throughout its metal length.

Inside the cockpit, the deck canted with a tremulous metallic scream. Locked in mortal combat, Rain and Mina lurched and slammed against the bulkhead as the plane went into an uncontrolled dive.

Out on the beach at the Ulithi naval base, jogging soldiers whirled at the distant boom and stared out at the morning sky, disconcerted.

It was an approaching burning bomber, presumably a captured Japanese Ki-21 "Sally" painted in American colors. One engine ablaze, the rear of the approaching craft was aflame. The doomed plane began to crash in earnest, trailing dark billows of smoke.

Arcing down, it sank towards the ocean, not too far away from the moored ships in the docks.

Out on the beach where the soldiers had been playing volleyball, the men stared at the flaming plane in dismay. Squinting, one square-jawed man visored his hand to his brow, peering at the sight.

---

with an enlarged trigger guard for easier firing with gloved hands. This is the model Rain is using here.

Inside the cockpit, their surroundings shook and rattled with the strain of uncontrolled descent. Mina felt her stomach rise. The muscles in her arms corded as the two wrestled over the pistol.

Rain was winning. His heavier weight and upper body strength gave him the advantage, and Mina felt the handgun slipping from her grasp.

Mina braced her foot back, gaining additional leverage to compensate. She tried to twist the gun out of his grip. Rain strained, inching the muzzle of the gun inexorably towards Mina's malevolence-filled face, his finger on the trigger.

He gritted his teeth, seething with hate. "*Jigoku e ochiro...*" Go to hell.

Pushing her muscles to their limits, Mina changed the direction of her struggle, shoving perpendicular to his efforts. She grabbed his wrist, slamming his hand repeatedly against the console.

He didn't drop it. His resolve was too strong, and he only grunted with the pain. The two continued to wrestle over the firearm even as they plunged towards the waves.

Visible through the cockpit window behind the struggling pair, the sea seemed to rush up to meet them. The force of the impact slammed them against the console even as the window shattered in a blast of broken glass and the ocean rushed in, starting to flood the cockpit.

Sprawled against the controls, both of them momentarily stunned by the concussive shock, they stirred. Mina staggered to her feet as water rose to her knees and kept rising.

First to regain their senses, Mina grabbed Rain by the sides of his face and tried to jam her thumbs into his eyes to blind him. Grimacing, instead of trying to shove her away, he extended a trembling finger towards the control panel, trying to reach something -

Mina glanced in the direction - and panicked. It was the detonation button. They were already in the middle of the anchorage.

Rain slammed his fist down on the button.

Mina's eyes widened.

"No!" she shrieked.

61 KAPPA, PART II

There was the sound of grinding machinery within the bowels of the plane - followed by a dying screech of gears. Machinery damaged and waterlogged, the bomb wouldn't blow.

Rain yanked the lever on the emergency bomb release. There was a metallic squeal of machinery as the bomb bay doors opened, but no detonation.

Cursing, Rain shoved her away and swam out of the sinking cockpit. "Damn fucking water!"

Still reeling from the blow, Mina staggered back on the canted, flooding deck. She doubled over and coughed out a mouthful of pink froth. Lung damage from the impact trauma, she realized. Damnit. She could taste the coppery tang of blood in the back of her mouth and a foamy texture.

She looked around. The crewman she killed first with the single-shot pistol floated towards her. She frisked the body and found a bayonet knife jammed in the boot.

Determined, knife in hand, Mina paddled out of the plane, going after Rain.

Swimming out the broken cockpit window, Mina clambered atop the sinking plane and looked around.

She surveyed the surrounding waters urgently, looking every which way. The bubbles surrounding the sinking plane gurgled and popped as air pockets flooded, obscuring her view of the water below. Damnit, where was he?

Under the surface of the water, the sunken atomic bomb lay beneath the plane, in the relatively shallower waters of the atoll.

Face contorted with effort, bubbles escaping from his clenched mouth, Rain already had the maintenance hatch open. His hands worked frantically as much as protracted movements in the water would allow, trying to hotwire the detonator manually.

Atop the sinking plane, Mina peered into the waves.

There. She saw a hazy man-shaped shadow near the plane's submerged bomb bay area.

Mina surveyed the scene with an analytic eye, tracking his movements. Feeling confident, even borderline predatory, she had no problem with the water anymore. Ever since the U-Boat incident, this was a newborn Mina of the high seas, as proficient in the water as any frogman.

She hastily put her loose ponytail back into a bun to keep it from becoming a liability in combat.

"Oh no you don't get away that easy," she muttered under her breath.

Like a pirate, she put the salvaged knife between her teeth and readied herself. She clasped her hands together like an Olympic swimmer and dove into the water.

She broke beneath the waves, sweeping the cool water past her in an adept breaststroke towards the sunken bomb and its attendant. Spurred on, she swam onwards, a feminine form silhouetted against the sun-dappled waves above.

Motion slowed by water resistance, Rain turned his head towards the petite commando swimming his way. Sound travels faster underwater than in air, and he had heard the splash.

Swimming towards him, Mina took the blade from her

lips and gripped the knife in hand, ready for combat. She took up no set posture.

One key thing about fighting underwater was that no "stances" *per se* could be used, since there was no solid footing. Instead, the opponent's body or some other sturdy object had to be used as a base, for most actions. The basic trick about positioning in an underwater fight was to ideally approach an opponent from only one side. Preferably, she'd try to maneuver to his rear whenever possible.

Mina glanced down at the situation below. Ordinarily, for underwater fighting it was best if one forced her opponent to come to them. Unfortunately, in this case Mina had no choice but to go to him. She had to stop him from detonating the atomic bomb. She couldn't depend on the submersion short-circuiting the detonator.

Approaching Rain, she didn't bother trying to swim around him. Their movements were too slowed by water resistance. There was little opportunity for surprise or sudden moves, as drag factor made most movements immediately apparent. Instead, she approached his flank and jabbed with the knife, feinting.

As she had hoped, Rain lunged for her, lured away from the bomb on the ocean floor. Mina dodged the grab, and Rain's momentum carried him past her.

Rain swept back with his arms and legs, channeling his momentum circularly to turn around. Using the sunken plane as a push-off point for leverage, he grappled with her for control of the knife. The two exchanged a series of arm sweeps, evades, and leg pushes. She ducked a swipe from Rain as he clawed at her head. She parried a few blows.

Mina braced her legs against the side of the sunken plane – and gained enough leverage to grab Rain from behind in an arm lock. Underwater, in the near-weightless environment, most holds had to be joint locks, on pressure points, or on nerve points. Unfortunately these were Rain's specialty in hand-to-hand combat.

Using his free hand, his knuckle jabbed out and struck

her temple, and the blow sent her reeling back.

Taking advantage of her disorientation, he managed to wrestle the knife from her grip.

He stabbed at her throat. Mina raised her arm, trying to fend off the blow with an arm sweep.

Mina let out a gurgled scream and bubbles gushed out of her mouth as the fifteen-inch blade impaled her forearm all the way through. Seeping blood formed a scarlet cloud in the murky blue water.

Out on the surface, just a few meters away from the almost completely submerged bomber, a triangular fin of white cartilage protruding from the waves threaded its way towards them ominously.

Underwater, Rain and Mina were locked in combat. The salt in the water made her pain particularly intense.

Mina caught the flash of gray-white motion out of the corner of her eye. Then she saw it full on. Being from Hawaii, Mina recognized it immediately.

It was a great white shark, sometimes seen in Pacific waters and off the coast of Japan.[144]

She realized it must have been drawn by fresh blood and from the dead crew inside the sinking plane. Unintentional chumming of the waters. Using her distraction, Rain maneuvered under and behind Mina. A dangerous predicament for her.

Rain glanced to his side, seeing the predator undulate, cutting a swift path. It'd be upon them in less than a minute.

Cruel, he gripped her wounded arm from behind and squeezed, forcing out puffs of crimson. Mina let out an involuntary gurgle of anguish and a gout of bubbles escaped her lips.

Fighting through agony, in protracted underwater movements, Mina grabbed the bayonet impaling her arm and

---

[144] Among other places in the world.

yanked it out. An inky cloud of red pervaded the area near her open wound.

Seeing Mina re-armed with the blade, Rain immediately grabbed Mina in a rear bear hug to keep her from using it. His arms compressed her chest like a boa constrictor and forced the air out. A massive torrent of bubbles surged from her mouth, precious air escaping.

Struggling, Mina pitched forward in an underwater somersault and the entangled pair rolled.

Mina's expression grew frantic. Air, air. She needed air. Her lungs screamed with the crushing deflation and the purge of oxygen.

Mina reached back and jabbed her fingers into his collarbone. Then under his armpit, into the nerve clusters there. Rain's face contorted with pain, the agony forcing him to relinquish his grip on her.

She broke free. Gripping his shoulder as an anchor point, she used her free hand to punch him in the stomach. He let out a gurgling moan and a long gush of bubbles escaped his mouth. Mina immediately clamped her lips over his to capture the bubbles in a perverse kiss.

Pulling away from him, Mina grabbed him by the legs and hauled herself under and behind him. Now she was in the optimal placement in an underwater fight - directly behind her opponent. Any effort on his part to face her would be delayed by the water.

Gripping a protruding part of the sunken plane to brace herself, knife ready, Mina considered slitting his throat right then and there - then stopped.

Sharks were attracted to motions of excessive splashing and thrashing. Better to keep Rain alive and use him as a lure for her getaway.

Instead, Mina administered the *coup de grace* in a different way. From behind, using her medical knowledge of biology, she jabbed Rain in the throat, not too deeply, just enough so he'd bleed profusely into the water. Blood seeped out.

She stabbed him in the collarbone, puncturing the artery there. Liquid red suffused the water about his torso.

Finally, she jabbed him in the back of the thigh, nicking the femoral artery, hoping he'd bleed faster. A gushing red plume suffused the water around his leg.

Rain began to flail wildly, and soon he was engulfed in a spreading vermillion cloud in the murky blue sea.

His eyes went wide as he saw the great white converge on them. Looming as it drew close, the shark threaded near, voracious, mere meters away.

Mina swam under Rain, to control his legs, the main method of propulsion underwater. She should have done it earlier but hadn't had the opportunity.

Mina sliced the knife across the back of Rain's thighs. Like running on land, the hamstring muscles were used for swimming, and this hampered his ability to do so tremendously.

Mina braced herself against the sunken plane's wreckage with her arms. She lashed out with a final double kick to the top of Rain's head as she swam off, using his cranium like a springboard.

Momentarily stunned, Rain shook off the confusion and frantically tried to swim towards the surface. Trailing scarlet plumes, kicking awkwardly, his face contorted with pain from the saltwater wounds and desperation.

Both of them swam upwards, trying to reach safety. Growing up on Hawaii, Mina knew since childhood it was impossible to outswim a shark. In this case, one of them only needed to be faster than the other to evade the predator - and Mina was in the lead.

Mina glanced upwards. Silhouetted against the sun-dappled waves, surrounded by smaller debris was some piece of buoyant wreckage. It looked like a jagged sheet of insulation or cargo crate, and from this distance, looked roughly seven feet on all four sides.

Pumping her legs, Mina swam upwards, towards salvation, glancing back over her shoulder.

Thrashing about, Rain flailed in the water. The looming shark overtook him, opening its mouth wide in a great, gaping maw of razor-sharp teeth. Disappearing in a scarlet inky cloud, Rain let out a gurgled agonized scream that was abruptly cut off. The massive, silent bite either swallowed him whole or chomped him in half so fast she couldn't tell. The shark continued towards her, leaving only behind a cloud of seeming crimson ink and scraps of floating cloth in its wake.

Hurrying, stretching her arms outward, Mina kicked on, glancing back. The shark, eager for a second meal, nudged its way closer, just a few meters behind her.

Glittering sunlight played upon the waves just a few inches away. Straining, Mina stretched out her fingertips, and grabbed the edge of the floating wreckage -

Sopping wet, her head broke the surface and Mina clambered aboard, taking in a massive gasp of air. Fortunately, the piece of insulation was as buoyant as it had looked and supported her weight.

Mina crouched into a fighting stance, balancing herself on the makeshift raft. She raised the knife in an overhead reverse grip, ready to stab the shark at the eyes, snout or gills. They were really the only vulnerable parts of the shark.

The great white's head roared out of the water and rammed her raft, tossing about nearby waterborne debris and nearly knocking her off. She hastily got back on her haunches, ready to stab at it.

It circled once. Then, losing interest, it swam off. Its fin cut a threading path through the waves, receding into the distance.

Mina let her hand drop. Panting, haggard, and completely exhausted, she flopped back onto the raft. Chest heaving, she closed her eyes, completely spent.

Suddenly, she heard the sound of an approaching motor and the bow of a boat breaking the waves.

She immediately got up and took up a knife-fighting stance, looking warily in the direction of the sound.

She looked off to her side. Bobbling, the body of a dead gunner from the plane floated facedown. Reaching out, she pulled it to her and patted it down. She grabbed a pistol tucked inside the flight jacket pocket.

Armed, she took a one-kneed firing stance, pistol held down in a two-handed grip, ready to shoot.

Fast approaching, a motorboat[145] skimmed the waves, manned by seven U.S. Marines armed with rifles[146].

As soon as they saw her, one of the armed marines pointed at her in warning.

"Jap, Jap!"

It was only then Mina realized she still wore the soaking wet, Imperial Japanese Navy uniform.

Stony-faced, hard creases around their mouths and eyes, the marines leveled rifles at her, save the one in the lead. The sergeant fixed eyes on her.

"Drop the gun! Drop the fuckin' gun!" he bellowed.

A third one yelled at in her in barely understandable Japanese. "*Hanase! Hanase!*" Drop it! Drop it!

Stern-faced, the lead marine racked back the bolt on his rifle with an intimidating metallic clack, meaning business. He snap-raised it to his shoulder, drawing a bead.

Mina's eyes widened in shock as she protested in English, letting the gun slip from her fingers -

"No wait! Wai -"

The crack of a rifle shot rang out, her release of her weapon a split-second too slow. The impact hit her chest like a bucking bronco and she felt herself thrown her backwards into the water with a splash.

From high above, one could see three other motorboats with armed men as they approached in grim solemnity. They encircled the petite form as it bobbed up and down with the current, limp. Unknown to the crewmen of the

---

[145] An LCPL "Shark Tooth" motorboat.

[146] The famed M1 Garand was the mainstay firearm of the U.S. armed forces after the M1903 Springfield rifle was phased out.

moored ships and those stationed at the naval facility not too far away, they had just gunned down the person who had singlehandedly saved their lives.

62 NEW BLACK SHIPS

August 15, 1945

The hospital room looked as if it had been converted from a hotel room - which it had. The 25th floor of the Edison Hotel had been repurposed and revamped into a small but efficient clinic. The War Department[147] had initiated a deal with the hotel owners for wartime use. Such conversion of civilian facilities was rare outside of great country estates, especially in New York City. However, Lockwood and some other members of the OSS wanted to make sure their own people were given proper, and if necessary, discreet care.

Lying in bed, Mina opened her eyes wearily for the first time in weeks. The ceiling had been recently painted, the first thing she saw. Her chest ached where she had been shot. She guessed the bullet had glanced off her ribs. There was the quiet droning of a radio nearby in an adjoining room.

Sudden loud screams and cheers erupted from the other room.

---

[147] The War Department, or the United States Department of War as it was also known, was renamed to its modern moniker, the Department of Defense, in 1949.

Mina bolted out of the bed by reflex. Sitting in the chair next to her bed, Lockwood immediately held up a hand to assuage her. She hadn't even noticed him at first.

"It's okay, it's okay!" he reassured her.

"What's going on?" she asked, confounded.

Lockwood grinned ear-to-ear, brimming with near-boyish excitement. In all the time she had known him, she had never seen him smile like that.

Mina felt a stir of anxious anticipation well inside her. Naw…it couldn't be. Mina hoped against hope, desperately wishing that she wasn't wrong.

"It's over! The war is over!" he cried out, overjoyed.

At first, she didn't think she heard him right and felt a sense of unexpected disbelief. After three years of bloody fighting and nerve-wracking turmoil, the idea was almost inconceivable. Then a tidal wave of relief washed over her in pure unadulterated joy and elation.

The wellspring of emotion burst out of her and she let out a cry. She squeezed Lockwood in a bear bug that hurt her still-aching ribs but she didn't care.

Locked in her embrace, still beaming, his beard tickled her ear as he spoke. "Japan just gave their unconditional surrender. It's all over the news."

Still somewhat unsteady on her feet, Mina broke away from him and fast-limped to the window. She drew both curtains apart in a single gesture and peered at the street below.

Mina was inundated with the spectacle. Down in Times Square, it was pure jubilation. Confetti and streamers thrown from the high-rises filled the air, drifting down. From corner-to-corner, the streets were packed almost shoulder-to-shoulder, filled with a teeming throng of cheering people.

A boy in a newsboy cap yelled exuberantly, throwing confetti into the air. She saw a sailor grab a nearby nurse and dip her in a passionate liplock. Ecstatic, one man in a business suit popped the cork on a bottle of champagne, spraying foam all over a pair of gleeful women in flower-print dresses.

Down at street level, at the skyscraper of One Times Square where the ball fell almost[148] every New Year's, the electronic ticker scrolled across. It read: "***OFFICIAL TRUMAN ANNOUNCES JAPANESE SURRENDER***"

Still standing at the window, Mina continued looking down, mesmerized by the sight. It was only now really beginning to sink in. She could go home. She could meet some nice boy and settle down. She could actually have a life outside of the drudgery of blood and mud.

Approaching her side, Lockwood spoke. "Last Monday, we dropped the Gadget on Hiroshima. Then another on Thursday, on Nagasaki."

He put his hand on her shoulder and she turned to him.

"Thank you, Mina. If it weren't for you, they might have beaten us to it. Hirohito himself announced the surrender this morning."

Mina felt as if she were about to faint. She stumbled towards the bed. Lockwood looped his arm around her and aided her steps.

She lay down as he spoke, settling back onto the bedsheets.

"They're already sending ships to officially accept the surrender," he told her.

Reflective, Mina processed what he said. She spoke musingly.

"New black ships," she said in a soft contemplative voice.

Lockwood looked momentarily confused by the reference. "I'm sorry, what?"

"New black ships," she repeated. "When European powers first arrived in Japan in the sixteenth century, the

---

[148] The first ball drop was held on December 31, 1907, to welcome 1908. The ball drop has been held annually since then, except in 1942 and 1943 in observance of wartime blackouts.

wooden ships were coated with pitch for waterproofing. Heralds of a new age."

Mina blinked as the realization came to her.

"It's the end of an era," she said softly.

Lockwood smiled genially. "And a beginning of a new one," he added.

He put a hand on her shoulder comfortingly. "Get some rest Mina. A new age is upon us."

Tucking her in with near-fatherly disposition, he pulled the covers up to her shoulders and turned to leave.

Quiet, alone, Mina lay back in the bed in solemn reflection. She closed her eyes, a gentle smile curling her lips.

63 FATHER'S HAT

Washington DC
September 16, 1945

The stars-and-stripes flew over 1600 Pennsylvania Avenue. Outside the main gates of the carefully manicured White House lawn, men in black fedoras and trenchcoats walked the perimeter.

Oval Office
The light gleamed off the four polished Purple Heart medals. They were pinned on her brown Army dress uniform with skirt. Next to those medals were two Distinguished Service crosses and three Silver Stars, burnished to a high sparkle. Adjacent to those was a Legion of Merit, a Bronze Star, and a Soldier's Medal, the last awarded for her translation work. Officially, Mina was part of the Army Nurse Corps, and held the military rank of Captain. Her insignia reflected that.

Trying to remain stoic, Mina stood patiently on the soft blue carpet of the Oval Office, waiting for the bespectacled older gentleman before her to finish speaking. Part of her still couldn't believe she was standing here, in *this* office full of legacy and tradition.

Well dressed in a sharp, dark gray suit, President Harry Truman finished recounting her trials and tribulations over the past few months.

Mina glanced out at the small invitation-only crowd of two dozen people. In the front row, dressed in a cream-white suit, Lockwood beamed at her.

As the President neared the conclusion of his speech, Mina went ramrod-straight, trying not to smile.

Truman spoke. "Captain Mina Sakamoto. For your extraordinary heroism above and beyond the call of the duty, I hereby present you with the Congressional Medal of Honor, issued in secret, and effective immediately promote you to the rank of Lieutenant Colonel."

Standing in front of her, Truman tied the blue-ribboned medal around her neck. It was a gold, five-pointed star, each point tipped with trefoils. He shook her hand warmly.

Grinning from ear-to-ear, Lockwood was among the first to stand, cane barely necessary. Rising in a standing ovation, the attending crowd burst into raucous cheers and applause. Lights flashed from photographer's bulbs, illuminating Mina and the suited leader in a barrage of bright light.

As Mina stood side-by-side with the President, one photographer took a picture with his camera. The bulb flashed, capturing an image of black-and-white that froze that moment in time. It would be a photo Mina would look back on fondly for years to come.

Afterwards, at the open reception held in one of the White House's numerous ballrooms, the crowd mingled in a quiet hubbub and refreshments were served.

Wearing a formal western dress, Mrs. Sakamoto embraced her daughter, overflowing with pride. "I'm so proud of you honey. I heard it was a very brave thing you did in the Philippines. The soldiers tell me you saved many patients from a hospital under attack and brought them to safety."

Mina had a smile plastered on her face, struggling not to laugh. "Erhm…yes. Hospital. Patients." Wow, her mom really had no idea.

Her mother beamed. "My little girl. Such a brave nurse."

Mina just smiled back. Little did she know.

Her mother perked up with delight as she recognized an old friend from Hawaii across the room, excusing herself. Mina smiled after her.

Making his way through the crowd, Lockwood hobbled over to Mina and gave her a great big hug. He wore the white Panama hat and matching cream-white suit.

Mina grinned, fingering his suit's lapel. "I love the new suit," she remarked. "Goes well with the hat."

Gentle, almost tender, she touched the brim of the Panama hat on Lockwood's head. Growing wistful, she whispered. "You wear my father's hat. In more ways than one."

Lockwood gave her a wan smile. "I know I can't ever replace your father Mina."

"I know," she said, still smiling. Grinning, Mina wrapped her arms around him in a great big hug, looking up at him with her doe eyes. "I'm saying I found another one."

Lockwood squeezed her tight in a warm embrace. After a long moment, they stepped apart.

"So, what are you going to do now?" he asked.

Mina gave him a fond smile.

"I want to go home."

64 HOMECOMING

The horizon over the Hawaiian sea glowed a fiery orange-violet in the Pacific sunset. Amidst the cry of seagulls, the waves lapped at the shore.

Standing near the rustling palm trees waving in the breeze, was a familiar figure. Surfboard tucked under her arm, Mina stood at the shoreline, a fond smile on her face. She wore a pink two-piece swimsuit, raven hair tied back in a ponytail that swayed in the warm wind. It was her first time back to this particular beach since childhood. This time, it felt damn good. A warm sense of homecoming wrapped around her like a blanket, unencumbered by the struggles and turmoil of the last few years.

Wearing ivory-white swim trunks with dual-black stripes on the side, Lockwood stepped in next to her, his own larger surfboard under his arm.

Grinning, Mina spoke as she looked out to sea. "Sure you wanna take me up with that bum leg of yours?"

Lockwood was facetiously defensive, smiling. "Hey munchkin, I can take you on any day, leg or no leg! Besides, I actually do better in the water."

Mina's tone turned mischievous. "Oh really?" she said playfully. "Let's see!"

Grinning ear-to-ear in eager anticipation, she took off at a sprint, running out into the waves with her surfboard under her arm. Splashing out into the swelling sea, she lay down on the board and paddled out, her surrogate father close behind.

The warm seawater caressed her body like the hands of a gentle lover's, washing over her. It had been worth it. She stood atop the board, balancing atop the white froth as the wave crested, the orange glow of the sunset behind her.

Over the sound of surf and the waves, she heard Lockwood call out behind her. "Ride out the wave, Mina. Ride out the wave."

Beaming, Mina rode out the wave, without a care in the world. She grinned from ear-to-ear as she angled side-to-side. All of her toil and hardships of the last few years had finally culminated in triumphant freedom. Victorious, ecstatic glee filled her body as she surfed the waves, content satisfaction flooding her heart. Of all the things she had accomplished in the past few years, of all the things she had learned, there was one adage she had learned to follow above all else.

Ride out the wave.

65 AFTERWORD AND AUTHOR'S HISTORICAL NOTES

Mina Sakamoto is a fictional character. Although Mina is not a real person, there are a number of individuals she is partially based on.

As is normal in wars, wars are not fought just at the frontline, but behind enemy lines as well. This novel is written partially as a tribute to those who really did serve in such a capacity during the war and in subsequent wars. This book thanks them for their courage, dedication, and sometimes, their ultimate sacrifice.

Japanese-Americans OSS agents and the shadow war

During World War II, there actually were a small number of Japanese Americans that served in the OSS, going behind enemy lines in the style Mina does. However, they were mostly sent to the China-Burma-India theater, not Japan as was initially planned due to concerns that the risk of capture was too great (as was demonstrated by Mina's brush with counterintelligence in Tokyo).

The following is an excerpt from the CIA official web site[149], the successor to the OSS mentioned in the story. The excerpt discusses the real-life Japanese-American OSS agents.

"Japanese-Americans enlisted in the US Army during World War II even though the US government forced many of their families into internment camps in the wake of Imperial Japan's attack on Pearl Harbor. In late 1943, an OSS representative visited the military's Japanese American combat unit, the 442nd Infantry Regiment, at Camp Shelby in Mississippi. The representative asked for volunteers who could read and write Japanese and were willing to undertake extremely hazardous assignments. More than 100 men volunteered, but only 14 were ultimately selected for OSS missions. All were Nisei, the US-born children of Japanese immigrants.

The volunteers underwent rigorous training for operations behind enemy lines. For most of 1944, they studied Japanese language and geography,

---

[149] Staff. *Japanese Americans in World War II Intelligence.* CIA.gov, 11 May 2012. Web. 6 Oct. 2013. ⟨https://www.Cia.Gov/news-information/featured-story-archive/2012-featured-story-archive/japanese-americans-WWII-intel.Html/⟩.

survival skills, hand-to-hand combat, explosives, and radio operation. They were assigned to OSS Detachments 101 and 202, special operations units that operated in the China-Burma-India Theater. Once deployed, they were to interrogate prisoners, translate documents, monitor radio communications, and conduct covert operations. They left the US in November 1944."

According to the CIA website, some notable real-life Japanese American OSS soldier-spies and their deployments, (those made public) include:

China deployments:
    Chiyoki Ikeda
    Takao Tanabe
    Susumu Kazahaya
    George Kobayashi
    Tad Nagaki

India deployments:
    Dick Betsui
    Wilbert Kishinami

Burma deployments:
    Calvin Tottori
    Tom Baba
    Fumio Kido
    Shoichi Kurahashi
    Ralph Yempuku
    Junichi Buto
    Dick Hamada

(If any of you guys are still alive, kickin', and happen to be reading this novel by any chance, I just wanna say, "Thank you for your service!")

One notable factoid about the character of Mina is her proficiency in languages. It is well known that even to this day, American field operatives are often carefully selected from a pool of candidates known for academic achievement and proficiency in languages. Study hard! ☺ Oftentimes, students who are being considered for recruitment don't even know they're being interviewed.

Japanese Americans during World War II

Internment

As mentioned in the excerpt, unfortunately, due to unproven fears of sabotage, most Japanese Americans on the Pacific coast were forcibly relocated and detained in internment camps. They had to endure great hardship and loss of financial assets.

Hawaii was a special case. The vast majority of Japanese Americans and their immigrant parents in Hawaii were *not* interned due to socioeconomic and law enforcement reasons.

In Hawaii, the number of Japanese Americans relative to the rest of the population was considerable. Japanese Americans comprised over 35% of the territory's population with about 150,000 inhabitants. Economic pundits had predicted that detaining a third of the territory's population would have caused the entire economy of Hawaii to shut down.

During the entire war, there was not a single documented case of treason committed by a Japanese American.

Military Service

Later on, many people interned in the camps served during the war in various capacities and proved their loyalty. Notably, their deeds included translation in the Pacific and frontline combat in the European theater.

Units of service included the Military Intelligence Service, the 442nd Regimental Combat Team, the 522nd Field Artillery Battalion, and of course, a select few joined the OSS.

Before going further, it is important to note that on the *Pacific* front of World War II, with few exceptions Japanese-Americans generally did not serve in a *frontline* combat capacity. (One such exception was Ben Kuroki, the only Japanese-American in the United States Army Air Forces known to have served in combat operations in the Pacific theater of World War II.) Most served as translators. Unfortunately, they generally were not trusted to fight the Japanese despite their record-breaking service record in the European theater.

One of the most famous units is that of the aforementioned 442nd Regimental Combat Team and its component 100th Infantry Battalion, comprised almost entirely Japanese Americans, many of whom were volunteers.

Not being trusted to fight initially, the top brass had sent the 442nd through training several times as a delaying tactic. This bore fruit however, as in the end, members of the 442nd received training several times that of ordinary soldiers and became incredibly proficient.

One famous accolade of theirs is when they saved a lost battalion surrounded on all sides by German forces. This was the 1st Battalion, 141st Infantry (36th Infantry Division, originally Texas National Guard), which was surrounded by German forces in the Vosges Mountains on October 24, 1944.

After several rescue attempts by other units had already failed, the 442nd was sent in for a third attempt. After five days of intense fighting, the 442nd broke through the German lines, screaming "*Banzai*" at the top of their lungs and scaring the living hell out of the German troops. The 442nd rescued the battalion which had been stranded with little hope of salvation.

As of the writing of this historical notes section, the 442nd Regimental Combat Team is still the most decorated unit in American military history, having served with great distinction.

Other Allied spies of Asian descent

Other than the Americans, a number of Allied spies in

Japan were from Australia, presumably of Asian ethnicity. (No real surprise, given Australia's proximity to Japan).

Additionally, oftentimes, spies behind Japanese lines were Chinese. Dai Li was the spymaster in China who worked with the OSS. These spies were active in Burma and other areas of Southeast Asia, operating behind enemy lines.

As a fun side note, there have been rumors of Korean and second-generation Japanese-American infiltrators being airdropped over the Japanese countryside in black-painted planes. (As mentioned in the novel, Korea had been occupied by Japan for several decades prior to the war and there were Korean conscripts in the Japanese army. Ethnic Koreans in Japan would not have attracted much attention.) However, these rumors have never been substantiated.

Notable real-life female spies in World War II

A number of spies in World War II were young and female. In France, children even younger than Mina were used to smuggle firearms to French resistance fighters under their coats due to their innocent appearance. Oftentimes, Nazi soldiers would summarily dismiss them during roundups and let them pass by.

Of the female spies that served the Allies in World War II, here are some notable ones:

Nancy Wake (a.k.a. the White Mouse) - This woman was known for both her femininity (silk stockings, expensive face cream) and brutality (killing men with her bare hands).

Krystyna Skarbek, a.k.a. Christine Granville - Granville had a unique skill set - she was an excellent skier. She put her skills to good use by transporting information back and forth from Poland to Hungary through the mountains.

Virginia Hall - This woman is notable because she had a disability, a prosthetic leg. Quite famously, she was one of the Nazis' most wanted ("The woman who limps is one of the most dangerous Allied agents in France," one German poster read.)

Violette Szabo - If you are a gamer, you may have already heard of her - the video game *Velvet Assassin* is inspired by her story. Szabo was only 23 years old. She parachuted into France, where she aided in the sabotage of a railroad, disruption of enemy communications, and passing of strategic information back to her handlers. Szabo is contentiously known for her final, brutal gun battle. She made a heroic last stand in a farmhouse against Nazi soldiers, providing cover fire so her French resistance handlers could escape. Wielding her Sten gun, she killed multiple soldiers and fought until she ran out of ammunition, whereupon she was captured. (German records state they incurred no casualties in the incident.) Unfortunately, she was taken to Gestapo headquarters where she was tortured and raped repeatedly. She was then transported to Ravensbrück concentration camp and later executed in the snow. Her life story was later turned into a book and then a movie, both entitled *Carve Her Name with Pride*.

The Japanese atomic weapons program(s)

Japan really did have an atomic weapons program during World War II (actually, *two* competing projects, one run by the army, one by the navy.) In 2002 it was discovered that Japan had completed blueprints for a 20-kiloton bomb. However, there are varying accounts of how far the Japanese got in terms of actually constructing it or how much uranium they were able to enrich. Accounts vary from simple uranium enrichment to plans for launching an atomic strike on the Allied Pacific fleet as it entered Japanese waters, just two weeks prior to Hiroshima (the latter being the premise of this novel).

As mentioned briefly in the story, the Japanese focused more on spending funds on radar technology instead of atomic weapons development. This was due to Japanese projections that their weapon could not be completed prior to the end of the war. The case was similar with the Germans, although both of these Axis powers made at least some progress in its development.

The inception

As mentioned in the story's prologue, in 1934, Tohoku University professor Hikosaka Tadayoshi's released his findings on "atomic physics theory." Hikosaka noted the massive amounts of energy contained by nuclei, as well as the possibility of creating both nuclear power generation and weapons.

The (real) egghead

Also mentioned very briefly in the novel during Mina's initial mission briefing, the real-life leading figure in the Japanese atomic program was Dr. Yoshio Nishina, a close associate of Niels Bohr and a contemporary of Albert Einstein.

(In terms of hierarchy, the character of the Owl in the story is supposed to be a subordinate of Dr. Nishina.)

In 1931, Nishina established his own Nuclear Research Laboratory to study high-energy physics at the Riken[150] Institute (the Institute for Physical and Chemical Research), which itself had been established in 1917 in Tokyo to promote basic research. This is the same facility featured in the story.

Riken still exists today, at a new location, in Wako just outside Tokyo.

The hardware

Cyclotrons are particle accelerators used for conducting nuclear research, and were a vital part of atomic weapons development.

In 1936, Nishina built his first 26-inch (660 mm) cyclotron.

In 1937, he built another 60-inch (1,500 mm), 220-ton cyclotron.

In 1938, Japan also purchased a cyclotron from the University of California, Berkeley.

…and they have a plan

In 1939 Nishina recognized the military potential of nuclear fission, and was worried that the Americans were working on a nuclear weapon which might be used against Japan.

In the early summer of 1940, Nishina met Lieutenant-General Takeo Yasuda on a train. Nishina told the general about the possibility of building nuclear weapons.

The Japanese fission project formally began in April 1941 when Yasuda acted on then-Army Minister Hideki Tojo's order to investigate the possibilities of nuclear weapons.

---

[150] As mentioned earlier, sometimes spelled "Rikken" with another "k"

Yasuda passed the order down the chain of command to the director of Riken, who in turn passed it to Nishina, whose laboratory division at Riken had over 100 researchers.

Ni-Go Project

The Imperial Japanese Army thus had an experimental atomic weapons project at Riken, the Ni-Go Project. Its main goal was uranium-235 enrichment.

However, the separator project came to an end when the building housing it was destroyed in a fire caused by one of the USAAF's raids on Tokyo. As mentioned in the story, the Riken facility was destroyed in a raid in April, one month after the Great Tokyo Air Raid. (More details on this in the following sections.)

F-Go Project

In 1943, the Imperial Japanese Navy commenced a different nuclear research program, the F-Go Project, under a different scientist, Bunsaku Arakatsu at the Imperial University, Kyoto.

A student of Einstein at Berlin University, next to Nishina, Arakatsu was ostensibly the most notable nuclear physicist in Japan.

One major center of the F-Go Project was its facilities in Konan, modern-day Hungnam in North Korean, featured in the story.

Heavy water was processed as a byproduct from nearby ammonia plants and used as part of Japan's nuclear reactor experiments. (Also, more details on this in the following sections.)

Postwar aftermath

After the conclusion of the war in August, on November 24, 1945, the Riken's remaining cyclotrons were dismantled and thrown into Tokyo Bay by occupation forces at the behest of the US Secretary of War in Washington D.C.

Would you like to know more?

A good source for further reading on Japan's atomic bomb project(s) during the World War II era is the non-fiction book *Japan's Secret War: Japan's Race Against Time to Build Its Own Atomic Bomb* by Robert K. Wilcox.

The Great Tokyo Air Raid a.k.a. Operation Meetinghouse

Operation Meetinghouse, or the Great Tokyo Air Raid as it was called, was a real event that occurred the night of March 9-10, 1945. It was one of the largest air raids in history, destroying fifteen square miles of the city. Many of the events depicted in the story, such as the intense fires, the white-hot bridge, were real and actually did occur that noteworthy night. (As to whether or not a teenage Japanese nurse single-handedly stormed an atomic research facility and took out the complex by calling in an air strike and shooting her way out, we may never know.) ☺

As mentioned, the Riken Institute was a real atomic research facility located in the Komagome district of Tokyo, which conducted atomic weapons research during World War II. However, the firebombing that destroyed it was a part of smaller raid that occurred on April 13, 1945. This was approximately one month after the massive firebombing of the Great Tokyo Air Raid depicted in the story. This smaller air raid demolished the building and severely damaged the cyclotrons used for atomic weapons research. In a disputed account, one of the supposed officers in charge of the project stated the air raid set their project back by three months. (This officer was partially the inspiration for the character Rain in the novel.)

For the purposes of the story, the Riken Institute was not the actual primary center of research for the project; Mina discovered most of the facility's project contents had been moved from Riken for security reasons and she had to take drastic measures to ensure their destruction.

The Konan Cave Facility (in Modern day Hungnam)

During World War II, Japan really did have a James Bond-style secret laboratory in an underground cave facility at Konan, (now called Hungnam, in present day North Korea). It was part of the aforementioned Imperial Japanese Navy's F-Go project. The hills above Konan were a major site of uranium ore. (Other searches for uranium ore conducted by the Japanese military range from Fukushima Prefecture in Japan, to Korea, China, and Burma.)

Here is where things get a little contentious - was there an actual atomic bomb test there? An American journalist named John Snell, wrote a contentious article in 1946 for the Atlanta Constitution, detailing a purported atomic bomb test. His article was immediately classified and not made public until years after.

What is *really* interesting is that there are (contradictory) reports of an atomic blast and ensuing mushroom cloud on the coast of Konan near the very end of the war. (The novel portrays a similar explosion occurring several months prior to this possible actual event, and at a slightly different location more inland. Also, there are confirmed accounts of the Japanese using prisoners as bomb test subjects arranged in the manner described in the story, although for non-nuclear weapons.)

The date of the purported real-life Japanese atomic test at the Konan site is particularly interesting: August 12, 1945, three days before Japan's surrender. This led to the oft-speculated rumor that if Japan really had a working atomic bomb, they were waiting to utilize it as a sort of last-ditch attempt at resistance. Possibly, this was to retaliate for Hiroshima and Nagasaki, which had occurred only a few days earlier.

However, for dramatic purposes, this event was not incorporated into the story, as it was thought the plot would be more interesting and the stakes higher if the planned attack took place prior to Hiroshima and Nagasaki. For most people, those atomic bombings mark the end of the war. Additionally, most analysts and military officials of the time realized that by the BEGINNING of 1945, Japan was already certain to lose the war due to heavy losses incurred in the Pacific and the encroachment of American forces.

What *is* confirmed however, is that just prior to the end of the war, the Soviet Red Army swooped in and occupied the Konan cave facility before other Allied forces could do so. Furthermore, just a few weeks after the war ended, the Soviet army shot down an American B-29 straying too close to the atomic facilities, in the name of "security" and airspace violations. The Soviets later deconstructed the entire Konan facility and transported it back to Russia. As of the writing of this statement, there is no clear indication what nuclear information they might have gleaned from the facility and its contents.

As in World War II, the cave facility at Konan once again became a hub of nuclear weapons development during the Cold War. This is because it is a site for uranium mining and enrichment, as the area is known to have uranium deposits. It continues to be part of the North Korean nuclear weapons program today.

U-Boat Uranium

Germany really did have a U-Boat submarine that attempted to ship uranium secretly to the Japanese, with two Japanese envoys onboard. The real-life submarine was named U-234, but unlike in the story, the U-Boat surrendered to Allied forces following Germany's capitulation, instead of just prior. U-234 was captured by the *USS Sutton* off of the banks of Newfoundland, on May 14, 1945.

However, the uranium found on board was supposedly not of weapons grade and still needed to be refined. Declassified documents, including the sub's manifest, show there were 560 kilograms of uranium oxide in 10 cases destined for the Japanese army. Two Japanese officers were aboard accompanying the cargo. Upon realizing they would not reach their destination, the two committed suicide by Luminal overdose (a barbiturate sleeping pill). They were buried at sea by the U-Boat crew. For the duration of the Cold War, the knowledge of onboard uranium captured from U-234 was classified due to the ramifications of such an fact.

Following U-234's surrender, the uranium onboard "disappeared." Supposedly, the uranium from the real-life U-234 U-Boat was sent to the Manhattan Project's Oak Ridge diffusion plant. After enrichment, the uranium (approximately one-fifth of what was needed for a complete bomb) was later used in the "Little Boy" atomic bomb dropped on Hiroshima.

The I-400 series submarines and Ulithi Atoll

Japan really did have their own mammoth "Death Star" type submarines in World War II. Designated the I-400 series, they were designed to launch sneak attacks on American forces. Admiral Isoroku Yamamoto, one of the major planners of the attack on Pearl Harbor, conceived of the original idea.

Instead of the atomic bomber as portrayed in this novel, the plan was to use the subs to launch trios of Aichi A6M Seiran seaplanes. The planes would bomb US coastal cities, including Washington D.C. and New York in an effort to terrorize the American populace. (The existence of these onboard seaplanes were actually not known to Allied intelligence until after the war ended, although Allied intelligence knew of the submarines themselves. Some other Japanese submarines could carry one or two seaplanes.) The submarine routes consisted of going around the tip of South America and heading north along the American coastline. Other plans utilizing the I-400 series included using the submarines' seaplanes to airdrop plague rats and bubonic-plague-carrying fleas on West Coast cities.

The planes really were painted over in American colors, much to the chagrin of the crew, who thought the tactic was dishonorable, not to mention breaking the rules of war. In the novel, the bomber is changed to a Mitsubishi Ki-21 for weight purposes, re-assembled just prior to launch. This change in the novel was needed because even stripped-down, it is unlikely a Seiran seaplane bomber could even lift off with the weight of a five-ton "Little Boy" type atomic bomb.

However, the Japanese seaplane-bomber plan was scrapped in the wake of Admiral Yamamoto's death and the advancement of American forces in the Pacific. The plan was updated to attack the American Pacific fleet stationed at Ulithi Atoll, as described in the story (sans the atomic aspect of the tale). The plan was to send these subs on a stealth mission to launch planes that would bomb enemy ships, including the fifteen carriers that would be at Ulithi preparing for the invasion of the Japanese home islands. However, following atomic bombings of Hiroshima and Nagasaki, Japan surrendered before the plan could be executed.

Following the end of the war, the two existing I-400 series submarines surrendered separately to American forces. Upon first seeing one, the boarding Allied sailors marveled at the gargantuan nature of the submarine, which was the largest of its time. ("Look at the size of that thing!") These advanced submarines were brought to Hawaii to be studied and reverse-engineered by the U.S. Navy. This led in part to the next-generation of American submarines, which bore more than a resemblance to the I-400 series.

In regards to the few specific ships of the I-400 series, their fates are detailed as follows:

As mentioned, I-400 and I-401 returned to Japan and were surrendered to the Allies. After the war, these two were taken to Hawaii for examination and studied. While there, the U.S. Navy received a message that the Soviets were sending an inspection team to examine the submarines. With the onset of the Cold War, to keep the technology out of Soviet hands, the submarines were scuttled in 1946 off the coast of Oahu, Hawaii.

The final resting place of these submarines was uncovered by deep-sea submarine crews of the Hawaii Undersea Research Laboratory in the new millennium. The I-401 was found in March of 2005 and the I-400 was found in August 2013 by the same team. The story was featured on CNN.

I-402 was converted to carry fuel to from the East Indies to Japan, but never performed such a mission. Along with other captured Japanese submarines, she was scuttled off Goto Island in 1946 as part of Operation Road's End. The submarines were taken to a position designated as Point Deep Six, about 60 km west from Nagasaki and off the island of Goto-Retto. They were packed with charges of C2 explosive and destroyed. Today, the subs rest at a depth of 200 meters.

Construction of two further ships of the I-400 design, I-404 and I-405, were stopped before completion, although I-404 was approximately 95% complete. A further 13 boats were canceled before construction started.

And what of the I-403 mentioned in the story? According to historical records, the construction of the I-403 was canceled in October of 1943. However, for the purposes of this story, the cancellation was a fabrication meant to allow its crew to carry out its secret mission.

Ooh, shiny!

Gadgets! Ah! The fun stuff! Most of the gadgets described in the novel really were used by the OSS and its British counterpart, the SOE, during World War II.

Everything from the thumbknives, fake latex callouses, secret radio, C2 and C3 plastic explosive, Lambertsen rebreather, Fairbairne-Sykes smatchet, Minox miniature camera, .22 caliber High Standard HDM silenced pistol, early version of the Fulton recovery system, etc. etc. are all examples of real-life OSS gear used at the time.

The only two exceptions are Lockwood's curare cigarette and Mina's exploding cookies (which are variants of real-life gadgets. These two exact gadgets depicted in the novel were invented for this story, although others may have had similar ideas). The OSS did have a .22 caliber cigarette gun, which was modified to be a curare dart. The cookies are based on real-life exploding loaves of bread, filled with "Aunt Jemima" described in the story. Again, Aunt Jemima powder is real-life explosive white powder similar in consistency to the namesake pancake mix. It can be moistened, shaped, and baked in an oven without detonating. (Presumably, into cookies!) The powder is often also called HMX or octogen. The substance can even be eaten, with relatively low toxicity in most cases.

Mina's trusty, low-tech slingshot doesn't really count as standard US-government issue. ☺ Nor are her roller skates, which had already been popular with kids for decades prior to the events of the book.

Final Words

Thank you, everyone, who has read this book. For those of you who have stayed to the end and are reading these words, there's a little treat in store for you. Read on! ☺

EPILOGUE

Out in the sun-dappled Pacific Ocean, the fin of the great white shark protruded above the waves as it threaded its way. Suddenly, the shark started to wriggle and struggle, surfacing as something registered within its primitive brain.

Something was churning inside its stomach.

Claw-like mangled fingertips burst out of the skin of the shark's belly. Blood-coated hands ripped out a gory tear along its underside, trailing a gash several feet long.

Floundering, tail flopping wildly in the churning white froth, the shark thrashed about as something inside its belly cut its way out in a perversion of birth. Its gaping maw of razor sharp teeth clamped open and shut, flailing in its death throes.

Straining, two arms protruded from the gash in its belly, tearing it even wider. The biceps were covered in gory, tattered shreds of a flight suit.

Wild-eyed, livid, Rain emerged headfirst, climbing free of his living entombment. Floating in the churning waves, he let out a livid scream filled with bloodlust and fury.

ABOUT THE AUTHOR

Clive Lee is the author of the screenplay *Darkfire Nova* which attained Semi-Finalist in the 2009 PAGE International Screenwriting Awards, within the top 25 in the Science-Fiction category, out of several thousand total entrants. His eclectic background of hobbies and academic interests include investigative forensics, psychology, and martial arts. He has worked full-time professionally in the realms of computer network security and web development, both in the federal and private sector. Clive often incorporates multiple elements of the aforementioned disciplines into his fiction writing and is a passionate hobbyist filmmaker and writer.

Facebook: http://www.facebook.com/coralhare
Email: coralhare@gmail.com

NOTES

NOTES

NOTES

NOTES

NOTES

NOTES

NOTES

NOTES

NOTES

NOTES

NOTES

NOTES

NOTES

NOTES

NOTES

NOTES

NOTES

NOTES

NOTES

NOTES

NOTES

NOTES

NOTES

NOTES

NOTES

NOTES

_____

_____

_____

_____

_____

_____

_____

_____

_____

_____

_____

_____

_____

_____

_____

_____

NOTES

NOTES

_____

_____

_____

_____

_____

_____

_____

_____

_____

_____

_____

_____

_____

_____

_____

_____

_____

_____

Valerie,
This isn't one of
those books that say
flowery things no-one ever
means - so many of these things
really hit home for me. You are *all*
of me and you always will be -
       I Love You -
              Judy
              1-10-00

*F*or there is no friend like a sister
In calm or stormy weather:
To cheer one on the tedious way,
To fetch one if one goes astray,
To lift one if one totters down,
To strengthen whilst one stands.

Christina Rossetti

Other books in the *"Language of"* Series... by

Blue Mountain Press ®

The Language of Love

The Language of Happiness

The Language of Friendship

The Language of Marriage

The Language of Teaching

The Language of Courage and Inner Strength

Thoughts to Share with a Wonderful Mother

Thoughts to Share with a Wonderful Father

Thoughts to Share with a Wonderful Son

Thoughts to Share with a Wonderful Daughter

It's Great to Have a Brother like You

The "Language of" Series...

It's Great to Have a

SISTER

like You

A Collection from Blue Mountain Arts®

Blue Mountain Press ®

Boulder, Colorado

The publisher wishes to acknowledge and thank Roxana Popescu for her extensive help in compiling the poems and quotations in this collection.

Library of Congress Catalog Card Number: 98-42677
ISBN: 0-88396-481-3

ACKNOWLEDGMENTS appear on page 48.

Manufactured in Thailand
Second Printing: May 1999

This book is printed on recycled paper.

Library of Congress Cataloging-in-Publication Data

It's great to have a sister like you : a collection from Blue
Mountain Arts.

     p. cm.
  ISBN 0-88396-481-3 (alk. paper)
  1. Sisters--Literary collections. I. Blue Mountain Arts (Firm)
  PN6071.S425 L36 1999
  808.8'0352045--dc21

                                    98-42677
                                      CIP
                                      Rev.

Blue Mountain Press INC.

P.O. Box 4549, Boulder, Colorado 80306

Contents

(Authors listed in order of first appearance)

Christina Rossetti

Ann Turrel

Donna Fargo

Theodore Roethke

Charlotte Brontë

Bonnie S. Hoffman

Barbara Mathias

Roxana Popescu

Susan Hickman Sater

William Shakespeare

Lea Marie Tomlyn

Casey Marie Mullens

Barbara J. Hall

Beth Fagan Quinn

Carey Martin

Laine Parsons

Mary Kunz

Linda Brown

Kelly Lise

Laurel Atherton

Geri Danks

James Rhodes

Joy Harjo

Lady Mary Wortley Montagu

darcy frances meese

Tim Connor

Ellen Goodman

Christine Downing

Letty Cottin Pogrebin

Alfonsina Storni

Ernestine Schumann-Heink

Olga Berggolts

Louisa May Alcott

Phyllis McGinley

Lord Byron

Nicole D. Myers

Laura Tracy

Marin McKay

Margaret Davidson

Patricia Ziemba

Paul Gauguin

Gwenda Isaac Jennings

Deborah Miller O'Bryan

George Eliot

Laurel Bosshart

Acknowledgments

My Sister Is...

Someone who helps me find my smile. Who accepts me for what I am. Who lets me know that my efforts really are worthwhile, and that my accomplishments are worthy ones. She lets me know that she will catch me if I fall. She's so much more wonderful than she will admit to being. She watches out for me and helps me through it all.

My Sister Is...

someone I'm very proud to be related to. Having her as such a special part of my family has given me memories that I wouldn't trade for anything — and hopes that I'll have for as long as I live. Even if there are times when the two of us are far away from each other, our thoughts will make sure we stay together.

My Sister Is...

a person who is great to have around. She's someone who laughs at my jokes (maybe because she has the same warped sense of humor!), and she understands the times when I need a shoulder to cry on. She is there for me in the exact same way that I will always be there for her. Our friendship will always remain, and our love will never depart.

My Sister...

deserves to know that even though I don't always get a chance to show it, she is absolutely essential to the happiness... that lives within my heart.

 — Ann Turrel

To My Sister, with Love

If I gathered up all my wishes for you
and put them in a pretty basket,
your multi-colored bouquet would look like this:

You'd have peace from every conflict you encounter in your life, all the love you need, and perfect health to enjoy this journey of life. Your basket would be filled with dreams come true, goals met, and satisfaction with your achievements.

There would be many friendships to enhance your feeling of community and belonging. A variety of meaningful relationships gives life spice and balance, so I'd fill your basket with the kind of friends you can call on, go places with, and care for.

There would be prayers for your freedom from everything that binds you and solutions to any problems you may have in life. In this pretty basket of wishes, you would have everything you need and want, and every situation and circumstance you encounter would enhance your potential for happiness.

May the time and concern you've invested in others translate into the kind of love and appreciation for yourself that you so deserve. You are worthy. You are beautiful. You are loved.

As I stir through the memories of what we've shared through the years as sisters, I want you to know that I have a bouquet of wishes for you... I wish you love, I wish you happiness, and I hope your every dream is coming true.

— Donna Fargo

To My Sister

O my sister remember the stars the tears the trains
The woods in spring the leaves the scented lanes
Recall the gradual dark the snow's unmeasured fall
The naked fields the cloud's immaculate folds
Recount each childhood pleasure: the skies of azure
The pageantry of wings the eye's bright treasure.

Keep faith with present joys refuse to choose
Defer the vice of flesh the irrevocable choice
Cherish the eyes the proud incredible poise
Walk boldly my sister but do not deign to give
Remain secure from pain preserve thy hate thy heart.

 — Theodore Roethke

You know full as well as I do the value
of sisters' affection to each other;
there is nothing like it in this earth.

 Charlotte Brontë

For there is no friend like a sister
In calm or stormy weather:
To cheer one on the tedious way,
To fetch one if one goes astray,
To lift one if one totters down,
To strengthen whilst one stands.

Christina Rossetti

Shells of Sisterhood

Seashells
   a remembrance of the past
   a salty familiarity carried forward

The ocean's past finding its way onto the sandy beaches
   into the hands of two small sisters — our hands

Our hands used to gather shells together
   memories collected and put in our bucket
   without much thought

Remember the times
   we searched the beach for our own unique treasure
   yours needed to be different from mine
   mine needed to be different from yours

Somehow as the sun set over the ocean
   our separate treasures became one in our shared bucket
   put away for safe-keeping

As time drifted by
 we each seemed to move farther down the beach
 looking for unique treasures and individuality

Realizing with each new wave
 our direction forward becomes full of newness
  new challenges
  new faces
  newfound treasures
  new uniqueness

But every once in a while a new wave will brush ashore
 a precious shell
 a shell of remembrance of a time of innocence
 and childhood faces

Connecting us to another time
 to a shared bucket full of shells
 a bucket full of sisterly memories
 a bucket we each cherish in our own way

Knowing that whatever new bucket of shells we may come across
 that old bucket full of memories will bond us for life
 giving us the strength and love to continue on our journey

 Bonnie S. Hoffman

Your sister is your other self. She is your alter ego, your reflection, your foil, your shadow. She can represent both sides of you at the same time, thus throwing you into an emotional tailspin. You are different in detail of how you live your lives, but not in substance.

 Barbara Mathias

My Sister

Do stars still shine brightly for you?
They've gotten kind of dim for me.
It's been so long since we've talked.
Every time I look at you you've gotten closer to the ceiling.
Do you realize that one day you'll be taller than me?
Your foot is already as big as mine. It's not fair —
I'm the big sister here.
Pretty soon you'll be passing me your outgrown clothes;
maybe you'll pass me your smile or your long lashes, too.
You are so beautiful; I'm proud to be your sister.
The words you sing fly out of your mouth like butterflies.
Your candied smile surfaces when I try to be dignified
   while tripping.
I love how you always have time to jump on the trampoline,
but when I try to squeeze in a dose of my typical philosophies,
suddenly the phone's ringing or your elbow itches.
I don't wish I were you, but usually I wish I were with you.
You are such an innocent optimist. No, a realist.
I am a pessimist.
Thanks for adding water to my glass.

 Roxana Popescu

It is a wonderful feeling to know I have a sister I can depend on, one who has stood beside me through everything, who loves me just for who I am, and who means more to me than I can ever express. There aren't many people who have gone through all that we have together and emerged with a bond as strong as ours.

 Susan Hickman Sater

A ministering angel shall my sister be.

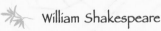 William Shakespeare

Sister, You Can Accomplish Anything You Choose...

I Just Know You Can!

If you could see through my eyes,
I wonder what you'd be feeling right now,
because I can see you as you really are —
powerful, sensitive, determined, and gracious.
I can see you achieving everything
 you choose to achieve.
I can see you being exactly
who and what you want to be.

Look through my eyes for an instant,
and you'll see yourself flourishing
and conquering all limitations.
Look through my eyes
and see who you really are
and what you are capable of.
You can accomplish anything —
 I know you can.

 Lea Marie Tomlyn

To My Younger Sister

I was four years old when we first met
And you had experienced only an hour of life
Staring into those two dark eyes
That peered at me from the depths of
   my mother's arms
I realized that I had a sister

At first I didn't like you much
You cried and fussed and stole my mother away
While I stood waiting, watching
Hoping that you would leave so things could
   return to normal
But you remained here

Time passed quickly in my child-mind
Soon we were playing together on the swing set
Making mudpies in the yard
And waging war on one another with
   winter snowballs
We became best friends

Then I reached my teenage years
Trading coloring books and sandboxes
    for "adult things"
I pulled away from you
To find my place in a world of false friends
    and identities
But you waited for me

Through the years we've grown together
With a love that only true sisters can know
Sharing good times as well as bad
And although we inhabit two different
    separate bodies
Within us beats one heart

I will be leaving this place soon
Embarking on a journey to find my future
But though I will be far away
Remember that you are my best friend
    and will always be
My sister

 Casey Marie Mullens

What a Family Is For...

A family is a special need inside the heart of us all.
In a family, you find
the cherished togetherness,
understanding, and unconditional love
that make life and keep it that way.
For a family accepts you as you are,
never focusing on your outside attributes
but on the many qualities within —
the person you are inside.
A family delights in every progress you make,
consoles your disappointments,
and stands beside you come what may.
Whatever happens, your family will be there
to urge you on, inspire you,
or put an arm around your shoulders
and let you know it's going to be okay.
A family's specialty is loving you
and providing a special place
to welcome you home with loving pride in all that you do.

That's what a family is for.

— Barbara J. Hall

My sister,
it's hard to imagine
my life, my secrets,
without thinking of you
and feeling your open warmth.
I know that we have
a lot in common
that brings us together as a family,
but there is more than that —
there is the bond of friendship,
of trusting, caring, being there,
of knowing our childhood memories
were created together.
I look back on the friends
that I chose long ago
and I wonder what I was looking for,
because the best friend
I could ever have had
was always right beside me.

 Beth Fagan Quinn

❧ A Sister Is... ❧

A sister is someone more special than words. She's love mixed with friendship; the best things in life. She's so much inner beauty blended together with an outward appearance that brings a smile to the happiness in your heart.

A sister is one of the most precious people in the story of your life. And you'll always be together, whether you're near or apart.

Together, you have shared some of the most special moments two people have ever shared. A sister is a perspective on the past, and she's a million favorite memories that will always last. A sister is a photograph that is one of your most treasured possessions. She's a note that arrives on a special day, and when there's news to share, she's the first one you want to call. A sister is a reminder of the blessings that come from closeness. Sharing secrets. Disclosing dreams. Learning about life together.

A sister is a confidante and a counselor. She's a dear and wonderful friend, and — in certain ways — something like a twin. She's a hand within your hand; she's so often the only one who really understands. A sister is honesty and trust enfolded with love. She's sometimes the only person who sees the horizon from your point of view, and she helps you to see things more clearly. She is a helper and a guide, and she is a feeling, deep inside, that makes you wonder what you would ever do without her.

What is a sister? She's someone more special than words; someone beautiful and unique. And in so many ways, there is no one who is loved so dearly.

 Carey Martin

A Sister Is...

...a friend and a smile and a rainbow
all rolled into one.

— Laine Parsons

...always the first person
I think of when I want to share,
or if I just need a special person
to confide in.

— Mary Kunz

...my closest companion... my best friend... the person
I most want to share the news with when things go right;
and the one I rely on when things go wrong.

— Carey Martin

...a friend who has the ability
to be impartial yet honest,
loyal yet independent,
true yet fair,
and always compassionate.

— Linda Brown

...a voice on the phone that calls me
at home to keep up to date on the news...
a happy dream from a distant day when
imaginations ran wild. My sister is a
beautiful woman — who's a reflection
of herself as a child.

— Kelly Lise

...the best there is. The absolute
best. And I appreciate everything
about her: her beautiful spirit, the
intertwining of our lives, and the way
she brings so many smiles my way.

— Laurel Atherton

...like a breath of spring
through the storms of winter,
a guiding star in the darkness of night.

 Geri Danks

To My Sister

You have such a heart for people.
No one else would listen
with such gentle tenderness
to the woes and worries of others,
and offer words of comfort
    and encouragement
that are always right on the mark.

You have a heart for laughter, too,
and for seeing the humor in this
crazy, sometimes bewildering world.
You have a heart full of love, too.
This probably is what brings you
so deeply into the lives of people.

May the love that you give away
come back to you
a hundred times over.

 — James Rhodes

All living things evolve and are involved in a pattern of struggle and release. This includes sisterhood. My sister and I came through the same door of our mother, we ate from the same earth... Our pattern of sisterhood makes an ongoing spiral, and within that spiral are our families, our communities, the earth, stars, all time. The spiral resembles two women carrying water through a battlefield in a rain of arrows. It resembles a long snake of relatives who walk through history, from the eastern hills of time immemorial. The light balances the dark. Wildness walks next to her steady sister. They make it to the other side together.

— Joy Harjo

There can be no situation in life in which the conversation of my dear sister will not administer some comfort to me.

— Lady Mary Wortley Montagu

"The best gift..."

the best gift you could ever give me
comes with neither ribbons
nor frilly, fancy bows
the best gift you could ever give me
does not fade with the times
it is not some passing fad
the best gift you could ever give me
is not wrapped in paper
nor encased in a box
the best gift you could ever give me
comes only with a smile
and a heartfelt hug

the only gift I could ever want
is the love that only sisters share

 darcy frances meese

My Little Sister

She came into the world my mother's prize
   after 3 boys and 40 years.
   She was a joy and a bundle of love and fun.
Her smile brought tears to my eyes as I gazed upon
   her porcelain-like body so radiant and glowing.
As I watched her grow into womanhood, I relished her youthful
   spirit and generous heart.
                  Now that she has a family of her own,
every once in a while I get to relive those earlier feelings and
   memories when I see her children, carbon copies of her mold.
She has been the glue in our family these past years
               that has held us all together.
In spite of careers, travel, other families and responsibilities
   she has done her best to see that we all never drift
farther apart than the nearest telephone.
     But however old she gets, she will always be my little sister.
Loving, supportive, giving and caring.
   She has never disappointed me in all these years and she has
always been there when I needed a friendly voice and sympathetic ear.
          Even though she is my little sister, she will
always walk tall in my life.

Tim Connor

The family... may be the one social glue strong enough to withstand the centrifuge of special interests which send us spinning away from each other... There, the old are our parents and the young are our children. There, we care about each other's lives. There, self-interest includes concern for the future of the next generation. Because they are ours.

Our families are not just the people (if I may massacre Robert Frost) who, "when you have to go there, they have to let you in." They are the people who maintain an unreasonable interest in each other. They are the natural peacemakers in the generation war.

"Home" is the only place in society where we now connect along the ages, like discs along the spine of society. The only place where we remember that we're all related. And that's not a bad idea to go home to.

 Ellen Goodman

Relationships between sisters seem
to be more intense and emotionally
intimate than between brothers, which
means that it may also be harder for
us to tolerate differences without
experiencing them as betrayal.

— Christine Downing

Sisterhood is such a complicated
subject for me; it's about biology
and family history, lies and love,
identity, secrecy, and the gut-level
truth that one distills not from facts
but from feelings. Most of all, for
me, sisterhood is about equality
and acceptance.

— Letty Cottin Pogrebin

My Sister

It's ten. Evening. The room is in half light.
My sister's sleeping, her hand on her chest; although
her face is very white, her bed entirely white,
the light, as if knowing, almost doesn't show.

She sinks into the bed the way pinkish fruit
does, into the deep mattress of soft grass.
Wind brushes her breasts, lifts them resolute-
ly chaste, measuring seconds as they pass.

I cover her tenderly with the white spread
and keep her lovely hands safe from the air.
On tiptoes I close all the doors near her bed,
leave the windows open, pull the curtain, prepare

for night. A lot of noise outside. Enough to drown
in: quarreling men, women with the juiciest
gossip. Hatred drifting upward, storekeepers shouting down
below. O voices, stop! Don't touch her nest.

Now my sister is weaving her silk cocoon
like a skillful worm. Her cocoon is a dream.
She weaves a pod with threads of a gold gleam.
Her life is spring. I am the summer afternoon.

She has only fifteen Octobers in her eyes
and so the eyes are bright, clear, and clean.
She thinks that storks from strange lands fly unseen,
leaving blond children with small red feet. Who tries

to come in? Is it you, now, the good wind?
You want to see her? Come in. But first cool
my forehead a second. Don't freeze the pool
of unwild dreams I sense in her. Undisciplined

they want to flood in and stay here, like you,
staring at that whiteness, at those tidy cheeks,
those fine circles under her eyes that speak
simplicity. Wind, you would see them and, falling to

your knees, cry. If you love her at all, be good
to her, for she will flee from wounding light.
Watch your word and intention. Her soul like wood
or wax is shaped, but rubbing makes a blight.

Be like that star which in the night stares at
her, whose eye is filtered through glassy thread.
That star rubs her eyelashes, turning like a cat
quiet in the sky, not to wake her in her bed.

Fly, if you can, among her snowy trees.
Pity her soul! She is immaculate.
Pity her soul! I know everything, but she's
like heaven and knows nothing. Which is her fate.

 Alfonsina Storni

What Is a Home?

What is a home? A roof to keep out the rain.
Four walls to keep out the wind. Floors to keep
out the cold. Yes, but home is more than that. It
is the laugh of a baby, the song of a mother, the
strength of a father. Warmth of living hearts, light
from happy eyes, kindness, loyalty, comradeship.
Home is first school and first church for young
ones, where they learn what is right, what is good,
and what is kind. Where they go for comfort when
they are hurt or sick. Where joy is shared and
sorrows eased. Where fathers and mothers are
respected and loved. Where the simplest food is
good enough for kings because it is earned. Where
money is not so important as loving-kindness.
Where even the teakettle sings from happiness.
That is home.

 — Ernestine Schumann-Heink

To My Sister

I dreamt of the old house
where I spent my childhood years,
and the heart, as before, finds
comfort, and love, and warmth.
I dreamt of Christmas, the tree,
and my sister laughing out loud,
from morning, the rosy windows
sparkle tenderly.
And in the evening gifts are given
and the pine needles smell of stories,
And golden stars risen
are scattered like cinder above the rooftop.
I know that our old house
is falling into disrepair.
Bare, despondent branches
knock against darkening panes.
And in the room with its old furniture,
a resentful captive, cooped up,
lives our father, lonely and weary —
he feels abandoned by us.
Why, oh why do I dream of the country
where the love's all consumed, all?
Maria, my friend, my sister,
speak my name, call to me, call...

Olga Berggolts

My Beth,

O my sister, passing from me,
  Out of human care and strife,
Leave me, as a gift, those virtues
  Which have beautified your life.
Dear, bequeath me that great patience
  Which has power to sustain
A cheerful uncomplaining spirit
  In its poison-house of pain.

Henceforth, safe across the river,
  I shall see for evermore
A beloved, household spirit
  Waiting for me on the shore.
Hope and faith, born of my sorrow,
  Guardian angels shall become,
And the sister gone before me
  By their hands shall lead me home.

— Louisa May Alcott

Sisters are always drying their hair.
   Locked into rooms, alone,
They pose at the mirror, shoulders bare,
Trying this way and that their hair,
Or fly importunate down the stair
   To answer a telephone.
Sisters are always drying their hair,
   Locked into rooms, alone.

— Phyllis McGinley

My sister! My sweet sister! if a name
Dearer and purer were, it should be thine.

— Lord Byron

A Promise of
Sisterhood

A promise of sisterhood
Lives in our eyes and
In our blood
It is present in our
Conversations together
Alone and among friends
It was born from our
First meeting and will remain
Until our very last day
On this earth
Our promise of sisterhood
Lives in unconditional acceptance
Without expectation or prejudice

It lives in the generation
Of wisdom that each of us brings
To the other's heart, trust, respect
And admiration
That constantly grows bigger and stronger
With each passing day —
Where the best of times
Are tucked away as memories
Free from grudges and regret

Our promise of sisterhood
Is as constant as the
Northern star shining in the night
It is a symbol of kinship, friendship
Loyalty, and love
And it will last as long as we
Breathe and remain one as family
I have this promise of sisterhood with you

 Nicole D. Myers

When sisters look into each other's eyes and see the mirror reflecting their "core," they really see only the little girls they once were. They do not see the women they have become...

In reality, most sisters share only a small portion of each other's lives. But since that portion, during childhood, was so powerful emotionally, often it seems that who we are depends on who our sisters are not. Often, sisters carry each other around inside themselves for the rest of their lives. No matter how geographically distant, a sister can remain the touchstone we use for our own identity.

 Laura Tracy

Sometimes on quiet mornings, and now and then on star-filled nights, I get to thinking of all the days gone by. There are beautiful, touching, happy/sad times when I find I have to turn away and brush a tear from my eye... a tear that comes from a loving place where my thanks is so full that it overflows from having a sister — like you.

 Marin McKay

My sister! with that thrilling word
    Let thoughts unnumbered wildly spring!
What echoes in my heart are stirred,
    While thus I touch the trembling string.

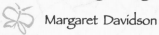 Margaret Davidson

We share so many memories —
both happy and sad — that we
don't have to talk a lot to know
what the other is thinking. A look,
a sigh, a hint of a smile... that's all
it usually takes to get across a
message that says "I'm glad today,"
or "I'm sad today... bear with me."
It's comfortable and it's comforting
not to have to say a lot.

 — Patricia Ziemba

Wherever people go,
whatever they may invent,
they will never discover
    anything better
than a family.

 — Paul Gauguin

We've shared everything, you and I.
Even a room
        filled with laughter and tears
        and all our hopes and fears.
We've shared secrets meant
        for no one but us.

Most of all, we've shared happiness.
There are so many wonderful memories
        with many more to come
        as we grow older... together
            as sisters...
                and as best friends.

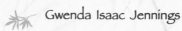 Gwenda Isaac Jennings

The Reality of Now

We are women in middle age, living in the moment,
our lives resting comfortably on the rich bedrock of our pasts,
sitting in our afternoon gardens, sunlight playing on our faces,
shadows dancing in the corners of our souls.

Shared loss and celebrations
bond us in experiences of the inevitable.
No longer separated by small jealousies and
society's competitions,
we accept with easy grace
the sisterhood that always was.

Our laughter resonates in softer tones, lower scales,
our smiles are given with lines etched by journeys well traveled.

Together we savor life's main course,
and consecrate this moment when past and future
blend into the reality of now.

 Deborah Miller O'Bryan

What greater thing
is there
for two human souls
than to feel that they
are joined for life —
to strengthen each other
in all labor,
to rest on each other
in all sorrow,
to minister
to each other
in all pain,
and to be
with each other
in silent
unspeakable moments.

 George Eliot

My Best Friend
Is a Very Special
Woman

Let me tell you about her:

She is someone who loves life
  to the fullest.
She loves the simple things in life,
like eating dessert
  and drinking flavored coffee.
She loves to watch romantic movies
  with a big box of tissues
    beside her.

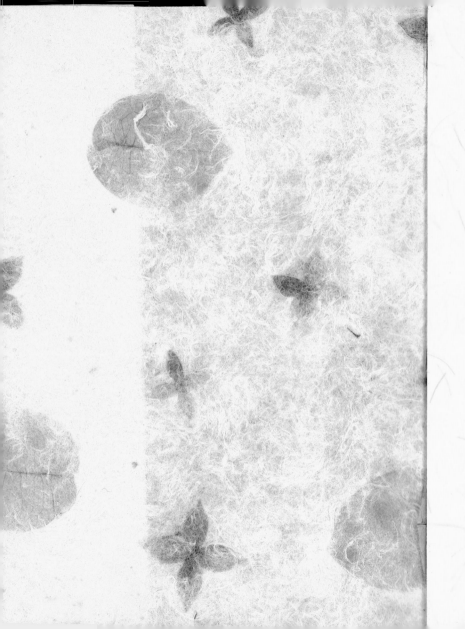

My best friend is someone
   I can always count on.
She is always there for me
   no matter what.
If I've just had my heart broken,
she's there to pick up the pieces.
Or if I just need a hug,
she'll come right over.

Even when we are apart,
we are as close as two friends
   can be.
And when we get together again,
it's as if no time has passed.

By now,
you must have guessed...
that my very best friend
   is YOU!

 Laurel Bosshart

ACKNOWLEDGMENTS

We gratefully acknowledge the permission granted by the following authors, publishers, and authors' representatives to reprint poems and excerpts from their publications.

PrimaDonna Entertainment Corp. for "To My Sister, with Love," by Donna Fargo. Copyright © 1999 by PrimaDonna Entertainment Corp. All rights reserved. Reprinted by permission.

Bantam Doubleday Dell Publishing Group, Inc. and Faber & Faber, Ltd. for "To My Sister" from THE COLLECTED POEMS OF THEODORE ROETHKE by Theodore Roethke. Copyright © 1948 by Theodore Roethke. All rights reserved. Reprinted by permission of Doubleday, a division of Bantam Doubleday Dell Publishing Group, Inc., and Faber & Faber, Ltd.

Bonnie S. Hoffman for "Shells of Sisterhood." Copyright © 1999 by Bonnie S. Hoffman. All rights reserved. Reprinted by permission.

Bantam Doubleday Dell Publishing Group, Inc. for "Your sister is your other self..." from BETWEEN SISTERS by Barbara Mathias. Copyright © 1992 by Barbara Mathias. All rights reserved. Reprinted by permission of Delacorte Press, a division of Bantam Doubleday Dell Publishing Group, Inc.

Roxana Popescu for "My Sister." Copyright © 1999 by Roxana Popescu. All rights reserved. Reprinted by permission.

Casey Marie Mullens for "To My Younger Sister." Copyright © 1999 by Casey Marie Mullens. All rights reserved. Reprinted by permission.

Barbara J. Hall for "What a Family Is For...." Copyright © 1999 by Barbara J. Hall. All rights reserved. Reprinted by permission.

Bantam Doubleday Dell Publishing Group and Patricia Foster for "All living things..." by Joy Harjo and "Sisterhood is such..." by Letty Cottin Pogrebin from SISTER TO SISTER by Patricia Foster. Copyright © 1995 by Patricia Foster. All rights reserved. Reprinted by permission of Doubleday, a division of Bantam Doubleday Dell Publishing Group, and Patricia Foster.

Darcy Frances Meese for "The best gift...." Copyright © 1999 by Darcy Frances Meese. All rights reserved. Reprinted by permission.

Tim Connor for "My Little Sister." Copyright © 1999 by Tim Connor. All rights reserved. Reprinted by permission.

The Washington Post Writers Group for "The family... may be..." from MAKING SENSE by Ellen Goodman. Copyright © 1977 by The Boston Globe Newspaper Company/Washington Post Writers Group. All rights reserved. Reprinted by permission of The Washington Post Writers Group.

Christine Downing for "Relationships between sisters..." from PSYCHE'S SISTERS: REIMAGINING THE MEANING OF SISTERHOOD, published by HarperCollins Publishers. Copyright © 1988 by Christine Downing. All rights reserved. Reprinted by permission of Christine Downing.

Penguin USA and Martin Secker & Warburg for "Sisters are always..." from TIMES THREE by Phyllis McGinley, published by The Viking Press, Inc., a division of Penguin USA. Copyright © each year 1932-1960 by Phyllis McGinley. All rights reserved. Reprinted by permission of Penguin USA and Martin Secker & Warburg.

Nicole D. Myers for "A Promise of Sisterhood." Copyright © 1999 by Nicole D. Myers. All rights reserved. Reprinted by permission.

Little, Brown and Company, Inc. for "When sisters look..." from THE SECRET BETWEEN US: COMPETITION AMONG WOMEN by Laura Tracy. Copyright © 1991 by Laura Tracy. All rights reserved. Reprinted by permission of Little, Brown and Company, Inc.

Deborah Miller O'Bryan for "The Reality of Now." Copyright © 1999 by Deborah Miller O'Bryan. All rights reserved. Reprinted by permission.

Laurel Bosshart for "My Best Friend Is a Very Special Woman." Copyright © 1999 by Laurel Bosshart. All rights reserved. Reprinted by permission.

A careful effort has been made to trace the ownership of poems and excerpts used in this anthology in order to obtain permission to reprint copyrighted materials and give proper credit to the copyright owners. If any error or omission has occurred, it is completely inadvertent, and we would like to make corrections in future editions provided that written notification is made to the publisher:

BLUE MOUNTAIN PRESS, INC., P.O. Box 4549, Boulder, Colorado 80306.